Also by Tracy Patrick:

Wild Eye Fire Eye

Praise for *Blushing is for Sinners*

Tracy Patrick employs an artisan's skill to the backdrop of the declining Paisley Thread mills and their world where she sets her tale of family relationships and industrial politics that span the backdrop of a 1960's Paisley. You can imagine you're walking the very same streets as Jean and Ava and Billy and Tommy, in juxtaposition to the contemporary setting of the Canada of the now where Ava's revealing reflection does indeed, reveal. As if weaving her own Paisley shawl from word patterns, Patrick uses an understated, consistently powerful narrative that always engages and brings an inner smile to this reader. Like most Paisley Buddies, and Patrick's characters, you can take the girl out of Paisley but never take Paisley out of the girl. An absorbing read that delivers, page by page by page.

– **Brian Whittingham**, Tannahill Makar for Renfrewshire.

Long Lost Family meets *Who Do You Think You Are?* in this ambitious first novel which is brimming with warmth, heart and soul. Humour and great dialogue mark this debut too, as do a cracking sense of place (including the workplace), a host of memorable characters & a deep-rooted political awareness. The Paisley chapters with their focus on the mills & a heart-breaking love triangle are to die for. *Blushing is for Sinners* is a stand-out addition to the growing body of literature suddenly emerging from Paisley.

– **Donal McLaughlin**, author and translator.

Faces glow and bodies feel the heat in this romantic thriller. Patrick has a poet's eye for detail and the book's strength is its insider's portrait of a Scottish town, with something of the dark malignity of Douglas Brown's *House with the Green Shutters* about it. The openness of the Canadian prairies, with its great expanses of forest rapidly disappearing to logging, provide contrast. This is a good quality first novel that promises much for the future.

– **Dave Manderson**, author and Robert Louis Stevenson fellow.

Tracy is very much a poet, and she has brought all her poet's skills into her prose to create a touching and humorous evocation of time and place and life. It's a story of people we care about, the choices we make and the choices made for us, played out against a backdrop of long-gone buildings, the destruction of man-made, and natural, heritage. It's a drama of complex 'ordinary' relationships; flawed people trying to discover who they are, what they've become. People with bits missing, emotional holes. But it's also a book full of genuine warmth and concern for the characters and their predicaments, a cautionary tale of not letting love go to waste. *Blushing is for Sinners* is an instant Paisley classic.

– **Graham Fulton**, poet and illustrator.

I could not put this book down! The tension running through each page kept me turning over, even though I was telling my sleepy self "right one more chapter and lights out." Tracy is a great teller of story. *Blushing is for Sinners* is one of the best books I have read this year. Highly recommended.

– **Donna Campbell**, poet and performance artist

BLUSHING IS FOR SINNERS

Tracy Patrick

CLOCHODERICK

First published by Clochoderick Press 2019
8 Townhead Terrace, Paisley, Scotland, PA1 2AX
clochoderick@gmail.com

A catalogue record for this book is available
from the British Library

ISBN: 978-1-912345-11-3

Cover design by Rebecca Johnstone
Typeset in Plantin Std by Andrew Forteath

Printed and bound by Imprint Academic
Seychelles Farm, Upton Pyne, Exeter,
Devon, EX5 5HY

For Doris McLachlan

PART ONE

1962
Paisley

There's a light rain on. It patters against the windows as we're finishing up.

'Right, girls, see you all tomorrow, sharp,' says Mr Green. He's been assistant manager in Twisting since forever; you'd think he'd get fed up. English, but we don't hold that against him.

On the way down the stairs, big Una starts again about the new high rises. She's been on about it for weeks. 'That Lizzie Naismith got one,' she says. 'You want to hear her. Thinks she's gone up in the world.' Una takes a near toothless drag of her cigarette.

'Aye, well, she has,' says Maggie Doyle, pursing her half-painted lips. 'She's gone up aboot a hundred feet.'

Laughter rings through the stairwell, a hollow steel sound. I take my plastic rain hat from my coat pocket. Wearing it makes me feel frumpy; but if I don't the rain turns my lacquer all sticky, then my beehive starts to sink. I tie it on just as we pour out of the twisting mill and straggle across the yard. Ahead, the faded cupolas of the old Victorian spinning mill look even more dreich under the hanging clouds.

'It's no that,' says Una. 'Do you know whit she said to wee Tam, him that's the foreman over in Spinning? She said, "I'll thank you to call me Elizabeth."' Una shakes her head. 'So guess whit? He started calling her "Your Majesty." That telt her.'

I think I might mention the new housing to Tommy when I get up the road; it's got indoor toilets. 'Here,' I say to Maggie. 'How do you get your name on the list?'

'Fur Foxbar?'

Una winks. 'Newton Street no good enough for you, is it, Jean McParland? You young folk are never satisfied.'

'That's no fair, Una,' says wee Aggie. 'Just cause you were born afore the flood.'

I try to catch Aggie's freckly face and smile at her for sticking up for me. That's when I see him, as we reach the gatehouse, leaning against the railings on the other side. My mouth clamps shut. He still has those sharp, green eyes, and that look, as though everything around belongs to him: the stones, the road, the rain and clouds, even the yard and the big hulks of the buildings. It's like I'm being squeezed from the inside. My brain goes all melty and my rain hat feels like it's tied on lopsided. I think about taking it off, then I remember the lacquer.

His hair is greased back, with that Tommy Steele flick hanging down between his eyes, the collar of his jacket turned up. He lifts his knee and presses his foot back against the wall, watching the girls stream past as though he owns them too. I try to shrink into the crowd, keeping my head down, but I feel his stare on me, the raised chin, the way he blows his cigarette smoke up into the air.

Una's mouth freezes for a second, and I know she's seen him too. Billy.

You can never go wrong with mince and tatties, or so my mother is never off telling me. I think of her face and start scrubbing the potatoes harder while Ava stands on tiptoes and sets the plates. I can hardly believe my wee lassie will be five next spring. I wanted to call her Scarlett, like in *Gone with the Wind*. But Tommy said that's a silly name and people would laugh, so we settled on Ava, like Ava Gardner. Frank Sinatra was the love of her life, and I always wanted to have a love of my life, though I didn't tell Tommy that.

My mother's voice starts up in my head, sticking in her two bob's worth even though she's not in the room: 'He's a good man is Tommy, and you cuid dae worse.' She always says this with a long stare that forces my eyes to the ground. I hum loudly, put the mince in a pot and set it on a heat. It's true, we've been happy here, me and Tommy and Ava. He's not much of a talker, but I can't expect everything. And he works hard. It's nice knowing I belong somewhere: here, in this wee house, making the tea with Ava.

I give her a big smile. 'Let's see whit's on the wireless,' I say, but it's only the news, something about the queen. We listen for a minute then I turn the dial. Buddy Holly comes on and I remember the shuffle step we used to do at the dancing, how it made your hips shake and your skirt swivel. Once a month me and Annie would save up and go to the Flamingo. She had all the records: Hank Marvin, Lonnie Donegan, The Everly Brothers. My mother hated that music. I'd have to hide my skirt and shoes in a bag and get changed at a café on the way.

That's how I first met Billy. Not in the Flamingo; boys like Billy didn't go to the Flamingo. It was on the way home. Annie was in a right giggly mood. Maybe it's because it was spring. She'd met a boy she liked and was already planning what to call their children. 'Whit aboot Peter?' she said. 'It's a kind name, don't you think?' I'd been stuck dancing with the pal. He was all big teeth and gums and kept standing on my toes. He apologised so often I felt like screaming. By the time we boarded the bus, I was hardly listening to Annie and had fallen into a daydream; then a voice from the back, loud so everyone could hear, broke into my thoughts: 'The Flamingo's full a kids. I only go tae the Barrowlands. It has better music.'

'Aye, and burds,' said another guy, but he was only talking loud to impress the first.

I turned round. Two boys dressed in white shirts and black ties were sharing a silver hip flask. One of them, with his feet up on the seat, looked at me, his eyes searching up and down until a wee shudder went through my body. 'I don't know aboot that,' he said. 'There's some fine lassies right here.'

I blushed. That was Billy.

My mother was right; blushing is a sign of sinful thoughts.

Turning up the wireless, I say, 'Come on, Ava. I'll teach you how to shuffle.' I take her hand and show her the steps in the wee space between the stove and the kitchen door. 'Cross, twist, and step to the front; cross, twist, and step to the front.'

Before the song is finished, the wireless gets turned down. It's Tommy. He's on night shift again, so he's standing in his vest and braces, rubbing his eyes.

'Hello, love.' I kiss his cheek. 'I wis just aboot tae wake you.'

He screws up his nose. 'Whit's that smell? Is something burning?'

In the morning, I meet Maggie and a few others on the road. There's no sign of Billy at the gates. Maybe it was just a one-off. He likes to put the wind up folk. Anyway, I'm married so that's that. I wonder if he knows about Ava. Well, good. I hope he does. And I hope he's thought the better of it and gone somewhere else. It's for the best. If I see him, that's what I'll tell him.

Una eyeballs me while we're getting into our overalls, but she doesn't say anything. The talk is quiet that time in the morning, except for Maggie complaining about her back again, sore from lugging her washing up and down the stairs while her man goes out on the randan till all hours. 'The only time I see him is ootside they railings every Friday when I get paid.'

'They want to pit glue oan they railings. That'll teach them,' says Una.

When we get up the stairs Mr Green tells me I'm on 14A, on account of Myra Brown being off sick and my machine being serviced. I don't hear him the first time and I have to ask him to say that again please.

'Her heid's miles away,' says Una.

'Dreaming of her man,' says wee Aggie.

'Mibbee he's needing serviced n'all,' says Maggie.

'Well he can have you all to himself when you get home,' says Mr Green, with a big daft smile. 'But, for the working day, you belong to us.'

I blush because it's not Tommy I'm thinking about. Una smirks but says nothing. The machines are double frames and we're usually opposite each other on number 12, with me on the B side. But I'm glad not to have her beady eyes peering at me between the cheeses of thread. Normally I can't stand the noise of the machines, the constant rattle of the frames, but today I let it drown out everything, inside and out. I wish I could work through dinner but I have to go with the rest of them to the canteen.

I take a bowl of soup, but I don't finish it. 'Skinny as a bit a threid,' says Maggie. 'It's a wunner they don't take you fur a spindle.'

'Her hair looks nice the day,' says wee Aggie, smiling. 'Is it a special occasion?'

'No, nothing special.'

'Only that's a new red lipstick too, in't it? I thought Tommy must be taking you oot somewhere after.'

'If anyone wid take his wife oot, it'd be Tommy,' says Una.

'I'd be happy if someone took my other haulf oot fur good,' says Maggie. 'In fact, I'd pay them no tae bring him back.'

'There's plenty worse than Frank,' says Una. 'Mind wee Jetta Smythe? Her man wis a shifty fella, cuid never look you in the eye. Anyway, he got sent down. She ended up in wan a they slums doon George Street. Damp up the wa's, wind blowing through the windaes, rats everywhere.'

'I hate rats,' says Aggie.

Una lights a cigarette. 'The trouble wae rats is you can never get rid a them. No matter whit you dae, they just keep coming back.'

My throat catches and I cough.

'Aye, they say prison changes a man,' says Maggie. 'Most a them come oot worse than they went in. If he didny use his fists on you afore, when he gets oot, he'll be swinging them left, right and centre. It's that and the drink.'

'That's the thing aboot prison,' says Una. 'Nothing tae dae but think. Who knows whit ideas come intae their heids? You canny be soft wae men like that.' She leans back, staring at me, and blows out a long tunnel of smoke. 'So how's your Tommy?'

'Fine,' I say, heat rising in my neck. 'Last night we had mince and tatties.'

I'm glad to get back to my machine. Una might have been talking about Jetta Smythe, but she was meaning Billy, I know it. I wish she wouldn't talk that way. I suppose I knew he would be getting out, but I didn't want to think about it. Anyway, I was just a wee lassie back then, crying for him in his cell, thinking how alone and frightened he must be. Every day I wanted there to be a letter, something to tell me he was alright, that he was thinking about me. Nothing came. I read about famous women betrayed in love. I even thought about becoming a nun. 'Don't be so ridiculous,' Annie would say. 'All you have tae do is find a good man, a kind man, and settle down.'

It was alright for her. She was still seeing that guy from the Flamingo. Then one night she wanted me to go to La Scala: 'There's a new Elizabeth Taylor film. Come on, it'll be fun.' I should have known she had something up her sleeve. There was an early autumn wind and, by the time we got there, my hair was like straw. Who was waiting for us at the door but Annie's beau, Archie, and his clumsy-footed friend. I told her right then I was going back home. 'Jist give it a chance,' she said. 'He's been best pals wae Archie since they wur weans. He's a good man and he'll treat you nice, no like...'

'No like some toe rag I met up the back of a bus?'

'I don't mean that. You cuid do wae a bit a fun. Come on.'

It wasn't as bad as I remembered. His teeth were still big but not that gummy. And now that he wasn't dancing he looked more confident, self-assured, like someone I could rely on. Before I knew what she was up to, Annie had taken a photo of me standing next to him like a daft lemon.

Billy would have laughed at him, of course; hated his type. Sheep, he called them. Waste half their lives slaving for a few shillings a week and then what? By the time they realise they've never lived, they're standing at the Pearly Gates with sweet Fanny Adams to show for it. Billy was a risk taker. Once he drove me in an Aston Martin, up and down the back roads, all the way to Irvine. He'd go right up to fifty miles an hour and I'd scream, but he never slowed down. I remember sitting on Irvine beach at ten o'clock at night, watching the summer sun sink into the sea, Billy's arm around my shoulders. But he couldn't sit like that for long. He was a restless sort. Got up and started skimming stones into the water. He tried to teach me to do it, but all my stones sank. 'You women are useless,' he said. I ran back to the dunes and started crying, while he stood chucking in stones, the burning sun framing his silhouette. It was always like that with Billy. In a single moment, you could go from the heights of happiness to the depths of despair. Eventually he came back, took my hand and kissed me, and everything was alright again as we lay down in the soft, soft sand. That night I had to climb in the kitchen window. My mother was waiting up. What a belting I got, but I didn't care.

In the end, there I was at La Scala with Annie and Archie and…

He held out his hand: 'Tommy. Pleased to meet you. Again.'

Blood gushes from my finger over the frame. The cut is deep, all the way to the fleshy part of my thumb. I shout for the supervisor. She's a right bitch. 'I don't know whit happened,' I say. 'I wis only trying tae take the end off, only I cut my finger instead of the threid. I didny mean it. I'm no used tae this machine…'

'Wan machine's the same as anither, Jean.' She inspects the damage then stands with her hands on her hips. 'This lot'll have to be chucked. There's blood all ower the frame. We'll have to get the fitters.'

The other girls start to snigger. 'Well, how long will it take?' I say.

'Dae I look like a fitter?' says The Bitch.

My nose nips as the tears well up.

'She wants tae know will her pay be quartered,' says Una. I don't know if she's sticking up for me or if she just wants to have a go at The Bitch.

'It'll no jist be quartered,' shouts Maggie. 'It'll be hung and drawn.'

My cheeks feel red and ugly. I'm glad when Mr Green comes over. 'The fitters will wipe your machine down quick as they can,' he says.

'I don't want to work the machines any more,' I tell him. 'I want a nice job, typing at a desk.'

The other girls snigger.

'Now, now. Let's get that finger to First Aid.'

Una volunteers to go with me. She wraps my hand in a handkerchief to stem the blood. 'It luks worse than it is,' she says. 'You'll no need stitches.' The First Aid Centre is in an annexe next to the Counting House. It smells of antiseptic but it's nice to be away from the noise of the flats. I sit on a chair outside one of the rooms, sniffling. 'Wait till you've been here thirty years, no three. Then you can stairt complaining.' Una snorts. 'Too many distractions, that's your problem.' She reaches out and pats my arm. 'Chin up, hen.'

When she leaves, the tears spill down my cheeks. Billy, aw Billy.

2013
Pickering, Ontario

Ava directs the driver off the main highway and into the heart of Pickering. Nothing has changed: the same flat landscape and boxed houses with concrete drives. Leaning into the back seat of the car, she draws the letter from her bag. J Langley & Co, Cissy's lawyers, wish to discuss matters pertaining to her estate, grand words for such a small legacy; all her aunt owns is that old house north of Whitevale with its creaky porch and battered sidings. The appointment is this afternoon, after the funeral. There's no point being sensitive about it; she might as well kill both birds while she's here.

The squat white chimney of the crematorium is visible beyond the trees. Its plainness gives her an attack of self-consciousness. She can't imagine any of Cissy's church fellowship friends rolling through the gates in a chauffeur-driven Mercedes. Besides, with the company name all over the headlines, they'll have enough reason to talk about her; she doesn't need to add another to the list. 'Stop here,' she says.

Outside the air is sticky and warm, but already the leaves are turning copper; in a few weeks it'll be October. This time of year always fills her with melancholy. Loosening a jacket button, she wipes her neck and forehead. It was quick in the end. Cissy fainted out back while she was watering the plants. Lung cancer. She'd never smoked a cigarette in her life.

The further Ava climbs, the steeper the path seems to grow.

The seclusion of trees offers no respite from the heat. Maybe if she rests awhile. A latticed gate leads into a neatly landscaped garden enclosed by hedges. Roses line a paved walkway ending in a covered gallery decorated with endless rows of plaques: so many names and dates, 'beloved' fathers and 'devoted' husbands and wives. Some people have taped laminated photographs to the posts: brides on the front steps of churches, young men in army uniforms, families gathered round Christmas trees. There are cards, flowers, poems, half-drunk miniatures of whisky. She doesn't sit down, doesn't want to be amongst this litter of bereavement. Cissy would call them gaudy, such open declarations of grief.

Her earliest recollection of her aunt is in Paisley, a brightly lit room with a piano, her own childish thrill at being allowed to tap the keys. The tenement where she grew up was dark by comparison, with small rooms and a narrow entrance leading up a dim flight of stairs. The school was only *down the road* as her aunt would say. The kids from the street walked there and back together. But one autumn day Cissy came to get her, her knuckles tight around her handbag, her face pale and drawn, and took Ava to her house with the piano. There was no school the next day, or the day after that. Her aunt was hanging washing in the garden, the ghostly white sheets snapping in the wind, when she removed a peg from her mouth and told Ava there had been a fire at the old house. Ava had started to cry and wanted to go and get her doll, Raggedy Jane. In her childish mind, she pictured smoke and flames huffing and puffing and poor Raggedy at the window, helpless. Cissy scooped her up and took her inside and said she had to be very grown up because things would be different from now on. They were going on holiday to a place called Montreal where she'd get a new Raggedy Jane and lots of other toys and friends. No one mentioned the word 'dead,' not then. 'Is Mammy coming?'

'We'll see,' said Cissy.

That evening, Uncle Alex brought colouring books and sugary tea cakes. Later Ava was looking out the window and saw a man in a peaked cap, his shoulders stooped, turn and walk away from the gate. 'Was that Daddy?' she said. But her aunt only told her to go back to bed. Soon after that, they moved to Montreal. Daddy couldn't visit because he was busy 'working.' Then one day, Ava's not sure when, her aunt told her that he'd *passed on*. 'You've got me and Alex now,' she said. 'We're your family, and we love you very much.'

Her memories of her mother are fragmented, yet clearer. As a child, Ava would stand by the window, watching the mill workers pour down the street, rows of women with their arms linked, taking over the sidewalk. She'd look for her mother in the crowd, that way she had of smoking while she walked, fastening her lips tightly round the cigarette and drawing out the smoke in quick sharp movements, her hair piled up under a scarf knotted at the chin. Ava would listen for her heels click-clicking on the stairs, then watch as her mother came into the kitchen, took off her coat and switched on the kettle. The wallpaper had blue and pink swirly flowers. Her mother sat at the small table, the cup of tea steaming in front of her. She remembers a feeling, too, of wanting to run towards her, lay her head on her lap and not let go. But she never did.

The gate clangs but it's nothing, only the wind. Ava hurries up the path, scuffing her shoe on a tree root. Cursing under her breath, she emerges from the garden to see the hearse rolling up the hill with a light-coloured coffin in the back, softwood, the cheap kind. She straightens. Leave the scuff. It's good to have a flaw, shows you're human. Other cars follow after with bumper stickers that read, 'God on Board!'

For a moment, she regrets dismissing her driver, but at last the small white-washed crematorium emerges between the trees. A woman struggles from the passenger seat of a rusty Ford. Her dress is black with short sleeves. She has thick ankles and fleshy arms, like the cubed women in Picasso paintings. She waves. 'Oh, my Lord, it's really you, isn't it?' Wanda has been Cissy's best friend for years. She wraps Ava in a tight embrace. 'Cissy will sure be glad you made it.'

She can hear the wheeze of air in and out of Wanda's lungs. A man in his early forties gets out the driver's side. He's wearing a beige anorak and black tie, hair combed neatly back. 'This is my son, Barney. You remember Barney?' Ava has memories of a shy kid who went through tortuous afternoons of Cissy trying to teach him piano. She offers her hand and he shakes it quickly, without looking up.

'Come and meet the folks from the Fellowship,' says Wanda, and leads her to a group of women who take turns at embracing her, some with genuine tears in their eyes. No one mentions Bruce, or the protestors massed outside the Parliament Buildings in Victoria. She felt guilty about leaving him in the midst of such a crisis, but it didn't seem right to forego her aunt's funeral for business.

The gaggle of women stand aside for the pastor in his crisp white shirt and Abraham Lincoln beard. His strong handshake is no doubt meant to be reassuring. 'You must be Cissy's niece. She played piano for us so beautifully. She'll be sorely missed.' The women murmur in agreement.

'She was a good person,' says Wanda.

'How's your son?' says the pastor. 'Scott, isn't it?'

The women exchange sympathetic smiles. No doubt they'll have prayed for Scott, along with all the other *afflicted*. 'Great,' she says. 'He's designing websites.' She doesn't mention that she'd had to tell him about the funeral by text. No answer on his phone as usual. Though it's not like he and Cissy were close. She tried to get him to call her Grandma, but it never caught on.

Condolences over, Ava takes her place in the front pew. 'You okay?' says Wanda. 'You look a little flushed is all.'

Ava nods. 'It's a long flight from Victoria.'

Wanda's rests her fleshy hand on Ava's as the light coffin is brought in and laid on the catafalque. Yellow chrysanthemums are blooming in vases all around the room. The pastor leans into the microphone and coughs, 'Through Jesus Christ our Saviour, we are forgiven –'

Wanda and Barney offer her a ride back to the old place. She has a couple of hours to kill until the solicitor's, and it's only natural to return to the house they shared, where Scott spent his childhood. It's almost like being a normal person again, *feet on the ground,* as Cissy would say.

Ava squashes into the back of Wanda's Ford, her knees at an angle, her ankles pushed awkwardly on their sides. Plenty of time to stretch out later in the limo. Wanda turns and smiles, her fleshy cheeks like eggplants. 'At least you got work to take your mind off things,' she says. 'Keeps the devil at bay.'

The protestors might disagree. This time it's not the usual bunches of dread-locked, pot-smoking brats, but the tax-paying middle classes, outraged by Borealis' application to extend logging around the old growth trees of Temple Grove. It's a PR nightmare. She switches off her phone.

They drive through the Nautical Village, past the pillared white balconies of Frenchman's Bay. Years ago, she offered to buy Cissy a place just like this, but her aunt preferred to stay put, said if it wasn't something she could pay for herself, then it wasn't worth having. Cissy never did lose that old Scottish Presbyterian streak.

Crushed in the zip compartment of her pocketbook, Ava finds the black and white photograph of her mother. It seems to have been taken on a windy day, her hair, which Ava used to imagine was the colour of honey, blown back from her face, a necklace glinting like a star at the base of her throat. When she was young, the photo was in a silver frame by her bed, her mother like a movie star or a princess, smiling across the ocean. There was something about that smile, not wide, her lips closed, but depending on which way you looked, on the brightness and angle of light in the room, it could be a smile of sadness, of someone haunted by a future that's not yet arrived, or it could be the most wonderful magical smile in the world, possessing all the secrets of the universe.

Outside, the sun ripples over Lake Ontario and its clusters of yachts. This was Cissy's favourite part of Pickering, beautiful if you can ignore the eight ugly nuclear reactors squatting on the shore. Not that most folks give it a second thought. Cissy didn't. Hadn't. She'd said: *It's not the place that matters, but the people.* Ava zips the photo back in its stuffy pocket, fetches her dark glasses from her bag and shields her eyes.

As they head north, there are newer houses with built-in garages and mown lawns, but most are the flat, one storey buildings she remembers, with whitewashed sidings, like Cissy's. She wonders if the piano is still there. A Steinway. Uncle Alex had to work overtime for months so Cissy could bring it over from Scotland, even though he said they had pianos in Canada, and what was the point? Ava recalls evenings in their small parlour back in Montreal, trying desperately to make one hand move independently of the other, while Cissy beat the rhythm with a pen. Later, when Uncle Alex died, Cissy earned a few bucks giving lessons to local kids, most of whom were better than Ava, much to her aunt's disappointment. By the time they moved to Pickering, just after Scott was born, the varnish had lost its shine and the keys turned a shade of nicotine. But lessons continued, despite her aunt's arthritic fingers.

They turn into the drive. The elms at the back of the lot are taller, but nothing has been allowed to get wild. Cissy always did have a knack for neatness. Ava gets out the car and Wanda hands her a set of keys attached to a little brown bear in a yellow t-shirt that says, 'I'm 4 Jesus.' The stairs creak on the porch, but the lock turns easily. There's a stale smell inside, though nothing is dirty: the shelves are dusted, the lampshades clean, and the cushions plumped.

Uncle Alex is still on the mantelpiece guarded by the two china dogs who've watched over him since his heart attack in 1972. Ava caresses the dark blue urn, then smacks her hands together, like Cissy ridding her gardening gloves of dirt. The undertakers have arranged for her to be delivered to the house in a matching vase. 'Just put her here when it arrives,' she says to Wanda, who's followed her inside.

Wanda disguises her disapproval with a smile. 'We can scatter the ashes in the Garden of Remembrance, can't we, Barney? It's no trouble.'

'No, it's fine. I'll work out what to do later.'

The ornaments, cushions, wallpaper have a sickly look about them. Despite the tidiness, there's an undernourished quality in the furnishings and window frames. A guilty cramp in Ava's stomach reminds her that she put off going to visit Cissy in hospital, believing she'd be alright, like she'd always been. The Steinway is in the same place, the corner by the window, shabby-looking, the upper wood bleached by sun. Lifting the lid, Ava presses one of the keys. It makes a click, the sound dampened by years of neglect. She decides not to waste any more time, refuses Wanda's offer of tea, and heads for the door.

A quarter of an hour later, she's stretching her legs in the back seat of the limo, the engine emitting a comfortable quiet hum. Telegraph poles and their parallel wires stretch endlessly past, framing the fields of stubble. Eventually they reach civilisation again, Pickering Main and the business district. The office is on the first floor of a white three storey building. The receptionist barely glances up as she points Ava to a carpeted waiting room, where a man in a white shirt and burgundy tie invites her into a cramped office with an oversized desk. 'Joe Langley,' he says, holding out his hand. 'Mrs Quail insisted that I speak to you personally.'

She sits on a red cushioned chair. There's a stain on the arm-rest so she clasps her hands around her knees instead. In a few minutes, all this will be over and she can get back to business in Victoria. Langley opens a box-file and takes out two documents: a notarised statement that Ava assumes must be the will, and a sealed white envelope. He asks if she wishes any tea or coffee before they proceed. She shakes her head.

It's pretty standard stuff: a bank account with a four-figure sum to be donated to the Church Fellowship; the house to be signed over to Ava; and all Cissy's possessions to be divided between her and Scott as Ava sees fit. Langley coughs. 'There's one final matter. Your aunt instructed me to give you this.'

He pushes the sealed envelope across the desk. The name scrawled on the front is not Ava Newport, or even her maiden name, Quail, but McParland, Ava McParland. The writing is messy, almost illegible, in a hand she doesn't recognise. A tight throb starts to form in her brow. Langley passes her a letter opener. It snags, and she rips the rest with impatient fingers. Inside is a single scrap of wrinkled paper, the words all jammed together.

31 January 1963

Beloved Ava,

I don't know what they've told you about me. I just want you to know that I'm thinking about you, that I will never stop thinking about you as long as I live. If I could change things I would. I wrote to Tommy and he said you'd gone to Canada. I'd hoped he'd look after you, that one day, maybe we could start again. Oh, I don't know. None of this is his fault. I suppose he didn't know what to do for the best.

I hope you can forgive me. You have always been the most important person in my life, and always will be, wherever you are. I want you to be like the actress I named you after, beautiful and full of spirit, never afraid to say what she thinks. All the things I never could be. Every day I imagine you living in that big country, seeing all those new things, all the things I'd hoped to show you myself. If only I hadn't been such a fool.

I want you to be a good girl for your Aunt Cissy. Remember to say your prayers. And don't forget me, oh God, don't forget me. I'll pray that you get this letter, and that one day soon, we'll be together again.

With all my love,
Mammy

It doesn't make sense. She looks again at the date. The envelope is too new for the yellowed paper within. Quickly, she shoves it back inside. She's getting a headache, a stabbing pain between her eye sockets.

'Would you like something to drink? A glass of water?'

'There's nothing more? A note, perhaps?'

Langley's face is impassive. 'I was simply asked by Mrs Quail to make sure you read it.'

'But she must have told you something.'

'I'm sorry, Mrs Newport. I have no idea of the contents.'

Ava resists the urge to grab him by the tie. 'But it's impossible.' Her lips quiver and her nose starts to sting. Shit. She's going to cry. This mediocre little lawyer is actually going to make her cry. She takes a deep breath and fumbles for her dark glasses. 'Mr Langley, my mother can't have written this letter. She's been dead for over fifty years.'

1962
Paisley

I've to keep my hand in a bandage for the next two days. It's a mess, the way it sticks out like a big paddle. I wonder what Tommy will say. Maybe I'll give the tatties a miss tonight and get a few pork chops on the way home. That's his favourite. I can serve them up with heaps of bread and butter.

At finishing time I keep my distance from Una and her lot, though I can hear her voice trumpeting up the stairwell. I hang back and listen to some of the single girls blethering about how they're off up the dancing. Even if it's only the Templar Halls with coffee and tea, at least they still get out.

When we get to the railings he's standing there, right in front of the gates this time, so that the women have to walk round him to get past. Keep moving, I tell myself. Don't stop. I'm trying not to look at him, though my heart is beating like a wild bird's. When I get level, he starts to walk backwards in front of me. Four years have taken their toll and it shows on his face, the skin not quite so smooth, the neck and chin fleshed out. But still the same old Billy. I feel breathless, like I've been running.

'Jean, doll,' he whispers. 'It's me.'

I try to find a space in the crowd where I can disappear.

He catches my arm: 'Jean.'

All the little hairs stand on end. 'Stop it,' I hiss. A couple of the girls turn their heads. I lower my voice. 'What do you want?'

'I'm back, Jean. See. You knew I'd come back, didn't you?'

'Where were you?' I glance up. He's stopped smiling and instantly I feel stupid.

'You know where I wis, Jean.' Billy laughs. 'That old cow, Una, is giving me dirty looks. Don't listen tae them, Jean. You're better than that, better than all of them.' His hand brushes the tops of my knuckles. I feel a piece of paper being pressed into my bandaged palm. He strokes my wrist, then he's gone.

'Mammy,' says Ava. 'Mammy.'

'Whit? I'm trying tae think.' I don't know how long I've been sitting at the kitchen table. My tea is cold. I light another cigarette.

She comes towards me, points at my bandaged hand. 'What happened?'

'An accident at work.'

'Did it bleed?'

'Not much.' She turns away so I say I'll buy her a nice dress, to take her mind off it. I decide I don't like the wallpaper. The colours are too old fashioned. Blue and pink. I imagine Una sitting in a kitchen staring at blue and pink wallpaper.

Ava tugs my sleeve. 'Can we do the shuffle?'

I turn towards her. 'The whit?'

She looks hurt. Then I remember yesterday, Buddy Holly. It seems like a lifetime away. 'The shuffle's old fashioned,' I say. 'Now everybody's doing the twist.'

'What's the twist?'

'I'll show you later.' It's like my brain has been emptied. I light one cigarette after another.

Ava is going in and out of cupboards, laying the table. 'What's for dinner?' she says.

'Oh, hell.' I forgot to buy the pork chops.

'You said a bad word.'

'Shut up, Ava.' I go into my bag and fetch my purse. 'Tell your dad we're having fish suppers.'

Tommy eats with his fingers. 'You forgot my pickles,' he says.

Tommy likes two pickles with his fish supper. 'They didn't have any pickles,' I lie.

Ava is excited like she always is when there's a fish supper. She swings her legs under the table. 'Fingers,' I say. She picks up her knife and fork.

Tommy doesn't ask about my bandage, but Ava starts going on about how there was blood everywhere.

'Where's the bread and butter till I make a piece?' says Tommy.

I fetch it and put it on the table. 'Bread and butter, your majesty.' Ava giggles.

'Were you at the pub this afternoon?' I say.

'Aye, what of it?'

'Well, that'll have to be stopped. I'm wanting wan a they high flats in Foxbar.'

'How does that mean I canny go tae the pub?' He bites into his butty, chews slowly. 'Anyway, they houses urny so good. You'll be bored stiff, stuck in the middle a naewhere, nae shops, nae cinema.'

'No pub.'

Tommy flashes me a look.

'We'll need a car,' I say.

'I don't drive, Jean.'

'That's why we need tae save money, so you can start. Do you think I want tae live here forever, Tommy? In this pokey wee flat wae this tiny kitchen, no enough room tae swing a loaf? Do you think I don't want something better fur me… fur us? Ava deserves a faither who's no afraid tae…?'

'To what, Jean? What?'

'Nothing.'

'Ach, I can't talk to you when you're like this. I'm away tae work.' He gets up, leaving his half-eaten butty on the plate. The door bangs shut.

Ava spits out a mouthful of chips. I give her a look and she starts humming a tune. She's mature for an only child. My mother could never keep me in one place. One time I got lost in

Barshaw Park. It was a holiday and there was bunting everywhere, and stalls where you could win a goldfish. My mother was at the white elephant stand. I shot off down the green when she wasn't looking. I was gone for hours. A neighbour told her she'd seen me going through Paisley Cross on the top deck of a tram. When she got home, I was waiting on the steps like nothing had happened. What a hiding that was! I brush a strand of Ava's hair behind her ear. 'Whit's that you're singing?'

'Nothing.'

'How would you like to visit your Auntie Annie?'

'And see the new baby?'

Annie's just had a boy. Only a few weeks old. Ava's been dying to see him. Annie won't mind. With a new baby to think about, she won't ask me any questions. 'We'll buy something fur him oan the way. Go and pit your shoes on, there's a good girl.' I don't bother clearing the table. I can do it later. I take the note out of my purse: *Tonight 7.30pm. You know where.*

2013
Victoria, British Columbia

In the airport lounge, she buys strong coffee in a cardboard cup. A flat screen TV shows footage of protestors, then switches to a press gang outside the headquarters of Borealis. She tries Bruce again, but his phone goes to voicemail.

A car is waiting. She climbs inside and shuts the door, glad to escape the noise. The driver says something polite but she doesn't answer. She's lost the energy for words, and her skin feels dirty, stale. The letter lurks inside her bag, like an intruder amongst her personal possessions; part of her wants to rip it up, toss it into an anonymous airport bin. But she can't.

They reach Downtown where the driver turns onto Government Street. Immediately, Ava regrets taking this route. The protestors have multiplied outside the Parliament Buildings. There's a carnival atmosphere, and on the steps a bearded man is playing a guitar, a woman with silver hair singing a dreadful protest song, applauded by violent cheers. Raised above the crowd, a cloth banner shows a giant cartoon bulldozer with carnivorous teeth, chomping its way through a grove of falling trees: the bulldozer wearing a cap that says BOREALIS. Woolly-hatted grandparents and shaggy-haired youths hold placards that bawl words like FASCISTS and TREES ARE NOT FOR SALE. How idiomatic: Bruce would laugh if he saw that one. Other people hand out leaflets on Government Street, while police officers cluster at the edges, not doing anything, just watching.

By the time she arrives at the house, her head is thumping. The gates close behind her and the car crunches over gravel, skirting the island of Trachycarpus palms. She remembers Cissy's face the first time she visited the house, her slowly widening eyes, her silence filling the car while Bruce eulogised over the architecture, the building's past life as a residence for attorney generals and governors. 'We're committed to keeping as many of the original features as possible,' he'd said. 'I can't stand it when these Asians come over from Hong Kong and replace all our historic buildings with monstrous condominiums.'

'Bruce is passionate about his history,' said Ava.

'Oh, we had history in Scotland,' said Cissy. 'Lots of castles.'

'Then it'll take more than a little place like this to impress you,' chuckled Bruce.

Her aunt had smiled then, a secretive smile with her chin tucked into her neck. Any outward display of pride was against her principles, but Ava could see she was quietly impressed. 'I like your dahlias,' said Cissy. 'We had dahlias in our garden back in Paisley.'

'Did we?' said Ava.

The smile disappeared. Cissy gathered herself like a darkening cloud, as though her earlier brightness had been a momentary lapse, an instance of forgetfulness. 'Oh, never mind, you wouldn't remember.'

Light cascades from the glass-domed atrium onto the stone floor. Ava kicks off her shoes. 'Bruce?' No answer. She hurries up the stairs, anxious for the warm soothing water of the shower. It trickles over her body, short and curved like her mother's. *Forgive me*. Forgive her for what?

Afterwards, wrapped in a towel, she looks down from the bedroom veranda at the flowerbeds, the ripe summer colours beginning to rust. Cissy loved the big terraced garden here. Her visits at the beginning of summer were like clockwork, until the long-haul flights became too much. Ava remembers how she'd book tours, dragging Cissy around museums and marinas, accompanied by an adolescent Scott, silent and brooding, until Cissy said that she was quite capable of taking care of herself, and began to go on her own solitary expeditions. When Ava returned home, she'd find her aunt sitting on one of the terraces, her eyes fixed towards the sandy beach and sapphire waters of the Juan de Fuca Strait and the hazy outline of America, as though she were watching, waiting, for a ship that never arrived. It filled Ava with a melancholy she found difficult to shake off.

It was Cissy who had given her that photo of her mother. If only she'd asked about it. She wouldn't hesitate now. She'd demand to know how Cissy could look her in the eye every goddamn day, letting her think that her mother was... She hurls her slipper over the veranda, toward the spot, near the roses, where Cissy used to sit. It misses and hits a statue of a chubby, childish looking angel. Originally there had been two, but the twin got destroyed. Ava always thought the remaining angel seemed lonely, abandoned. The slipper lands on the terrace with a quiet plop, and Ava sinks to the floor, small, insignificant, like a goose-bump on the shoulder of the world.

When she goes downstairs she's moisturised and dressed in loose linen pants and a matching cream shirt. The door to the TV room is open but she pauses, taking in the back of Bruce's head above the sofa, his thick brown hair flecked with silver. The TV room has always been his territory: dark panelling; a carpet that looks suspiciously, though not exactly, like leopard print; and a reclining sofa whose generous armrests remind her of airport lounges in the seventies.

She caresses his shoulder, then sits down, tucking her legs under her. His jacket is flung over the table, his face grimly absorbed in a way that suggests irritability, impatience. A reporter is comparing the scenes outside Parliament to a battle encampment, a modern-day crusade against nasty corporations. 'Kelly said he'd oil the wheels, push this licence through without a squeak,' says

Bruce. 'Now he won't take my calls, he's pedalling away faster than the kid that broke the window.' He loosens his tie. 'Do you know he hasn't made a single statement?'

'No doubt you'll ride out the storm. You always do.'

'That's not the point. Everyone said this would be easy, that it was the right thing to do. Even you.'

'We misjudged the situation.'

'Someone's to blame, and I want to know who.'

'The public care more than we thought.'

'About what?'

'Temple Grove. Some of the trees are nearly a thousand years old. Can you imagine what that will stir up?'

Bruce turns to look at her for the first time since she walked into the room. His eyes are still a pale, piercing blue, translucent in their brilliance, the one part of him that's never changed. 'You're beginning to sound like them. Next you'll be growing dreadlocks and smoking pot. I've planted more trees, created more new growth forests than these assholes have had birthdays, and they tell *me* I'm ruining the environment.'

Ava's fingers trace the letter in her pocket. Sitting next to Bruce, cushioned by the artificial light of an eighty-inch screen, it seems less significant, a scrap of paper and ink. Bruce will tell her to put it in the trash. Best place for it. But she needs to hear herself say the words. She strokes his arm through his shirt. 'Something strange happened,' she says. 'A letter from a solicitor.'

'What do they want to sue us for this time?'

'It was from Cissy's lawyer in Pickering.'

'Where's the remote? I can't listen to this guy anymore.'

She slides the remote from under his jacket sleeve. Noticing the pouch of her belly through her shirt, she pulls the material and shifts position, thinking how great it would be to suck out the excess baggage. 'Cissy wanted me to have this.' She takes the small square of paper from its envelope.

Bruce stands up, his trousers brushing against her knees, and disappears through the arch that leads to the bar. There's a chink of glass and ice and he reappears, leaning against the wall, swirling his whisky. 'Do you want one?'

She shakes her head. 'Bruce, listen to me.'

'What?' he says, his neck coiling.

She tries to conjure the words, but hesitates too long and his attention is sucked back to the screen where a bunch of self-righteous kids are promising to bring down the 'system.' They don't know companies like Borealis are practically indestructible, so many arachnid legs she's not sure even Bruce knows what each of them is doing. 'Read this.'

He tosses back the drink and smacks his lips. 'What is it?'

'Cissy left it to me. Just tell me what you think.'

'Not now, Ava. I've got the press on my back, people outside Parliament waving banners with my fucking name on them.' His phone vibrates. Escape route. He paces round the room. She can tell from the amount of nodding that it's Sue Brash. The only person Bruce ever defers to: his PR star. 'Sue's got me a spot on that current affairs show tonight,' he says. 'Big audience.'

'It's about my mother.'

His eyes meet hers, softer this time. 'I know it's hard, losing Cissy like that. But you're not alone, you've got me.' He lowers his gaze briefly. 'And Scott, why don't you call him? Look, I need to go back to the office. We'll talk about it tonight.' He lifts his jacket, slams his empty glass on the table.

'But, Bruce...'

He's already out the door, the tic-tac of his footsteps fading then returning. He's coming back; maybe he's changed his mind. But it's only Susi, carrying a tray with a silver teapot and cup. 'Camomile tea,' she says.

'I need coffee.'

'Camomile tea is better. No caffeine.'

'I don't want any.'

The housekeeper nods in that patient way of hers. There's a Scottish twang in her voice, softer than Cissy's. Ava doesn't know why, but it makes her want to cry. Through the linen pocket of her pants, the letter grazes her flesh. She thinks of Langley's office, the stained armchair, the envelope snagging when she tried to open it. The coffin, her aunt lying inside, the downwards turn of her mouth, all the answers locked inside that motionless flesh.

'You okay?' says Susi. 'You look a little flushed.'

'It's nothing.'

'I could boil some sage leaves. It helps with hot flushes.' Susi follows her to the kitchen.

Ava rifles through the cupboards stacked full of boxes: jasmine tea, elderflower, Turkish apple. Where does Susi get all this and why, in a kitchen this big, is it so hard to find a clean mug?

'Have you tried tai chi?' says Susi. 'It's works wonders for anxiety –'

A bright yellow cup shatters onto the tiled floor. 'Shit and damn.' But before Ava can think what to do, Susi has swept up the mess and told her to sit down. She observes the thin lines around Susi's eyes, the grey veins in her square-cut hair. 'Any kids?' says Ava.

The housekeeper places a silver teapot in front of her. Its steam has a bitter, woody smell. 'No.'

'Must be nice, no one to look after.'

Susi's smile is tense. 'Just my mother.'

This time Ava can't stop the tears. 'I'm sorry,' says Susi, and passes her a tissue, thin and transparent, like it could float off on the slightest wind.

1962
Paisley

Annie lives with her mother on the ground floor. My mother is in the top flat, been there thirty years, nearly as long as she worked in the mills. She retired five years back, her and Isa, both pally with big Una. They were never off telling me what a great mammy I had and what a hard job it was bringing me up, like it was my fault my father had died in the war.

I keep in tight to the buildings and tell Ava to be quiet, watching in case my mammy sticks her head out the window and shouts to Isa next close down. I don't know why they can't chat indoors with a cup of tea like normal civilised people. Annie's mother is no trouble, never pulls her up for streak marks on the plates, or creases in her man's shirts. Not that my mammy doesn't like Tommy, that's the problem; she loves him like the son she never had, all that fussing over him with biscuits and tea. He goes round every day and sees her after work. Imagine calling on your mother-in-law before you've come home to your own wife and child. 'Tommy fair likes my tea,' she tells me, with that wee glint in her eye as though it's some sort of competition.

She never visits us; we always go round and see her. The last time she came to our place was just after Ava was born. She had on that navy hat that she pulls down over her ears like a helmet. Tommy told her he was going out to paint our window frames. 'Una's got some white paint left from when she got hers done,' said my mammy. 'I'll get her man tae drop it roon.'

'I don't want white paint,' I told her. 'We're daein them baby blue, urn't we, Tommy?'

'Baby blue? Do you see anybody in this street wae baby blue frames?'

'Aye, that's the point, Mammy.' I wanted our windows to be different, like the pastel-coloured houses in Millport or Largs.

'It'll look daft, Jean. Everyone'll talk.'

'Let them talk. We don't aw huv tae be the same, Mammy: same claithes, same jobs in the mills, same bloody white windows.'

'You'll no rest, Jean McParland, until you've made a great big bloody fool of yourself.'

'It's only a bit a paint.' I rocked Ava in my arms. 'Whit if everyone painted their windows baby blue, whit wid you dae then?'

'I don't know, but I can tell you whit you'd dae, Jean McParland. You'd paint yours rid or green or bloody big dots because that's you all over. Selfish.'

Ava had started to cry.

'Maybe yer mither's right,' said Tommy. 'We'll keep the windaes white, nae sense in making a fuss.'

I said nothing. Ava was all teary and red so I went and got a bottle ready. When I came back, my mother was in the hall putting on her coat. 'That's settled then,' said Tommy. 'Everybidy's happy.'

'Oh aye,' I said, bouncing Ava on my hip, but looking square at my mother. 'You can be sure she's very happy, Tommy. She's the happiest wumin in the world.'

We're standing outside Annie's door and Ava is waiting for me to knock. 'Hurry up, Mammy.'

I try and gather my thoughts, check my bag to make it look like I'm busy. 'Where's the teddy?'

'Here.' Ava holds up the other bag and rolls her eyes. I see the teddy's brown fluffy ears and the ribbon round its neck. Baby blue. I laugh. 'What's funny?' says Ava.

'Nothing.'

She frowns. I'm about to chap the letterbox, then I hesitate. Do I really want to do this? Before I can change my mind, Ava shouts through the flap, 'Auntie Annie. It's us.'

Annie opens the door. Her hair is pushed back from her face with Kirby grips, and the buttons on her cardigan are done up wrong. I can smell it straight away, that baby milky smell. I feel sick. Wee Peter is in a pram in the hall. She tells us to come in and whisks him out as she passes, his wrinkled face gazing at me over her shoulder, his eyes half shut. We go through to the front room. Archie is out, thank God. Same shift as Tommy. Annie's mother is in the corner near the fire, eating a double nugget, chocolate and ice-cream all over the sides of her mouth. 'Hello, Mrs Fraser.' She doesn't answer. There's a low humming sound, like the murmur of a distant river.

'She sits there singing tae herself aw day,' says Annie. 'I don't think she knows whit tune.'

'Ava wanted to see the baby,' I say.

Ava is standing, one leg twisted behind the other. 'Can I give him his teddy?'

I nod. Annie pats the couch, inviting Ava to sit beside her. 'Meet baby Peter,' she says, dangling him by his oxters. Ava holds up the teddy and makes it dance. He drools and reaches out his fat wobbly fist. 'Can I have a baby brother, can I?' says Ava.

I pretend not to hear. I take my hairbrush and my purse out my bag, then put them back in again. 'Will you watch her a minute, Annie? I won't be long.'

'Where are you going?' Ava pouts.

'Mammy left her cigarettes in the house.'

'Take wan a Archie's, he'll no mind,' says Annie.

'It's the filtered wans I like,' I say. 'Plus, I'm savin up the coupons.' I didn't really need to put in that last bit, but she doesn't notice.

'I'll pit the kettle oan and we'll catch up.' Annie turns to Ava and smiles. 'Do you want to hold the baby?'

Ava jumps off the couch. 'Yes, please.'

'Let Mammy do it first,' I say. 'So you learn not to drop him.'

Annie hands me the baby wrapped in his blanket. I can't move, can't go anywhere. I smile down at his gurgling face, then glance up at the clock on the mantelpiece. Quarter past seven.

'Good as gold,' says Annie. 'Out like a light every night at eight o'clock. Archie spiles him rotten. Every week he buys him a new toy. Last week it wis a big yellow rattle…'

I nod, desperate for another reason to get away. I'm thinking of saying I left the gas on, but just then the quiet murmur of her mother erupts like a waterfall, '*Will ye go, lassie, go, to the braes o' Balquhidder? Where the blaeberries grow, 'mang the bonnie bloomin' heather.*' The slab of ice cream slides out between the chocolate-coated wafers and drops onto her lap, spreading in a milky puddle. 'Annie! I've wet maself.'

'You've no wet yourself, Mammy. You just spilt your ice cream.'

'My ice cream, my ice cream!'

'I'm away tae get my fags,' I say. 'I'll bring her back anither nugget.'

Ava tilts her head to one side, like she always does when she wants something. 'Can I get a nugget? I'll share it with baby Peter.'

'*Will ye go, lassie, go…*'

'Mammy, will you shoosh!' Annie takes a handkerchief from her skirt pocket and wipes her mother's singing lips.

I whisper to Ava to take Peter, and I belt it out the door.

It's half past seven and I've not even reached Paisley Cross. I feel all sweaty and pink and my heart is banging like it wants to leap outside my body. It's been like that all day. I must look a right hawgaw, with this stupid bandage. Anyway, I don't care what he thinks. I won't stay long. I check my reflection in the window of Watson's, the butcher's, wetting my fingers to flatten my fringe, and quickly powdering my cheeks. Billy always liked my cheeks, like two pink rose petals, he said. You didn't expect that sort of talk, not from someone like Billy. No one ever saw that side of him. 'I canny help it when I'm wae you,' he'd say. I made him feel that romantic. I thought about telling Annie the truth, but I knew it would be no use. 'Nice enough looking,' Billy always said about her. 'Gorgeous eyes, bit she'd bore you tae death in haulf an oor. Bit you,' he'd say, slinging his arm round my waist. 'You're jist right fur me, you've got potential.'

We used to meet at Abbey Bridge. It was near enough to the Lighthouse pub where Billy used to drink, and just out of sight of Paisley Cross and busy eyes. I thought it was like a fairytale, me and Billy with the turret of the abbey in the background. Billy never took me to the cafés or the pictures or any of the other places boys took their girlfriends. I would never know what was going to happen. Sometimes, we'd go out in a car with his friends. We'd drive up to one of those big houses in Thornly Park or Calside Road, with gravel drives, bay windows and gardens that sloped all the way down. Billy said he was looking for work, gardening, that sort of thing. We'd park right up behind the house then Billy and his friends would go and knock on the back door while I waited. I asked why I couldn't go with them but he said it didn't look good, scouting for work with a lassie in tow, and didn't I want him to get a job so he could take care of me?

The best times were when we used to walk round town. Billy liked to talk and I liked to listen. We'd go past the Lighthouse and along River Cart Walk where the Anchor Finishing Mill sits on the riverbank. You weren't supposed to, but Billy would lift me over the fence and we'd lie on the grass near the Hamills, watching the water rush and tumble over the rocks. The clanging from inside the mill was quieter there, the rows of windows a little more distant. Billy would tell stories about tailing the linn: 'Ye'd jump in where the watter gushes ower the falls, and swim fur yer life tae the ither side.' They stopped it because it was dangerous, but he did it loads of times. Billy said that one day he would be rich, and that he was a distant relative of Al Capone, whose ancestors came from Scotland. 'Wasn't it Italy?' I said.

Billy lowered his head. 'Aye, but some were from Scotland. Not a lot of people know that. Don't you trust me when I'm talking to you?' I felt Billy's finger lifting up my chin, tilting my face to his.

'How can I be with you when you don't trust me?'

'I'm sorry,' I said. He kissed me and I was flying again. We walked round town watching the women in dull overcoats and rain hats shuffling along with their string bags; the men with their sunken faces, lifeless eyes and cloth caps, all looking as miserable as each other. Sometimes, Billy would stick his tongue out right in front of somebody's face and baa like a sheep. It put the wind right up them. Once, this daft old guy in war medals chased him all the way round the cenotaph and up the High Street. But he was no match for Billy, who ducked him at every turn. I knew it was wrong but I couldn't help laughing. It was Billy all over.

Twenty-five to eight. The thought of seeing him face to face after all this time turns my legs to jelly. I'll tell him I'm not the person I was, and neither is he. He can't be. Like Una said, prison changes a man. We've just got to knuckle down and accept our lot. I hurry along to the corner and turn onto St Mirren Brae. Before I see them, I've run right into them, my bag and make-up spilling onto the pavement. 'Watch where you're gaun,' says a voice.

'Aye, why don't you get a pair a specs?' says another.

I look up and it's wee Aggie and her pal, Angie, from Spinning.

'Ach, it's you, Jean,' says Aggie. 'Angie, it's Jean, you know Jean, fae Twisting?'

Angie smiles, 'Oh aye, that Jean.'

'Aye,' says Aggie. 'Where you going anyway wae yer pants oan fire?'

I scrunch Billy's note up in my hand. 'Nowhere... I wis jist... anyway I've left Ava at Annie's and I've got tae get back. We're visiting the new baby.'

'Who? You and Tommy?'

'Naw, Tommy's at work.' I gather everything up, and I'm about to rush off.

'Your hair looks nice,' says Aggie.

'Aye, a bit well turned out tae go visiting a baby,' says Angie. 'I widny wear a suede jeekit like that tae huv a baby be sick all ower it.'

'Well, Tommy likes me to look nice. Where are you two off

tae?' I say, trying to change the subject.

'The Regal. We were jist at the Anchor Rec watching the fitbaw. Aggie likes that, whit d'ye cry him, Jim Shepherd. She's hoping when he catches sight of her stockings, he'll make her his goal.'

'Shut up, Angie.'

'It wisny that hauf an oor ago. Whit were you shouting? "Come oan, Jim, geez a goal ya big sweetheart, ye."'

'I didny say it like that,' says Aggie.

'It wis all I could dae tae stop her throwing her knickers. We're going tae the Regal tae calm doon. Fancy coming? They're showing a Gary Cooper film.'

'Another time. I've got tae go.' I wait till they turn the corner, then cross over the square, past the statue of Queen Victoria with her dour stare, up the side of the river, and out of sight. It's nice, that wee stretch of water. Even though the river is dirty, there are still the green banks and the trees framing the abbey on the other side. I used to imagine walking under its big arched doorway in a wedding dress.

When I reach the bridge there's no sign of Billy. I glance towards the Town Hall. The clock says quarter to eight. I go to the end of Abbey Close, then turn and walk across the bridge, the big Anchor Finishing Mill staring down at me. The acrid smell of the soapworks on the opposite bank chokes my nostrils. The river flows thick and brown, tumbling from the Hamills, wee grey and brown bubbles floating on the surface. I peer down and watch them gather and burst on the banks. A few men are standing outside the Lighthouse. If I ask nicely, one of them might go inside and look for Billy, but, halfway there, my stomach knots up and I turn back. I try to work out how much longer before I need to get back to Ava, and I decide to give it another five minutes. The skin on my lip snags where I've been chewing it. Still no sign of him. Just like Billy to pick you up and drop you again. Why do I never learn? Tearing up his note, I drop it into the river, watch the pieces float downstream with the bubbles and the scum.

2013

Vancouver, British Columbia

The Helijet sweeps over the shimmering roofscape. From its comfortable interior, Ava looks down at the double-B of the Borealis logo rising out of the city's heat haze. Bruce has called an emergency meeting. The TV interview didn't go well. Catastrophic is the word he used. Clips of it are trending on social media as an example of everything that's wrong with the world. He enacted all the right gestures: mimicking the interviewer's body language, hypnotising her with those blue eyes. He even told *the* story, how his ancestor, Captain Hastings, used to haul logs with nothing but donkeys. Ava's heard him tell that one a million times: 'When old Hastings ran out of line, he unwound a steel cable he found in an abandoned mine with his bare hands till he had a five-strand main line and a one-strand haulback. Sure as hell wasn't the best but it worked. They got those damn logs out. That's how this great country was built. By men like that.'

At the harbour, she rushes from the jet towards her waiting car. It speeds through the early morning traffic and lets her out at the entrance, where she click-clacks through the foyer, past the central bronze statue of the indomitable Captain Hastings pointing blindly at the distant forests of British Columbia, then takes the elevator to the top floor.

The boardroom is full of the usual faces: finance, marketing, PR, eyes glued to their phones. She's never liked this room. The dark wood panelling always makes her feel claustrophobic. She walks to the cooler and fills a jug with water, afraid that if she sits down she'll congeal. Bruce is sweating and his face is red. He thumps the table. 'Okay, so there's two issues here,' he says. 'I want that licence and I want rid of these protestors.'

Sue Brash shakes her page-boy brown hair. 'Well, the good news is I think we can swing the effects of last night's interview. Melanie has some ideas.'

Sue's assistant, a young woman with black-rimmed glasses and a tight skirt, the kind of skirt that used to look good on Ava when she was that age, lifts her head. 'I think we're overlooking the positives. Bruce did a great job. We should build on it, get that guy who does the heritage section in the local rag to do a feature on Captain Hastings: any churches he funded, schools, hospitals, parks. We need the public to see Bruce as a working man, someone who learned the business hands-on.'

Ava can't blame her. She did the same thing when she started out, buttering up the boss. Bruce grins. 'It's good, but it's too soft. I want preventative action.' The grin fades. 'Target Green Alliance. I need an injunction against the ringleaders. And I need the public to back me up.'

Bernard Bentley folds his hands – Ava doesn't like lawyers: they know too many secrets, and have no qualms about handing someone a letter from their supposedly dead mother. 'Legally speaking, we'd need to convince the court that the protests will damage the economy,' says Bentley, neatly.

'Why not get Kelly to put a stop to it, then it keeps our hands clean.' Sue leans forward, elbows on the table. 'You just have to persuade him it's in the public interest.'

Bruce reddens. 'Of course it's in the goddamn public interest. I'm backing Kelly in the upcoming election. I want some kind of return.'

Bentley crosses his arms. 'Kelly will never go for an injunction.'

'Then we'll get someone who will,' says Sue.

Ava shakes her head. 'The last thing we need right now is pictures of elderly protestors in handcuffs all over the front pages. If you want to get the public on side, you need to keep pushing the jobs issue. Extending our licence will save jobs. I think Bruce made that clear last night.'

'It's not enough.'

'Sue's right,' says Bruce.

Sue leans back, a smug crease on her lips.

There was a time when Bruce would back Ava up, when they'd back each other up. Human Resources used to be exciting, dramatic even. She'd have pay disputes, strikes to sort out, but over the years her position grew less important, the workforce dwindling and 'strike' becoming a dirty word. The most exciting thing to come her way these days are memos about canteen menus, parking spaces and vending machines.

Ava half-listens to the exchanges round the table, nodding her head at appropriate moments. Her eyes drift to the wall and a map of the BC interior, its rivers and creeks coloured dark brown so that, from a distance, they look like tree branches. When she was a teenager in Montreal, she'd dreamed of being an artist. She'd go on languid walks down touristy streets, dressed in flared jeans and a bandana, sketching monuments and churches, doing caricatures for a few dollars apiece. Once, she attempted a likeness of her mother's photo, but crumpled it almost immediately, as if nothing she drew could come close.

Faces float up from the past, mill women in long coats and scarves. Her mother had come into the kitchen one day wearing a white PVC raincoat that shone like it was made of light. She'd kissed Ava's cheek and fixed her a banana sandwich, laughing as she put sugar on it, like she was doing something naughty. Then they sat in the kitchen with the blue and pink swirly walls, her mother watching her eat and smiling between puffs of her cigarette. Ava had wanted to go out and play that day, but her mother wouldn't let her. Instead, she made her sit beside her on the couch all evening, running her fingers through her hair. Maybe she should call Cissy's lawyer; perhaps there was something he forgot to tell her, some small detail that was overlooked.

It was December 1962 when they arrived in Canada. She remembers the liner, its two big red funnels with black coronets, the strange smells, pleading with Cissy to *please, please, please* let her sleep on the top bunk, and sulking when Cissy refused. It was on that boat, out on the wild Atlantic, far away from Paisley, that Cissy finally told her her mother was dead. 'The fire took her away,' she said.

'Will she be coming back?'

'No. That's what dead means.'

Ava had sobbed till she was out of breath, her aunt rubbing her shoulders, promising everything would get better once they got to Canada.

Bruce shoves his phone in his inside pocket, signalling the meeting is over. She leaves him deep in discussion with Bentley. 'I'll see you at home,' she says, as efficiently as her tired mind will allow. Last night, she couldn't sleep. Susi had made her some kind of healthy tea, a night-time remedy that smelled of liquorice. Ava catches her reflection in the foyer, her body sagging inside her expensive suit. God, she feels shitty. She hails a cab and dials Scott.

'Yo,' he says.

'Be a sweetheart and put some coffee on. I'll be there in ten.'

His condo is in Vancouver West, near an early twentieth century church that once dominated the street. She buys some milk just in case. There's a delay when she presses his buzzer, then a click that takes her into the bright lobby and the elevator to the twenty-fifth floor. The door is already open. It's not a big apartment, just a room and kitchen, with a mezzanine and a balcony, the view obscured by tall buildings. Scott gets a monthly allowance to cover his bills, but he usually overspends. The black leather couch is strewn with clothes, the table piled with magazines, books, an overflowing ashtray. The veranda door is open and a draught blows through the room. She pulls it shut. 'Scott,' she calls, and heads to the kitchen. The coffee percolator is silted with brown gunge, a pile of unwashed plates and cups in the sink. Might as well wash them.

Scott comes hurrying down the stairs in black skinny jeans and a t-shirt of some band she's never heard of. His feet are bare.

He runs a hand through his hair and gestures at the sink. 'Leave it, Mom.'

'You can't drink coffee from this.' She lifts up the percolator.

'It's alright, Ginny left some instant in the cupboard.'

She doesn't ask who Ginny is.

He lights one of his black cigarettes and sits on the sofa. She wonders if he does it to annoy her, living like a teenager at the age of thirty-six. God, what is she thinking? It's not as if she hasn't spoken to enough doctors. It's only in the last ten years they managed to get a diagnosis. Bi-polar. Such a funny word, but it sums it up in a way: a person of opposite extremes, geographically distant.

Ava sets two cups of coffee on the table. 'I wish you'd give that up. I know a great hypnotherapist in Victoria. Remember Bruce used to have that god-awful habit of grinding his teeth?'

Scott sighs. 'Smoking is the only pleasure I have in life.'

She scuffs his knee playfully, drapes a shirt over the back of the sofa, and sits down. 'How's the Internet business?'

'It's web-design, Mom.' He rubs the heel of his palm into his head, making his hair stand up like straw. 'People have no imagination, that's what happened. All they want are the basics. Any monkey can do that.'

'Well, that's business, Scott. People get what they can afford.' It's no use, she can't stop herself. Ava sets down her cup and starts picking up clothes from the floor, turning the shirts the right side out, folding them into neat squares.

'Don't do that.' Scott stares at her, like she's just pencilled obscenities on his walls. 'I don't like people touching my stuff.'

She stops, half-flustered. 'But I'm your mother.' An image of his room in Pickering flashes through her mind, the Superman poster on the wall, tidying away his comics, hanging up his clothes. 'I'm only trying to help.'

'You're not listening, Mom. Shit, it's always the same with you. You never listen.' He gets up, takes several rapid drags of his cigarette (just like her mother used to do), and paces back and forth, not looking at her. 'Why didn't you give me a shot, Mom?

You know I have good ideas. If people knew I had experience, that's all it would take, you know?'

Ava takes a deep breath. 'It's not that easy. We can't just go cancelling contracts and handing them out to someone else. But there's still time. Prove yourself, like Bruce said, and who knows? This time next year, a contract could be yours.'

'Too late.' Scott stares at his feet. She's not sure if he's waiting for her to reply, or having some kind of silent dialogue with himself. The weight of concern settles about her shoulders. But before she can say anything, he looks up again, his face animated. 'Anyway, it doesn't matter. I decided I'm going to do what I do best.' He shifts into a cross-legged position and grins.

He's been through so many incarnations, a series of bands with names like Boiled Entrails, Subversive Clones, and White Phosphorous. Then it was the Canadian College of Performing Arts. After that he gave up being an actor and studied directing at the film school in Vancouver. He sits down. 'I'm ready to make another film.'

'So what's the script?' She almost says, 'this time,' but stops herself.

'Scripts are so predictable. It's more of a docu-drama.'

'What's the subject of your, um, docu-drama?'

Scott grins. 'Me. I'm going back to the beat-era. Fuck the Vancouver Film Festival, fuck the Vancity Theatre, this thing is going to Europe, man. I'm talking Venice, Cannes. I really think they'll understand me there, Mom.' He furrows his brow. 'Ginny thinks it's a great idea.'

Well, Ginny must be a genius.

'All I need is a camera. Maybe two. I want to shoot in real film. Old style. That's the beauty of it.'

'Scott, are you sure this is what you want?'

That hurt look again. 'Are you serious? You know I've always dreamed of being a director.'

She stares into the bottom of her empty cup. 'Well, if you're sure. But I wish you had something to fall back on. Something less irregular.'

He presses his head into the back of the chair, his teeth clenched and his upper body arched, the way he used to do as a child, stiffening his muscles to prevent her from lifting him in and out of his pushchair.

'Scott?' she says. He taps his forehead with the heel of his fist, then holds it there as though stemming a blood-flow. 'Scott, we need to talk about this.' Without saying anything, he gets off the couch and slides his feet into a pair of moccasins. 'Where are you going?'

He heads for the door. It closes in her face.

We've been here before. He'll come back. She'll wait. There's a chair on the veranda. She sits down and folds her arms, thinking of the flat in Pickering, the empty rooms where Scott took his first wobbly steps, the endless washing and ironing, and skinned knees, the way his laughter always made her smile no matter what. It wasn't Scott's fault. The years had flown by and, in all that time, she couldn't really say if her son was happy. Bruce had done his best, but it wasn't the same; there was none of the adhesive warmth that comes from sharing the same genes. Scott never expressed his resentment, not outwardly, but it was there on a subterranean level, in his childish eruptions, usually over some trivial matter, but the accusation, for her, was always the same – all he had for a father was an idea, a chance encounter that had taken place one afternoon in her life.

August 1975. She'd gone to sketch the Basilique Notre Dame, that famous tourist attraction of Montreal, whose Gothic arches and carvings were a test of precision and interpretation. Philippe (she never asked his surname) was busking in Place Jacques Cartier. He had dark collar-length hair, wore an open shirt and a red bandana. In his top pocket was a pack of Gauloise cigarettes. All she had was a couple of dollars, but she gave him it anyway. He made an elegant speech about how the Colonne Nelson should be replaced with a statue of Lenin. She was seventeen. He was twenty-one, a pillar of maturity and wisdom. She agreed with everything he said, and they ended up in his friend's flat in The Plateau. That was it, the whole story. No sketch, not even a photo.

Scott looks a lot like him: dark and lean, the same impatient gleam in his eye. Perhaps even the same flaw; the latest research says it's hereditary, a loose wire in the brain chemistry that causes that painful imbalance, those dangerous mood swings. She knows already that she'll sign the cheques, hoping half of it won't be spent on skinny cocaine-addled girls, or whoever Ginny is. But it's more than that. She sees it every time she drives down the street, sitting in cafes and under the enclosed domes of shopping malls: a son and his mother, the warm glances and easy laughter. That's what she wishes for. Normal. All she wants is for things to be normal.

The door clicks. He's back, a cardboard cup from Costa in his hand. She stands up. 'You should have got me one.'

'You're still here?'

'Where else would I be, Peanut?'

He shrugs, lights another Kretek, and steps through the veranda doors. 'It must be a disappointment, Mom, having an irregular son like me.'

'You're not a disappointment.'

She looks down at the streets below, the flowing streams of traffic winding round her like an unsolvable puzzle, its meaning precise, yet unclear. She's only being half-truthful. When Scott was a teenager, things got bad. He'd sit for hours and hardly say a word. He'd forget to turn up for lectures, appointments, he'd miss assignments. No one knew what was wrong, least of all him. The doctors gave him Prozac, Xanax, a whole cascade of anti-depressants, most of which he refused to take. They went through various diagnoses. In the early days it was depression, then hysteria. One doctor thought a year in the military would *soon make a man of him*. Others wanted to do tests. But she knew the diagnosis already: it was her fault. Still, the latest concoction of anti-psychotics seems to be working. For now. 'All the best directors started out in steady jobs,' she says. 'Wasn't Ridley Scott in advertising?'

'Yeah, Ridley Scott is so fucking regular.'

'I just want you to be happy. To have that feeling of really achieving something.'

'Face it, Mom. Just because we're related doesn't mean we have to like it.'

It's worse than a slap, worse than getting a letter from your long-dead mother. It's like the ground underneath her has begun to shake and split around her feet. Scott's words fall like debris, but she must pretend it doesn't hurt. What was that tune Cissy used to play? A sad lamenting song, full of mist and tears, singing in that strange mysterious voice, then closing herself up again as she shut the lid over those luminescent black and white keys. 'Come to Pickering with me,' says Ava.

'No. I'm not going anywhere near a funeral.'

'That was last week. I need you to help me clear out some of Cissy's things. We'll hire a skip.'

'Why can't you pay someone to do it?'

'Because there might be some stuff we want to keep. Come on. If you're making a docu-drama it's the best place to start. I'll get you that camera.'

'I'll need film.'

'Sure.' She smiles. Soon the house in Pickering will be gone, its memories packed into boxes, and abandoned in tips. It's her last chance to find something of herself, an explanation, some memento wrapped in her aunt's possessions. It'll be a family trip. Just the two of them. Normal. Maybe she'll find nothing. In which case she'll chuck the letter in the trash, forget it ever existed.

1962
Paisley

I trip over one of Ava's dolls in the hall. 'Will you put that away?' I shout. 'I've spent all day cleaning this place.' Shirts, sheets, skirts and trousers are washed and drying out the back. I want the flat to look spotless. Tommy appreciates coming home to a clean house.

Ever since we were at Annie's, I've had this horrible feeling inside me, like I'm getting smaller and smaller. My eyes were stinging when I got back from going to meet Billy, but I don't think Ava noticed. 'You forgot,' she said.

'Whit?'

'My double nugget.'

'The shop wis shut,' said Annie. 'I could've telt ye that if ye hudny jist belted oot the door.' She had Peter slung over her shoulder. When she patted his back, he let out a burp.

'I got my cigarettes.' I said.

Ava gave this big long sigh that made me feel like I was shivering all over. I wish that feeling would go away, but it gets stronger every time she looks at me. She's lurking in the corner, her doll that she calls Raggedy Jane tucked under her arm. 'Away you go outside and play,' I say. 'Go on. It's Saturday efternoon and it's no healthy, a lassie your age being in the house.'

'But, Mammy, it's raining.'

'Do whit you're told. Now!'

When she's gone, I lie on the couch and look out the window. The rain is heavier than I thought. No doubt Ava will run round to one of her pal's. It's difficult to get peace sometimes.

Yesterday, on my dinner break, I went to the library to get away from Una and her cronies. When I was there, I got a book on Mary, Queen of Scots. It's got seven hundred pages. It looks like a doorstop and weighs a ton. Mr Webster, the librarian, says she's one of history's most tragic figures, worthy of Shakespeare, though, being an Elizabethan, Shakespeare could never have written about her without ending up in the Tower himself. 'Fascinating,' I say. Mr Webster is the only person I use words like that around. If I said it to Tommy, he'd just look at me funny. There's not much Tommy says that's fascinating. My bag was bulging when I went back to my shift. 'Whit you got in there?' said Una.

'Nothing.'

'Disny look like nothing.'

'A book, that's all.'

She wrinkled her face. 'Wish we had time tae read a book, eh, Maggie.'

I told her it was for Tommy, and that shut her up. The annoyance on her face means I do the rest of my shift, smiling.

I try reading on the couch, but fall asleep before I finish the chapter. When I wake up, the rain is lashing off the window. Tommy is in his chair and Ava is on the floor, cradling that silly doll. 'I found her on the steps,' he says. 'She'll catch her death.'

'Ava.' I sit up and pull her towards me, wrap my arms around her body. 'A bit of rain never did a wean any harm. They like it, Tommy. It's natural.'

He gives me one of his looks.

I smile and shrug it off. 'You worry too much.'

Sunday is the worst day of the week. At least Tommy isn't one for going to church. It was bad enough going to church with my mother. Even so, the day still drags. I spend most of it staring out the window. Occasionally, I think I see Billy, but the fella ends up being too short, too old or too fat and, anyway, Billy doesn't know where I live.

All day I'm tired, but at night I don't sleep much, and when I do, I dream I'm at the Abbey Bridge, only when I look down there's no water, just wet mud and a fish lying in it, gasping for breath. I feel repulsed. I look up and see Ava coming towards me. I call her name but she walks right past, as if I wasn't there. Then the rain pours down and I'm soaked to the skin.

In the morning, I wait until the lassies have passed on their way to the mill before I run downstairs. I can't be bothered. All I want is to do my shift and go home. I get there in the nick of time. 'Morning,' says Mr Green, looking at his watch. 'How's the hand?'

I hold it up to show him. I've replaced the bandage with a plaster. The wound is a bit sore if I press on it, but I'll get through the day. I go to my own machine this time, with Una on the other side. I keep watching the clock. When the trolley comes to take away the cones, I jump. It's a feeling I've had all morning. It's a bit like thinking you're pregnant but not knowing for sure; life going on as normal though deep down you know that peace could be shattered, taken away forever, broken into a million fragments.

Soon the frame comes down again and the twisting threads start to blur. I ask Myra to watch my machine and I put up my hand for a toilet break. There's a couple of cigarettes in the pocket of my overall. I wish I could hide in the cubicle and smoke for the rest of the afternoon, but there's no one to keep watch and it's three days' suspension if you get caught. I've only had a few puffs when a voice says, 'Is that you, Jean McParland? I thought I seen you leaving your machine.'

It's Una. I open the cubicle door, and she slides in. 'I might as well have one too,' she says, lighting up and leaning against the door so no one can get in. 'Mind and flush the dowt. The Bitch will be in here quicker than Maggie's man at the sound of a bottle opener.' Una laughs. I don't, and her face goes serious. 'How's the baby?'

'What baby?'

'Wee Aggie said she ran intae you up the toon.'

'Peter's fine,' I say. 'Ava wis dying tae see him. She loves babies.'

'You should have anither wan,' says Una, right out the blue. 'Tae keep her company.'

I want to tell her it's none of her business, but I take another puff and make a 'humph' noise.

'Did you go and see your mither?'

I shake my head.

'Aggie says you wur all dolled up.' There's a knock at the cubicle. Una opens the door and Maggie squeezes in.

'Who wis dolled up?' says Maggie.

'Jean.' Una gives me a challenging look. 'Aggie saw her up the toon.'

'I wisny dolled up,' I say. 'Anyway, it's nobody's business whit I do, no yours, no Aggie's.' The words are out before I can stop them.

Una folds her arms, her cigarette poking between her fingers. She looks at Maggie.

Maggie raises her eyebrows, and lights up. 'That's no way to talk to Una.'

I reach for the lock.

Maggie steps in front of me: 'You owe her an apology.'

They're standing shoulder to shoulder, blowing smoke out their noses like an ugly two-headed dragon. 'Why should I?' I stammer.

'Tae think I go back years wae her mither. Whit that poor wumin went through, bringing her up on her own.' She's shaking her head at me, but talking to Maggie. 'Fifteen we wur when we started in here. You didny huv much, but you had friends. And her mither wis the best.'

'It's no my fault she never married,' I say.

Una comes up close to my face. 'There wis a war on.'

'Aye, and she's been at war wae me ever since.'

'If it wisny fur her, you wouldny huv a joab in this mill. Jist remember, it's your mither who got you where you are.'

'Do you think I want to work in this place all my life? Well, I won't, you'll see. And Ava won't either. Jist because you're unhappy, jist because you had a bloody rotten time, don't take it out on me.'

'Your mither's right. She always said you thought you were a cut above the rest.'

'I know what I'd do if she wis my lassie,' says Maggie.

'Well, I'm not. Now let me go, or I tell Mr Green you're giving me bother.'

They let me go and I rush into the corridor, just in time to see The Bitch waddling towards me. 'I said a toilet break, Jean, no a trip tae Saltcoats.'

'Sorry.' It crosses my mind to get Maggie and Una three days' suspension without pay. But things are bad enough. They're already on my case. Anyway, the supervisor might be a bitch, but even she knows better than to tangle with Una McMenemy.

I give the canteen a miss and go for a walk instead. My stomach's empty but I couldn't eat a thing. I go past the warehouses and the old spinning mill, its domed shadows stretching along the ground and merging with my own. I'm near the gatehouse when I hear a whistle, but I don't look up. Instead, I bow my head and keep walking. I know it's him but, even so, the touch of his hand on my shoulder still makes me jump. Then he's in front of me, so close I can smell the leather of his jacket, a whiff of smoke. I forget all about work, about Una and my mother and, for a moment, it's like nothing has changed, like time hasn't moved at all.

'You're not supposed to be in here,' I say, trying to cover my drab green overalls with my coat.

'I sneaked past the guard.' He glances over his shoulder. 'I waited for you the other night. You didn't show.'

'You couldny have waited long. Things got difficult. Anyway, you said you'd understand, that if I didn't want to come you'd leave me alone.'

Everything is so familiar, those green eyes like magnets. 'I know whit I said, bit I hud tae see you. You look good, Jean, better than ever.'

He grins, and the heat rises to my cheeks. I'd forgotten that smile, the way it slants, one corner higher than the other. 'I'm on my dinner.'

He shrugs. 'I know. I wis hoping fur a glimpse a you. Crazy, isn't it? But I canny help it.' He bends his knees till his face is level with mine. He looks stupid, standing there bow-legged with his hands in his trouser pockets. I try not to smile. But it's too late. 'I've missed you, Jean. I've missed that smile. I know it's daft, but that's me. Your big daft Billy.'

'You should go before someone sees.'

'Just give me a chance, that's all. Five minutes, Jean, come on. Five minutes then you never need tae see me again.'

'I don't know. I need tae git back.'

His back stiffens. For a moment, everything is still. Then he takes a run and boots the railings, a hard rattle that makes my heart jump. People are turning their heads. 'Billy!' He goes towards a van parked part way down and I think he's going to boot that too: 'Billy. Billy, stop!'

He spins round. 'You've nae idea whit it's been like. Aw they years withoot ye. Thinking about you – where you were, whit you wur daein. It's enough tae drive a man mad.'

'Okay.' I glance about the place for anyone that might recognise us. 'Five minutes.'

That grin again. 'Thanks, Jean.'

We follow the canal that runs past the spinning mill, round the backs of the warehouses and the big chimney. It's quieter down there, apart from a few girls who feed the ducks. Ever since the mills started up, the ducks in Paisley have got fat. That's what Tommy says, but I try not to think about Tommy. The sky is low and greyish, but at least it's not raining. Still, the nearer we get to Twisting, with Una and her cronies inside, the more I feel like I'm gasping for breath. 'How's work?' says Billy. 'Dae you like it?'

He never could stand a silence, always had to find a way to break it.

'Okay,' I say, not looking at him. 'You know.'

He starts to whistle a tune. 'Dae you like The Beatles?' he says. '*Love me Do.*'

This time, I let the smile happen.

We reach the part of the canal where the water spreads out like a big fan. I stop and Billy leans against the railings. There's no one else here; the girls who feed the ducks don't usually come this far up. I couldn't stand it if someone saw us. The air around me is heavy, crushing me, and I just want it to stop. I look between the railings to the smooth grey of the water. 'Things are different now, Billy. You canny jist turn up after all this time and expect –'

'Dae you think I don't know? You mairrit Tommy McParland.' Billy's face is serious.

'Yes, I did.'

'Why, Jean? Someone else, and I might've understood, bit Tommy?'

'We're happy, Billy.'

'Gaun tae work every morning, and coming hame at night? Listening tae Tommy snoring?'

'What, Billy? What are you trying to say? That Tommy is boring?'

'You said it, no me.'

'You've nae right tae talk aboot Tommy. He's my husband. He's a good man and he's there fur me, Billy, which is mair than you ever were.'

Billy takes a deep breath. 'I deserve that. But, when you didny answer my letters, I –'

'Whit letters?'

'From the prison. Believe me, it's no easy fur a man in there. Some of those blokes, the things they've done. I wis scared. Fur the first time in my life, I wis really scared. All I wanted wis one letter, jist a word –'

I feel the tear escape down my cheek. 'I never got a letter, Billy. I swear, not a single one. If I did, I'd have wrote, I promise.'

He wipes my cheek with his thumb. Billy's thumb, his skin, his warmth, his closeness. Once, the most natural thing in the world would have been to take his hand, kiss it, hold it. But not now. I turn away. 'If you know aboot Tommy, then you know aboot Ava.'

I hear Billy's breath, shallow at first, then deeper. 'I bet she looks jist like you.'

I turn again to face the water, hold onto the railings with both hands. It's like a wave rising up inside me, and the noise that escapes from my throat sounds like grief, like the sound people make at funerals. My shoulders, my whole body starts to shake.

His hand touches the small of my back. 'Ach, Jean, don't, eh?'

I've never wanted to be held so much as I do now.

Then his arm is round my body, the grip tightening, pulling me towards him. 'Don't, Jean, please.'

My head is pressed against his chest, the smell of leather and aftershave, familiar yet strange. He strokes my neck, my ears; then it's his mouth kissing my forehead, his breath on my cheek, searching. I pull away. 'Don't, Billy.'

His voice is a murmur. 'We belong thegither, you and me. Billy and Jean. Jean and Billy. That's the way it is. Like nature.'

My hand covers my mouth. 'I can't, Billy. It's wrong, I'm married. I can't –'

'Listen to me, Jean.' He touches my shoulder. 'Who says whit's right and whit's wrong? Them oot there? Your mither? Who makes up the rules?'

'Stop it, Billy. Stop it. People will talk. You know they will.'

Billy laughs, a harsh sound. 'Who, Jean?' He sweeps his arm behind him, towards the mill buildings, the chimneys, the warehouses, the distant rattle of trucks. 'One day, nane a this will exist. All gone, like cardboard in the rain. And the people tae, wae their cardboard lives, where will they be, big Una and them? All we've got is the day, Jean. Here and now. Are ye gauny let they people run yer life fur ye? You're better than that and you know it. The world is changing, and this place is stuck in the past.'

'It's no that easy.'

'Are you happy, Jean?'

I don't know what to say. That I'm a mother, I have responsibilities? Do I even have the right to be happy? But the words are so difficult. I take my hands from my face and try to speak with my eyes.

'You're no happy. One look at you and I know. I can take you away fae aw this, jist say the word. Have you seen whit's happening aroon ye? America, Jean. That's where we'll go. We cuid have it aw. Jist think, no one telling us whit tae dae. I realised something in prison. You create it aw yersell. You make your own prison, your own freedom. Naebody can tell you whit tae dae except you.'

'This isny fair, Billy.'

'Come wae me. You and me. We can make it, I promise. Away fae here.'

'Whit about Ava?'

'Ava too.'

I can't stay still. I start walking the length of the railings. A family of ducks follows me in the water, a row of babies and their mother. I know it's madness but part of me is thinking, why not? If you try hard enough, you can make something happen. 'At least I huv a job here,' I say. 'I can pit food in my mouth and buy clothes fur my daughter. It might be a prison bit it pays. Whit wid we live oan? Where wid we live?'

Billy is walking beside me. 'Don't worry, Jean. I've got it aw worked oot.'

'Whit dae you mean?'

'This place, this is how we'll do it.'

His eyes have a faraway look. 'You're no making sense, Billy.'

'You know how it works here.'

'How whit works?'

'Whit time do they pay you oan a Friday?'

'Aboot three o'clock. Why?'

'Good. Aw I need to know is when they start making up the pay packets.'

'I don't know, do I? They do it in the Counting House.'

'So we can hit them there, or in transit. Who brings the pay ower?'

'I don't know, Billy. Stop it, you can't be serious.'

His jaw is tight. When he's not speaking, he's grinding his teeth and running his hand through his hair. He stops, looks at my tearstained face and laughs. 'I know, I'm aff my heid, you're right. Whit wid a nice girl like you want wae a ned like me? But I know you, Jean. The real you. You're wasted in a place like this. You were made fur better things. And you're wrong. I do understand. I understand why you mairrit Tommy, why you settled. It's because I wisny here. But I'm here noo. And I hate tae see you working your fingers tae the bone. That's no my Jean. My Jean wis meant tae be someone.'

I shake my head, biting my lip to hold back the tears. There's a ball of cramp in my stomach. I suppose I always knew, just didn't want to admit it; never questioned why he made me wait in the car when he went round the backs of the houses with those friends of his. I just accepted it: the Aston Martin, the little presents of jewellery. That was Billy. As soon as I felt his arms around me none of it mattered. Until he went to prison. Burglary is one thing, but this? 'Dae you know whit you're saying, Billy?'

'Aye, I know. Think it over; don't make a decision right away. Once you've made up your mind, you can find me in the Lighthoose.'

'No, Billy. I can't...'

'When the time's right. You know where I am.'

2013
Pickering, Ontario

Scott is asleep in the passenger seat. Ava kills the engine and brushes his hair from his forehead, smiling as he blinks and starts to focus. 'You always did wake up as soon as the engine stopped.'

Fetching Wanda's key from her bag, she climbs the stairs to the porch. Scott lags behind on the path. Soggy elm leaves have fallen from next door's lot onto the paving. He picks one up, holding it away from him like a piece of rotting flesh, then lets it drop, wiping his fingers on his jeans. 'Can you get the cases, hon?' she says, and throws him the car keys.

He lets them clatter at his feet. 'Why didn't you ask *before* I got out of the car?'

'Sorry.'

Inside, the house smells of polish. She goes down the hall to the L-shaped room where she used to sleep, and slings her hold-all on the bed. Through the window there's an empty patch of earth where Cissy grew lavender, dahlias, gladioli: a flower for every season. She imagines her aunt tugging up weeds, that small grunting sound she made as they came loose from the earth. The way her body must have folded as she collapsed among the dirt.

Ava changes into sweatpants and goes into the kitchen. On the table is a casserole dish with a note stuck to the lid: *Thought you might be hungry, love Wanda.* Scott leans over her shoulder and sticks his finger in it, then opens the fridge stocked with milk, butter, eggs, and cold meats wrapped in cling film. He jingles his way through the drawers, picking out knives and spoons till there's a small pile of cutlery on the counter. Eventually he chooses a spoon and sits down. She's about to ask where hers is but thinks better of it, and lifts one from the pile.

On the counter is a loaf. She heats the stew, ladles it into bowls and tears off a chunk of bread. Scott is talking, something about how he's not going to use a tripod because hand-held is so much more real, and how she should carry on as normal if she sees him filming. She was worried he might be in one of his silent moods. It's been ages since they went anywhere together, just the two of them. In fact, she can't remember the last time; probably in the days before eBay, when she'd take him round the stores. She nods and smiles, trying to focus on his lips, his words. They've sat at this table together so many times. She'd feed him sitting on this very chair, watching his tiny mouth suck at the bottle while Cissy cleaned around her, wiping the table, rattling the dishes, voicing her permanent disapproval with a multitude of subtle gestures and sighs. It was her fault – Ava's – that they'd had to move to Pickering in the first place. This was how Cissy punished her, by taking her away from her friends, her school.

Ava had been so scared in those early months. At first, nothing had happened: no morning sickness or swollen ankles. She'd thought the whole thing might be a false alarm until, one day, she couldn't fasten her jeans. Her reaction was to hide it from Cissy as long as possible by pretending to put on weight. She'd ask for extra portions at dinner, go up to her room brandishing king-sized bags of potato chips, then flush them down the toilet. It wasn't until she was nearing the end of her final year, when Mrs Kingston, deputy head teacher, took her aside one afternoon, stared at Ava's slowly growing belly and asked if there was something she wanted to tell her. Ava shrugged and Mrs Kingston said she would speak to her mother.

'My mother is dead,' said Ava, the tears flowing shamelessly down her cheeks. She ran to fetch her friend, Emile, who sympathised and stroked her hair in the toilet cubicle. 'That baby's going to come out sooner or later whether you like it or not,' Emile said. 'You have to tell Cissy.'

Ava looks at Scott wiping his plate with a piece of bread. Of course, she's never told him about any of that. She always tried to make his entry into the world sound respectable, like a beautiful accident that was meant to be – his biological father gave her the most precious gift: her son. If it hadn't been for him, then they wouldn't have each other.

Scott used to like hearing all that stuff. But now, if she mentions it, he shrugs and avoids her gaze, and she doesn't want to drive him away. He mounts a sound recorder onto the camera. In the end he opted for digital; real-film can apparently be recreated in an editing suite these days. Bruce says it's laziness, but as Scott chatters about pixels, resolution and sensors, and the required megabits for broadcasting quality, she realises it's not as simple as point and shoot. 'Pretend I'm not here,' he says.

'I can't. It's kind of creepy. Like being watched.'

He circles her chair, holding the camera. 'Every director puts his audience under a spell, and if you break the fourth wall you're spoiling that illusion. And you can't break someone's illusion without having a good reason. Can you, Mom?'

She realises he's expecting an answer. 'I guess not.'

'So, we're agreed?'

'On what?' She starts clearing the plates.

'That we won't break the fourth wall.'

'What's the fourth wall?'

'Jesus, Mom, haven't you listened to a thing I've been saying? Just don't talk to the camera while I'm filming, okay?'

'Sorry, you know I don't get all that technical stuff. I'm in your hands, director.'

He rolls his eyes. She smiles. It's nice to hear him use the word 'we' and know that she's included.

In the front room, she tries to figure out what can be put in boxes and what can be chucked in the skip. Scott is outside in the yard. He wanted to film what he could before the light died. She watches him train the camera on a crack in the paving, though she can't figure out what he finds so interesting about it. Then he focuses on the Japanese willow, crossing Cissy's flowerbed and trampling petals on the way.

He told her not to move the objects in the room before he has a chance to film them, so she puts little yellow stickers on the items that Wanda can give to charity: the sideboard, carriage clock, sofa suite. She hasn't told Scott why she's really here. She spent half the plane ride wondering whether to show him Jean's letter. In the end, she decided to discuss it with Bruce first, though it's difficult to talk in the five-minute windows he has between phone calls. All he did was advise her to keep busy. That's his remedy for everything. Goals. Achievements. He thinks all Scott's problems, the mood swings, the medication, can be cured by a regular nine to five job.

Anyway, it's not Bruce, it's her. She's never been great at saying what needs to be said. She remembers being seventeen and lying on her bed in Montreal repeating the same phrase over and over and trying to make it sound normal: 'Can I have a biscuit? By the way, I'm pregnant. What's on TV? By the way, I'm pregnant.' Every time she summoned up the courage, she'd balk at the sight of Cissy's face, and run back up upstairs. Then, a few days after her eighteenth birthday, she was sitting in the kitchen. Her aunt stopped washing dishes and wiping counters, and said, 'There's something we need to talk about.'

God, how her heart lurched. Mrs Kingston must have called already. This was it, there was no going back. 'I'm pregnant,' said Ava. Cissy dropped her dishcloth. A wet plop. She crossed the room and swung her hand in the air, bringing it down inches from Ava's cheek. She can still recall the fine cracks on her aunt's face. 'After everything I've done,' said Cissy in a low voice. 'I should have left you in Paisley, let you rot like your mother.'

A few days later, Cissy made the announcement they were moving to Pickering. They didn't know anyone there, but Cissy insisted she wasn't going to stay in Montreal and be gossiped about by any Tom, Dick or Jane. So while the rest of Quebec was preparing for the 1976 summer Olympics, Ava was packing her suitcases.

She's about to put a yellow sticker on the piano, but Scott tells her to wait. He aims the camera towards her hand as she lifts the lid. 'Play a tune.'

'I can't. It's broken.'

'Doesn't matter. Just do it.'

The melody is only faintly audible beneath the flat dead notes. *Merrily we roll along, roll along.* She can't remember where she learned it. It must have been Cissy. Turning to the mantelpiece, Ava glances at the dark blue urn. Wanda placed it exactly as Ava requested, her aunt and uncle, side by side, the china spaniels at either end. The urns are darkened globes, slippery stones that vanish beneath a rising tide. She thinks what it would be like to lift Cissy's urn from the mantelpiece and let the whole thing drop from her fingers, clay, dust and bone smashed to the floor.

Scott picks up one of the dogs and dangles it by the head. 'I never could stand this ugly junk.' She should tell him not to talk that way, but instead she tries to hide her smile. 'Do you remember that time she spanked me for breaking some stupid china lady with a parasol?' he says.

'Uncle Alex bought her that. She was upset.'

'She hated me because I was a bastard.'

'That's not true, Scott.'

He shrugs, but the words hurt. She can't stand to hear him talk of himself that way. She watches while he finishes filming the room, then she's allowed to start packing things in boxes: an orange teaset Cissy's kept since the seventies, glass vases, an ashtray no one ever used. Junk. In the sideboard, she finds two photo albums with padded covers, one labelled 'Scott' and the other 'Ava.' Each is full of Polaroid snaps: Scott in the garden in his pram; Scott wide eyed before his first birthday cake; photos of Ava and Emile in Montreal; Ava standing with Cissy beside Niagara Falls; the three of them, Alex, Cissy and Ava, on a tartan blanket near the lake at Saulte St Marie. She remembers that day: her perfect white dress with the lace frill, Uncle Alex in his jacket and tie, and Cissy in hat and gloves. They ate sandwiches and drank from a flask. Alex said it was just like going up the coast back home, only there were more mountains, more sand, more of everything. Cissy tutted that it was no use going on about the past and, if he wanted to talk about that other place, he should call it the Old Country like everybody else. Alex got annoyed and said the past was the past whether Cissy liked it or not and that sooner or later the lassie would need to know. The picnic was cut short and they drove all the way home in silence, Ava wondering, in her childish way, who 'the lassie' was.

Behind the double doors of the sideboard, there's a black accordion folder where Cissy kept all her important papers: mortgage statements, insurance documents, bills and receipts. Ava goes through them, separating new from old. Scott picks up a folded square of paper that's dropped onto the floor. He starts to laugh. 'I didn't know your middle name was Scarlett.'

'Give me that.'

He holds it up, then yanks it away, giggling as he dodges her grasp. 'What else haven't you told me, huh?' He mimics a Stasi accent. 'How can I trust you if vot you are telling me iz lies?'

'Just give me the thing.' She can hear the annoyance in her voice, tries to swallow it back, but it's too late. Scott scrunches the paper and stuffs it in his mouth. Her emotions swing between the need to stay calm and the urge to scream. That paper could have been her only clue, her only link to her mother. Anger wins. 'That might have been important, Scott. Didn't you think of that? Don't you think of anybody but your goddamn self?'

He spits the sodden ball out and laughs. She picks it up and flattens it on the floor. It's a birth certificate. Typed neatly inside the red-lined boxes are her father and mother's names: Jean and Tommy McParland. Underneath is her own name, the name with which she began her life, her original self: Ava Scarlett McParland.

How many people knew her by that name? No one in Canada. Here, she's always been Ava Quail, or Mrs Bruce Newport.

She tips the folder upside down. A yellowed photograph floats onto the carpet: Ava as a little girl seated in front of a piano, looking over her shoulder. Cissy's front room. She remembers it more clearly now, the green wallpaper and net curtains. In the corner is a woman's leg, wearing a heeled brown boot. Cissy, maybe? No. She couldn't imagine Cissy wearing boots like that. Her mother? Ava tips the photo as though she could peer sideways past the piano to the woman who nursed her through her first few years of life, who comforted her when she fell, who tucked her into bed and gazed at her sleeping face the way Ava used to gaze at Scott's. She stuffs it in the pocket of her sweatpants.

On the coffee table, Scott has laid out the saliva-soaked certificate and is filming it. 'Why didn't you tell me you had a middle name?'

'I don't use it.'

'Tommy? That's my granddaddy, isn't it?'

It's strange, hearing it put like that, the notion that this person she barely knew is Scott's granddad. 'Cissy didn't talk about him much,' she says.

'Well, I guess not talking must be a tradition.'

'What do you mean?'

Scott puts the camera aside and lights a Kretek, with its distinctive smell of cloves.

'You know your Aunt Cissy doesn't like smoking in the house.'

'She's dead, Mom. And she's not my aunt.'

Her foot lands on the creaky floorboard in the hall – the one she used to tiptoe over so she wouldn't wake Scott. When he got older, they converted Cissy's walk-in wardrobe into a box room for him. It hasn't changed: his set of drawers is still there, with the hockey stickers that she gave up trying to peel from the paint. His prized possession was his Superman costume. When he wore it she had to ask where Scott was, because more than anything he wanted her to believe he *was* Superman. She can't imagine what it would have taken for her to leave him. To walk away knowing she'd never see him again.

Her mother knew she was in Canada. *She knew.* Yet, she never came.

'Mom.'

Scott is calling her from Cissy's room. 'Look what I found.' He's holding a book, with a hardback mahogany cover discoloured at the edges. On the spine, in gilded script: *The Life and Times of Mary, Queen of Scots.* 'Catch.' Scott throws it to her.

There's an old strip of paper on the inside that someone has tried to peel off, leaving a stamped date and the words: 'Pais Library.' The title page is missing, but the rest is in good condition. 'It's a library book,' she says. 'I think it's from Paisley, the town where I was born.'

'Who'd have thought it, Cissy was a book thief?' He films over her shoulder and narrates: 'In Pickering lived a woman with a deep dark secret, a woman no one would ever suspect.'

'Oh, stop it. Cissy didn't steal this book. She's never even mentioned Mary, Queen of Scots.'

'Then how did it get here?'

She shrugs. 'Uncle Alex, maybe.' Though she can't imagine Uncle Alex reading that kind of thing. 'Who knows why people keep stuff? It'd be a shame to throw it away.' She pauses. 'Find anything else?'

'Like what?'

'I don't know.'

She shrugs and starts to pack up Cissy's clothes. Some of her jackets and skirts are of good quality, but too old fashioned to be any use, so she puts them into bags for the trash. Scott fetches the camera again and films her movements. It seems intrusive somehow, but she doesn't want to risk upsetting him. It's the first time in ages she's seen him so enthusiastic.

There's a set of drawers built into Cissy's wardrobe that contain her jewellery: pearl earrings and matching necklace, a rose brooch in three shades of gold. There are hatpins, cufflinks belonging to

Alex, and other bits and pieces. Ava should be crying, filling up with nostalgia and family memories. But she can't. All of it is no good. It tells her nothing.

Scott leans towards a suitcase, yellow with a big buckle. Ava has seen it before. It came with them on the boat from Scotland, and again from Montreal to Pickering. He tosses aside the souvenir matchboxes and sugar sachets Cissy collected from those rare outings to expensive restaurants, and focuses on a navy blue tie with small gold letters emblazoned on it: *J & P Coats*. 'What does this mean?'

'It's the name of the company that owned the mill where Cissy and Alex worked.' *And Jean, her mother.*

Scott stops filming to knot the tie around his neck and rummage in the suitcase. He's whistling a tune. It starts to irritate her, that and the noise of trinkets being swirled around. Occasionally he lifts something up: newspaper clippings of the queen's visits to Canada, tickets to museums, a brochure for *The Canadian* passenger train. 'Why in hell did the daft old coot keep this?' There's even a piece of paper with a list of Canadian towns and cities scribbled on them, and a circle round 'Pickering, Toronto.' Cissy was 'daft' for anything Canadian, as Alex used to say. Ava has the urge to push Scott aside and look through the suitcase herself, but she doesn't.

'Hey,' he says. 'This is cool.' It's a model of a boat, about the size of a pencil case and made of metal. It has big red funnels, the same as the boat they sailed on from Scotland.

For a moment, her heart lifts. 'I didn't know she'd kept that old thing.' It was their first Christmas in Canada. The boat was 'Santa's gift' to Uncle Alex. 'Isn't it wonderful?' Cissy had said. Ava had got a book about Canada which was 'wonderful' too, filled with pictures of bears, mountains and waterfalls.

'Look, there's a photograph,' says Scott.

It's of Ava, sitting on Alex's knee. Behind them she can see the bright glow of the coal fire. She remembers how little sparks had flown up from the flames and how she'd asked Cissy if it hurt.

'Did what hurt?' said Cissy.

'My mammy being in the fire. Did it hurt?'

Alex sat her on his knee. He promised her that her mammy hadn't felt a single flame touch her body, and that she should never worry about these things again.

Now the tears start to fall. Before she can stop him, Scott has thrust the boat into her hands. He's filming her, actually filming her sitting there, a pathetic, middle-aged woman crying over a stupid boat. 'Scott, please. Stop.'

'This is great, Mom,' he says. 'Just the kind of thing I'm looking for. Don't move.'

She drops the boat. 'I'm sorry, I can't do this. I need a coffee.'

In the kitchen, Scott takes a flask from his jeans' pocket and tips whisky into two mugs. He's talking so quickly she can hardly keep up, something about how they're going to break the fourth wall after all. 'What you did back there was great. That stuff is gold. We need more of the same.'

She shrugs. 'I was upset, Scott. How can that be good?'

He ignores her and places the sound recorder on the table, then flutters his fingers. 'Just start talking. Your memories, that kind of stuff.'

'What's got into you?' She can never keep up. One minute he's sullen, the next manic, full of ideas that he thinks will take over the world. Bruce says the drugs Scott took at university made his head soft, that's the reason why he can't focus.

'Come on, this was your idea, remember? That's why we're here, aren't we? Bond with your son in the old family home. Reminisce about all those happy memories. I want to find out more. What was she like?'

'Who?' She takes a sip of scotch.

'Your mother.'

'I don't know, do I?' Her muscles contract and the whisky stings the back of her throat.

'Try. Something, anything will do.'

She might still be alive. 'She was very beautiful. You look like her around the eyes.' She reaches to brush a strand of hair from his forehead, but he ducks.

'Talk into the camera, Mom. I want to capture a genuine moment, like when you were holding that boat. Say whatever comes into your mind. As long as it's authentic.' He takes his eye away from the LCD screen to look at her. 'As long as it's the truth.'

'Don't be silly.' She shifts her gaze. 'I can't do anything while that thing is pointing at me.'

'It's not on. Not yet. What about when you first came here? Tell me about that.'

She takes another sip of scotch, twists the cord on her sweatpants round her finger, then lets it go. 'I remember running in and out of automatic doors because I thought they were magic. I'd never seen anything like that before.' Scott doesn't laugh, but she does.

'Didn't you ever want to go back?'

'No. Cissy said this was our home now, and if I wanted to talk about Scotland I should call it the Old Country. I guess I always thought of it as this historic place, like in medieval paintings.'

'What about your mother?' He shifts angle, so she's in profile.

'I thought you said that thing was off.'

'I lied.'

'Nothing. I don't remember a lot about her.'

The two of them dancing in the swirly blue and pink kitchen. Tagging after her brisk steps in the street. Reaching up to take her bandaged hand. Jean's angry look, 'Ouch, Ava.' That sense of distance, wanting to hold onto her forever and ever, but never quite knowing how. 'Look, can we stop now? I've got a head coming on.'

'Cissy used to get heads, didn't she?'

'What's that supposed to mean?'

'What about your father, then? Remember anything about him?'

She shakes her head.

'Wow, the legacy of fathers is really lacking in our family.'

It's always the same. Just when she thinks everything is going good between them, it turns out like this, Scott baiting her, trying to push her buttons. Why can't he be grateful that he has one parent who truly loves him?

'How old were you when he died?'

'I don't know. I don't remember.' It's back, that irritation in her voice. She sounds like Cissy, warning her that spoiling Scott won't make up for his lack of a father. 'Sorry, I can't.' She rubs the corners of her eyes.

'What's the matter? Not so many happy memories as you thought?'

'This isn't about you, Scott.'

'Communication is about body language, Mom. The silence between words. Based on that, we're making real progress, me asking questions, you not answering them.'

She gets up from her chair.

'You can dole out your shit advice; you're good at that, but as soon as we start to have a real conversation, you can't deal with it. What are you so afraid of?'

'Oh, grow up, Scott.'

She goes to her room and shuts the door.

1962
Paisley

I steer clear of Una all afternoon. She's eyeballing me from behind her machine, daring me to put a foot wrong. I set myself a new task. Myra Brown is off sick again and this time Mr Green asks me to do her machine as well as my own. At first I'm all nervous that I'll make a pig's ear of it, but soon I've got the two machines running at once. Not like Una who can do six, but she's had years of practice. Still, I've the satisfaction of knowing me running two machines will get the wind right up her.

It keeps my mind off Billy. After the canal, my heart was hammering and I had to smoke four cigarettes in a row. It's always been like that with Billy, like I'm noon and he's midnight; when one is asleep, the other is awake. I glance down the rows of frames, and wonder if life is the same for everyone: my mother, Una, even Annie; that feeling of all the good things having slipped away.

With Billy it was exciting. He always told me to sit in the front of the car because that was the only place for a lady. One night, when we were at one of the big houses in Thornly Park, he came down the drive, running. We drove at speed up the Braes, along narrow roads, till we came to the back of an abandoned farmhouse. His knuckles were bloody. When we stopped Billy burst out laughing. 'Whit happened?' I said. 'Tell me.'

'Dog nearly bit my baws aff.'

'Are you hurt?'

He laughed.

'Dae ye need first aid, Billy?' I could feel the red creeping into my neck.

He grinned. 'Aye, I need first aid, Jean.' His hand slid above my knee and his mouth covered my lips.

It was a week before I saw Billy after that. Billy's da didn't like people coming round the house. A week I spent crying into my pillow thinking Billy had gone off with someone else. Then, one day when my mother was at the mill, he showed up. 'Where've you been?' I said.

'It wis my da. He took ill.'

'And you couldn't come round and let me know?'

'I couldny lea the hoose, Jean, wae him coughing his lungs up. I thought he wis fur it this time. Anyway, ye know whit your mither's like; how cuid I come roon tae yours?'

'I'm sorry. Is he alright now, your da?'

'Aye, don't worry aboot him. I brought you this.'

He opened his fist. In his palm was a silver necklace with an engraved locket. I lifted the catch with my nail. Inside was a picture of Billy and the words, *Forever Yours*. 'Oh, Billy, it's beautiful, I love it.'

Just then, my mother came marching up the path.

'Mammy, you're hame early.'

'I'm home wae my sore knee. Not that you wid care.' She turned to Billy. 'Go on. Scram. I know your kind and don't think I don't. You might be able to get past my Jean, but you'll no get past me. Rotten, that's whit you are. Now get afore I take my broom tae ye.'

'Mammy!' I shouted. She pushed me back inside with her big hand, but not before Billy got a chance to mouth: 'Tonight. The bridge.'

I glance over at Una, thinking of all the times her and my mammy have sat talking about how I'll come to no good. As if my mother never made a mistake. I think of the wee oval black and white photo of my father in his soldier's uniform, the way she looks at it with teary eyes. I hate that. I bet he couldn't wait to get away; I bet he was glad there was a war on because it meant he didn't have to come back and marry *her*. But I'm not supposed to talk about that because he died in the war; I'm just supposed to shut up.

I hated the way she treated Billy. 'I'm no a wee lassie,' I told her. 'I can see who I like.'

'I brought you up to be decent, Jean, and whit do you do? You throw it back in my face, cutting about with that, that no good toe rag.'

'Folk like you don't give him a chance.'

'A chance? You don't gie men like that a chance. One chance is aw they need. If I catch you wae that Billy again, I'll throw you out on your ear, do you hear?'

I ran to my room, kissing the locket Billy gave me. I knew it was knocked off, but I didn't care. I said nothing, not to Billy and especially not to my mother. It would've stuck in my craw, all the 'I told you sos,' and 'just like you, Jean, you never listen.' She never could stand it if I was happy. I wore the locket under my collar, taking it out whenever I went to meet Billy, and tucking it in again before I went home.

The vibration of the machines courses through my body, shuddering through every bone and muscle. Billy's never been a proper criminal, not like in the films. He could never do a big robbery. People say daft things when they're not thinking straight, things they don't mean. Best just forget it. These mills have been here for a hundred years, the thick walls and high ceilings, the machines clanking and clattering day after day, and no one's tried it yet. They wouldn't dare, not even Billy.

The pork links look like burnt twigs, but Tommy cuts them up anyway and dips them in his blob of ketchup, grinning like they were the best sausages on earth. He's looking right pleased with himself. 'I did it,' he says.

'Did whit?' I butter a slice of bread and wrap it round one of my sausages. I'm not hungry but it's best to look like I'm making an effort.

'I pit oor name oan the list.'

'Whit list?

'Foxbar, Jean.' His eyes droop for a second, that way he does when he wants to look hurt, but then he keeps going. 'You were right. They high flats have got everything, central heating, the lot. Nay mair lugging coal up and doon the stairs. We're going up in the world.'

'Can we live at the very top?' says Ava. 'As high up as a bird?' She claps her hands.

'Don't get her hopes up,' I say.

'Aye, your mammy's right,' says Tommy. 'We have to wait and see whit they offer first. Bit you can start thinking aboot wallpaper, curtains, even a carpet; soon as you like, we'll be living in a new hoose, looking ower the Gleniffer Braes.'

'I want a blue carpet and gold curtains and silver wallpaper,' says Ava.

Tommy is finished his links and starts mopping up the grease, cramming the bread in his mouth so his lips look all shiny and wet. 'Don't lick your fingers,' I say.

He takes his handkerchief from his shirt pocket. 'Ye cuid look a bit mair happy aboot it, Jean. Whit's the matter? I thought that's whit you wanted.'

Ava turns to me with wide eyes, like I'm the big bad fairy come to take everyone's lollipops away. 'I am happy,' I say. 'I've got a bit of a headache, that's all, listening tae they machines aw day.'

'Never mind, love, it'll be worth it when we're in the new place, eh? Queen of your very own castle.'

'Princess,' says Ava. 'Princesses are prettier than queens, just like Mammy.'

'Well, then, I'll be Rapunzel in her very own ivory tower.'

Tommy gives me a funny look, but I pretend not to notice. Ava shoves a few half-chewed mouthfuls of sausage to the side of her plate. 'Are you not going to finish these?' I say.

She makes a disgusted face and shakes her head. Tommy steals one and laughs like nothing can spoil his mood. 'You shouldn't encourage her,' I say. I clear away his empty plate and steep it in the sink. Tommy and Ava exchange father and daughter giggles behind my back. I stare out the kitchen window, across the park, at the towers of the old Victorian spinning mill like shadows behind the trees.

After I finish work, I go straight home and tell Tommy we're going to my mother's. Tommy's only half awake, pulling his braces up over his vest. 'Whit's the grand occasion?'

'We should tell her thegither,' I say. 'Aboot the new place.'

'Don't you think we should wait? We're no even in it yet.'

Tommy knows just as well as I do that my mother will have something to say about it. I can see it coming, the poor old woman act. 'The sooner she gets used to it, the better.'

I got the idea while I was at work. The machines get hypnotic after a while. When I started this morning, my hands were shaky and I could hardly think. All night, Billy was in my dreams. I'd wake up every now and then, my heart giving me wee jolts, my stomach tied in knots. During the day I tried to put new thoughts into my brain, good thoughts. Tommy was right, Foxbar is a new start for us. Standing at my machine, watching the web of threads winding onto the cones, I decided I wasn't going to be selfish Jean anymore. Tommy deserves better.

I dreamed up wee scenes of us in the new house. We'd have potted plants, and a table with a rug under it, not for wiping your feet, but for decoration, and cushions on the bed, and a twin tub washing machine, and I'd tell everyone, 'My Tommy did this. He did it because he loves me.'

'Whit you smiling at?' says Tommy, pulling on his shirt.

I lean over and kiss his cheek. 'My husband.'

'You're daft, you are,' he says. 'Anyway I wis going tae tell your mither the nicht on my way hame.'

'We'll do it how it should be, as a family.'

Ava tugs at my legs. 'Where are we going?'

'To your nana's. Pit oan your dress. I want us to look our best.'

I take Tommy's arm and smile. I'm wearing my good suede coat with the double row of buttons, and Ava's got on her favourite red and white shoes. The curtains twitch and I sense eyes watching me from behind the netted folds. The door is open as usual. Ava runs straight to the cupboard where my mother keeps her biscuits. 'Wait till you're asked,' I say.

'Ach,' says my mother. 'The lassie can have a biscuit. How about a wee coconut mallow? Pink or white?'

'Both,' says Ava, jumping up and down, a coconut mallow in each hand. 'Can I watch the television?' I take her to the front room and switch on the screen. The white dot appears, a wee sun that bursts into life. 'Weed,' says the sunflower, and the flowerpot men wave their puppet arms. Ava laughs.

When I go back to the kitchen, Tommy and my mother are sitting with a plate of biscuits and mugs of tea. I pour my own and sit down. 'So you're down for wan a the new places?' says my mother.

I feel annoyed that Tommy told her without me. I flash my eyes at him but he just shrugs. 'Aye, that's right,' I say. 'We decided we needed more space.'

'We decided,' says my mother, as if talking to herself.

'The views are lovely,' I say. 'I can even get one a those twin tubs.'

'It'll be a trek getting tae the mill,' says my mother. She's not looking at me but staring out the window, her hands fidgeting inside the apron of her pinny.

'That willny matter; Tommy's saving up fur a car.'

Her head turns sharply, 'A car? You never mentioned it afore, Tommy.'

'Aye, well, I wis jist thinking aboot it, you know. But now we're really moving, I might as well. Nothing expensive, it's no like we can afford an Aston Martin.'

I cough. 'Anyway,' I say. 'It means we might see a bit less of you once we're moved. When we get the car we can bring you up tae visit, can't we, Tommy?'

'Oh?' She stops eating her bourbon cream and puts it beside

the cup. 'I don't know, wae my knees. The doctor has me oan water tablets.'

'Not at all,' Tommy says. 'I can still pop doon efter work, jist like always.'

She demolishes the rest of the bourbon cream. 'Well, only if you're sure. I don't want to be a trouble.'

'Don't you worry, Senga. That's whit a motor's fur. We can go anywhere we like: Saltcoats, Ayr, Irvine.'

'I don't like Irvine,' I say.

'Ach, I'll no want tae come,' says my mother.

'We'll see aboot that, Jean, won't we?' Tommy winks. 'Moving up tae Foxbar will be the best thing that's happened in a long while, tae all of us.'

Next day, I go to the library at lunchtime. I'm not looking for a book, I just want a bit of peace. There's a map of America on the wall. Mr Webster sees me looking at it and starts on about the Cold War and Cuba and how America is the land of opportunity and JFK is the greatest American president since Lincoln. I say I don't know how anyone could find their way around America let alone know what to do when they got there. 'Thinking of visiting, are you?' He says it as though me and Tommy could just pack our bags and jump on an aeroplane without a second thought.

'Me? Definitely not,' I say. 'Why would I want to go to America? I'm perfectly happy where I am.'

At home later, I get that itchy feeling in my bones. Ava is out playing. I see her from the window, laughing with her friends in the park, sliding down the chute. Watching her makes me feel sad. I wish everything didn't happen so slowly. I wish we could move tomorrow. The longer it takes, the further away things seem to get. I feel like I'm dissolving, and all that will be left is the mist from my cigarette. Tommy is getting ready for work. I go into the bedroom and sit at the dressing table, staring at my jewellery box.

My mammy got me it for my fifteenth birthday. It has a kitten dressed in a pink bow on the lid. When I open it, a little ballerina pirouettes to the tune of *Swan Lake*. Not that I've much jewellery, mostly beads and brooches. Underneath them is a glint of silver thread, the locket Billy gave me. I'm tempted to take it out, but I don't. Instead, I smother the ballerina and her tinkling tune. 'I'm sick of it, Tommy, looking out at the same auld view a that stupid mill. Can't you do something, get us moved up the list?'

'Whit can I dae, Jean? It's up tae the council, isn't it?' He brushes a hair from my cheek. 'Don't worry, we'll get there. Jist be patient.'

He moves to kiss me and I turn my head.

'Cissy came roon the day,' he says.

I stiffen. Tommy's stuck up older sister is the last thing I need. She's something to do with pensions in the mills, though you'd think she'd cut the ribbon when the place opened, the way she walks about in her navy suit and pearls. 'What did she want?' I say.

'Her and Alex invited us fur dinner, a week on Friday.'

I sigh. Cissy lives in one of those two-up-two-downs on Green Road. When me and Tommy first got together, he took me round there. Her and her man have a room for sitting in and one for eating. The dinner was all that polite way, with napkins and different kinds of spoons, though no one said much. After it was finished, when I was helping clear away the plates, I walked in on them in the kitchen, Cissy speaking to Tommy in a low voice, all tight-lipped and serious, something about voicing her concern. I used to go round with Billy McBride, that's what she was saying. I didn't have to hear the words.

'Dae we have tae?' I say to Tommy.

'You're my wife. That means we should aw try and get along. And you know how she feels aboot Ava.'

Cissy doesn't have any of her own. I asked Tommy about it once but he just shrugged and said it was none of our business. Every Christmas Eve, she pops round with her man, the two of them dickied up for church in coats and hats. They always have a present for Ava, usually something useful like a nice coat or pair of shoes. Expensive, too, like I couldn't look after my own daughter.

'We can tell her aboot the new hoose,' says Tommy. 'That'll stick a craw in her bunnet.'

'Alright,' I say. 'We'll go.'

After dinner, I tell Ava about Mary, Queen of Scots, about how beautiful she was and how many men were in love with her. We're sitting long-ways on the couch, Ava next to me, all light and warm. Even when she's lying still, part of her is always moving, a knee or an arm, or just her head, tilting to look up at me. 'Did she have hair like yours?'

'I don't think so,' I say. 'She wis a queen and wore a crown, made of jewels and gold, and she had a hundred servants to wash her clothes, and horses to take her wherever she wanted to go.' I smile and twine a strand of Ava's hair round my finger. 'And Mary, Queen of Scots didny have to work in a mill.'

Ava sits up on her knees. 'I think you're a queen, Mammy. You know why?'

I shake my head.

'Because you have make-up and high heels and you look pretty.'

I turn away so she can't see my face. Anything sets me off these days. This afternoon I burst into tears while I was peeling the potatoes and had to put powder on to cover my ugly red nose. I wipe my cheek with my sleeve, kidding on I've just sneezed, then I rub Ava's chin. 'I promise you, Ava, you'll never be a mill girl, you'll never live in a rotten tenement, or wash your husband's vest in the sink.'

She looks puzzled. 'Can I go out to play again?'

'Aye, off you go.'

When she's gone, the itchy feeling returns. A thudding in my chest, like I can't breathe, like I'm running from some nameless thing, pushing with both hands on a great big wooden door, only it won't open. I'm trapped behind it and the thing I can't see is getting closer; the longer I'm trapped, the more I can't breathe.

I open the window and stick my head outside, taking in long

cool gulps of air. I light a cigarette and take puff after puff, the smoke curling round my head till I can hardly see a thing and the big brick outline of the mill disappears. When I'm finished I throw the stub onto the street and through the blue and grey wisps I see a figure crossing the road, up past the park. There's an empty can in the middle of the pavement and he kicks it into the grass. Even from here, I know it's Billy. His hands are in his pockets, his shoulders hunched. When he reaches the corner, he turns and looks over his shoulder. I can't see his eyes but they're flashing my name. Then he turns the corner, out of sight, obscured by the mill's dark hulk.

2013
Vancouver, British Columbia

From her glass-fronted office, Ava peers down into the street below; it's always disturbed her that the only thing between her and a several-hundred feet drop is a pane of tinted glass.

The letter stares up from the shiny surface of her desk. It was in the mail this morning. No address. Just the name, Ava McParland, scrawled on a pristine white envelope. Inside is a square of discoloured paper with that same neat script crammed between the lines. She buzzes her secretary to hold all calls, then reads the words again, as though, if she scans them often enough, something will start to make sense.

August 1963

Dear Tommy

Every day I imagine how big she's grown. How is she at school? Is she clever? No doubt she will have got that from you, not me. Please send her my letters, Tommy. I'm begging you. I know I was a rotten wife, but don't do this, don't keep me from my daughter. I know you loved her too. We loved each other once, remember? Send me her address, Tommy. Then I promise I will never bother you again. Whatever my mother says, don't listen to her or anybody else. Billy could never be Ava's father. I'm telling you the truth. She only ever had one father,

Tommy, and that's you.

Jean

Ava coughs when she says it out loud. Billy. No one ever mentioned a Billy. She dials Langley, and in a patient telephone manner he assures her that there were no more letters from her aunt, no further instructions. 'So how do you explain this?' she says. 'Some kind of joke?'

He's very sorry he can't be of more help. 'Maybe you could ask a friend or family member?' She's tempted to ask if he can recommend a good medium. Instead, like in the movies, she hangs up without saying goodbye.

Outside, the shiny skyscrapers are like glaciers dragging their weight through a dark sea. Sometimes she marvels at how much time she spends suspended in air, all these people kept afloat by layers of glass and flimsy partitions. Part of her wants to rip the letter into pieces and watch it float into the streets below.

Tommy. A pale man who went out at night and slept during the day. Ava had to be quiet and not play in the hall. She remembers bringing him a cup of tea, her mother's voice telling her to be careful, the warmth in her hands as she set the cup by his bed, then tiptoed out. *You loved her too*, that's what the letter says. Past tense. Which means at some point he ceased loving her, the word 'love' becoming meaningless.

She'd not long started high school when she asked Cissy how he'd *passed on*. Her aunt was kneading dough, rolling her knuckles into the soft whiteness. 'He had a weakness,' she said, her mouth forming a tight line. 'There were complications.' Ava can still hear the oven door click shut, feel the heat as she stared through the glass, crying for the father she barely remembered, but most of all crying for herself.

She thinks of the letter Jean wrote her, how Cissy would have read it until one of her heads forced her onto her bed with it face-down on her chest. So much weight in those small pieces of paper.

Not a small lie, but a terrible, robbing, cheating lie; so bad that she couldn't bear to look Ava in the eye, that she'd rather be dead before she faced up to what she'd done. But someone out there wanted Ava to know. She just has to find out whom.

She arranges to meet Bruce for lunch in a Japanese place downtown. He arrives fifteen minutes late, still on his phone, and sits down. She can tell it's Bentley on the other end, Bruce hissing into his ear that Kelly needs to get his finger out his ass. He ends the call and smiles, switching into husband-mode, 'You might have picked a place nearer the office.'

She stares at the centrepiece of the restaurant, a giant ice peacock. 'We had our twenty-fifth anniversary in here, remember?'

'Did we? Are you sure it wasn't that touristy place over in Gastown?'

'No, it was here. Only back then it was Thai.'

He studies the menu and summons the waiter. Bruce orders scallops and she asks for the same; one kind of food tastes much like another lately. His phone rings again. His voice is more grovelling this time. One of the directors. For some reason, Bruce resorts to cowboy metaphors. He's still in the saddle. Nobody knows this horse like him. While he's holding the reins, they'll get results.

'It's not good for you, all this stress,' she says, after he hangs up. 'Maybe you should take some time off.'

'Yeah, our investors will feel a lot better if I have a goddamn suntan.'

'Come on, Bentley can take care of things.'

'Is this why you dragged me out here, to talk me into a vacation?'

'Just consider it. With Cissy dying and all, I feel like I could use a break.'

Bruce pours them both a glass of iced water. 'Look, I know it's been hard. None of this, the protests, the media, helps exactly, but I can't step away now. I need to feel things are back on track, and then we'll go on a long hop. Rome. Barbados. Anywhere you like. I promise.'

She smiles. If she tells him now, then he'll realise just how much she needs this, *him*. 'Bruce, there's something you should know.'

'Well?' She recognises that look, the frown followed by the arched eyebrow; he doesn't want to hear anything inconvenient.

'Nothing.'

Bruce sighs and shakes his head. 'You know I hate nothings.'

'This film of Scott's,' she says. 'It's a kind of self-portrait. Don't be surprised if he asks you to be in it.'

'Why can't he get a job with one of the TV stations, something that pays money? Sue has contacts at CBC; maybe she could help move things along.'

'You know how he is about doing things off his own back.'

'Face it, Ava. He's not a kid anymore. There's a younger, brighter crop of talent that would give their fucking eyeteeth for an opportunity like that.'

'Just give him some encouragement, will you? That's all I ask.'

One of the stories she and Bruce tell at functions, after everyone has been acquainted with the heroic deeds of Captain Hastings, is how Scott brought them together. It was the summer of 1981, and she was on the promenade in Pickering, taking Scott to a puppet show, when her worst nightmare happened. She lost him. Instinct and panic drove her across the beach, kicking over sandcastles, tripping over bathers. As she was scanning the water, hoping and not hoping to see a pair of tiny arms break the surface, Bruce came striding towards her. 'Newport. Bruce Newport. I found something of yours.'

Scott was clutching a silver coin. Bruce had caught a stranger giving it to him. God knows what they were about to do. Here she pauses the story to let him bask in admiration. Yet she'll never forget the sick feeling in her stomach as she hugged her son, then scolded him for nearly giving her a heart attack, while all he could say was *na-na-na-na*. That part usually gets a laugh. Afterwards, Bruce invited them onto his yacht. She'd never been sailing before. They cruised around Lake Ontario, while Scott drank cola, and she had a Martini with an olive on a stick. Well, it was the eighties. Bruce tells their audience she was a hippy-artist, and they have a mock argument about whether he had a rat-tail hairdo or not. He did. 'How can I ever repay you?' she'd said. He'd asked for her phone number.

Twenty-eight years later, here she is, sitting in a restaurant in Vancouver, watching Bruce shout into his phone. Ava can't say she isn't pleased to hear Sue getting her ears singed. 'I've already said it's not true,' says Bruce. 'I don't need a press conference.' He hangs up, wipes his mouth with his napkin. 'They're calling it a slump. Can you believe that?'

'Calling what a slump?'

There it is again, the eyebrow. 'Twenty per cent is a slump. This is just a blip. It happens all the time. The markets are so gullible these days, it's like dealing with a bunch of hysterical women.'

'Why, what happened?'

His ears are red. He's angry. He throws his napkin over his empty bowl. 'Where have you been all goddamn morning? Mars?'

'I was in my office.'

'First you drag me here for 'nothing.' Then you tell me you've no idea what's going on, though it's on every news channel in the country. Are you on medication? Help me out, Ava, because I'm doing my best here.'

'I'm sorry. Since Cissy died, I've discovered some stuff about my parents and I don't know what to do –' There, that wasn't so bad. She sags in her chair, like someone has cut the strings that were holding her up.

Bruce sighs. 'Look, it's only natural that Cissy dying will dredge up unpleasant feelings. But you've got to snap out of it. I need you by my side.' He gives a strained smile, peers at her with those seductive blue eyes. 'Have a cup of tea, do some deep breathing, and I'll see you back at the office. Alright?'

He stands up. She watches him stride between the tables and out the restaurant, the phone at his ear. 'Alright,' she says. 'Alright.'

She hadn't bothered to read the papers; she'd been so preoccupied with that damned letter. The story is on every front page. Apparently Green Alliance has posted an online video of Borealis employees carrying out illegal logging in the Interior. They're calling for an enquiry. The case is pretty watertight. It's inspired a wave of articles about soil erosion and the decline of rivers, salmon populations and other food sources for First Nations communities. One tabloid has a borderline-libellous spread about how Bruce persuaded the government not to hand over ancestral land rights if it meant giving away lucrative logging territory.

If the enquiry succeeds, it could affect the licence application for Temple Grove. How could she have missed this? She used to live and breathe her work, just like Bruce. That's what he liked about her. Bruce helped her transform from the hippy artist of 1981 into a sharp-edged executive. Art was all very well as a hobby, but she was a mother with responsibilities; she had to act like it. She went to night school, got herself a first-class business degree and had just landed a job in a plastics company when a vacancy for personnel manager came up in one of his subsidiaries in North Ontario. Bruce offered her a rate slightly above industry average. Pleased with her work, he invited her to take a post at head office in Vancouver. She and Scott moved out there in 1985. The boom years. Business was good. Bruce secured those all-important government subsidies and the company embarked on large-scale logging, creating hundreds of jobs, which reflected well on the politicians whose hands he shook. The Midas touch. When he proposed to her at a conference in Whistler, they'd been sleeping together for months. He booked a private dinner in the honeymoon suite. The waiter brought the ring in a box, a pink diamond. 'Seal the deal?' said Bruce.

They dined with ministers, had sex in a dome-ceilinged room in the Prime Minister's house in Ottawa, a portrait of the queen gazing down on them; but, by 1993, the boom was over. New regulations were introduced; the government went on the back foot, leaving the company to face accusations of improper dealing and environmental destruction. The bad publicity necessitated an image overhaul. Canada West, as the company had been called, was dismantled and Borealis was born.

She has to hand it to Green Alliance. They won't let them forget it. Bruce will have to fight back.

Ava arrives at the meeting ten minutes early. The boardroom's plasma screen shows a drop in shares of another five percent. Officially a slump. The company is on anxiety alert. Directors have been calling, investors, analysts. Borealis's share price is being dissected on a minute by minute basis. Now that it's been revealed Kelly has a stake in one of the subsidiaries, they're down again, the word 'corruption' being tossed from one reporter to another.

'What's the progress on that injunction?' says Bruce.

Bentley squares his papers, tapping them on the table. 'Kelly's sources say that, before he'll side with us publicly, we have to prove that the allegations are false.'

'Of course they're fucking false.'

Ava clears her throat. 'I've looked into the records, and it was a private contractor who carried out that logging.' It's not much, the result of a few minutes research, but better than nothing. 'We hired them to clear roads. I'll have someone look up the contract and pass it to Bentley.'

Bruce barely glances at her. Her redemption will depend on results. 'Don't be put off by this bleating for an enquiry, folks,' he says. 'Take it for what it is, smoke and mirrors. Our goal is Temple Grove. Give me an update, Dave.'

Dave Winterbourne is their new Forestry and Environment Executive. A Richard Branson clone, as Bruce calls him, with fair hair down to his collar and a corded bracelet on his wrist. He uploads a Power Point display, flashing complicated statistics on the effects of increasing the cut zone around Temple Grove. 'At the moment we're getting away with ten percent, but as you can see the probability of windthrow increases in relation to –'

Bruce gives an exaggerated sigh. 'Just get to the chase, Dave.'

'I'm afraid Green Alliance is right. Our environmental report shows that anything above a ten percent cut will expose the old growth trees to damage. I've emailed you all a copy.'

Bruce drums his fingers on the desk. 'Who compiled this?'

'We did,' says Winterbourne. 'And the government.'

Bentley and some of the other execs look up from their phones. Bruce gives Winterbourne a hard look. He's not been in the job long enough to know never to present a problem to Bruce if you don't have a solution. 'Well, compile it again. And this time make it sing to our tune; let's push that cut zone to forty percent. I might not have gone to university, but I know probability isn't fact.' He looks round the table. 'Any other works of genius to present?'

Sue leans forward. 'Melanie has ideas on how to launch a media counter-attack.'

Ava wonders who Melanie is, then Sue glances at her assistant. Melanie lowers her eyelashes and smiles. 'Mrs Newport could do one of those daytime chat shows. You know, offer up family anecdotes, talk about motherhood, baking, that sort of thing; show the friendly face of the corporation.'

'I hardly think a bit of baking is going to put across the right professional image,' says Ava. 'We're not trying to win *MasterChef*.'

'I like it,' says Bruce. 'It reaches out to the ordinary public. People who have no idea about business, who'd vote for Kermit the fucking Frog if the papers told them to. That's the kind of people we're trying to convince.'

She casts her eyes at the photographs on the walls: Bruce accepting industry awards; Bruce presenting cheques to various charitable causes; a photo of all three of them at Emerald Lake, dressed in shorts and backpacks, surrounded by tall pines and snowy-peaked Rockies. That photo used to be on Bruce's desk. She wonders when it was moved. 'Okay. I'll do it.'

The plasma screen has resumed its news coverage of scenes outside the government buildings: linked protestors chanting anti-capitalist slogans; drivers blasting their horns in support. A man in a light canvas jacket is filming the demonstrations, a distinctive black cigarette in his mouth. He raises his fingers in the peace sign.

Sue gives a derisive snort. 'Isn't that your son?'

1962
Paisley

Una's been off with me ever since that day in the toilets. But this morning she's asking how my hand is, even though it was two weeks ago and all that's left is a wee red welt. Maybe she wants something, but I can't think what. 'You need tae be careful wae they machines,' she says. 'There wis a lassie once, got her finger took right aff. That wis afore your time, mind, when we used tae work the belts wae wur toes.'

The older women start reminiscing about who had it the worst, and how you couldn't get a job if you had fleas, and what a laugh it all was. I feel sorry for them. Most of them have never been out of Paisley, except on mill outings down the coast. I don't say anything. It's Friday and Una's always happy on payday. She's singing, '*There was a mill-girl, a Paisley mill-girl who travelled far away, she was on holiday; she had a rare time – it was the fair time –*' The more The Bitch glares, the louder Una sings. Every Friday she brings in sweets. Today it's rhubarb and custard drops. I take one and stick the sweetie in my pocket. My mother told me in the old days Una used to smuggle tuppenny cakes of chocolate in her drawers and sell them. I've been suspicious about eating anything Una's brought in ever since. At the dinner break I've run out of fags and she offers me one of hers. 'No doubt you're saving up, hen,' she says.

'Saving up for what?' says Aggie.

'Her and Tommy pit their name doon fur Foxbar.'

Una's been talking to my mother. I might have guessed.

'Next you'll be working in embroidery, turning up tae the mills wae yer hat and gloves, like Lizzie Naismith.'

'That's Elizabeth to you,' says Aggie.

'I'll no,' I say. 'Tommy and I thought it wid be good fur Ava.'

Maggie puts on a posh voice, 'My husband and I, Tommy and I...'

'Gie the lassie a break,' says Una. 'She's only trying tae dae whit's right.'

'Well, I'm happy where I am.' Aggie tips half the salt shaker over her chips then pulls her cardigan shut in a bristly way. 'Anyway, how're you supposed tae see the fellas fae a hunner feet up in the air?'

'Depends whit fellas,' says Maggie. 'There's some cuid be ten thoosand feet away and it widny be faur enough. Isn't that right, Jean?'

Una gives her a hard stare. 'She's talking aboot her own man, isn't that right, Maggie?'

Maggie takes a loud slurp of tea but says nothing.

'Maggie!'

'Aye, that's whit I mean.' She looks across the table at Aggie.

Aggie clears her throat. 'You'll never guess who I saw the other night, coming oot the Lighthoose, pished as a fart.'

'Lizzie Naismith,' says Una.

Everybody laughs.

'Naw.' Aggie takes a slow draw of her fag just to keep us in suspense. 'That Billy McBride. And d'ye know whit he said?'

I take my compact out my purse and start putting on some lippy, like I'm only half listening.

'"You're a sight fur sair eyes wee Aggie Burns. I've a good mind tae run away wae ye. Whit dae ye say, Aggie, you an me, eh?"'

I put another sugar in my tea and stir, even though there's two in it already.

'She telt him tae dae one, of course,' says Angie. 'He had a lassie in tow.'

'A lassie?' I can't help myself. Maggie smirks. Una's eyes are like a hawk.

'Aye, the common sort, bleached hair and a laugh that could curdle milk.'

Everyone is staring at me, but I won't give them the satisfaction. I'm choking for a cigarette. I look at Una but she doesn't offer. Questions fizz inside my mouth. What was her name? Did they leave the pub together? Did they kiss? I clamp shut my jaw, pressing my teeth together to stop the words from getting out. Just when I can't stand it anymore, Una says, 'So I hear you're huvin dinner ower at prissy Cissy's.'

Trust Tommy to tell my mother everything. Anyway, I like that Una called her prissy. No one else does.

'Ask her aboot this pension thing, will ye, hen?' Una nods towards the notice board.

There's been an announcement up for a fortnight, something about calling round to the office to discuss options. So that's why Una was being so nice. I knew there had to be a reason, though I don't pay much attention to the notices. I'm too young to start worrying about pensions.

I glance at Una's pack of cigarettes. 'Aye,' I say. 'I'll ask her.'

Una sits her box of matches on top of the pack. Her good mood seems to have reached its limits. 'You do that,' she says.

Once I've got my pay, I go straight up the town and buy new shoes for Tommy, the black slip-on kind with pointed toes. When I get back to the flat, he's sitting on the kitchen chair, polishing his old brown lace-up brogues. 'Whit's this?' he says. 'Looks like something you'd clean yer teeth wae.'

'You've nae style; that's your problem. They're aw wearing these, Tommy. Have you no seen The Beatles?' I playfully swipe his hair. 'And we'll need tae dae something aboot that an all, Tommy. How aboot a quiff?' Gathering his hair in both hands, I sweep it so it sticks up.

'Jean!'

I laugh. Since I finished today, I've been feeling light, like a sweet breeze blew me out the mill and up the streets. Maybe it's the feeling of having money in my purse and cigarettes in my pocket. I wish I could spend it all at once then I remember we're saving up for Foxbar. I feel like dancing and try and pull Tommy up from the chair. *'Love love me do, you know I love you.'*

'Jean, I'm busy.'

I dance on my own in front of him, snapping my fingers and bopping my head, *'So Plea- ea – ea –ease.'* He laughs but stays put. 'I want us to look smart tonight,' I say. 'You know whit prissy Cissy's like.'

'Don't call her that, it's no nice.'

'Sorry,' I say. 'But wear the shoes, will ye, Tommy? For me?'

The hedge next to Cissy's gate is perfect, like her man has cut and measured each twig and leaf to make them even. A light grey Triumph is parked outside, so shiny you can see your face in the bonnet. I take Ava's hand as we walk up the path. Cissy has Venetian blinds instead of nets. There's a gleaming brass nameplate above the letterbox that says Mr and Mrs Alex Quail. Ava touches it and leaves a thumbprint that I try to rub off. I feel frightened to move, and we're not even inside the house. Tommy chaps the door. 'It's us.'

Cissy appears, wearing a navy blue skirt, a blouse with a brooch at the neck, and a cream cardigan with pearl buttons. 'There's a bell, Tommy,' she says.

'Excuse me,' he says, and rings it. Ava giggles and Cissy gives her a disapproving look.

'Ava,' I say, though I don't know what for.

Cissy hangs our coats on the stand just behind the door. There's a raincoat on it already and a brass-topped cane. 'Is Alex having trouble with his legs?' I say.

'The manager in Spooling gave him it as a gift,' says Cissy, as if I should know that already.

In the front room, her man is smoking a pipe in a high-backed chair with a dark green velvet cushion. He looks up and nods his head. 'Tommy.'

Tommy nods back. 'Alex.'

The decor is changed since the last time I was here. There's a green carpet with Paisley swirls, and light green wallpaper to match, patterned with leaves that look like ferns. On the mantel-piece, there's a brass carriage clock. But there's something else that wasn't here before, in the corner by the window: a piano, the wood all polished and red-looking. On top of it, a cut glass vase filled with yellow flowers. Ava's eyes light up. 'A piano, Mammy.'

I keep a tight hold of her hand. 'Don't you touch it, it's your Aunt Cissy's.'

'That's alright. Would you like to try it, Ava?'

'Aye,' says Ava.

'It's no, "aye," it's "yes, please,"' I say. 'Mind yer manners.'

She drops my hand and rushes over like a shot. She looks right dainty standing there at the piano, in her red and white shoes and the dress with the wee satin bow tied at the back: one that Cissy bought her last Christmas. Cissy opens the lid and I can almost hear the wood creak. The keys shine like a row of per-fect teeth. Even I want to touch them. I've never been at a piano before. Cissy sits down at the stool and lifts Ava onto her knee. Her cheeks bunch up and even though I can't see her face I know she's smiling. Cissy starts to play on the piano with one hand, one of those nursery rhyme tunes. It's only four or five notes, so, in a few minutes, Ava has got the hang of it. 'Look, Mammy.'

'That's great, hen,' I say. 'Jerry Lee Lewis, eat your heart out.'

'I was thinking more of Mozart,' says Cissy.

'Well, it disny matter. It's no like we can afford a piano anyway, is it, Tommy?' But Tommy isn't listening. He's standing by the window with Alex while he starts on about his lawnmower or something. 'Come here, Ava, till I fix yer hair,' I say.

She rolls her eyes and slides off the stool. I take my comb out my bag and start brushing. There's not much wrong with her hair. I just need my hands to be busy. 'Have you been playing long?' I say to Cissy, to make conversation. 'Tommy never mentioned about a piano.'

'Since I was a lassie,' she says. 'The organist at the kirk gave lessons: hymns and sonatas. I thought I'd take it up again, start teaching.'

'Aye,' I say, thinking it's alright for some. When I've finished brushing Ava's hair, Cissy puts her on the stool again and asks if she can take a photo. It's one of those expensive cameras that take an instant picture. Ava is enjoying herself, so I say yes.

For dinner we have beef olives, roast tatties and neeps, just as if it were a Sunday. We eat in the dining room. The window looks onto the back green; there's no washing hanging out, just a concrete path with clipped hedges running up the sides, and a neat carpet of grass. There's a hut, too, with nets in the window just like a house, and a big tree hanging over it.

The wooden table is so gleaming with polish that I only eat wee forkfuls at a time, afraid of dropping any food. Ava picks up her napkin ring and tries to put it over her wrist: 'It's too small.'

'Put that back,' I hiss. There's another vase of flowers, just like the ones on the piano, 'Begonias,' says Cissy. 'From the garden.'

'Tommy's never been much of a gardener,' I say. 'Anyway, we won't need to worry about keeping a green when we're in the new place.'

'New place?' Cissy dots the sides of her mouth with her napkin. 'Where?'

'We're on the list for Foxbar,' says Tommy.

'Oh.' She puts down her napkin.

'The new high flats,' I say. 'They've got central heating.' Even Cissy doesn't have central heating.

'What about the rent?' says Cissy. 'How will you manage?'

Trust Cissy to try and spoil it. 'We'll manage,' I say. 'We're saving up, aren't we, Tommy? I can always do more shifts.'

'You'll be lucky,' says Cissy.

'How do you mean?'

'They're downsizing,' says Alex.

'What?'

'Scaling back operations.' Alex looks at Tommy when he's speaking, not me. 'Outsourcing to foreign places where the labour is cheaper. Mostly it's in Turning. They'll no be making the spools in Paisley anymore. They're using a plastic moulding from America instead. There's already been layoffs.'

I take a drink of water to cool the flush of heat to my cheeks. 'But that'll no affect me, will it, what happens in America?'

'They're cutting back in Spinning, ring frames and speed frames. Two whole flats are about to go. That means less yarn for Twisting.' He wipes his hands on his napkin as if that'll tidy things up.

'Aye, but surely that'll no be for a while?' says Tommy. 'There's time yet.'

'There might no be layoffs, but they're asking for voluntary redundancies. That's what this pension thing is about.'

I picture Una chaining herself to the machines rather than give up her title as queen of Twisting.

'When that starts,' says Alex. 'Mark my words, there'll be no guarantee of a future in the mills. If you've sense, you'll start looking elsewhere.'

'Alex is taking his pension in one lump sum,' says Cissy. 'That way we'll have some capital.'

I nod, though I don't know what she's on about.

'Can you do that?' says Tommy.

'Aye,' says Cissy. 'Used to be you had to take it in monthly payments. Did Jean no tell you? There's a notice up about it.'

'It's so you can have the option if you volunteer for redundancy,' says Alex.

Cissy glances at me, then at Alex. 'But we don't know anything for sure. No point in spreading rumours.'

I remember what Una said earlier. 'If it's true,' I say to Cissy. 'Will they no ask the older workers first?'

She shrugs, trying to keep it in, not wanting to be the one to give away management secrets, but her mouth is twitching. Eventually it's too much for her. 'Put it this way, if the worst comes to the worst, it's last in first out. So I wouldn't go buying Tommy any more new shoes.'

For pudding, we have ice-cream and tinned fruit. Ava leaves

the cherries till last and makes a face out of them in her bowl. 'Can I have yours, Mammy? I need them to make a happy mouth.'

I fish around, trying to scoop them out but Cissy gets there first. When we're finished eating she lets Ava play on the piano again. Tommy and Alex go outside, stalking around the Triumph like it's a ship just landed from outer space. I help Cissy clear up in the kitchen. She's got a right face on her. No doubt it's because Tommy just shrugged off all that talk about the mills, said he'd do extra shifts and soon we'd have a car just like theirs, only a Cortina because Fords are the best. I smile to myself and whistle under my breath, but it makes her clatter the plates even louder. Then, right out the blue, she says, 'Don't think I don't know what you're up to, Jean Owen.' She uses my maiden name, instead of Tommy's.

I keep on wiping the plates, watching the dishcloth in my hand. 'What do you mean? I'm no up tae anything.'

This time Cissy stops scrubbing so I don't have another plate to dry. She leans her hands on the sink. 'I saw you both. A fortnight past, walking round the back of the mill, up towards the canal.'

My heart gives a quick thud but I act like nothing's up and put the clean plate on the worktop. 'I really have no idea what you're talking about,' I say, all posh like her.

She turns to face me, with her back to the sink, still leaning on it, her body shaking like she's about to pounce. 'Well, I canny say I'm surprised. That's just like you, Jean, isn't it? To stand there brazen as you like and lie to my face when I've seen you with my own two eyes, you and that Billy McBride.' She spits his name like it's making a bad taste in her mouth.

For a moment I stand stupidly, staring through her, the dish-cloth in my hand, like she might pass me another plate from the sink. But she doesn't. She's waiting for me to say something. 'It's no whit you think, Cissy. I promise. He just turned up, wanted to talk. That's all it wis, just talk.'

'Aye, there's always plenty of talk where you're concerned, Jean Owen.'

'I'm sorry. I wish I never spoke to him. And I've no seen him since. Honest.'

'I don't care for your honesty,' says Cissy. 'What I care about is Tommy and that wee lassie, believe it or no. It's no her fault she's been brought into all this.'

'Whit's Ava got to do with it?'

Cissy takes a deep breath and clenches her fists.

'Billy's going wae a lassie fae Glesga,' I blurt. 'Ask Aggie Burns.'

'I'll do nothing of the sort.' Cissy walks towards me, close enough so I can smell the ice cream and neeps on her breath. 'Hear this, Jean Owen. I don't care what you do. In fact, the farther away you do it the better as far as I'm concerned. But for Tommy's sake, I'm giving you one more chance. If I ever see you with that McBride piece of rubbish again, I'll be telling Tommy and let him see you for the wee trull that you are. Are we clear?'

My pulse is hammering like a bloody marching band. In the parlour Ava is playing *Merrily we Roll Along* but she keeps hitting all the wrong notes. I don't know whether to cry or scream. In the end I do neither. 'Aye,' I say. 'We're clear.'

2013

Victoria, British Columbia

Government Street is thronged with TV crews and reporters. The whole scene is being beamed live into Ava's phone while she sits in the back of the car. Kids, who five years ago had never heard of Borealis, are being asked for their opinions, their earnest unblemished faces filling her screen. One claims that Borealis is a sword of Damocles above the heads of British Columbia; a bit overblown, she thinks.

Her car pulls up outside the Victoria Conference Centre. Five minutes later Scott comes strolling along the pavement. He's accompanied by a skinny woman in cropped jeans and a checked shirt knotted at the waist. Her hand floats through the window of the car like a limp bird. 'Hi, I'm Ginny.'

Ava takes it briefly, then turns to Scott. 'Can I talk to you a moment? In private.'

Ginny rubs his back, and signals with her thumb and pinkie for him to call her. Nice to meet you, Mrs N.'

'Mrs N?'

'Leave it, Mom.' Scott climbs in and sits opposite, fidgeting with his camera, not looking at her. 'So what is it you want?'

'I'm fine, thanks for asking.' She tells the driver to make his way round the block. 'What's going on here, Scott? What are you trying to prove?'

'Isn't it obvious? I'm making a film.'

'I mean this.' She gestures out the window. 'The protests. Why do you need to get involved?'

'It's a free country.' He points the lens towards her. 'Or it's supposed to be. Maybe that's what my film will prove, whether it is or it isn't.'

'Do you realise how this looks for me, for the company?'

'No. How does it look?'

'Don't play games, Peanut.'

'Don't talk to me like I'm a character in Snoopy.'

She turns away. 'Things are bad right now. Bruce is concerned, we all are. It was a private contractor who carried out that illegal logging. We're dealing with it.'

'Great, you have a scapegoat. Heads will roll, just not the right ones.'

She sighs. 'They want me to appear on one of those daytime shows. Present the family face of the company, get the public to see us as real people.'

'So?'

'So, we have to show a united front. If you're on the protests, well, do I have to spell it out?'

'Ah, the smiling face of the corporation. You want me to play happy families, is that it?'

'Yes, just for a while, until things calm down.'

'Shouldn't be so hard. We've been doing that for years, haven't we, Mom? Playing happy families.'

'What do you mean?'

'You want me to come on this TV show?'

'No.'

'Why not? It'll be fun.'

Why does he always do this, put her on the spot? 'I don't want you under that kind of pressure. They ask questions. Sometimes not very nice ones.'

'Afraid of what I'll let slip? Which would they be more interested in: my not-so-cosy father-son relationship with Bruce, or the fact that I've never set eyes on my real father?' He affects a *thinking* pose, then slides down, filming her from the floor.

'Put that thing away. I'm serious. I want you to stop this, Scott.

Stop it now. Let's talk like civilised people for once.'

'Like we did in Pickering?' The eye inside the lens narrows, like she's being measured, judged. 'Maybe you could tell them how you never visited Cissy, your only living relative, in hospital, or that my grandma perished in a house fire in Scotland before I was born. That's the truth, isn't it?'

Her face is burning. 'What do you want from me?'

'Everything with you is lies. Why don't you just shoot the protestors? At least that would be more honest.'

'Don't be ridiculous; no one's going to get shot.' He edges towards her and the camera's snout bumps against the bridge of her nose. It hurts. Anger surges through her. 'Bruce is right; you've too much time on your hands. It's my fault; I've spoiled you. If you knew what it was to earn money for a living, you wouldn't waste your life with all this – this nonsense. Face it, Scott, do you really think the board at Cannes is going to call you up? There are kids out there who'd sell their blood to have the advantages you've got. You're too old, Scott. Your time has come and gone, and you were so wrapped up in yourself you never saw it happen.'

Scott is laughing. Filming her and laughing. 'Brilliant, Mom. You've really broken the fourth wall.'

Her bag drops to the floor, spilling its contents. She instructs the driver to stop. 'Get out. This conversation is finished.'

'So soon? And I was having such a good time.'

They've reached the harbour. Scott opens the door, and the glare of water makes her eyes screw shut. Then he's out on the wharf, his figure growing smaller in the rear-view mirror, the camera pointing accusingly at her slowly retreating car.

Susi is cracking eggs into a bowl. Ava collapses into a chair and blinks away her tears. It's as though she's been storing up salt in little mounds. Sniffing, she tells herself it was just another of Scott's absurd provocations, anything to get a reaction, to satisfy whatever mood he's in at the time.

'How was your day?' The bowl rests in the crook of Susi's arm. She whisks the contents and looks at Ava with sympathetic green eyes. 'Did something happen? You look awful.'

'It's nothing.' Ava loads cutlery and plates into the dishwasher. Bruce hates it when she does housework but she needs to occupy her hands, her mind. What if Scott is right and she's part of the problem? What if her whole life has been one big lie?

Susi is singing quietly in Cantonese, or maybe it's Mandarin, Ava isn't sure. The tune has a calming, lilting quality. 'Where did you learn that?' she says.

'My stepfather taught me it.'

'It must be nice – to have him around, I mean.'

'He's from Hong Kong but has a restaurant in Chinatown. He's very old now. Almost blind, but still working.' Susi places the bowl on the table and washes her hands.

'So, what's the song about?'

'Almond blossom, how it's nurtured by the branch, then blows away in the wind.'

'Nature?'

'Actually, it's about family.' Clipping a few leaves from a silvery green sprig, she puts them in a teapot.

Ava sighs. At least she had some sort of connection with her father; Scott has nothing, a blank space, a question mark. She took it for granted he'd be like her, that he could get through life without thinking about it, but he's not; he's different. 'What if the blossom doesn't blow away?' says Ava. 'What if it's taken?'

'The result is still the same. It's our roots that make us who we are.' Susi pours some of the liquid into a cup, and stirs. It has that same bitter smell as before.

'How did you get this job anyway?'

'Sorry?' The spoon makes a high-pitched rattle.

'Bruce mentioned he'd hired you, but he's always been lax on detail.'

'Mr Newport frequented my father's restaurant for business lunches; I was looking for a job and – well – here I am.'

It makes sense. A third of their buyers come from China and, despite Bruce's dislike of the Asian diaspora, it's his job to keep them entertained, or as he puts it: 'If they want to eat fucking fried octopus balls, I don't mind tucking in their napkins, so long as the money keeps flowing.' Still, there's something Ava likes about this woman, a sort of steady calmness. She presses her lips in a smile, and takes the warm cup of sage tea from Susi's hand. 'Thanks.'

Ava stretches on the sofa with the Mary, Queen of Scots book on her lap. Bruce is working late again, thrashing out legal stuff with Bentley. Ironic that she's sitting in what they call the 'family room,' when she spends most of her time in it alone.

The book's pages are strangely reassuring, a mystery of marks and smudges: tea stains, the translucent shine of grease, an inky thumbprint. The tell-tale signs of people's lives, book borrowers, perhaps dead now, who read about Mary, Queen of Scots during lunch-breaks, or on Sunday afternoons with tea and biscuits, or, like her, stretched on their sofas, thumbs sweaty enough to smudge the ink.

On 15 June, 1567, Mary, Queen of Scots, accused of the murder of Lord Darnley, her syphilitic husband, was captured, and imprisoned in a small dilapidated room in the Provost's house in Edinburgh. Denied her servant women and the usual protocols afforded to a queen, she appeared at the window, only to be jeered at by the crowds below. Enraged, she screamed, tore at her hair, and stripped herself to the waist.

The words begin to blur. Ava shuts her eyes but her head is too full to sleep, so she opens the book at the beginning again. Some of the pages have fallen loose from the binding. There's a serrated edge where the title sheet should be, as though it's been ripped away. Holding it under the table lamp she can see little dents scored into the blank page below, indecipherable, but there, like footprints.

In school they used to make rubbings of maple leaves and bark. She runs downstairs to the TV room: there's a pencil that Bruce uses for keeping billiard scores. She grabs it and, rushing back upstairs, holds the book flat under the lamp and starts to gently rub the fine grey nib across the paper, blowing away the excess particles until the indentations reveal themselves, forming slowly into words:

To Ava on her 18th birthday. I hope you'll read this book and think of me.

Love always, Mammy xx

An acrid taste rises in her throat. She smudges the pencil marks with the side of her fist, trying to make the words vanish, but it's too late; they're etched into her brain. She lets the book drop and runs to the bathroom, retching tea and bile into the pristine white bowl. Her stomach aches and her chest feels empty. It's not true. It has to be some kind of sick joke. She sinks onto the cool tiles. Footsteps echo in the hall and stop outside the door. 'You okay?' It's Susi.

'Go away. You have to stop giving me that tea. It's making me ill.'

'I have a message.'

'Whoever it is, I'm not in.'

'It's Bruce. He's been taken to hospital.'

1962
Paisley

At dinner time, Una plonks her tray next to mine and sits down. The younger crowd are chatting about what they did at the weekend. Aggie was up the Barras with Angie. I wait to see if she mentions Billy and the woman from the Lighthouse but she says nothing and I'm not going to ask. 'In oor day aw we had was tea dances,' says Maggie. 'Mind you, the cakes were good, weren't they, Una? Lovely cream buns. Men never respected a woman that drank.'

'They still don't.' Una stirs her tea. 'So how did it go at Prissy Cissy's? Did you ask her aboot the pensions?'

I flinch. I'd rather not think about Cissy. I've had enough of it from Tommy; I've lost count of the amount of times he's said: 'See, Jean, whit wur ye worried aboot, my sister's no that bad, is she?' I tell Una about the downsizing.

'The whit?'

'It means cutting back on work.'

Maggie laughs. 'My man's been doonsizing fur years. If he doonsizes any mair he'll be horizontal.'

Una lights a cigarette. 'That means there'll be layoffs.'

'No layoffs. Voluntary redundancies. And Alex says it might no be fur ages.'

She's not listening. It's like the wind's been sucked out her, her eyes small and tired. 'That stuff aboot the pensions, they're trying tae pick us aff. Well they'll no get rid a me afore I'm ready, that's fur sure.'

On the way back, I wait till the others have gone to the toilet and Una's on her own. She's walking slower than usual, her shoulders slightly stooped. Her hips roll like they're stiff and she holds her palm to the small of her back. I see her ageing and I feel sorry for her. 'Thanks,' I say. 'For being nice to me, you know, after that time in the toilets.'

Una turns towards me, her arms folded. Sun glints through the tall arched windows of the corridor and glows through the silver edges of her hair. 'I'm a good Christian woman; it's how I wis brought up. And I'm nothing, if not fair. You mind o that Jean McParland, and you'll do alright. Bit try it oan wae me again, and you'll no be so lucky, mark my words.'

She walks away and her posture has shifted upright again. I wonder how I could have let her fool me. Una McMenemy might be old but she's plenty of spite left in her yet. I feel stupid. My feet are frozen to the linoleum floor. Out the window, an office worker in a blue suit is going towards the Counting House: Cissy. Tommy says she went to night school for six months to learn typing and shorthand. He says she can type eighty words a minute. I imagine her saying it, her writing pad on her knees and her pearls round her neck. 'Yes, Mr So-and-so, I can type eighty words a minute.' I watch her till she disappears, then I turn away, Una's fire and brimstone still ringing in my ears.

I tell Tommy that I hate Mondays. 'I'm finished wae the mill. I want to get a job in an office.'

Tommy laughs. 'You, in an office, Jean? You need tae have a certificate for that.'

'So it's alright for Cissy tae have a certificate and no me, is that whit you're saying, Tommy?'

'No, I'm no saying that. It's jist, it costs money, Jean. If we're moving house –'

'You said yourself that'll no be fur a while. I just want an opportunity, Tommy.'

Ava's gone that way where she's staring at her plate, making a wee landscape out of her dinner, a river of peas flowing through mashed potato mountains. I feel like my body's burning inside, like I could grab my plate and smash it against the wall. But I don't. I've just got to sit here. If I say I'm going out, Tommy will ask where. Or I'll have to take Ava. It's not her fault, but sometimes I wish that, just for a wee while, I could be free to do what I like, no questions asked. 'You know fine well they're laying people off, Tommy. I'm thinking aboot the future. There's no point sitting in a fancy high hoose if I've nae job.'

'Sometimes there's no pleasing you, Jean.'

I scrape my dinner into the bin, clattering the knife against the plate, then I fling the dishes in the sink.

'Your mither's right, Jean, you don't think aboot anybody but yourself.'

'Will you shut up, Tommy?'

'And I'm no wearing they shoes anymair either. They hurt my feet.'

'Fine,' I say. 'Stick yer heid in the midden while you're at it.'

He says nothing, just gets up and puts on his jacket. When he's leaving I shout after him, 'Say hello to my mother on your way home.'

I'm sick of these four walls, but the only place I can go is Annie's. I tug Ava behind me. 'Mammy, you're going too fast.' When we get there, Annie sends Ava to the shop to get a double nugget. Ava can hardly believe her luck. Annie goes to make the tea and I sit with her mother, wondering what it's like to get to her age, what's going through her head, if she's remembering all the things she wished she'd done but didn't. It seems like ages before Annie comes back. I pour, and she bounces Peter on her knee, going on about how he's getting a bit gurny, but not any trouble really.

I'm about to start talking, when she gets up from the couch. 'Mammy,' she says. 'You're too close tae the fire again.' She hands me Peter while she shifts her mother's chair. I look at Peter's big round face. There's a bit of yellow sick trickling out his bottom lip. I pat his back and catch the rest with a rag that's on the couch.

'Ta,' says Annie. 'Between the two a them, I don't know whether I'm coming or going.'

I nod. But, the more Annie talks, the less I understand. She never asks about me, not really. It's always Ava, or Tommy or my mother. How does Tommy like his mince? Does he like a lot of gravy like Archie?

When Ava gets back, she asks if she can go upstairs and see her nan. I say yes, then I listen to a bit more of Annie's talk before I say, 'I suppose I'll go and see whit Ava is up to.' I know my mother and Ava will likely be in the front room watching television, so I slip out the back, jump over the wall, then run across the greens and out the close two blocks down. At the corner of the pavement, I turn right and head into town. By the time I reach Abbey Bridge my whole body is pulsing and dizzy. The door of the Lighthouse is open, but I stop on the corner and gather my breath.

I had to get them all out of my head: Cissy, Tommy, Una. But now I'm here I don't know what to do. I take a deep breath and cross over to the pub. The ladies' lounge is through the other door but I pretend like I don't know and start walking towards the bar. The light is warm and red on the sandstone outside, but inside it's all cool and dark like a cave. I can hardly see for the smoke. A few men are drinking at the bar and others near the window but I can't make out their faces. I go right up the back, near the toilets, before I find Billy sitting with a man I've never seen before, burly with a bushy moustache. The man glances at me, says something to Billy, then slips away to the bar. Billy grins. 'Jean. You're here.'

'Aye,' I say, checking over my shoulder. 'I'm here.'

'Get me doon by the Hamills in five minutes.'

I practically run outside. The barman shouts after me: 'Ladies' lounge is through the other door.' I pretend not to hear.

'Jist like old times, eh, Jean?' says Billy. We're sitting on the bank of the river, in the lee of the big finishing mill, the water skimming low over the rocks.

I hug my knees up to my chest. 'No quite.'

Billy stretches his legs, lying long and relaxed, not worried about his feet getting wet. He turns towards me, leaning on his elbow. 'We made a right mess of things, didn't we?'

I can feel him watching me. He's searching for something but I don't know what. 'I don't have much time,' I say. 'I've left Ava wae my mither. They don't know I'm gone.'

He smiles. 'I knew you'd find a way.'

Further upstream, the water is tumbling down the falls like a big valance sheet, all frilled and foaming. 'Go away, Billy,' I say.

'Bit I jist got here.'

'I mean go away fur good. Leave Paisley.'

'No withoot ye, Jean. Dae you no mind whit I said? The two of us? America?'

'Tommy's my life now, and Ava. You've got tae understand.'

He sits up, chucks a stone into the water. 'Do you think I'd say all that stuff if I didny mean it? If it wisny the only way?' He's picking grass from the wee cracks in the stone, not looking at me. 'Aw they years in the jail while you were with him, wae Tommy. It kills me knowing he's the one who gets tae hold you at night. But I don't blame you, Jean, dae I? I've no even thought aboot anither lassie aw that time. You're the only one fur me. Dae you no know that, Jean?'

'You're a liar, Billy McBride. I know you were wae a lassie last week. And don't try and deny it. Wee Aggie told me whit you said.' I stare into the water, but I can feel his eyes on me, coaxing me to turn round. 'So don't think you can come here asking me tae run away wae you when you're chasing every bit of skirt you find.'

He starts laughing, like he's embarrassed. 'She's nobody, a pal.'

I stand up. 'I've said whit I had to say.'

'Sit down, eh?'

I try to shake off his hand but he holds tighter. I sit down.

That smile again. 'Alright, I wis winding Aggie up because I knew you'd be jealous. Have you heard the mouth on her?

I'd rather kiss my da's dug.'

His hand touches my neck, and it's the best feeling I've had in ages. Tommy never strokes my skin. I know I should move but I can't. Billy's breath is getting closer. He tilts my face up to meet his. The river rushes in my ears, flowing so fast I can't hear anything else, not even my own thoughts. Billy's lips touch mine, soft at first then harder. I shudder and pull him close, pressing my body into his, breathing in leather and beer and Billy, his jacket wet with my tears, wrapping my arms so tight around him I think it must hurt. 'Oh, Billy.'

Tommy calls it 'that bloody book.'

'Will you pit that bloody book down, Jean? I canny find a clean shirt.'

Sometimes I think he makes things up just to annoy me because he can't stand the sight of me having five minutes to myself. I don't get up from the bed, just turn the page and tell him to wear the old one till the others are washed. Tommy pokes his head round the bedroom door. 'The other fellas in work don't have tae pit up wae this. Dougie Broon turns up every day wae his shirt spotless.'

'Aye, and Myra Broon turns up tae the mill every day wae a black eye. How did you no marry her insteid?'

'Don't be daft, Jean.'

'You should think yourself lucky, Tommy. No every fella has a wife who's trying tae better herself.' I take a deep breath. This moment is as good as any. 'I've decided tae take classes,' I say.

'Classes? At the mill?'

'I spend enough time there already, Tommy. No, shorthand and typing. Down at the Grammar School. Every Tuesday night.'

Tommy sits on the edge of the bed, runs both hands through his hair. You'd think I just told him somebody died. He says nothing, so I keep talking. 'I could get a job in an office, Tommy. Like Cissy. I'm thinking aboot the future, setting an example fur Ava.'

'It's hard graft that does that, Jean. Anyway, that stuff aboot redundancies is all talk. The mills pay well. Best thing you can do is stick in there and Ava will get a job, jist like her mither. Then she'll no need tae worry aboot getting an education.'

'It'll only be a couple of hours a week.'

'I said no. How are we supposed tae pay fur it? Whit aboot the car? Motors urny cheap, you know.'

'Once I'm an office girl we can get any kind of car we want, even an Aston Martin. We can holiday in Spain, take Ava oan an aeroplane. And when one vest gets dirty we'll buy you a new one.' I shut the book, move close to him and run my hand down the centre of his back. 'Come on, Tommy. I'm doing this fur us. Can you no see that?' When I say it, I really believe it, like I've never been so sure of anything in my life; a bit like being a teenager again, thinking that when you grow up you'll have everything you want, that you'll be happy. It's a long time since I felt that certainty. I kiss Tommy's neck. 'Come on,' I say. 'I like a man in a dirty vest.'

'Jean!'

I silence him with my mouth. 'I have to go tae work,' he says.

'Not yet.' I close the bedroom door, undress down to my slip and get under the covers. Tommy takes off his trousers and gets in beside me. 'We'll have to make it quick,' he says, climbing on top.

After he goes to work, I sit down with my book. Mary, Queen of Scots is married to Lord Darnley but in love with her servant, David Rizzio. I say his name out loud, elongating the first syllable like the Italians. I decide the name would suit Billy. 'Billy Riiiz-io.' Then I say, 'Jean Riiiz-io,' but that just sounds silly.

Passionate. That's how Mr Webster described Mary, like a Shakespeare heroine. And what's so wrong with passion? I imagine Tommy finding out I kissed Billy and me saying, 'But I'm a passionate woman, Tommy.' And Tommy nodding, 'Aye, right enough,' just as if I'd said I was hungry or sleepy; a simple need that had to be satisfied. It's not that I don't love Tommy. I do. But differently. I used to wonder if it was possible to love two people at once. Now I know it's possible, but that you love them in different ways. Mary knew it, too, and it pained her just as much as it pains me. I want to tell Billy I could live happy for the rest of my life knowing only that he loves me. It doesn't matter that we can't be together; our love will always be pure, passionate, perfect. But he wouldn't understand. 'I'm no letting you go this time,' he said, when I left him under the bridge. 'Telephone the Lighthoose. When you find a way, I'll be waiting.'

'What if you're not there? What if someone knows it's me?'

'I'm always there. It's where I do business.' He tugged the edges of his jacket, pulling up the collar. 'Use anither name if you're that worried.'

I kissed him once more, awkwardly on his teeth rather than his mouth. 'Mary,' I said. 'I'll say I'm Mary.'

My mother doesn't say much the first time I drop Ava off. I know it's because of Tommy. He'll have mentioned Cissy and downsizing and typing classes and my mother will have sat there fidgeting with her hands in her pinny pockets, not saying anything, but mountain-like in her silence. 'It's only seven till nine on a Tuesday,' I can picture Tommy saying. 'There's a lot of money in office jobs. More than a mill lassie gets.' Though my mother will never disagree with Tommy or upset him or be seen to be the one who spoils things, I can imagine her looking at him with her martyr's face, and how Tommy will have taken it to mean concern for Ava, replying, 'She'll be no trouble at all, Senga. You jist let me know if she is.'

My mother looks me up and down, her eyes flitting off my suede jacket, my lipstick and earrings, her tongue wagging silently inside her head. 'Getting above her station, full of flighty ideas about shorthand and Foxbar and Ford Cortinas.' Ava is already stuffing her face with a caramel wafer. When I'm about to leave, she looks up and says, 'Have a nice time typing, Mammy.'

Something inside me swells. I make a big show of kissing her, cupping her face in my hands, feeling my mouth quiver. 'That's my girl,' I say. Then I straighten my skirt and I'm out the door, but not before I catch my mammy shaking her head.

All along the street, and on the bus, I still have that feeling of being full to the brim inside. I've never loved Tommy and Ava so much as I do now. A stray tear spills from my eye and I catch it before it streaks down my cheek. The feeling doesn't go away until I reach the Grammar with its sober red sandstone and big windows. I give my name at reception and go along corridors and past classrooms, the heels of my boots echoing along the wooden floors.

I find myself in a room with rows of desks and typewriters. I sit down nearest the window. Most of the other girls are younger than me. I think of when I first met Billy and suddenly I see myself like I was then, all ankle socks and rosy cheeks. It feels like a lifetime ago. I look down at the typewriter. There is a board covering the keys. The teacher is tall and dressed in a plaid skirt. Her glasses hang from a chain round her neck. She takes the chalk and writes Q W E R T Y in big letters on the blackboard.

After the class is finished, I walk to the corner. When Billy sees me, he turns and walks up a road past big houses with huge windows, sweeping lawns and driveways. I follow silently. No one I know lives up this way so we don't have to worry about being seen.

Yesterday, I went to the phone box at the end of Newton Street and called the Lighthouse. I put on a posh voice. 'I'd like to speak to Billy McBride, please. It's Mary.'

'Mary who?' said the barman.

I hadn't expected him to ask for a surname. 'Mary Stuart,' I said. 'Tell him Mary Stuart.'

Billy takes the first on the right and waits for me at the end of a street that leads to the back wall of a church. My heart is thudding. 'This way,' he says, and nods. 'I'll gie you a hand up.'

'My tights,' I say, but he takes my bag and lifts me up by the waist. I grab onto the top of the wall and swing myself over and down the other side, scuffing the toe of my boot. My bag lands beside me, then Billy. We're surrounded by trees. Laughing, he leans me against the wall. Then he's kissing me, his tongue reaching into my mouth. I push back, deeper, until there's nothing in the world except the smoky taste of Billy's lips. 'I wish it wis jist you and me, Jean,' he says. 'Away fae here. We can dae it. One afternoon and we can be oan a plane, away. America; jist think.'

'You don't even have a job. How cuid ye look after Ava?'

'The mill, Jean. It's full a money. There's nothing to hold us back.'

'Stop it, Billy.' I'm annoyed he had to bring it up. It was fine when we were kissing.

He looks at the ground. 'If you don't want to, if you don't think enough of me.'

I go to kiss him again but he pulls away. 'Don't you like it?'

'Aye, I like it, Jean. But I feel like I'm being eaten alive. I'm thinking Tommy disny kiss you enough.'

'Don't talk aboot Tommy,' I say.

'How can I no? Every time I look at your hand, I see his ring.'

I look at the gold band and see my eye reflected in it.

'Take it off, will you?'

I take off the ring and slip it inside my brassiere. I feel like a feather, swept along in the air, only to land and be trampled in a puddle. Billy slides his hands inside my pockets, pulling me towards him, the taste of his lips all smoky and soft. 'Good girl,' he whispers.

Una marches straight past The Bitch and chaps on the glass door that says 'Manager' in black letters. Ten minutes later it's dinner time and she's still not back. I'm fair hungry and I get pie instead of soup, and an extra helping of mash. 'Whit's that you're singing?' says Maggie, when I sit down at the table. 'It's driving me bloody mad.'

'Sorry, I didny realise I wis singing.'

'It's The Beatles,' says Aggie. 'Love Me Do.'

'Is it?' I say, feeling a slight flush.

'Gie me Andy Williams any day.' Maggie starts singing and some of the older women join in. They sound like a bunch of quacking ducks. Una's appearance makes them stop. 'Well?' says Maggie.

Una sits down and lights a cigarette. 'You'll no get anything out of him. Oh, I'll be alright for a pension on account of my long service but I'll not get a certificate. Imagine that? Doing away wae long service certificates. It's a sign. It'll be jist like the end a the trams, only naebody'll be lining the streets tae wave *us* goodbye. That tells you something. Anyways, I went by the Turning Shop on the way here.'

Some of the younger girls giggle. Everyone knows they walk by there to get the wolf whistles from the young apprentices.

'The foreman says he's no taking on any mair young lads.'

The girls drop their eyes and look sheepish.

'Something tae dae wae plastic bobbins fae America. I'm telling ye,' says Una. 'It's the beginning of the end.'

There's a lot of head shaking and tutting amongst the older lot whose mothers and grandmothers all got long service certificates that they pinned on their walls; and it wasn't like that in their day; and the Americans can build rockets but they canny save the mills. 'We should never have got them involved in the war,' says Una, as if that's got anything to do with it.

'Whit's wrong wae Americans anyway?' I say. 'Life disny end wae the mills, you know.'

Una looks like she might spit on the floor. 'I'll have you know the mills are all some folk have got. Look at Myra Broon. The mills is the only place she can get away. Whit she'll do when they're no here I don't know.' Myra is sitting at the end of the table. She looks up at the sound of her name, a fresh bruise spread across her cheek like a squashed tomato. Una eyes me up and down. 'I suppose it's America you'll be going when ye've finished yer night school.' She says it like it's something disgusting.

They're all looking. 'It's good to have something to fall back on,' I say. 'Just in case.' That's what Mr Webster said when I told him I wanted to take classes. It was Mr Webster that told me about the Grammar. The only thing I don't like is the teacher, Miss MacDiarmid. If you hand back your text with typos she calls you a stupid girl and makes you sit at the back like a naughty child. But I don't care because, afterwards, there's Billy, waiting with his smile and his mouth full of kisses. If I'm late back I tell my mother I stayed behind chatting to the other girls about vowels and diphthongs, heavy strokes and light strokes. That's when she usually stops listening.

'Well, it's good of your mother tae take Ava,' says Una. 'Though I don't know if she's up tae it, mind. I wis there yesterday and she wis looking awfy pale.'

'It'll be her knees again,' I say. 'She's on them water tablets.' But I know it's nothing to do with her knees. She can't get to me through Tommy so she'll be laying it on thick for Una. 'Don't worry,' I say. 'Ava's no trouble fur my mammy.'

'What do you think of Jacqueline Bouvier Kennedy?' I say to Tommy, while I'm making the tea. It's eggs, chips and beans. I turn away to butter the bread so I don't have to watch Tommy eat, the wee glimpses of food inside his mouth. I wonder what people in America have for tea and I'm sure it's not egg and chips.

'Who?' says Tommy.

'She's the President of America's wife, Tommy.'

'Whit aboot her?'

'Do you think she's, well, attractive?'

'I've never thought aboot it,' says Tommy, dipping his chips in yellow yuk.

I sit down and practise cutting my food into smaller mouthfuls. I read somewhere that's the mark of a lady. 'I'm thinking of getting my hair like hers, that's all. I wanted to know if you'd like it.'

'I like you jist the way you are,' says Tommy. 'Anyway, we can't afford to go spending any mair money.'

'What's Jacqueler Boover Kendy like?' says Ava.

I tell Ava she has the loveliest clothes, elegant and sophisticated, and lives in a great big white house, and rules over the richest country in the world.

'Where's that?'

'It's a big big place, ten million times bigger than Paisley, with buildings a thousand times as high as the chimneys on the mills.'

'Higher than Foxbar?'

'Much higher, and you can do anything you want there. That's why it's called the land of the free. The president's even going to put a man on the moon.'

'Don't fill the wean's heid wae rubbish,' says Tommy.

'It's no rubbish,' I say. 'Dae you no listen tae the news? At least one of us is educated.'

'Jist cause you can type a few words, Jean, don't get carried away.'

'And we should eat healthy food. Stuff ye can pit in the oven that's no fried and greasy. Like beef olives.'

'I don't think much of beef olives,' says Tommy. 'Egg and chips will do me.' He mops the plate with his bread and looks at Ava. 'When ye're finished, goan oot and play. I want tae talk tae yer mammy.'

The breath lingers in my body, filling every bone with dread. When I stand up to clear the dishes, my head feels dizzy. I watch Ava leave the room, like she's part of a film or television programme, and wonder whether to call her back.

'I've been thinking,' says Tommy. 'It's no fair on the wean.'

'What isn't?' My voice comes out all breathless.

'I think it's aboot time we gave her a wee brother or sister.'

I can't say anything. I sit back down on the chair, put my palm against my forehead and start laughing.

'Whit's so funny, Jean?'

'Nothing.' I remember what Una said that day in the toilets. 'Have you been talking tae my mammy?'

'No. Well, she might have said something, but I'd been thinking the same thing. It wid be nice, wouldn't it? All of us staying up in Foxbar, you, me, Ava and the new baby.'

'Oh, is that right? Is Ava no enough fur ye then?'

'You know that's no whit I mean. I love Ava. It's the right time, that's aw I'm trying tae say.'

I get up and start running the tap. I hear Tommy push away his chair. He's standing beside me. I can feel the hesitation in his breath before he puts one hand round my waist and kisses my cheek. 'Jist think aboot it, Jean. That's all I'm asking.'

I nod without looking at him. He pats my shoulder then he's gone. I lean over the sink, not moving, just staring into the bubbles. I wipe my face with my arm and some of them stick to my cheek, bursting in little white circles where Tommy's kiss has been.

2013
Vancouver, British Columbia

A consultant leads Ava past the signs for cardiac, coronary units and intensive care wards, her heels clicking efficiently on the sterilised floor. Ava listens, trying to make the connection between Bruce and words like hypertension, atherosclerosis, aneurysm. She bites the skin around her thumbnail. 'So is he going to be okay –?'

The doctor turns to Ava. 'Your husband's doing fine. We're running tests and we'll want to keep an eye on him for another twenty-four hours. He'll have to make some lifestyle changes: diet, exercise, that sort of thing. He insists he's well enough to go home, but if you could persuade him to co-operate. Just for now.'

They start walking again. At the door to Bruce's room, she hands Ava a leaflet and recommends an exercise programme at the hospital, then retreats with her clipboard. Bruce is sitting up in bed, circular pads and wires attached to his chest, his heartbeat a steady stream of bleeps on a screen. There's an overbed table with a jug of water and a plastic glass. On a chair next to him, leafing through papers, is Sue Brash.

'Sue, could you leave? I'd like to talk to my husband alone.'

Sue glances at Bruce and he nods, 'I'll see you back at the office. Keep me informed. I want to know who Kelly's talking to, even if I'm on the fucking operating table.'

The door closes and his eyes slide back down to his tablet. Ava straightens Bruce's pillow. 'You shouldn't be working. You've had a heart attack.'

He yawns. 'I hate that word. It's a little chest pain, is all. I'm fitter than an Alaskan brown bear.'

'I brought some things.' She folds his pyjamas and toiletries into hospital drawers, and drapes his robe over the end of the bed. The wall-mounted TV is tuned to CBC News: people are travelling from outside the province to join the protests. Ava picks up the remote and turns down the volume.

'Hey! I was watching that.' He tosses the straw out his glass and glugs the water. 'So, did you speak to Scott, find out what he's playing at?'

'That can wait.' She tucks in the sheets where they've come loose. 'Shouldn't you try and sleep?'

'I'm not dead yet.'

'Don't say that, Bruce.' Ava folds her arms. 'So what happened, exactly?'

'Kelly called last night. Son of a bitch was drunk. I told him I'd hang him out to dry: my dollars got him into office, and I can get him out of office too.' The monitor bleeps faster, the peaks and valleys ganging together. 'I had a few chest pains. You shouldn't worry. Everyone my age has heart disease, hon, unless you're a goddamn lazy bum.'

She sits down in Sue's empty chair and takes his hand. It feels cold. She rubs it between her palms. 'It makes you think, something like this, huh?'

He grunts.

'I'm serious, Bruce. Take some time off. I just lost Cissy. I don't want to lose you too.'

They sit silently for a moment. Though silence is never truly silent. All those times she sat at the kitchen table in Pickering with her aunt, making inane comments about the weather to fill in those yawning gaps. At least when Scott was little they could talk about what to feed him, or how he'd cried when the neighbour's dog licked him. But when they were alone, the silence swallowed her whole. She doesn't want things to go that way with Bruce; another one of those couples with nothing to say to each other.

'I only want what's best. The doctors say you should rest up –'

'Yeah, it'd suit them fine if I was on my knees before the Pearly Gates. Have more tests, take more pills. That's how they make money. It's a business, Ava, like anything else.'

It's embarrassing sometimes, how little influence she has over him. But that's just Bruce, stubborn as a railroad mule; she knew what she was letting herself in for. The yawning silence gathers slowly round her. 'What am I going to do with you?'

He pats her hand. 'Don't worry. When this is all over, we'll go somewhere together. I promise. How about that spa place up in Whistler?'

'I remember when Uncle Alex died,' she says, 'I came home to find Cissy waiting for me on the steps; it looked like someone had kicked a ball into her stomach. She took me inside and propped herself against the worktop like it was the only thing holding her up. "Alex is gone," she said. "There was nothing anyone could do." It was the only time I saw her cry.' Ava pauses. 'I guess what I'm trying to say is you've got a second chance.'

Her speech is met with the sound of deep breathing. She pushes the overbed table away and tucks his hands under the sheets. Too tired to sleep herself, her thoughts turn to the Mary, Queen of Scots book and her mother's inscription like pale scars through the smear of grey pencil dust. Taking the book from her bag she looks for the page, but it's not there. 'Shit.' She gets to her knees, scanning the floor under the hospital bed.

'What's happened? What are you doing down there?'

'Nothing. Go back to sleep.'

'I can't. I'm bored.'

'I've lost something, that's all.'

'What?'

'It's not important.'

'If I'm going to be stuck in this bed, I need unimportant things to think about.'

This wasn't how she wanted to tell him. 'Okay. Remember Cissy's lawyer, the one in Pickering? He gave me a letter from my mother.'

'That two-bit clerk? So what?'

'My mother's been dead since I was four, you know that.' She rambles on about mailboxes, stolen library books and ghostly inscriptions, blurting out her sentences in broken fragments.

'I don't understand. Why would your mother give you a book about Mary, Queen of Scots?'

'That's not the point.'

He heaves a tired sigh. 'So what have we got here? An old library book and two anonymous letters written by someone pretending to be your mom.'

'Not necessarily pretending.' She sits on the edge of the bed. 'I'm sorry, Bruce. I shouldn't be springing all this on you, not now.'

He gently nudges her cheek. 'You're being melodramatic. It's obvious. It's a hoax. Someone is trying to wind you up.'

'A joke? Why?'

'Ava, money makes people jealous, and you've got lots of it. You should expect this sort of thing. If I had a dollar for every time someone claimed to be a long lost relative… Don't react. Eventually they'll tire of it.'

'But what about Cissy's will? Why would she leave me that letter if she didn't think it was true?'

'She was a gullible old coot. You know what old people are like; they get senile. Look at you.' A jokey smile, though she notes the subtext: he thinks she's past it.

'It's not funny, Bruce. I'm not senile. One of the letters was meant for my father, Tommy. My mother wanted him to give her my address, but he wouldn't. He thought –' Her voice cracks. 'He thought I might not be his child.'

'Look, Bentley knows someone who sits on the Police Foundation. Work out a list of people you've told about your past that might know your father's name; we can probably trace it to a few gossips down at the yacht club: nothing to worry about. Right? I'll get him to make enquiries.'

She's never exactly been open about her past, skilled in directing the conversation anywhere but herself. There's no one who knows enough to set up such an elaborate hoax. Only Cissy, perhaps Wanda, but she wouldn't hurt a fly... A hollow throbbing starts around her eyes. The front room in Pickering. Scott shovelling the birth certificate into his mouth. No, he wouldn't do something like that, not even in a manic phase. It's too cruel, too callous. He's her son. 'Forget Bentley,' she says. 'You're right. There's no other explanation. My mother is dead. She has to be.'

But she can't shove the idea from her mind. It's all this stuff with Bruce, hospitals. She'll get some fresh air and coffee. Decaf. 'Bruce –'

'Hold on.' He turns the volume up on the TV. A line of flashing police cars is parked along Government Street. It's chaos. The camera pans to a little girl crying while her mother is questioned by a police officer. Other protestors are being dragged forcibly towards cars, feet scraping on the grass. Men and women, old and young, are spread against vans, officers searching their pockets.

Kelly's face appears on screen, red and hot under the collar. His chest is puffed under his shirt. Beads of sweat shine on top of his bald head. 'This is a government building,' he says. 'Not an open-air festival. It's my job to ensure our citizens aren't subjected to the unlawful and disruptive behaviour of an unruly minority.'

'Did you know about this?'

Bruce is smiling, not a wide beaming smile, but a small self-satisfied twist of his lips. 'About time Kelly did something. I'm not backing him for his good complexion. There were reports of drug taking amongst the protestors, apparently. Looks like Kelly decided to send in the ole boys in blue. It's not an injunction, but it'll have to do.'

Ava walks the block to Scott's apartment. If only Bruce had told her sooner, she could have warned Scott, got him out of the way. His phone is off. She has to see him with her own eyes, make sure he's safe and not in the back of some police van being carted off God knows where. The streets are busy: office workers sipping coffee, joggers with iPods, rich elderly ladies and their pampered dogs. The world is full of hackers, jokers, hoaxers. Any one of them could find out about her past. Letters can be made to look old, and perhaps she misread the inscription; it's hard to tell without the missing page.

A storm is gathering, wind whipping round the side of the building. She doesn't press the intercom, but follows a resident inside. The elevator is like the quiet eye of a tornado. With each floor, the knot of dread in her stomach tightens. Ginny answers the door, her eyes squinting against the brightness of the hall. 'Mrs N?'

Cissy used to show her disapproval by saying, 'I'll give you McDonald's,' or 'I'll give you pierced ears,' or whatever forbidden thing it was that Ava had asked for. As she enters Scott's apartment, she's tempted to flash her teeth at Ginny and say, 'I'll give you Mrs N,' but the scene that greets her pushes her intentions aside. The curtains are drawn, giving the room a mouldy dank feel, like mushrooms. Scott is sitting on the floor, a blanket over his head and a half-finished bottle of Jack Daniels at his side, the brand that rock stars drink. On the table in front of him a projector splashes images onto the far wall. She recognises Highway 401, Cissy's driveway, the orange teapot. She turns to Ginny. 'When was the last time he ate?'

'He's been up all night.'

'Scott, you're not on something, are you?'

He sighs. 'Fuck off, Mom. What do you want?'

The blanket makes his head look small and round, like when he was a baby, her own little Peanut. For a moment the letters, the book, don't matter. All she wants is to reach out, pull him to her, comfort him. 'Can I sit down?'

'I'll make some coffee,' says Ginny.

Ava crouches on the floor next to Scott. 'What are you watching?'

'My life.' The screen shows images of alleys and shops in Chinatown. Scott on the ferry going across the Georgia Strait, seagulls in a blue sky (that one looks quite nice; a special effect has been added, the gulls changing from pink to green).

'It's quite good,' she says.

'It's shit.'

'Why don't you add music?'

He strikes a match and lets it burn to his fingertips. 'My life is nothing. A dried-up old stick. It has no soul.'

'Staying up all night won't help.' She should know. She hasn't had a wink of sleep since the call from the hospital. The images on the wall get faster, busier. There are lots of people now. Government Street. Parliament. Protestors filmed from below so they look like they're growing out of the grass. More blurriness. Then a car. Her face at the window. God, she looks angry. Scott's feet. The inside of the car. Her frown. The camera zooming in on her. Mouth tight. Holding up her hand to block the lens. 'I told him this is the most interesting part,' says Ginny, returning with the coffee. 'But he won't listen.'

Scott clutches the blanket round him. He looks at Ava, his eyes intense. 'Just some talentless has-been, that's what you said.' He grits his teeth like every word and gesture is an effort, excavated from some deep, dark place.

'I was angry,' she says. 'I didn't mean it. Of course you have talent. You just need –'

'What?'

'None of us are perfect, Scott. Least of all me.'

'You can't say it, can you?'

'Scott, I'm trying to help. I –' Her thighs hurt from crouching.

'You hate having to be here right now. You hate having to deal with me. And, do you know what, you're right. I hate myself. I fucking hate myself. I hate what you've made me.' He stands up, his arms like pale twigs, the blanket drooping around them like raggedy wings. 'I'm nothing. And it's your fault. You never wanted me. I remind you of some cheap teenage fuck you wish you'd never had. You'd have flushed me down the toilet if you'd had the guts. Do you know what that's like, not to know who you are, to have one part of you always missing, just a great big FUCKING BLUR?'

She can't speak. Her eyes sting. Don't cry. He doesn't mean it.

He's not well. She sinks down so her bottom touches the floor. The car in the film is driving away now, turning to a black dot, shrinking, shrinking. Then blank. 'You're wrong, Scott. I do. I do know what it's like. I didn't mean what I said –' It's happening again. Pickering was his manic episode. Now it's the crash, the fall back down to earth. She takes Ginny aside, whispers in her ear, 'Maybe he should see a doctor, change his medication.'

Ginny looks at the floor. 'I'm not sure it's a doctor he needs.'

'So it's drugs, he's on drugs.'

'No.'

Scott looks up at them. 'We've decided, if Ginny has a girl, we'll call the baby Una. Has a nice ring to it, don't you think?'

'What?'

'Ginny likes it, don't you, Ginny?'

'It was a false alarm,' says Ginny. 'I'm not pregnant.'

'See,' says Scott. 'I've failed again.'

'Scott, what are you talking about? Please, honey, say something that makes sense.'

He's grabbing the matchbox, lighting several at a time, the rest tumbling across the floor. He drops the blanket and grabs the bourbon, heading towards the glass veranda doors.

She can't get rid of it, that terrible shadow of doubt at the back of her mind. What if her son hates her so much that he would do something so unthinkable –? 'Okay. I admit it,' she says. 'It's my fault. Just promise you'll tell me the truth, Scott.'

He turns round. 'The truth about what?'

'I've been getting some letters lately, personal letters. You don't know anything about them, do you?'

'What kind of letters?'

'Stuff about the past, my past. Bruce thinks they might be some kind of hoax.'

'You think I'm writing you hoax letters?' He sticks out his neck, vulture-like, staring at her with an open mouth.

'Do you really hate me so much, Scott? Whatever I've done, all this, writing letters, drinking, won't make it any better, will it?'

He holds up the bottle. 'You think I'm doing this to hurt you?'

His body sags against the railings. 'That's what you think?'

She gathers her breath. 'That book at Cissy's. Where did you find it, exactly?'

'First you accuse me of writing you hoax letters. Now you're asking me about a fucking stupid book.'

'Please, Scott. It's important. I need to know.'

He turns and leans over the edge of the rail, only the tips of his toes keeping him from falling over. One slip, a gust of wind, that's all it would take. He throws the empty match box, watches it float down, down, and out of sight. She's pulling her son by the loop of his jeans. His weight sends her staggering, but his body gives way and he's back on the veranda again, sitting on the ground with his head tucked against his knees. Ginny is beside him, rubbing his back, cooing into his ear.

Ava wheezes, out of breath. When he looks up, his mouth is a straight line, his teeth clenched. 'You can't say it, can you?'

'What? What do you want me to say?'

He tugs his blanket round his shoulders and stares at her with owlish eyes. 'I want you to say sorry.'

1962
Paisley

For days all I can think about is Tommy and the new baby and how to stop the new baby. I never realised before how much the lassies at work talk about weans. All week Maggie's been on about knitting a blanket for her grandwean's cot. It'll need to sleep in a drawer on account of lack of space. What's the point in having weans if there's nowhere to put them? But I don't say anything. It's nothing compared to Una. She had ten weans. I can't even imagine what that must be like. Decades of nappies and sick and knitting. 'When one lot left,' she says. 'The other lot were growing up.' At dinner break she starts on about her old wives' cures. 'They doctors know nothing wae their fancy pills,' she says. 'When mine got coughs, I'd soak broon paper in vinegar and stick it ower their chests. They'd be right as rain in a few days.' I imagine Una's man, some wee sickly soul who sat by the fire, occasionally coming to life for a quick how d'ye do. 'Did you never just feel like running away?' I ask her.

Una looks at me like I'd just smacked her one. 'Whit would I want tae dae that fur?'

I shrug. 'It must've been hard looking efter aw they weans. Ava's no trouble but she can be a handful. I canny imagine whit I'd dae wae ten.'

Una gives me a sharp look. 'Ye just get oan wae it, hen. That's whit ye dae. Just like before yer fridges and medicine and type-writers pit fancy ideas intae lassies' heids. Ye just get oan wae it.'

After work I get the bus to Well Street and go to the doctor's. It's at the top of a narrow flight of stairs. There's a separate waiting room for pregnant women. I try not to look at it, the sight of their swollen bellies. The receptionist is a sort of Cissy person, only fatter and with horn-rimmed glasses. I ask to see the doctor. 'I can give you an appointment next week,' she says.

I almost burst out greetin, but then I remember a word we type a lot in class. Smoothing over my coat I say, 'Urgent. Tell him it's urgent.'

'What's it about?' she says.

I don't know how to explain. I overhead some of the younger ones at the mill talking about it when I was having a fag break in the toilet. 'You take it every day and you don't get pregnant,' said one. 'I widny trust a pill,' said another. 'Honestly, it's true. All you have to do is ask your doctor.'

I stare at the receptionist, open my mouth, but the words don't come out. 'It's nothing,' I say, and run back down the stairs.

Ava is dancing rings round me. While I'm making dinner, I hear *Swan Lake* and go into the bedroom to find her with her fingers in the jewellery box. Quickly, I spank her hand. 'Whit have I told you about touching Mammy's expensive things?'

She cries that she only wanted to see the ballerina dancing.

'Ach, Jean, it's no like you've got the crown jewels in there,' mumbles Tommy from his pillow.

The whole thing puts Ava in a huff. At dinner, she picks pieces of mince off her tongue and gets her hands all greasy. 'You'll stay at the table till you clean yer plate,' I say. 'It's no like I've mince coming oot my ears.'

Tommy just smiles. 'The wean's no daft. This stuff is fae the knacker's yard; there's mair gristle than meat.'

I can't stand another minute. I take Ava to my mother's early and phone the Lighthouse. 'I need tae see you now,' I say. Ten minutes before the class starts, I'm waiting for Billy round the back of the church. When I see him coming I go running to meet him, one hand on my chest and the other clutching my bag, like in the movies. He flicks his cigarette and starts to kiss me. His lips taste of beer. I pull away. 'Whit's the matter?' he says. 'I thought you couldny wait to get yer hands on me.'

'It's Tommy,' I say. 'He wants another baby.'

Billy kicks away a stone.

I shake my head. 'Billy, whit am I gauny dae? I can't have a baby – can I?'

'Ye know whit you have to do, Jean. You've got tae leave him. It's no fair to you, or to me. And it's no fair tae Tommy.'

'Since when did you care aboot Tommy?'

'I don't. Bit the longer you leave it, the harder it's gauny get. Do it now, Jean. At least gie him a chance tae rebuild his life, it's the least you owe him.'

I can't believe what I'm hearing. All this was Billy's idea and now it's as if I'm the bad one. I thought he'd comfort me; at least tell me it's going to be alright. But this – this is worse than I thought. I blink back the tears but it's no use.

'It's now or never, Jean.'

I shake my head. 'It's too soon. I'll hold him off. I'll tell him I've a headache, anything.'

Billy sighs. 'I'm fed up waiting. I won't be around forever, Jean. There's plenty a lassies I cuid go wae.'

My head feels like a black cloud about to burst. 'Who? Aggie Burns?' I spit out the words.

Billy laughs. 'Jist do me a favour, eh? Go intae the payroll on Friday and see how many people work there. That's all you have tae do. I'll take care of the rest.'

'No, Billy, I can't.'

'Do you love me, Jean?'

'You know I'll always love ye.'

'Then whit do you want? Fur things tae be like this forever? I can't do that, Jean. I've tried finding a job. As soon as I mention the jail, that's it, they don't want tae know.' He thumps the wall and little scrapes of blood seep from his knuckles. 'If you don't want me, Jean, I'll find somebody else who will.'

When I reach for his hand he snatches it away. In one bound, he's over the wall. 'Billy,' I call. 'Billy. Billy!'

I'm off sick for three days. That's the good thing about the mills. If you're off sick you still get paid. But any more than three days and I'd need a line off the doctor. I decide to go back on Monday: that way I'll have the weekend too. I tell Tommy I'm getting terrible headaches and lie on the settee with the lamp off and a wet towel over my eyes. When Ava asks what's wrong I say it's the noise of the machines. It's raining most of the time so she's always in the house pestering me to read her a story or colour in pictures. 'Not now, Ava,' I say.

'See,' says Tommy. 'If she had a brother or sister she could play wae them, gie you peace.'

I don't answer. Instead I send Ava to the shops to get stuff for the tea; I couldn't stand running into any lassies from the mills. At least I'm keeping on top of the housework, making sure Tommy has clean vests and shirts, and fresh towels. At night I tell him I'm exhausted with all the effort. 'You jist concentrate on getting better,' he says. 'Wid you like me to take some washing tae yer mither's?'

'No,' I say. 'I'll manage.'

Sometimes when Tommy's at work, I let Ava lie beside me on the settee after school, and I read to her about Mary, Queen of Scots and how she was imprisoned in a big castle in the middle of a lake. 'Why?' says Ava. 'Was she a bad lady?'

'No. She wasn't bad. She was in love. Only the man she married wasn't as nice as she thought he was. He did many cruel things. Then, one day, Mary met a handsome earl who promised to take her away from all that. They ran away together but were captured by her enemies and they put Mary in a big stone castle in the middle of a lake.'

'Was she by herself?'

'No. There were people there to make sure she didn't escape, because they were mean and narrow minded, just like her husband.'

'What's narrow minded?'

'It's when someone thinks that life only happens in a very small place, like their house or the street where they live. They don't realise there's a big world out there with lots of people and places and countries, and even planets. Who wants to stay in one place when you can reach for the moon?' I stretch my arm as if I'm grabbing the moon out the sky.

Ava laughs and copies me. 'Reach for the moon,' she says. After a minute, she goes all quiet. 'Did Mary ever escape?'

I sigh and put my arm around her. 'Well,' I say. 'We'll just have to wait and see, won't we?' I know then that I'll never forget that moment, lying on the settee with Ava next to me, like two crescent moons. I run my fingers through her soft hair and close my eyes. She still has that new smell, not like the sour milkiness of babies, but a fresh smell, strong yet fragile, unspoiled by disappointment, by life. In those short moments I forget everything: the mill, Tommy, my mother, even Billy. There's only Ava and me, and it's perfect, as close to perfect as I'll ever get.

Six o'clock on Monday morning and Mr Green is being nice as ever. He asks after my health and says it's good to see me back. He's so gentlemanly about everything, I can feel myself blush. 'Remember and wear your ear plugs, ladies,' he says. 'We have to look after our girls and we don't want any more sore heads.'

Una hates that he's making a fuss of me. If it was her getting fussed over that would be different. She'd be all smiles and 'yes sir, no sir, Mr Green.' When we're walking over to our machines, I hear her say, 'If I'd took time aff whenever I had a sair heid I'd never have got oot my bed.'

'Mr Green,' shouts Maggie. 'My nail's broke. I'll be off for a week till I convalesce.'

'That's enough,' says The Bitch.

Mr Green goes back to his office like he hasn't heard.

The next day, things aren't any better. At dinner time, they keep cracking jokes about not speaking too loud when I'm near.

If Maggie bursts out laughing or Aggie drops her knife and fork, Una says, 'Sshh now, you'll gie Jean a sair heid.'

Looking at the same faces makes me feel depressed: Maggie with her baggy eyes, Una's stained teeth, Myra Broon and her permanent bruised cheek. Angie tells us wee Aggie finally got Jim Shepherd to take her on a date. The jokes start about winching in the back row of the Regal but I think, what's the big deal? She'll only end up like all the rest, having babies, washing clothes and working in the mills.

'You still going tae the night school, Jean?' says Una out the blue.

'Aye,' I say, my voice squeaky. 'Probably.'

'How's Tommy?' says my mother, the next night, when I drop off Ava. She doesn't ask me how I am or if I've been to the doctor's.

'Fine,' I say, then I add, 'I might be a wee bit late the night. Depends if I go wae the ither lassies fur a tea.'

Miss MacDiarmid gives us text we have to type without looking at the keys. There's a record player on her wooden desk. We have to type along to a special version of the William Tell overture. Miss MacDiarmid taps the beat with a ruler and when she shouts, 'Carriage return!' she says she wants to hear 'all those bells ringing in unison.' I don't know why I can't get the hang of it. My fingers keep slipping off and tripping over each other, and my carriage returns several beats after everyone else's. By the time the class is finished I've been called a 'stupid girl' more times than I can count, and my head really does hurt. I can't wait to see Billy but there's no sign of him across the street. I walk up Mansionhouse Road and peer over the wall of the church. A man goes past, walking his dog. 'Can I help you?' he says.

'No,' I say and hurry past, thinking, 'stupid girl.'

This time I don't go to the canteen for dinner. Instead I go down by the canal and feed the ducks. It's one of those bright autumn days with yellow leaves floating on the surface of the water. I think about when I was here with Billy and he first talked about going away together. Yet here I am, alone again. That's always the way with him. He's like a shooting star that bursts through your life in a haze of light then he's away, leaving you alone in the darkness. Not like Tommy. He's more like a sixty-watt bulb, always there when you need him, ready to light up the way, reliable, dependable. But even light bulbs burn out and have to be replaced. I wonder when Tommy will burn out, when he'll look at me and decide he's had enough.

The family of ducks has grown bigger. They don't follow their mother any more, but swim off to the sides, distracted by ripples, curious, exploring a little further each time before she calls them back. Most of the ducks have families but there's always a few drakes diving round the edges, the ducks who haven't managed to find mates and settle down, or don't want to. Maybe they prefer it that way.

I wonder where Billy is. With the woman with the bleached hair? I'd like to see her. I try and imagine what they talk about: music, *Z Cars*, his time in jail, me. But nothing seems real enough. Billy said she was the wife of a friend. Which one? That's the trouble with Billy. He'll say anything he needs to at the time, whatever gets him out of a pickle. But even though I know what he's like, I still can't help myself. And that makes me worse than him. At least he doesn't pretend. He just is what he is. My life is made up of lies. I think of going round to his house, but I'm not even sure what number it is. He's never taken me there, says his dad drinks and the house is no place for a woman. I even think of calling the pub, asking him to meet me in town and bringing Ava, telling her not to say anything. If we really are going to run away, she should meet him, shouldn't she? But it's too risky. The thought of it makes me feel sick, of taking Ava and just leaving. Billy's right. I have to make my mind up one way or another. I don't blame him for being impatient. The twisting mill stares back at me from the water. The line of ducks swims across it, cutting the reflection in half. I throw them the last of my stale bread, and wish life could be that simple, like the ducks.

On Friday, I ask if I can be excused ten minutes early. 'This isny the number twelve bus,' says The Bitch. 'You canny just ring the bell and get aff whenever you like.' But Mr Green is there. He asks me what it's for and I tell him, 'It's to go by the Counting House and see about the pensions.'

'Oh, yes,' he says. 'Well, seeing it's a matter of importance, I'll allow it.'

The Bitch stamps her feet and thunders off. She's got it in for me now. Soon as I put a foot wrong she'll be waiting to jump on my back, but I don't care. I put my coat on over my overalls and run down the stairs, out the side exit and towards the Counting House. It's the only place in the mills where there's trees. It has two floors with rows of big windows, cleaner than all the other buildings. I go in through the main door. It's heavy and wooden with fancy columns at the side. In the lobby, there's a desk girl who asks what I'm there for, and I tell her it's to see about the pensions. She takes me to a row of chairs along the wall and says someone will be out to see me. I hope it's not Cissy. There's a set of stairs with a carpet and people going up and down with folders full of papers. I wonder where the room is that they make up the pay packets. Eventually someone comes down the corridor and introduces himself as Mr Thomson, the Finance Manager. He has glasses and a thin moustache, like Clark Gable, though he's much older. He takes me into a room, shows me to a chair, and sits opposite me behind a big wooden desk. I tell him I'm from Twisting and I saw the notice and I'm wondering what to do about my pension. I use the word 'options.' He telephones an office girl and asks for a file to be brought through with my name on it: my service record. I wait while he glances over it then he clasps his hands and says that there are factors I need to consider. 'Will there be scaling down?' I say. 'Like in Spinning?'

Mr Thomson says he doesn't know about that. 'Let's look at the situation hypothetically,' he says, though I don't know what that means. For older people, in the case of redundancy, he usually recommends the lump sum option, but for someone my age, unless I'm planning to emigrate or start a business, the monthly payment plan would be fine.

'What if I just leave?' I say.

'Then you only get back what you've paid in. The full pension is only payable in the case of redundancy or retirement.'

'Is there any way I won't get a pension?' I say.

'Of course there are circumstances. Anyone caught stealing from the mill will have their pension revoked without further discussion.' He smiles. 'But a nice girl like you won't have to worry about that.'

'Well, I think I'll just leave my pension as it is.'

'Very well.'

He closes my file, but, before he stands up to show me out, I say, 'Do you get a bigger pension for being an office girl, only I'm learning typing and shorthand and it might sound silly but –'

'Go on.'

'I've always wanted to work in the Counting House. You know, making up the wages. Do you do that in here?'

'Oh, that's upstairs,' he says. 'In the back room. It's a very responsible job and requires training.'

'That's what I'm doing,' I say. 'Training.' I imagine myself in a twin-set and heels, and Mr Thomson calling me into his office to take dictation. Instead of sitting in my overalls, I'd have a notepad and a pen and lovely twelve denier American tan tights. I'd make enough money for me and Billy to run away and live for a while on my pension.

'Well, why don't you work hard and when you get your certificate come back and we'll see what we can do?'

'Thank you, Mr Thomson. Thank you.'

We stop early to clean up the machines. Una's all over me wanting to know what Mr Thomson said. I don't tell her much. I'm enjoying that she has to be nice to me. Plus Una works much faster than I do and ends up doing my machine as well as hers. All I say is that older workers are better off with a lump sum. 'You could use it as capital,' I say.

She frowns. 'Aye, well, I might go and see about it then – Ta, hen.'

Later, before I go home, I go to the phone box at the end of the road. 'It's Mary Stuart for Billy McBride.' I quite enjoy putting on my posh voice. It takes ages for Billy to come to the phone. When he does I don't mention about him not being there on Tuesday. I just say, 'How are you?'

'Better fur hearing you,' he says.

'I did that thing you wanted. Can you meet me after my class next week?'

Silence.

'Please.'

'Don't say any more,' says Billy. 'I'll be there.' He pauses then says, 'Wear something nice, eh?'

'Okay.'

'That's my girl.'

On Saturday I take Ava to Cardosi's for an ice cream. Then we visit baby Peter. I tell Annie I'm preparing a surprise for later that night and ask if she can watch Ava ten minutes while I go up the town. After I get back, I go and see my mother though I don't know why I bother. She sits there and hardly says a word. I show Ava how to pretend type on the kitchen table. I do the William Tell overture and she hums along. She likes it when I make the ting noise and shout 'carriage return.' My mother shifts in her seat, glancing at us now and again, annoyed because she can't join in.

When we go home, Ava shows Tommy how she can type. He laughs and says, 'You're having a good time.' It's his night off. 'I'm away out for a drink, love,' he says. 'I'll no be long. I'll get my tea in the pub.'

'Take as long as you want,' I say.

Ava and me have mashed potatoes that we make into castles. The gravy is a lake. Then I go and get my surprise. It's not much, just a red cloak with a plastic sceptre, and a gold crown with coloured plastic jewels that I got out the fancy dress shop on George Street. But I tell Ava I'm going to do her up like Mary, Queen of Scots. I brush her hair and tie it up in a bun with ringlets coming down the sides. I even give her a bangle from my jewellery box and let her look at the spinning ballerina. Next, I watch while she puts on some of my make-up. She gets it all over herself so I do it for her, making her cheeks all rosy and putting on a bit of pink lipstick, but not too much. Then I do the fanfare for her entering the living room. 'Good evening, your Royal Highness.' I bow down. 'May I say how sophisticated you look.'

'Don't forget elegant,' says Ava, and taps me on the head with her sceptre. 'You may rise.' Then she struts around the room waving to imaginary subjects while I hold up the edges of her cloak like a lady in waiting. Afterwards she wants to go outside and show her make-up to her friends. I stand at the window and give the royal wave, but she disappears across the park like she's forgotten me. I make a cup of tea and smoke a cigarette, staring onto the street, watching twilight fall and the outline of the mill darken through the trees.

When Tommy comes home I'm already in bed, even though it's just gone half past nine. I'd thought of putting Ava in next to me and telling him she had a nightmare, but then I imagined her sticking me in it and saying, 'No I didn't, Mammy.' So instead I just lie there, pretending to be asleep. I hear him bumping around in the hall. 'Jean.' He comes into the room and stumbles across the dressing table. 'Jean, it's no even ten o'clock.'

I don't move. The wardrobe door clatters open as he hangs up his jacket. I feel annoyed he doesn't have the decency to be quiet while I'm asleep. The bed squeaks as he sits down to take off his socks. Tomorrow I'll find them inside-out on the floor. 'Jean, love.' His hand is on my shoulder, shaking me gently at first. 'Jean.' He's not going to let go. 'Oh, Je-an.'

I open my eyes. 'Tommy, you're drunk. Whit time is it?'

'It's no late. You alright?'

'I had a headache. Where've you been?'

'Out for a few pints like I said.'

I sit up on my elbows. 'More than a few, by the looks of it.' Trust Tommy to need Dutch courage before he can lie with his wife.

'You know whit Archie's like. He's been wetting baby Peter's heid for months now. I said, "Archie, you'll need tae give it up. You canny go oan like this till he's twenty-one."'

'Annie'll have his guts. As if she's no got enough on her plate wae her mither tae worry aboot.'

'Ach, Annie's fine. It brings it out in a wumin, having a wean, don't you think? Makes her all curvy and rosy faced.' He slides up and pinches my cheek. 'I hope you don't mind, but I said to Archie, me and Jean are thinking aboot it, having anither one. "Archie," I said. "Don't pit yer whisky away jist yet, if you know whit I mean."'

I picture Annie in her old cardigan and Kirby grips and push his hand away. 'Whit are you going and telling people that fur, Tommy? Noo they'll aw be expecting the news.'

'I wis hoping it wis you who wis going tae be expecting.' He puts his hand under the covers and over my belly. 'Whit's wrong wae that? I wis only telling the truth. Why no give them something to look forward tae? Hmm?' He makes a mushy sound and nuzzles his face into my neck.

'I suppose ye telt my mither tae? Next thing it'll be all over the mills. How no just put an ad in the paper, Tommy? Dae ye realise whit ye've done?'

I push his hand away, sit up and turn on the lamp.

Tommy blinks. 'I never told yer mither. Honest. Jist Archie, that's aw. And maybe a few a the boys in the Lighthoose.'

'What?' My throat closes, like a hand is pressing against it. I swallow hard and say, 'You were in the Lighthoose?'

'Aye. Whit of it?'

My skin goes cold. I get up and put on my dressing gown and take my cigarettes from the bedside table. I light one up. 'I don't like that place, Tommy. It's full of the wrong sort. I don't want you going in there. It's a bad example tae Ava.'

'Whit dae you know aboot who goes in the Lighthoose?'

'Nothing. Wee Aggie told me. They aw talk aboot it in the mills. Some guy wis leering at her fae the door as she walked by the other day. Gave her a right fright.'

I walk to the window and open the curtains. There's nothing there, only my reflection, one hand holding the cigarette, the other cupping my elbow. Tommy comes up behind me. The drink has made him bolder. He kisses my shoulder. 'Come on, Jean, you don't really care about that do ye?' He tries to take the cigarette from my fingers.

'Leave it,' I say.

'Ye can finish it later. Kiss me, Jean. I'm your husband.'

'I'm no kissing ye, Tommy. Ye're reeking a drink.' I shut the curtains. 'Who else were you drinking wae in the Lighthoose besides Archie?'

'A few lads fae the work. Does it matter?'

'It matters tae me.'

'Anyway, I left them in the pub. I wanted tae come home and see my wife.' He squeezes my breast. My muscles contract. I want to reach out, slap him away. I turn from the window. 'Not now, Tommy, I've a headache.'

'A headache, Jean?' He clenches his fists and kicks the wardrobe door. It doesn't suit him. 'You've always got a bloody headache.'

As I brush past, he grabs my wrist, turns me towards him. 'Do you love me, Jean?'

I don't answer.

He tightens his grip. 'Answer me.'

I laugh. 'Course I do. You're my husband, aren't you?'

Neither of us moves. Ash drops from my cigarette onto the carpet.

'I need the ashtray,' I say.

He lets go. I walk round the other side of the bed and stub out my cigarette. 'Are you getting in then?'

A wee knot forms in the middle of his forehead. He lifts the lid of the ottoman, takes a blanket and leaves the room. A few minutes later, I hear the radio's muffled drone.

2013

Vancouver, British Columbia

Ava sits on a large red sofa, opposite Phil and Penny, presenters of *Good Morning, British Columbia*, favourite daytime show of students and stay-at-home voters. Phil is a tall black man with immaculate hair, grey at the temples, and Penny a sun-tanned blonde twenty years his junior. Phil reads from an autocue, introducing 'today's controversial guest whose corporation, Borealis, is at the centre of a storm of protests.' Then he fixes her with a patronising stare. 'Mrs Newport. Ava. Is Borealis engaged in illegal logging?'

She keeps smiling. Guilty people don't smile, apparently; at least, that's what Sue Brash said when she briefed her on the way to the studio: 'Avoid having to give an opinion on anything political – stick to children, gardens, domestic bliss.' Sue even handed her a recipe for home-baked lemon cheesecake. 'Tell them it's been in the family for generations; even the dog likes it.'

'We don't have a dog.'

'Make one up.'

Ava carefully inserts the interviewer's name in all her answers: 'Well, Phil, I'm not at liberty to discuss legal matters.' She listens to herself waffle on about how the company is investigating the situation; viewers can be assured that every detail will be given the utmost consideration. 'As head of Human Resources, Phil, my main interest has always been jobs. We're a family company and I care about the families of British Columbia.' Big smile.

Cue Penny. The conversation moves predictably onto domestic issues: the perfect opportunity to introduce the Bruce meets Ava story. Viewers love a romance, don't they? The presenters exchange sympathetic looks as she describes the moment of Scott's disappearance on the beach: 'It's every mother's dread.' Relief when she moves onto the happy ending, and then big laughs all round as she finishes by poking fun at Bruce in a wifely way: 'He always wanted to be a knight in shining armour.'

Penny's expression becomes serious. 'We understand you came to Canada after tragic beginnings.' Ava grits her teeth. The only person privy to her so-called tragic start in life is Bruce. He must have given Sue the details, her childhood the subject of some boardroom brief. 'Well, when I was very young... my mother... she died in a house fire. And my father passed on a few years later. I was brought up by my aunt, who succumbed to cancer recently.' Jesus, why couldn't they stick to handbags and make-up tips?

'She was all the family you had.' Penny hands Ava a tissue, even though she's not crying. 'So meeting Bruce must have been like a fairytale.'

Right now, Ava wants to kill Bruce, but smiles and says, 'Yes, you could say that.'

Next come the photographs, her private moments flashed into homes all across the province: her wedding picture, the photo from Bruce's office of them all backpacking. Penny asks her what makes the perfect family, and Ava spouts banal advice from women's magazines about how it's important to spend time together, careful to add that each of them has an unwavering commitment to British Columbia's natural heritage and enjoys nothing more than family trips to the mountains. When was the last time they did that? Thankfully, no one asks and she's spared having to invent stories of adventure holidays and white-water rafting.

Phil leans forward. 'So what do you think of your son's involvement in the recent protests?'

She stays cool. 'We've always encouraged Scott to express himself. Like all families, we have our disagreements, but there's nothing we wouldn't do to support each other.'

'I don't know if you're aware,' says Phil, eyes glinting, 'but your son, Scott, got in touch with us before you came on the programme. Here's what he had to say.' Her breath pounds in her ears, her hands are sweaty, *clammy* as Cissy would say. The presenters turn to look at the screen behind them: tree trunks filmed from below, light filtering down through a high canopy. A man is lying on his back gazing up through the trees. Scott. There's a bedraggled air about him, his shirt collar sticking up. He sits and looks directly into her eyes. 'Hi, Mom.'

Ava holds her breath and smiles, aware that her reactions are being transmitted to thousands of strangers, customers, voters. Her grin feels stupid, plastered on. She has the feeling she's about to be sacrificed.

'I suppose you're wondering where I am,' says Scott. 'Well, these trees above me are Douglas Firs, over five hundred years old. There's a lot of wood here, as you can see. Big demand for old growth, especially in the Asian market.' He pauses. 'Since Europeans first arrived, we've lost 80% of our old growth forests, and they continue to be decimated at an unprecedented rate. That's why we're moving our protest to Temple Grove. We need to blockade the logging routes directly. If Daddy wants access, he'll have to get past us first. Sorry to spoil the whole happy families thing, but I feel real strong about this; guess I've found my vocation.'

The screen dies and the presenters turn to Ava. They don't speak, just stare with pasted-on concern. She grins inanely, so much that it hurts. 'All families have differences. It's how we deal with those differences, how we resolve –'

'Did you know your son had such strong feelings?'

'We tend not to discuss work at home.' Her heart feels like it's trying to pound its way out of her body. She glances at Penny; her down-turned lashes make her look at least partially sympathetic. Ava coughs and swallows the lump in her throat. Home-baked lemon cheesecake won't save her.

The drive from the studio goes by in a haze, her stomach tied in an anxious knot. As a child, when she was upset, Cissy used to make her pancakes with maple syrup. The secret was to separate the yolks from the whites, beating the whites into stiff peaks and adding them to the batter just before cooking. Ava could never get the hang of it. She always mixed the ingredients so that her batter was lumpy or rubbery and her pancakes had to be peeled like stuck wallpaper from the pan. She tried all the tips: a drop of oil, even a dash of cream soda, but nothing worked. When she served them, Scott would stick out his tongue and pretend to barf. 'Yuk.'

Ava asks the driver to stop the car, and gets out. She's sweating, her clothes sticking to her. Unbuttoning her jacket, she lets the cool air waft through to her skin. It keeps her alert. The worst thing she can do is let people think it's got on top of her. The aroma of coffee drifts from cafes and bistros. She contemplates finding one that sells pancakes, but already she feels eyes lifting towards her, office workers on stools turning their heads, glancing from behind bagels and paninis.

Perhaps if she'd been more disciplined with Scott when he was young. Cissy taught her to fold laundry (always at the seam), and stack dishes (cups bottom up), but when Scott left home, he'd no idea how to do the most basic things. She'd arrange for his laundry to be picked up and delivered. If the flat got too messy, she hired a cleaner. He needed to learn responsibility (another of Cissy's favourite words). But it was easier said than done. She remembers when Cissy bought him a BMX for his fourteenth birthday; a few days later he left it in the park, nose out of joint because another boy beat him in a race. Ava lied for months, eventually making up a story about the bike being stolen, so she didn't have to deal with the guilt, the hurt look on Cissy's face.

It's not easy getting it right, knowing which decisions are inconsequential and which will affect the rest of your life. Ava should have waited till she had proof before she accused Scott of sending those letters. Now he's punishing her, humiliating her in public.

She reaches the Borealis building and looks up, the glass and steel structure stretching impossibly high. She pushes back a mounting feeling of dread. Some of the elevator's occupants ignore her, others make commiserating faces: the ones who've watched the show. She smiles politely. The only person she has to explain herself to is Bruce. He relied on her to sort things with Scott, at least stop him stirring the waters, and she couldn't even do that right.

His secretary glances up from her desk, a neat-looking woman in her mid-thirties. Ava doesn't wait for an exchange of pleasantries. She pushes open the heavy door to Bruce's office. It's empty, save for his jacket over the back of his chair. A set of sliding wooden panels leads through to his private quarters: two rooms panelled in the same dark wood as the boardroom, complete with a walk-in wardrobe, ensuite, and leather sofa; everything he needs to freshen up after a long night at the office.

His feet, in the navy socks he prefers, poke over the arm rest. 'Honey, are you awake?' Silence. 'Listen, I'm sorry about the show. Scott... he's not been himself lately.'

There's a muffled noise, and Bruce's face appears over the back of the couch, red and blank-looking, his hair slightly dishevelled. 'What time is it –?'

'Are you alright?'

'I was dreaming. Can you give me a minute?'

This time the noise is more of a squeal, followed by a thud onto the floor. Ava walks across the room and Bruce holds his hand out to stop her. Too late. It only takes a moment to piece together the jigsaw: the woman lying on the rug by the sofa, clutching at her open blouse; Bruce with a hand over his naked groin. Ava opens her mouth but nothing comes out.

'Bruce and I –' says the woman. 'We –'

'Melanie was just going, weren't you, Melanie?' says Bruce.

Melanie. Sue's assistant, short hems and long legs. All of nineteen. She flashes her eyes at Bruce. 'But, baby, you said –'

Baby. Honey. Pet names. Marks of possession. Ava turns and calmly slides the door shut behind her. Her body feels like one of those shells on the beach, hollow yet full of the noise of distant waves falling and rising. She walks up to the glass and looks out at the steel and concrete buildings opposite, thousands of invisible people going from floor to floor, office to office; others on the streets below, hurrying to meetings, all oblivious to her thoughts. She thinks of Mary, Queen of Scots baring her breasts to the jeering crowds, a woman pushed to the edge, her heart exposed like an open wound for the world to see, to do with it what they would.

Spreading out her arms, she feels the coolness of the glass on her palms. In one breath she releases from her lungs all the trapped noise, wave after wave, until her ears ring and her throat stings. This high up, there's no one to see, or hear. No one that matters. As soon as the scream leaves her mouth, her body empties, lightens. The doors behind her open and Bruce rushes out, barely giving her a glance, Melanie behind him, pinning up her hair as she runs. The corporate towers and distant mountains stare impassively back, like nothing out of the ordinary has occurred.

1962
Paisley

When I get off the bus Billy is already there, waiting at the corner. His hair is slicked back, neater than usual, and he's grinning. I didn't know what to wear so I put on my best stockings, polished my brown boots and chose the pink blouse with the black collar that I usually wear for nights out – not that there's many of them. I had my cardigan over it so my mammy wouldn't notice, then took it off on the bus, shoving it into my bag, like I was sneaking off to the Flamingo all over again.

I quicken my steps into a wee half run. Billy says, 'Follow me,' out the side of his mouth, and walks ahead. Halfway up Mansionhouse Road there's a black Morris Minor. He stops beside the passenger door and makes a show of opening it, sweeping his hand like a magician: 'Yer carriage awaits.'

I shake my head then get in. He slams the door, spoiling the effect, then jumps in the driver's side and leans over to kiss my lips. 'Whit dae you think?'

'I think I want another kiss.'

'I mean the car, daftie.'

'You're crazy.'

'I'll tell you whit's crazy. Snatching a winch wae yer bird roon the back a the church. We're no teenagers anymair, Jean. Tonight, I'm taking you tae Glesga.'

'Whit aboot my class?'

'Ach, they'll no miss ye for one night. This is mair important.

Whit dae you say?'

'Aye, alright, you're on.' I fasten my seatbelt. 'So I'm yer bird, am I?'

He starts the engine. 'That's right, Jean, you're my girl.'

I pause. 'Billy, where did you get this motor?'

He laughs. 'Don't worry, doll. It's no a stoler if that's whit you're thinking. A mate of mine lent it tae me.'

'Whit mate?'

'He's no fae around here. I'll introduce you tae him some day.' He spins the wheel and then we're driving up Whitehaugh and along the back way onto Arkleston Road. I like watching Billy's knuckles as he changes gear, the way the muscles in his neck move as he turns to look over his shoulder at junctions. While he drives he taps the wheel and hums, *'It's Alright Now, Mama.'*

'The Beatles are good,' he says. 'But they'll never beat Elvis.' I feel the urge to kiss him but I don't. Soon we're driving past fields and along streets I don't recognise. In the distance I can see the big ships so we must be near the River Clyde. He pulls into a street with red sandstone tenements and stops outside a close. 'This is it,' he says.

I feel a bit disappointed. I thought he might be taking me to a café, a place no one knows us, where we could sit and talk and eat ice cream and drink tea, like a proper couple. He opens the door and this time there's no magician's wave. He's looking around him as if he's watching for something. It's a bit like Newton Street only greyer, with no park or trees. There are a few children hanging around one of the closes. Their faces are sullen. The whole street feels sort of oppressive, as if the buildings are closing in, their windows like eyes, inspecting the comings and goings, taking note of any new faces. A curtain twitches and is still. 'Who lives here, Billy?' I say.

'Same guy who loaned me the motor. Gave me his keys, see?' He jangles them in front of me and walks into the close. 'Don't jist stand there.'

The air inside is heavy. I feel like I have to wade through it as I climb the stairs. From the dusty windows I see women leaning out their kitchenettes, smoking and shouting to each other across the back courts. They catch sight of me and Billy going up the stairs, and the chatter stops. I know they're watching and I keep my head down. At a bend in the stairs a man comes down from the floor above. He stops and presses against the wall to let us past, nodding at Billy. 'Who wis that?' I say.

'Nobody, jist a neighbour.'

The flat is on the top floor. Billy turns the key and pushes open the door. There are pictures all along the wall: four different Chinese ladies peeking out from behind fans. The carpet is thick and brown and my feet don't make a sound. In the front room there's a fan on the ceiling. Billy switches it on and grins as the black and gold blades rotate. Against the near wall, there's a big sideboard of dark wood with crystal glasses on it and a decanter full of whisky. The settee is black and leather, and the seats at either end have wooden ashtray holders on metal stands. On the sideboard are photographs. One of them shows a woman with bleached blonde hair and sunglasses. I wonder if it's the woman Aggie saw in the pub.

Billy gestures for me to sit down. He pours whisky from the decanter into two crystal glasses. 'Cheers.'

I take my glass. 'Are you sure it's alright?' I say. 'Us being here?' There's a soft white rug under my feet and I feel like I should take off my shoes.

'Course it is.' He sits beside me with one foot crossed over his knee. 'Whit dae you think?'

'Lovely,' I say.

'Jist think, this could be us one day, Jean. You and me.'

'And Ava.'

'Aye.'

He talks for a while about the settee being real leather and how the carpet is the best money can buy. Then he puts his arm around me and, stroking my shoulder, says, 'So you had a look around the payroll office then?'

I shrug and take a sip of the whisky, but don't say anything.

'Look, I don't mean tae put pressure on you. Maybe you're

right, it's a stupid idea but you know me, Jean, once I've got a hold a something, I can't let go. That's why you're stuck wae me. I can't let go of you.'

I tell him all I know. Maybe once he realises, he'll get it out of his head once and for all. I tell him about Mr Thomson and the desk girl, the stairs and corridors and the back rooms on the upper floor. Billy nods and pours himself another whisky. I've never seen him this way, so alert, attentive. He starts grinding his jaw. 'Whit time wis this?' he says.

'I don't know, just after twelve or something. How?'

'Because after that it'll be too late. All the money will be split up. Whit time does yer shift start, Jean?'

'Six.'

He pours me another drink even though I've not finished my first. 'Here's whit I need you tae do. Watch the Counting House, Jean. Find out who goes to the bank and when.'

'Billy.' I sniff. I'm crying. I can't help it. 'I don't want to, Billy, don't make me do this. I'll do anything you ask, I'll tell Tommy. We'll run away thegither. I'll get a job. I promise. But no this, Billy. I just can't.'

He takes the glass out my hand and puts it on the table next to his. 'I'm sorry, Jean. Don't cry. I'll shut up. It's crazy, all of this. Don't listen tae me. We'll wait. Don't tell Tommy yet. I'll say when. You're right, we need mair time.' He kisses my face, my lips, wiping my tears, telling me how sorry he is. There's an intensity about him, careful and deliberate, like I'm a precious object, all shiny and delicate. He takes off his jacket, keeping his eyes on me the whole time. 'It's you I can't let go of,' he whispers. 'You're my girl.' I feel myself folding under him, his warm body pressing down on me, his fingers under my blouse, against my bare flesh. I slide my hands under his shirt and up over his back. 'Not here,' he says. 'There's a spare room.'

This time he lifts me up in his arms. I feel like a bride. He carries me onto a large double bed with a white counterpane. 'Won't they mind, your friends?'

'Nah,' says Billy, taking off his shoes. 'They said tae treat the place like it wis oors.'

'I wish it was,' I say.

'Soon, Jean, soon.' He shuts the curtains.

Billy drops me off at a bus stop on Glasgow Road and I watch the Morris Minor till it disappears. I feel like I'm glowing inside, like I'm the candle and Billy's the match; two flames shining for each other in the darkness. Because what good is a candle without a match, or vice versa? We need each other, Billy and me, it's destiny.

I get off the bus and walk down Lady Lane. It's exactly quarter past nine. I'm on time, even early, for picking up Ava. When I turn into Argyle Street I see Annie standing outside the close, Peter balanced on her hip. Isa is there and a few other of the neighbours. As soon as they see me coming, they stop talking and watch me walk up the street. It feels like my legs are going funny. My cheeks start to redden. I can't make out their expressions. When I get closer, I see they're tense, concerned, like they're all waiting to let out breath. 'Ava? Is Ava alright?' I say.

Annie rushes towards me, puts her hand on my arm. 'She's fine. She's playing inside.' I've barely let out a sigh of relief when she says, 'Jean, it's your mother.'

'She's had a stroke,' says Isa, dying to put in her tuppence worth.

'A stroke?'

'Well, that's whit they think,' says Annie. 'We don't know yet for sure.'

'It wis the exact same wae my mither,' says Isa. 'And I'm telling you, I know a stroke when I see one.'

'When did it happen?' I say.

'1955,' says Isa. 'She wis barely a day over sixty-three.'

'She means Senga, you daft bat,' says Annie. 'It wis a while back. We tried phoning the Grammar but they couldny get hold of you. Don't worry, we got Tommy to come down fae his work. He's up there wae her now, in the Infirmary.'

'Whit dae you mean, they couldny get hold of me? There must be a mistake. Where else wid I be?'

'Don't worry aboot that.' Annie gives me a soft look, not suspicious or accusing, just concerned, like all there is is now, this moment. Before I can stop myself, I'm hugging her so hard I nearly squash wee Peter.

She hugs me back. 'Off you go, away up and see her. And give her my love. Ava will be fine wae me till you get back.'

I run all the way along George Street and get the bus on Causeyside to take me up Neilston Road. I should be thinking about my mother but all that's going through my head is when did they phone the school, and what am I going to say to Tommy when he asks why I wasn't there and why he had to come all the way from his work. By the time I reach the Infirmary, I feel like I'm going to be sick. My palms are covered in a cold sweat. My mind is all over the place and I can barely read the signs for the wards. I stop a nurse in a starched white cap. She tells me to take the lift to the fourth floor and ask the sister. The folding iron doors of the lift close me in like a cage. I feel like shaking it with all my strength. I get out and there are patients everywhere, being wheeled along the corridor in chairs, or on stretchers. I think of all the lives that have been put on hold by burst appendixes, broken legs, heart attacks. Only my mother could do something like this, only my mother could arrange her stroke to turn my life inside out at the worst possible moment.

The sister is a bony woman in a navy blue uniform. She takes me into a poky room with six other patients. There's a beige curtain drawn round my mother's bed. The sister pulls it back and there's Tommy sitting beside her on a chair. The sister puts another chair on the opposite side. 'I'll leave you to it,' she says, and closes the curtains.

Tommy turns long enough to glance at me but doesn't say anything. I sit down and look at my mother, lying with her eyes closed. Her skin is grey and there's a rattle in her throat. Her face looks sunken on one side, like her mouth has been pulled down over her jaw. I wonder if I should take her hand, but I don't. 'How is she?' I say.

'She's how she looks,' says Tommy.

'Whit's that supposed to mean?' I shake my head. 'Sorry, I don't know why I said that.'

'Doctor says there's no much movement on one side.'

'Will she get better?'

He shrugs. 'She might, but it'll take time. She'll no be like she used tae be.'

I'm about to say, but who'll watch Ava on a Tuesday, but I stop myself just in time. 'How long?'

Tommy's eyes flash. 'How should I know, Jean? I'm no a bloody doctor.'

'Sorry,' I say.

He nods.

'Whit happened? Is Ava alright? Did she find her?'

'She saw yer mither oan the kitchen floor and ran down tae get Annie.'

I take off my coat and hang it over the back of my chair. When I turn round Tommy is staring at me in a funny way, a look of disgust almost, as though I'd just swore or laughed out loud. It makes me feel self-conscious and I go to tuck in my blouse, a nervous reaction. That's when I realise I'm not wearing my cardigan. It's not in my bag either. My mother is in hospital and my cardigan is lying on the carpet in the bedroom of some stranger's house. Ten out of ten, Jean. I feel like I'm going to retch. 'My other blouse has a rip in it,' I say.

The look in Tommy's eyes turns from disgust to hatred. Where did it come from, that look? When did he learn to hate me so much? 'Imagine our Ava acting like a grown up,' I say. 'When did she get so clever?'

'What else could she do, Jean?' he snaps.

I wonder when he'll get round to mentioning it: that he was called out from his work. In the end I can't stand the suspense and decide the best thing to do is bring it up, get it over with. 'Will they dock your pay?'

'Trust you tae think aboot money at a time like this.'

'That's no whit I mean. I'd have got here quicker if I could. I don't know how Annie couldny get through. They must've checked the wrong list or got the names mixed up. Maybe she cried me Jean Owen, instead of McParland. She does that sometimes. We've known each other so long.' I can hear myself prattling, but once I've started I can't stop.

'Give it a bloody rest, eh?' says Tommy. He speaks through gritted teeth. 'Can you no think aboot someone else besides your bloody self fur a change?'

'I'm sorry, Tommy.'

'Right, I'm away. I've a shift tae finish.' He does what I couldn't do and takes my mother's hand in his. Her fist is all curled up like a claw. 'Don't worry, Senga, they'll take good care of you here. Get some rest and I'll be back the morra.' Then he's gone. No kiss, no goodbye. I look at my mother lying stretched out on the bed. Her nostrils make a snorting sound and, God forgive me, the first thing that comes into my head is, 'Aye, mammy, I bet you're enjoying this.'

All week at the mills it's: 'Tell your mither I wis asking fur her' and 'Give her my best.' The management sent her a bouquet of flowers, even though she's not worked there for years. 'Isn't that nice?' said Una. 'Course, your mither got her long service certificate. Nice tae see it stands fur something.' When my mammy gets out the hospital a week later, I take the day off and drop Ava at Annie's house. They bump my mother up the stairs in a chair, just like a baby in a pram. I tell them to put her in the living room by the fire. 'I've got it all nice and warm for you, Mammy,' I say. 'Winter's coming on so you'll want tae be nice and cosy.'

Her breathing is sharp and quick, like she's trying to say something but the words won't come out. I put a blanket over her. 'Don't exert yerself, Mammy. You know whit the doctor said. You've tae take it easy. Now you sit there and I'll make us a nice cup of tea.'

I fill a pot and bring it through and set it on the table. 'Do you want to watch a bit of telly?' I say. She shakes her head. I realise I'm shouting even though there's nothing wrong with her hearing. Her tea is in one of those plastic baby cups, the same one I used to use for Ava. I dribble some on the back of my hand to test the temperature. Mammy sees it and her eyes go all wide and bulging, like I'm coming towards her with a knife. 'Come on now,' I say. 'You want a drink of tea, don't ye?'

Her good arm shoots out from beneath the blanket and she grabs the cup and fits it into the corner of her mouth. Tea drools down the slack side of her face. I don't know if she can feel it so I get a tissue from my apron to soak it up. But she twists her head away. 'Mammy!' I say. The cup drops and the lid bounces off, tea fanning out over the wooden floor. Mammy sits there, watching me defiantly. I start mopping it up with the tissue when the door opens. 'It's only me: Isa.'

She's wearing an overall, and a scarf over her rollers. I can never understand how women like Isa and my mammy still dress like they're in the mills long after they've retired. Isa puts her hands on her hips, surveying Mammy in her chair, tea dripping from her chin down her front, and me on my knees trying to mop up the spillage with a wee handkerchief. 'Right, Senga,' she says. 'Let's get you tae rights.'

Mammy's eyes light up. She lets Isa wipe her face. 'She's best drinking out of this,' I say. Mammy gives Isa a strained look.

'It's a wunner they didny go the whole hog and jist gie you a bottle,' says Isa. 'Mind you, my Jimmy cuid dae wae one a those. Seventy-two year old and he still manages tae get haulf his dinner doon his claithes. It's a miracle he can find his mooth.'

Mammy pulls one side of her face into a grimace. Her lips remind me of a twisted piece of string but I can tell from her eyes that it's a smile. Isa fetches a cloth from the kitchen and cleans up the spillage. I sit down. She doesn't ask for my help and I don't offer. When the door opens again, it's another one of the neighbours from down the street. Then Una. Her voice soars above all the others: 'Yoo hoo!' She opens her bag and there's a bottle of sherry. 'This'll have you jiggin in no time.' She looks around at the others and puts her finger to her lips, 'Jist don't tell the doctor.'

No one asks what I think. It's like I'm a wee part of the universe cut off from all the rest, like that bit of the moon no one ever sees. I cough. 'Do you think that's a good idea?' I say. 'Whit if it makes her ill?'

They all stop and turn their heads. Isa laughs. A look passes from Mammy to Una, as if to say, 'See what I have to put up with?'

'Here,' says Una. 'There's nothing they doctors prescribe that'll put you tae rights hauf as well as a drop of the auld medicinal. Isn't that right, Senga? Those doctors don't know their elbow fae a hole in their troosers. Away and get us some glasses, Jean.'

I come back with a tray and Una pours my mother's sherry into the plastic cup. 'It's no the ship that matters,' she says. 'It's the cargo. Here's tae you, Senga. God bless.'

The women raise their glasses. This time my mother doesn't shake her head. There's no defiant look. She even lets Isa tilt her face so the dribbles go down the right way. 'Doon the hatch.'

After a while, the working side of Mammy's face begins to look almost like herself again. The women talk about the old days: 'Mind that mill trip tae Portobello and Isa nearly missed the bus trying tae see up that piper's kilt?'

'I did not.'

'If he stops playing, we said, we'll know he's taken her for a winch.'

Mammy doesn't try to speak, just listens. When she nods, her head goes side to side instead of up and down; and sometimes the muscles on her face stretch, and I'm not sure if she's trying to laugh or if she's in pain. Occasionally her eyes linger on me but she always looks away. The way they're all sitting round laughing and talking you'd think nothing had changed: that Mammy wasn't half a mammy with half a body, and that half of those women's lives hadn't long since slipped away.

Someone else comes in. This time it's Annie. 'Hello, hen, don't mind us,' says Una. 'We're just having a wee natter. We'll no keep her up long, I promise. Just you say now, Senga, when you're ready for a wee rest and we'll be away.' Anyone would think Annie was her daughter and not me. But it's not Annie's fault. She sits down beside me. 'Ava's out the back. I just came tae see if you needed a hand.'

I nod towards the kitchen. 'Come oan and I'll make us tea.' The pot's still warm. We sit at Mammy's table and I pour us both a cup.

'How you coping?' says Annie.

I sigh. 'She hates me. I wis only trying tae help her but – it was like she wished I wisny there.'

Annie reaches across to pat my hand. 'It's no you, Jean. Your mammy, well, she's used tae daein things herself. It's gauny take a bit a getting used tae, that's all.'

'I suppose so.'

'And ye've Tommy tae help. And I'm always here; you know that, don't ye?'

'Ta,' I say. We sit for a minute in silence. I look at Annie's round, trusting face and think I don't deserve it, this kindness. Maybe it's better that people treat me like my mammy does, maybe she's been right all along. I'm selfish and that's all there is to it. Soon I'm sniffing back the tears.

'Ach,' says Annie. 'Don't worry, she'll pull through. Look at my mammy, hardly knows where she is but we manage, don't we?'

But it's not my mother I'm crying for, not really. This isn't what I had planned; this is not how I wanted my life to be. I go to the sink, splash cold water on my face. 'You're right,' I say. 'It'll be fine.' I take the hanky out my pocket to blow my nose, realise it's covered in tea, but use it anyway. 'I think Tommy's annoyed at me,' I say. 'For not being there when it happened.'

'You know whit men are like,' says Annie. 'They don't know whit tae dae in that kind a situation. He'll come round. He probably jist panicked.'

I take off my earrings, white plastic hoops, and rub my earlobes with my thumb, as if eradicating invisible dirty marks. 'I don't know whit happened,' I say. 'There are lots of different classes at the Grammar. Did you give my right name when ye phoned?'

'Me?' says Annie. 'It wisny me who phoned.'

I stop playing with my earrings and look at Annie. 'Not you? Who wis it then?'

'It wis Tommy,' says Annie. 'I couldny remember where you were taking the classes. Heid like a string bag, me. In one ear and oot the ither. And your mither wis in no fit state tae talk. So we called Tommy. He said tae leave it tae him and then – Jean, are ye alright?'

A cold tremor runs through my body. It starts at my head and finishes in my toes. My mouth is dry and my lips feel colourless. I remember Tommy's look in the hospital. Why didn't he say anything? Why did he just let me go on talking? All that stuff about Annie getting my name wrong. 'I don't know,' I say. 'I'm no feeling very well.'

'It's been a hard day. Why don't you go on home, take Ava, and I'll finish up here? Me and Isa can put your mither tae bed.'

'Aye,' I say. 'Tommy jist forgot tae tell me. That's it. It's no important.' I put my earrings back in. The heat returns to my body in quick pulsing waves.

Annie narrows her eyes. 'You're awright aren't ye? You and Tommy?'

I nod. 'Aye, everything's fine.' I say it too quickly. Annie looks at me wide-eyed, waiting for me to say something else. My fingers are twitching by my sides. I wonder what would happen if I told her everything, about Billy, the classes, the Morris Minor, the flat in Glasgow. For a brief second my mouth opens. Then I look at Annie sitting there with her soft eyes and her kind, tired heart, and I can't do it. She's got enough to cope with, between her mother, Archie and the weans. Suddenly it all seems so ridiculous that I'm overcome with a kind of weariness so strong I feel like I could collapse. In that moment, I truly love Annie, as much as I ever will or ever can. I put all that love into my smile and say, 'Don't worry, Annie. I'm that grateful fur all you're doing, really I am. You're like a Godsend, I don't know where I'd be without you. And don't mind me, I'll be awright the morra, honest. A good night's sleep does wonders.' I get my coat from the chair, and my bag, and go out into the hall. In the front room, Una's on the final verse of *There Was a Mill Girl.*

'*And fine as these green foreign hills may be, they are not the hills of home.*'

I think about going in to kiss my mother goodbye, but change my mind and head out the door.

2013
Vancouver Island, British Columbia

The road narrows over inland passes and widens again as it falls towards the coast. Ava's driven this way so many times, the Strait of Georgia glittering in the sunlight, the horizon hugged by the distant Olympic mountains; yet today they seem dark and foreboding, the summits concealed in cloud.

When Bruce first brought her here she'd thought it breathtaking, the light tinted with hope. Most Scottish immigrants ended up in the east; it had a grittiness about it. Uncle Alex used to say it reminded them of home. Her phone flashes a call from Wanda. The third in as many days. She lets it ring out.

She's not sure where home is anymore. All her life, she's had a sense of waiting for something. It started in Paisley, at Cissy's house after the 'fire.' One day, she'd come downstairs to find her aunt carrying bags of clothes from the car to the midden: miniskirts, tights, plain turtle neck sweaters, a pair of brown boots. 'Are those my mammy's?'

'A pigsty,' Cissy had said. 'That's what this is, a pigsty.'

That afternoon, when the sky was darkening, Ava had waited in the car with Alex while Cissy went to the shops, and she saw a shiny flash of white in the crowd. A woman in a PVC coat, just like her mother's, went into a café and sat by the window, drinking tea. How Ava had wanted to go to her, as if the thing she'd been waiting for had finally arrived. The woman lit a cigarette but didn't smoke the same way as her mammy. Her puffs were too long and slow, like she had all the time in the world. Even then, Ava had twisted her neck as the car moved off, just to make sure.

It was that same feeling that drew her out of Cissy's the following day. Not to her old home in Newton Street; she was afraid to see it all blackened and burnt, Raggedy Jane lying in a pile of ash. Instead, while Cissy was at work, and Alex snoring in his chair, she ran to the gatehouse of the spinning mill with its forbidding windows and towers. There was a lot of noise, men shouting from depots, and big chimneys belching out smoke. Vans splashed muddy water up from the puddles. She felt small, invisible against the railings. Then, out came the mill women from all the different buildings, threading into a single strand. She'd picked out a big lady with ankle boots and a heavy wool coat, and tugged at her sleeve. 'Scuse me.'

The woman leaned forward and smiled. 'What's your name, hen?'

'Ava. Ava McParland. I want my mammy.'

There was a whisper of urgent voices.

'She's no here,' said a woman with small dark teeth.

'Away back to Cissy, hen. She'll look after you.'

Ava had started to cry. The big one moved to touch her, but didn't. Instead, she reached into her apron and pulled out a sticky penny caramel. 'Here, huv a wee sweetie.'

Ava turned and ran.

A snowy peak emerges briefly, then returns to shadow. Off the Alberni Highway, the landscape has an undernourished look, as though the early settlers had thought better of the place and moved on, leaving scrappy telegraph poles, abandoned storage lots and unused railroads.

The land rises and turns to forest, green hills with serrated patches where the slopes have been shorn of trees, the earth below red and slack, the way tired muscle sags on the bone. A trail of logging trucks sits idly at the foot of one of the narrow passes. Further along, a small encampment has sprung up, people perched under makeshift tents like something from the gold rush. A few have attached banners to the surrounding trees: *Save Our Ancient Forests.*

Ava drives on to where Cameron Lake spoons out between the hills, and pulls in at the entrance to Temple Grove. She gets out and follows the trail through the interior. The air is cool and moist, the earth powdery and red beneath her feet. Giant cedars enclose her in a womb-like space, light filtering in soft green spirals through their protective branches. And there's a presence, like a heartbeat she can't hear, but is there all the same.

Sitting in the curve of a mossy trunk, she takes out her sketch-pad, the one that's been lying for years at the bottom of a drawer next to an old charcoal pencil, and holds the nib above the page. The blank sheet is intimidating. It would be easier to shove the pad back in her bag and never find out if she can still do it, give life and permanence to a moment that would otherwise disappear. Opposite her a forest giant has been blown down by a storm, its massive roots ripped out of the earth. Breathing deeply, she makes her first tentative mark, sketching its proportions, building up areas of light and shadow.

Last night, she'd waited for Bruce to come home, shame spreading through her at the realisation that the entire board-room must have known about Melanie. Unable to stand it, she'd sought the fresh air of the veranda, staring across the lonely sea, her mind churning out the same tired thoughts. In the dusk, she saw a silhouette down on the terrace, making fluid shapes like the outline of a bird. Susi returned her wave then headed along the flagstone path. A few moments later she rapped gently on the bedroom door.

'What were you doing?' said Ava.

'Tai chi. Good for –'

'Anxiety. I remember you said.'

'Yes. My father did it every morning.'

'And your mother?'

'She said there's nothing a glass of wine couldn't cure.'

'I'm on her side.'

There was something comforting about the way her eyes searched Ava's face. 'How was your day?'

'Fucking awful. I screamed until I couldn't stop.'

'Right,' said Susi. 'Stand up.'

'What?'

'Watch carefully, then copy me.' She proceeded to make the same bird movement as earlier, brushing one arm past the other, then repeating the gesture on the opposite side.

Ava mirrored the shapes, Susi instructing her which foot to lead with, and when to breathe in and out. 'This is called white crane flashes its wings.'

'Hey, this is easy.' Ava let out a Bruce Lee screech and kicked the air, then fell onto the bed with a giggle.

Susi shook her finger. 'Sensei say caterpillar must grow wings before it can fly.'

Maybe it was her Scottish lilt that gave Ava a kind of nostalgia, but she liked this woman, and there weren't many people Ava actually liked, not in the real sense. She lay back and stared at the ceiling. 'So why did you come to Canada?'

'To get away I suppose. And visit family.'

'Your stepfather?'

'And my sister.'

Ava rolled onto her tummy, gazing through the veranda at the grey expanse of the Strait. 'I'll tell you why I came here. I had no choice. My mother died, and my father – well –' Her throat closed.

There was the light touch of Susi's hand on her shoulder. 'So long as there is someone in your life who cares about you, you can get through anything.'

'Do you know how to make pancakes, Susi?'

'Pancakes?'

Ava sat up. 'Someone once told me that after a good helping of pancakes and maple syrup you see the world with different eyes.'

'It works?'

'It did when I was twelve.'

Susi smiled. 'Then let's give it a try.'

Ava uses her thumb to blend the charcoal lines. That's all it is, light and shade, the entire world made up of gradations of perception. Her fallen trunk is slowly emerging from nothingness, becoming three dimensional, something she can touch and feel.

In the savage storms a few years back, hundreds of trees were toppled by high winds. The government established a buffer zone around Temple Grove, giving the cluster of ancient trees protection from the elements. But Borealis argued for a ten percent selective cut – to satisfy the Asian markets which, according to Bruce, are 'as hungry as a soldier in a cheap brothel.' Green Alliance protested; windthrown timber is salvageable so it's as good as going in with chainsaws. But Borealis played the economic stability card, and that wins voters. Now Bruce wants the cut increased to forty percent. The trees are old men who've had a good life, he says, so no one should feel sad when they're gone. Yet if Green Alliance is right, thousands of hectares are lost every decade to windthrow, and it won't be long before ancient trees are a relic of the past. Ava sighs and brushes charcoal dust from the paper. Surrounded by the massive Douglas Firs and Red Cedars, it's hard not to think they can feel their world being slowly cut away.

A drumming sound vibrates through the earth and echoes in the high branches. Voices. Slowly they get nearer, then condense to a steady rhythm until she can't concentrate. Stuffing her sketchbook in her bag, she hurries back through the trees and out into the carpark. A crowd is marching along the highway, winding its way towards the protest camp, row after row of people surging past, all ages and backgrounds, some angry, others carrying placards. A paper mâché dummy of Kelly as the grim reaper towers above their heads, chains of protestors chanting with their arms linked: 'Hands off Temple Grove.'

Ava glances at her car. It's too late to go back now. Her feet are already walking, following the crowd. Isn't this what she came for, after all? It's a gamble and she has no idea how on earth she'll find him in this sea of faces, but she has to do this. She has to be near to Scott.

In the row in front a grey-haired woman and a man with a beard hold hands: man and wife, protesting together. Ava keeps her head down, her heart beating faster. The air is filled with electricity. It's like being young again, the whole world at her feet. No, it's more than that. The protestors want something other than low taxes and decent pensions. They have ideals, aspirations. A belief that they can change things. She was like that once. She has to see if it's still there, deep down within her. Hope.

The encampment comes into view, the protestors making their way towards it, like festival goers with a higher purpose. Beneath her feet, the road is rutted with muddy brown pools and the wheel marks of logging trucks. She's out of breath but she doesn't care. A banner stretched between two trees reads: *Borealis Out!* Another has a print of Kelly's face, the word *Criminal* emblazoned underneath. Chains of people are sitting on the track, holding hands, forming a barricade. A man with straggly hair and a high-viz jacket with a Green Alliance logo points to a space near the edge. 'You go there.' Ava's palms break out in a cold sweat. She searches for the elderly protestors but they've disappeared. Turning back she tries to squeeze through the crowd, but there's no way out. The press of bodies pushes her forward and she has no choice but to move along. If she keeps her head down they might not recognise her. There's a lot of shouting, someone she can't see on a loudspeaker, issuing instructions. A shaven-headed woman in high-viz tries to guide her towards the barricade, but Ava sees a gap and makes her way along the edges. The woman consults with her straggly-haired colleague who then walks towards Ava and takes her aside. 'We know who you are. This is a peaceful protest. We have a right to civil disobedience.'

'I don't want trouble.' Ava holds up her hands. 'I'm just looking for my son.'

'Scott's not here.'

'But he must be. Please, I only want to talk to him.'

He confers with his associate, who nods and disappears into the crowd.

Ava folds her arms. From within the barricade there's a flutter of agitation, the chants rising: 'Borealis Out!' She spots the man and wife protestors in one of the rows, their fists in the air. At last she sees the shaven-headed woman coming back. Someone is with her. In the crush of people, it's difficult to make out whom. 'Scott,' she calls. 'Scott!' But it's not Scott. Winding languorously towards her is a thin girl with long straight hair. She's wearing a massive rainbow-coloured jumper that looks home-knitted and as though it might have fleas. Ginny. 'Mrs N. Didn't expect to see you here.'

'Where's Scott?'

'You can't stop him, you know. He believes in this. He's at the bypass further back. It was him who gave us the tip off.'

Ava looks around. 'What tip off?'

The sound of distant sirens sparks a restless surge through the crowd. 'We can't trust her,' says the shaven-haired woman. 'Who knows what she'll tell them?'

More groups come down from the encampment, squeezing into the human barricade, arms linked. Maybe the woman is right. She shouldn't be here. What will it look like, what will Bruce say? In the jostle Ava drops her bag, the sketchpad tumbling into the mud.

'If you want to go, go now,' says Ginny. 'They'll arrest as many of us as they can.'

Ava grabs the sketchpad, clumsily shoving it into her bag.

'Temple Grove?'

'Don't look so surprised.'

'Hey, it's not bad, you know. Scott told me you used to be an artist.'

She's surprised Scott remembered. No one ever called her that before, an artist, like she had a right to it. The protestors stand in unison, still chanting, all eyes on the track leading down to the highway. 'What's it to be, Mrs N?'

The siren screeches get louder. Ava thinks of the Borealis building, the tall rows of steel and glass, the way her voice emptied into air. She thinks of Mary, Queen of Scots imprisoned in Fotheringhay, awaiting execution, of her mother walking every day to that big stone mill, her soft sad face, nothing but a fragment, gone. Of Scott, grasping at the bones of his identity, just like her. Clouds cut across the sun, like a great dark bird about to swoop over the camp. The time comes when you have to make a decision. She turns to Ginny. 'I'm not going anywhere. Show me where to stand.'

1962
Paisley

Every day after work, I go and check on my mammy. I wipe the table, mop the floor, do the dishes. I feed her soup and cut up bread into wee squares small enough for her to chew. She lets me do it, though her eyes still glare at me from beneath her brows, telling me that if she could have it any other way, she would. I don't talk much while I'm there. I put the wireless on to drown the silence. If there's washing to be done, Annie helps me hang it out the back. Then I go up the road to Newton Street and get half an hour to myself, a cup of tea and a cigarette at the kitchen table, before it's time for Tommy to get up, and then the same routine of cooking, washing and cleaning starts all over again.

I've not seen Billy for weeks. I called the Lighthouse just after the stroke happened. 'I've a surprise planned for you when all this is over,' he said.

'No the flat again?'

'No, I can dae better than that for my Jean. Call me soon as you get the chance. But don't leave it too long, eh?'

'I'll try but I canny promise.'

'Tell me you're my girl.'

'You know I am.'

'Say it.'

'I'm your girl.'

It's a Friday, so normally I should be out getting a bit of shopping before I go home. But my body feels like an empty sack. Even if I wanted to move I don't think I could. My head's hammering with the sound of the mill, and my nerves are raw with scrubbing. I climb the stairs slowly, like an old woman, go into the kitchen, make a cuppa and sit down. Tommy says my mother's getting better. The other day she made him a cup of tea using her good hand. 'Well, aren't you the bloody Pope?' I said. He didn't answer, just sat behind his paper. That's all he does these days, sits reading the news and shaking his head.

It feels like I've barely lit my cigarette before I hear him getting up and moving around. The first thing I do is fill the basin with water so he can have a shave. I look at my hands. The nails are ragged. Even my wedding ring looks dull, like all the shine's come off. Tommy never mentions the Grammar and I don't bring it up. I just never go back. Sometimes I wonder how they're getting on, the 'stupid, stupid' girls and Miss MacDiarmid and her William Tell Overture. It wasn't all about Billy. I was actually learning something. I tried scribbling shorthand in the margins of Tommy's paper, trying to translate the paragraphs, remember short forms, heavy strokes and light strokes. But I never could. He thought it was Ava. 'Tell her to use her colouring-in books,' he said. Eventually I gave up.

We live in silence, only speaking to each other about the necessary things like, 'Sausages awright?' or 'I'm doing an extra shift,' or 'I'm out of razors, Jean.' There's no mention of Foxbar or the new baby. One night, he rolled on top of me in the dark, his hot breath shuddering against the side of my face; then it was over. I remember Mr Webster going on once about how I should read the Greek myths. He said life was like some rock that a Greek bloke had to spend eternity pushing up a hill. Well, I think he had it easy; try pushing a sick mother, a crabbit husband and a wean. Give me a rock any day.

When I'm finished filling the basin, I light another cigarette and lean against the sink. I stare at the clock. The minutes tick by and I think of all the things that are happening everywhere else: the lovers lying in each other's arms; wedding bells ringing; babies being born. I think of planes flying across the sky to far off cities like Paris and New York: the glasses clinking in cafés; the big shops with their mannequins and bright lights. I think of mountains and oceans and giant forests with trees taller than buildings. I think of JFK and Cuba and important people marching down corridors and how with one push of a button it could all be gone. There's so little time. Here, nothing seems to change. No matter how long I stand and stare at the clock, everything here is the same.

'Tommy,' I shout. 'That's yer basin ready.' While he shaves I start dinner. There's nothing in the cupboard except a tin of meat, bread and a turnip. My mother likes mince and mashed up neeps. Sometimes I make her a wee bit fish cooked in milk to make it soft. I should have brought some home. I decide to give Tommy and Ava the turnip and I'll just have a piece. I spread the slices of meat across the plate to make it look more than it is. 'I thought it wis payday,' says Tommy, sitting down behind his paper.

'Aye, well, I've no had time for the shops. I'll go the morra.'

Ava has brought that overgrown doll, Raggedy Jane, to the table with her. She sits it on her knees and pretends to feed it with a spoon. It has eyelids that blink when it moves. It's something Cissy bought her. I find it creepy. 'Put that doll down till you're finished,' I say. 'And, Tommy, I'll no have that newspaper while there's food on the table.'

'This isny food,' he says, from behind the sports section. 'Wheesht, wumin.'

'Wheesht,' says Ava. 'Wheesht, wheesht.'

'Ava!'

She whispers something to the doll and sits it on the floor beside her chair. Tommy doesn't move from behind his paper. I don't remember the last time he looked at me. Sometimes I feel like sticking out my tongue, making faces at him to see if he's watching. Occasionally, the paper rustles then smacks as he straightens out the page. Each time he does it my bones jump. I want to snatch the bloody thing from his hand and shred it to pieces. Instead, I search for words to stuff the silence. 'We'll have to get new dishtowels,' I say. 'For when we move to Foxbar.'

I expect him to reply, 'Whit's wrong wae the old ones?' Instead, there's a pause while he reaches round to hook his cup of tea. The cup disappears behind the paper and there's a slurping noise before he puts it back on the table. 'We'll no be moving tae Foxbar,' he says. 'I took oor name aff the list.'

'Whit dae ye mean, aff the list? Bit you promised –'

'Who'll look after yer mither?'

'She's improving, you said so yerself. She made you a cup a tea.' I feel like I'm being pushed under water, gasping for air. 'How cuid you do that, Tommy? Withoot telling us. How cuid you do that and no say a word?'

'Did I no tell you?' he says. 'Maybe I forgot.'

I bang my fork on the table. 'I've a right tae know. I'm your wife. Or did you forget that tae?'

Tommy folds the paper, finishes drinking his tea and stands up. 'Aye, and I'm your husband. And whit I say goes. I've made my decision.'

That's it. He's out the house without another word. Whatever strength I had left inside me dissolves. It's like that rock is rolling towards me, crushing me. I lean over and let my cheek feel the cool Formica surface of the table. 'Mammy,' says Ava, but I wrap my arms round my head, squeezing tighter and tighter, shutting out the light, burying myself in the blackness.

I've already been up three hours. I spend it standing at the window, smoking cigarette after cigarette, watching the silhouette of the spinning mill, dark and blind except for the corner domes, silver in the moonlight. Mary, Queen of Scots was only twenty-eight when she was imprisoned in Fotheringhay Castle. I think of her shut up behind its dreary stone walls, watching the same moon scud across the sky, waiting for a freedom that never came.

At a quarter to six, I go down the stairs to join the others and make my way across to the gates. Three years I've been working here. When my mother retired on account of her bad knees, she'd been working thirty-six. Her long service certificate hangs framed above the mantelpiece. I remember the day she left, how the front room was filled with flowers and all the women she worked with came round for sandwiches, cake and tea. After they left she cried like somebody had died, like it was a funeral. Una's coming up for forty years' service in December. She's been on about it for weeks now. I can't imagine Una without the mills. She wouldn't know what to do with herself. Institutionalised they call it, like men after they come out the army or prison: they can't adjust.

After an hour on the machine, the threads start blurring into each other, the bobbins like white blobs before my eyes. 'Jean,' says a voice. 'Jean.' I look up. It's Maggie. 'That's the third time I've asked you tae keep an eye oan my machine. If I don't pee I'll burst.'

I nod. Outside, the sun is starting to rise. I wish the machines would stop, that, just for a minute, everything could be still and quiet. When Maggie comes back, I put up my hand for a toilet break. 'Two minutes,' says The Bitch.

The corridor is empty. I find a patch of wall where the sun has illuminated the dull green paint, and lean against it. Then I stretch my arms along the stone as far as they'll go and close my eyes. The world around me is spinning. I want to sink to the floor, curl up and not move. But I know I have to keep walking, so I sidle along, keeping my back close to the wall, feeling like it's the only thing stopping me keeling over. In the toilet, I splash cold water on my face. My throat feels hoarse and my chest clogged. I've never needed fresh air so badly. I open the window and lean out, pushing my head through as far as it will go. My mouth tastes of the gluey water the thread passes through, and my head is full of the rattle of machines, the other women shouting over the noise, all of it spinning round in one big spool. I look down, down into the yard below, the foremen standing at the warehouses, the trucks going in and out, everything carrying on as normal. I'm six flats up and I feel like I'm the only person in the world. My stomach tightens to a knot, like I'm being strangled from the inside. I can't hold it in any longer. I open my mouth and scream as loud as I can, my breath pouring into the wind and over the canal, the storage depots, the gatehouses, the football pitch. I scream till my lungs empty and every last gasp of air is out my body.

No one notices. I could stand here screaming all day and all they would hear is the noise of the machines. I shut the window. When I get back, The Bitch is angry with two women arguing over their piece sheets, shouting that the weights have been mixed up; no one likes to be sold short. I walk right over; tell her I've just been sick.

Mr Green gives me the rest of the day off. From the phone box at The Cross I dial the Lighthouse. 'Billy's no here,' says the barman. 'Can I take a message?' I hang up.

Billy lives on Bank Street, but I've no idea which close. I don't bother with a bus. I run and run until I reach a couple of weans playing on the corner. They look about Ava's age: two wee lassies with a toy pram. I ask for the McBrides' but they go all shy and shake their heads. One of them says, 'My name's Nora, whit's yours?' I see a boy coming down the street on the other side, whistling with his hands in his pockets. He looks about eleven. I cross over and ask if he knows where Billy lives. He gives me a suspicious look.

'I'm a friend,' I say.

'Third down on the right. Don't say I told you.'

The close is dark except for a weak light filtering through from the back court. There's a smell of piss. As I climb the stairs, the smell gets stronger. There's a door with a dent where the wood splits as though it's been kicked. I knock. No answer. I knock again. A voice that reminds me of a spade being dragged through gravel, shouts, 'B-aa-lly.' It's somewhere between a slur and a roar. 'B-aa-lly.' Still no answer. I whisper through the wood: 'Billy, it's me, Jean. Are you there?'

Immediately a crack appears and half of Billy's face peers through. He's unshaven and wearing a vest. He looks at me like he's never seen me before. 'Whit?'

'I need tae speak to ye.'

He glances over his shoulder. 'No here, wait fur me downstairs.' The door shuts.

From inside, the rough voice starts spitting out words. I can't make them out, only Billy's reply: 'Nane a yer business, Da.'

I wait at the bottom of the close. When Billy appears, he looks like himself again, his hair greased back and his face shaven, a dark woollen shirt under his jacket. He nods for me to follow him outside to the midden. He leans against the wall, next to an old mouldy pram, lights a cigarette and stares up into the clouds. 'I told you no tae come here.'

'I had to see you.'

'Whit's so important?'

'I want to go away, Billy. As far away as possible. You, me and Ava, jist like you said. I don't care whit it takes.'

He raises an eyebrow. 'I don't know.'

'Bit you promised, Billy. Aw that stuff aboot America. You said I deserved better than this.'

He shrugs. 'How am I supposed tae get that kind a money?'

'I'll do it,' I say. 'The mills. I'll do whitever ye say.'

He stops looking at the clouds and stares me right in the eye. 'Dae ye mean it?'

'Mair than I've ever meant anything before.'

'Whit aboot Tommy?'

I shake my head. 'It's you I want tae be with, Billy. It's always been you. I know that now.' I think now he'll take me in his arms. My Billy. His warm smell, his crooked lips, telling me I'm his girl.

He doesn't. His jaw starts grinding and his eyes glaze over like shutters. I feel like he's slipping away and I wish he would let me inside. I want to know everything about him: his home, his life, where he goes when we're not together. 'I don't mind aboot yer da,' I say.

'When can you get away?'

'I could take the day aff the morra, leave Ava wae Tommy, tell him I'm at the doctor's. So long as it's only a couple of hours.'

'Meet me at the bridge. Twelve o'clock.' Billy stubs out his cigarette with his foot. If he kisses me, I won't care who's watching. We're going to be together and that's all that matters. But he turns and disappears back up the close, the crushed remains of his cigarette still giving off a faint spiral of smoke.

It's one of those clear, crisp days, too cold for what I'm wearing. I should have put on my long woollen coat with the pleat at the back, but it's frayed at the cuffs, so I put on my suede jacket and boots, a baby pink turtle neck and paint my nails to hide the fact that they're all worn down.

I'm barely at the bridge when a car pulls up beside me – the same Morris Minor Billy was in before, only this time another man is driving. He's older than Billy and wearing a suit and a thick gold watch. I recognise him from that day in the Lighthouse; he was talking to Billy before I came in. Billy is in the passenger seat and, in the back, is a woman with bleached blonde hair, cut short into her neck. She opens the door so I can climb in beside her. It all happens very quickly, and then we're off, driving up past the Anchor Mills and Saucel Hill. 'This is Harry,' says Billy. 'And his wife, Norma.'

Norma holds out her hand. She's wearing a leather jacket with a belt. 'How long ye been working in the mills?' she says.

'Long enough,' I say, and they all laugh.

We drive along the Barrhead Road, past the Hurlet. There's a big load of trees on the left that Norma says is Pollok Park. Then we're back amongst buildings and shops and down more streets I don't recognise. Harry goes into a side road and parks. We get out and follow him round the corner to a restaurant with two Italian flags above the door. We're hardly inside when a waiter rushes over to take our coats. He knows Harry and his wife and asks how they are. 'Usual table, sir?'

Harry nods. The waiter half-bows as he leads us to an alcove up the back, and a square table covered in a red and white checked cloth. All the time Billy is grinning, smiling at me like we're sharing a secret joke.

Harry orders white wine 'for the ladies' and whisky for the men. 'So, Jean, I hear you and Billy go back quite a bit,' he says, when we're seated.

I nod.

Harry winks at me and says, 'She's a looker right enough, Billy boy.'

I glance at Norma, but she doesn't seem bothered that her husband is paying me a compliment. Billy smiles but keeps his head down. I've never heard anyone call him 'Billy boy' before. After a pause, he says, 'Harry and Norma were kind enough to give us a loan of their flat.'

I blush, remembering the cardigan I left in the spare bedroom, but I don't mention it. When I look at Norma, I see she's glancing at my wedding ring. 'It's a lovely flat,' I say. 'I like your pictures.'

She doesn't answer.

'So how did you meet Billy?' I direct the question at Harry, turning my head towards him but not looking him in the eye.

It's Norma who answers, 'Jail. They were cellmates.'

'I looked out fur ye, didn't I, Billy boy?'

Billy nods and sips his whisky.

'But that's just me,' says Harry. 'Always happy to do a favour for a friend. And I'll tell you something aboot Billy here. He's got guts. This is a great business opportunity, Billy. Risky, mind, but all the best ones are. If it pays aff, ye'll be a rich man.'

The waiter returns with menus bound in dark leather. Most of it is in Italian and I've no idea what to order. Harry says not to worry about the expense. Norma chooses something called carbonara, so I get that too. Harry and Billy get steak. During dinner, Harry does most of the talking. First, about the number of times Norma changes her hair, and then about all the decorators he's had in the past year. 'If it wisny fur Norma's tastes, I could retire.' Then he says about the pubs he owns, and how he had to get rid of a manager for dipping his hands in the till. He gets angry when he talks about it. 'No place fur thieves in my business,' he says. 'If ye're a thief, ye're *finito*.' He tells Billy there's plenty business opportunities to be had around the dry docks 'if ye've got someone on the inside.'

Billy nods and laughs, while Norma drinks.

'Have you got children?' I ask her.

'Two,' she says. 'They live with my mother.'

I don't ask why.

After dinner, Harry says, 'Let's no beat around the bush, Billy boy. Tell me whit ye need and when. I can give ye a couple a guys.'

'That depends on Jean.' Billy looks at me and smiles, half encouraging, but with a nervous twitch I've never seen before. I notice he's hardly touched his whisky.

'I've heard of inside-men,' says Harry. 'Bit this is the first inside-woman.' He laughs out loud then his face straightens, 'So long as you know whit ye're doing.'

'She does,' says Billy.

'I hope so. We've seen enough a Barlinnie tae last us a lifetime, eh Billy boy?'

'Can we no talk aboot the jail again?' says Norma, pouring another glass. 'We're out for a nice meal.'

'Who do ye think pays fur yer nice meal?' says Harry.

Norma doesn't answer.

Billy starts to speak but Harry tells him to wait till we're in the car. It's cold when we leave the restaurant and my breath steams in front of my face. We get into the car and Billy and Harry turn in their seats to look at me. Billy speaks first, 'Are ye sure ye want tae do this, Jean? Because once ye're in there's no backing out. Understand?'

'Back out and ye're *finito*,' says Harry, and laughs.

I nod. 'I'll no back out.'

Billy looks at Harry. 'The payroll is upstairs in the back room. Jean'll find oot when the cash gets delivered, won't ye?' He turns to me, his face serious. Maybe it's the wine, but I can't stop smiling. 'Thursday,' I say. 'I mind Cissy mentioning it tae Tommy.'

'That's my girl.' Billy grins. 'Telt ye she wis good, Harry.'

'It's Friday I'm worried aboot,' says Harry.

'We need ye tae be careful, Jean. Find out who goes in and out the office on a Friday. Whit time they arrive, when they go for lunch, and whit time they come back. Can you do that?'

'Aye.'

'Good girl.'

'Once it's done ye'll need tae lie low fur a while,' says Harry. 'Understood?'

I nod.

Norma yawns. 'Harry, I'm tired.'

'Drunk mair like.' He starts the engine.

'Billy,' I say.

He turns round, pats my knee and winks, 'Don't worry, Jean.'

2013
Victoria, British Columbia

From the shouting and clanging of doors, she guesses it must be morning. There's no window and the cell is redolent with years of stale piss. Yet, despite the lumpen mattress, it's the best sleep she's had in days.

When the police stormed the barricade, she'd screamed and shouted with the other protestors, getting caught in the tussle and tangle of bodies; somehow it made her feel liberated, like she was part of something. She'd even tried to prevent the arrest of a young woman she'd never met. Next thing she knew, she was being thrown in a police van and taken to the station to cool off. A female officer with a bellowing voice unlocks the cell door and says, 'Come with me, Mrs Newport.'

'Am I being charged?'

'You're being released. Mr Newport is sending a car to take you home.'

The officer walks her briskly to the main desk and hands over her personal belongings. Her bag is muddied but with the sketchbook still inside. From a side door, Bentley appears in a dark wool coat. He glances at the officers, then runs his eyes over Ava's crumpled sweatpants and uncombed hair. 'Okay, let's go.'

'I need to get freshened up.'

'There's no time. I'll do the talking.' He manoeuvres her towards the exit. A bunch of reporters is gathered on the sidewalk. She's greeted by harsh daylight and a thick clamour of voices:

'Mrs Newport, will you be leaving the company? Where do you stand in the debate? What does your husband think of your right to civil disobedience?' Bentley's fingers dig into her flesh, guiding her towards the car. It annoys her. Since when was he *her* lawyer? 'Don't touch me,' she hisses. He forces her into the back seat just as a reporter thrusts her mike inside the car. 'Visit Temple Grove,' says Ava. 'Before it's too late.'

More media vans are gathered outside the house. A network of tyre tracks scars the gravel, shiny company cars stationed around the side entrance: Bruce is home. She half expects Bentley to put a blanket over her head and smuggle her through the doors. He accompanies her inside before breaking off in the direction of Bruce's office. The injunction will have made Bentley man of the hour.

Ava heads for the kitchen. 'Susi?' There's no one there but the kettle is warm. She scoops instant coffee into a mug. Bruce will be working out how to spin the situation round, how to 'deal' with her. She wonders if Melanie is there, if he's had the gall to bring that little prom queen into her house. Ava checks her phone. It's full of missed calls: three from Wanda and a voicemail from Scott. Ignoring the others, she clicks the voicemail, his words rushing into her ear: 'Wow, Mom, just saw you on the news. You were amazing. Love you.' He says it so quickly it could be a mumble or a cough. The words she's been waiting so long to hear. She wraps them round her like a warm blanket.

'Ava.'

The voice makes her jump. Bruce is standing at the entrance to the kitchen, his tie loosened, a glass of whisky in his hand. He fetches ice from the freezer then slams it shut. His face is red, slightly bloated. 'The doctor said you should cut down on drinking.' She winces at the sound of her voice. Force of habit, being Bruce's noticeboard, reminding him of anniversaries, cufflinks, doctor's orders.

The ice-cubes rattle in his glass. 'I've got to hand it to you, that little spectacle in the press. I underestimated you, Ava. But I'm not mad. Hell, I kind of admire you for it. You taught *me* a lesson, and there aren't many who can do that.' He walks towards her, arms slowly opening. 'I deserved it. I admit that. Can we get back to normal now? Please.'

If she wanted she could reach out and touch him, but she turns away. 'Deserved what?'

'Come on, Ava, don't push me. It's over. You had your fun. Listen to what I'm saying. I'm willing to forgive all this, get past it.'

'Have you ever been to Temple Grove, Bruce? Have you seen it?'

'Yeah, I've goddamn seen it. I'm not the bad guy here. If I hadn't kept this company afloat, the Chinese would have got their hands on it years ago.' He lowers his gaze, then looks up and flashes his blue eyes. 'Look, I'm sorry, alright? She meant nothing.'

'Is she here?'

'Of course she's here; it's just business, nothing more. But if you want to risk everything you have over some two-bit PR assistant, then you're losing focus.'

'Risk everything I have? What exactly do *I* have, Bruce? A husband who treats me like some goddamn secretary, stuck in this sterile house night after night, who's so fucking ego-centric he thinks I'm doing this out of some kind of petty revenge?'

He drains his glass. 'You have to understand, you've put me in a position. We've prepared a press release. You visited the protest camp in an effort to start a dialogue, see if some kind of compromise could be reached. Bentley used his contacts in the Police Foundation and they've agreed to say they arrested you by mistake. He's drawn up the papers. All you have to do is sign. Then we'll forget this whole thing ever happened.'

'That's ridiculous. I won't do it.'

Bruce checks his watch. 'Don't play me, Ava. I can make life difficult.'

She keeps her eyes on his. He won't break her down this way, she won't let him. 'You can't hurt me any more, Bruce. It's finished between us.'

He turns his back. 'I didn't say *your* life.'

Bruce pauses to let the words sink in. Her skin grows cold. 'No,' she says. 'You can't. He's your son too.'

'You know how things get done, Ava. There's a lot of itchy backs out there. Remember that producer Sue used to be engaged to, the one with the quiff who dumped her after she put up the money for some dodgy project of his? Never worked in media again.'

'You wouldn't. It could put Scott back years.'

'On the other hand, if you make the right call, the perfect offer could come his way.'

The sight of Bruce standing and smiling, like he's already won, ignites a fire in her belly. She won't be backed into a corner. The only way out is to leave a mark, draw blood. In a split second, she's lunging at him, clawing his face. His glass falls and shatters. He swats her aside, his lips curled in disgust. 'What in hell's name do you think you're doing?'

'What you deserve,' she says, her breath panting in her ears.

'Sign the statement.'

'And if I don't?'

'I want you out of this house.'

'I'll divorce you,' she says. 'I'll take everything you've got.'

'Remember what I said.' Straightening his tie, he backs towards the door. 'You've got twenty-four hours.'

Her body is shaking. She collapses in a chair, covers her face with her hands. She's seen it happen to others, watched executives rise and fall, but she was Bruce's wife, bulletproof. Maybe she should sign the goddamn thing. At least she'd be doing it for a reason. Scott wouldn't understand, but it's what he'd expect.

She hears tyres speeding over gravel. They're leaving now. Bruce. Melanie. He's right, she does mean nothing. There might have been a dozen PR assistants over the years. It's standard practice really, a husband's affair is a small price to pay for a house in Rockland and a bank balance with the right number of zeros. Maybe those women are right. Relationships aren't formed out of love, they're the product of convenience, of circumstance. God, she can barely breathe. She grips the table, fighting for air.

'Ava!' Susi drops her shopping bag. She rummages for a paper poke and holds it to Ava's lips. Apples and oranges roll under the chairs and between their feet. 'Breathe,' she says.

The wheezing subsides and Ava's breath slowly returns. 'Jesus, what's wrong with me?'

'You were having a panic attack.'

'It's Bruce... I...'

'Don't try to speak.'

When she stands her legs wobble. Susi catches her elbow, her presence warm and solid. 'Thanks,' says Ava.

'For what?'

'Being here.'

'It's my job, remember?'

The effort of smiling makes Ava feel heavy. Her phone rings. Wanda again. She cuts the call and asks Susi to help her upstairs. Outside, the sky is turning a deep shade of blue. In the bedroom, Ava resists the urge to crawl under the quilt and hide. Instead, she goes into her closet and tosses sweatpants, jeans and shirts into a canvas holdall, trying desperately not to look at Bruce's rows of suits and polished shoes, the polo shirts and perfectly creased pants. Susi's eyes narrow at the gaping bag filled with its crumpled cargo. 'You're leaving?'

'I can't stay here.'

'But where will you go?'

Ava doesn't answer. She upturns her jewellery box and takes out pearl earrings, a ruby necklace Bruce gave her for her fiftieth. Susi can give them to charity. Ava turns around, but Susi's not behind her. She's sitting on the bed, the Mary, Queen of Scots book open in her lap. 'Where did you get this?' she says.

'Don't touch that.'

Susi's look reminds Ava of a hare caught in the headlights. She drops onto the bed with a sigh, lifts the book from Susi's knee and runs her finger along the spine. 'It was my eighteenth birthday present. My mother sent it to Montreal. All these years I thought she was dead. They lied to me. What possible reason could people have for doing that to a child?'

Susi rubs her shoulder. She smells woody, like incense. 'Everything happens for a reason.'

'Really?' says Ava. 'What reason could someone have for sending me letters that were supposedly written years ago?' She fetches the letters from her bedside drawer and hands them to Susi. 'Bruce thinks it's some kind of hoax but –'

'You don't?'

For a moment, the only sound is the sea and her own breath. 'I thought it was Scott. I accused him, Susi. I accused my own son.'

'Oh, God.' Susi's voice is a whisper.

Ava's chest starts to tighten. Nothing here belongs to her anymore. It's Bruce's house, not hers. She grabs her holdall from the closet. 'I need to go; he'll be back soon.'

Susi springs to her feet. 'I'll come with you.'

'No, I have to do this on my own.'

'Wait –'

'If you need me I'll be in Pickering.'

Ava heads for the door, Susi's voice echoing after her, her accent thicker than usual, the way Uncle Alex spoke when Cissy told him to *talk proper*. 'See ye soon, right?'

1962
Paisley

It's a cold morning. I'm wearing my new white PVC coat, all zipped up. Ava has on her wool coat with the pleats and her matching grey hat and gloves. There's a few shillings in my purse, lipstick and a brush, and my jewellery box, because I know Ava likes it so much.

Act like it's a normal day, that's what Billy said. But I don't know how you can call this normal. There's a dull cramp in my stomach as I cross Canal Street over to Argyle Street. It's five thirty in the morning and there's hardly anyone around. Yesterday, Tommy said that's what the world would look like after a nuclear war. 'Like Paisley after the night shift?' I joked.

'No. Empty.' The way he said it made me feel sad.

Everybody says the world is on the brink of World War Three. It's the only thing Tommy talks about. 'The Communists have moved their missiles intae Cuba,' he said, from behind his paper. 'One push of a button, that's aw it takes. If they don't shift them, Kennedy will need tae follow through. Enough missiles tae blow us aw sky high.'

'Will you stop talking about it in front of Ava?' I said. 'It's giving her nightmares.'

She woke up the other night screaming because she'd dreamt she was a skeleton. 'If my skin comes off will I be dead?' she said. 'Can the bomb make it come off?'

'Never you mind all that,' I told her. 'In a wee while you won't have tae worry about any of it.'

'How, Mammy? Have they stopped the war?'

'There is no war,' I said. 'And if there is, your mammy will look after you. I won't ever let anything bad happen tae my Ava.'

'But Daddy says the Communists are coming. What's a Communist?'

'Never you mind whit Daddy says. Noo go tae sleep and I promise you, tomorrow, everything will be different.'

The past few days I've hardly let her out my sight. I find excuses why she can't go out and play. I even bought flour and eggs so we could bake wee fairy cakes. Maybe I should have encouraged her to spend some time with Tommy, though he hasn't taken much notice of her lately. I suppose it's for the best. This morning she wanted to go in and kiss him sweet dreams, but I said not to wake him. So she left a fairy cake on the kitchen table instead. I couldn't look at it. I put the rest of them in my bag to take to my mammy, to try and make things look normal.

My mammy's street feels different. As I pass the mouth of each close, I can smell the breath of the buildings, soot and smoke mingled with sour middens and rank cludgies; the whole street like a tired yawn reminding us that in this town we know all there is to know about each other, and there's nothing more to be said. I feel calm walking down there in the darkness, not the sadness or nostalgia I expected to feel, but a quiet forgiveness. The sleeping inhabitants are like children who'll never understand the hopelessness of their own lives, or realise that all you need to change it, is love.

There's a light on in my mammy's kitchen. She always did get up early, a habit she kept from the mills. I climb the stairs and give the door three knocks. They echo off the stone walls and for a moment I feel like I'm alone in a dark cave. I hear her shuffling to get to the door. It takes her a while to answer, though the doctors say she's improving better than expected. 'You'll be doing cartwheels this time next year,' Tommy always says. He's so predictable I can mouth the words behind his back. But Mammy just smiles like every time is the first.

When she opens the door, I'm surprised at the pinch in my heart. Her face still sags down one side, though not as much. Either that or I've got more used to looking at her. I want to tell my mammy not to worry, that everything will be alright, I want to tell her all these things, but she's looking at me, half-stooped, her eyes questioning. 'It's me,' I say, stupidly. 'Tommy's no awfy well. He's had his heid in the basin aw night. I couldny lea him wae Ava. You don't mind watching her, dae ye? Only I didny want tae miss another shift, no wae so many of the lassies doon wae flu. He said you widny mind.'

I nudge Ava in the door and give her the plate of cakes, covered with a dishcloth. 'We made you these, Nana,' she says, and skips through to the kitchen.

'If she's any trouble, take her doon tae Annie's,' I say.

Mammy looks at me and wipes one hand on her apron. It's a blessing she can't talk, though her eyes are still throwing out sparks. 'I'm sure Tommy will be alright again the morra.' After a brief pause, I add, 'He sends his love.'

She doesn't move. 'It's cold, Mammy,' I say. 'You should go back inside.' I imagine her in the future, standing in this same hall, opening birthday cards and Christmas cards from America, maybe with money inside and a wee picture of Ava. I step forward, put my arms around her and press my cheek to the side of her face. 'Thanks, Mammy,' I say. 'For everything.' She goes stiff. I let her go and step back. 'Are you alright, Mammy?'

She shuts the door.

Outside, I light a cigarette and start walking. A sweat breaks out on my palms, even though it's cold. I should never have given her that hug. A normal day, Billy said, and hugging my mammy isn't normal. She'll be wondering what I did it for. Anyway, I'll be back in a few hours. It's not like she can go anywhere. I'm worrying about nothing.

I don't want to go down Newton Street again, so I cut through Queen Street, past the Tannahill Cottage, then along Ferguslie Walk. I catch sight of my reflection in a shop window, my arms folded across my white coat, the trail of cigarette smoke. A couple of weeks ago, Billy told me to meet him on Mansionhouse Road. He turned up in Harry's car. That's when he gave me the coat, all wrapped up neat and folded. You could tell it had never been worn. He put the coat on me, holding it out like a proper gentleman, then twirled me under his arm and pulled me to him, kissing me hard on the lips. 'When you wear it I'll know ye're thinking aboot me,' he said.

'How could I no think about you, Billy McBride?' I paused. 'Where will we go when –?'

'We can stay at Harry's till things cool off. This is just the beginning, Jean. Trust me.'

I nodded.

'Say it.'

'I trust you, Billy.'

Tommy never asked me about the coat. Ava made a big fuss, telling me I looked like a lady out a magazine. I let her try it on. Tommy snapped his paper as he turned the page.

When I get to the Victorian spinning mill I stand for a minute outside the gate. I look up at the brick façade, the arched windows and columns and the fading cupolas. It would look quite nice if it wasn't a mill. I remember Mr Webster saying something about how it was in the style of the French Renaissance, whatever that is. He liked to go on about the 'exquisite' architecture in Paisley, and how nobody appreciated it except him. I'll miss him and his heavy framed glasses and pretend posh voice.

A hand slaps me on the shoulder. It's Aggie, 'Whit ye staunin there fur?'

'I'm looking at the building. It's quite exquisite, isn't it?'

'You been drinking?'

'No. It's in a French style, that's all.'

She frowns. 'Never mind the building. If you don't get in there and start yer shift, it'll be the guillotine.' She makes a cutting motion across her throat.

I laugh. I think about taking her arm, but don't.

It's a full two hours into the shift but I feel like I've only just blinked. The sun is starting to come up and soon the mill flat is filled with a creeping grey light. I watch it slither in the windows and over the floor, giving the machines a business-like look. The rhythmic clank and grind starts to drill into my bones. I feel like I'm a muscle in the body of some big beast with smoky breath and mechanical teeth that just go on rattling and thundering, each twist of the thread driving me to the point of no return. While it was dark outside, it felt like I was in a dream. But now that the sun is up, everything seems too real. Una is singing, '*We're working here in Coats', we're working hard all day, working the roses off our cheeks, for very little pay...*' A few others join in.

'Come on, Jean,' says Maggie, nudging my elbow.

I pretend, to make things seem normal, but my fingers are shaking. She passes me a poke of mint humbugs. I put my hand in but I can't prise one out. The poke drops to the floor and the sweeties spill out. 'Sorry,' I say.

She shakes her head and I put my hand up for a toilet break. As soon as I'm in the cubicle I throw up into the bowl, a mess of foamy tea-coloured liquid. All the hairs on my skin are standing on end. It's like my insides are boiling. My head is a jumble of thoughts. I wish Billy was here so he could tell me what to do. He makes it sound so easy. After he gave me the coat that day, we drove to a pub on Govan Road, near the dry docks. It wasn't much of a place, a few cheap Formica tables and chairs and some men, shipyard workers, gathered at the bar. Harry said there was no point spending money on furniture for it to get smashed up in fights every weekend. We sat up the back. 'How's our wee actress doing?' said Harry.

Billy did most of the talking. Mostly it was just stuff I'd told him already, about how I'd gone to the Counting House to tell Mr Thomson I'd had to leave the typing classes because of my mother. I said I could type forty words a minute to a speeded-up version of the William Tell Overture but that I could easily get faster if he'd only give me a job. He took off his glasses, steepled his hands and said that was all very commendable, but I'd still have to have a certificate. 'What if someone is off sick?' I said. 'You could give me a trial run. I'd do it for nothing.' I noticed he was looking at my knees so I made sure to lift my skirt a little.

He recommended I go back and finish my classes as soon as I get the chance. 'Come back and see me then, and I'm sure I can fit you in.'

'Thank you, Mr Thomson.'

The next time I went over, I pretended I was looking for Cissy, though I knew she'd been off with flu. 'Mr Thomson will see you instead,' said the desk girl. I told him I'd hoped Cissy could show me round the office. 'Did you know she's my sister-in-law?' I said. 'That's why I want to work in the Counting House, so I can be just like her. It's so much more exciting than working the machines, and I was really looking forward to seeing the upstairs, so I can imagine myself being there. Once I've got my certificate, of course.' I crossed my legs and smiled.

'Alright, Jean,' said Mr Thomson. 'Now I wouldn't do this for anyone else but you're Cissy's sister-in-law, so I don't see any harm.'

He led me up the stairs towards the back office. The room was surprisingly small, with a grey cast iron safe set into an alcove on the right. Around the walls were shelves filled with box files and big folders full of papers. In front of the safe was a table with a telephone and more papers arranged in a neat pile. 'This is where Cissy normally sits,' he said. There were two other desks, near the window and off to the left, also with telephones. There were two people at each desk, men in dark suits with concentrated, pained looks on their faces. 'These are our accountants,' said Mr Thomson. They glanced up briefly and smiled.

'How many people work here?'

'We have nine staff including senior management. That's quite enough to cover everything, and three typists in the other rooms. Myself and Mr Bell are downstairs, of course, though Mr Bell is only in on a Tuesday, and then there's Rose, our desk girl.'

'How interesting,' I said, in a posh voice. I said I'd go back to my classes as soon as I could and, who knows, then it would be me taking his shorthand.

'Keep up the good work, Jean,' said Mr Thomson. 'We could use an enthusiastic girl like you.'

The office goes for lunch at twelve o'clock. Except for Mr Thomson and Cissy. They don't go until one. Between twelve and one they lock the door. I know because you can see the Counting House from the bathroom window. The Bitch must think I've got the runs the amount of times I've excused myself for the toilet. Always on a Friday too. Billy said it has to be done quick. In and out. Harry will supply the van, make it look they're there to do a delivery. He knows someone on the inside who'll get them through the north gatehouse. My job is to make sure the door to the Counting House is unlocked and cause enough of a distraction to give Billy time to get up the stairs and down again to the van. 'Whit will I say?' I asked him.

'Don't worry, Jean,' said Billy. 'You'll think of something.'

When it's time for our break I don't eat a thing. 'I've made a decision,' says Una. Something about her pension. I stop listening. It's difficult to concentrate when my legs are shaking like Aggie's strawberry jelly. I wonder what Ava's doing. No doubt she's happy in front of the television eating my mother's coconut mallows. I imagine my mother sitting looking at her with that half-twisted smile. 'I jist want to make sure I'm getting whit's due,' says Una. 'It's the, whit dae ye cry it, the small print. They get you wae the small print.'

For a moment I think that all the commotion in my brain and body is going to rise up in a fountain of uncontrollable laughter, and once I start I'll never be able to stop. Una is looking at me and her mouth is moving but it takes time before I can make out the words. 'Whit's so funny?'

'Nothing,' I say.

'Take that smirk aff yer face then.'

'There's no a smirk on my face.'

'It's folk like me made this place, that's whit I'll tell them. And

I don't see there's anything funny aboot it.'

'Never mind,' says Maggie. 'It's payday, remember.'

'Aye, there's worse jobs than the mills.' Una sighs. 'Pity they're trying tae take it all away.'

When we go back to the machines, Mr Green says, 'You're looking very pale, Jean. Are you sure you're alright?'

I blush. 'Aye, I'm awright, Mr Green. Thanks.'

He smiles and walks away, his folder tucked under his arm, footsteps disappearing along the corridor. I think there must be something priestly about him; even though I'm about to do something terrible, he's still smiling at me like I'm the nicest person in the whole world. I wonder what would happen if I ran after him and told him there's about to be a robbery. I imagine him patting my hand and telling me to go and have a lie down and that I'll be alright in ten minutes. There's no going back, that's what Billy said. I hear his voice in my head, telling me how we're all slaves, how the mill owners make millions while we work our fingers raw. I remember Mammy telling me how her mother lost her big toes working in these mills. That's how they used to operate the twisting machines, with their big toes going up, down, up, down, shift after shift, day after day. When I was wee she showed me where they'd been cut off, two wrinkled purplish stumps. It still gives me the shivers.

But that's not really why I'm doing it, leaving my husband, my home, taking my daughter away. There's only one reason. Billy. I might not be a heroine, but I know Mary, Queen of Scots would understand. She gave up her throne, her country, even, all because she loved a man. Billy's no Earl of Bothwell, but I'd do anything to be with him, to have him by my side forever, no matter what; to love the taste, smell and thought of him so much it's like nothing else exists. If Mary, Queen of Scots could march proudly up to the execution block, then I can do this, and that's what I keep thinking about, keeping one eye on the clock, while the machines rattle and wind. And soon it's like somebody else is working my machine, someone I've never seen before, and I'm just standing, watching her.

I watch when she puts up her hand at quarter to twelve and asks to go home. I hear The Bitch say, 'No again,' and Mr Green say, 'I thought you looked a bit shivery earlier.' She replies that she thinks she's getting the flu and there's a lot of it about. 'Best go home early,' says Mr Green. 'I'm sure the other girls won't mind cleaning your machine.'

'Oh aye,' says Una. 'If you ask nice I'll come round and make yer tea as well.'

'See,' says Mr Green. 'It's all settled.'

I watch this other woman run down the fire escape. She flattens herself against the wall and waits until the Payroll staff leave for lunch. She counts them then crosses the courtyard to the office, keeping her head down, moving quickly, quietly. The door is locked. She bangs on it with her fist. 'Cissy, Cissy, come quick. Open up. It's Jean.'

She keeps banging and shouting until Cissy comes down the stairs, her face taut, her lips tight. 'For goodness' sake, you'll wake the dead.' Cissy unlocks the door with a key and the other Jean pushes inside, panting and breathless.

'I've something tae tell you,' she says, closing the door and leaning against it.

Cissy's eyes focus narrowly on the dishevelled commotion of a woman standing before her. 'Can't it wait?'

'No, it's important. You need tae know.'

The flicker of contempt in Cissy's eyes turns to concern.

'I'm leaving Tommy.' This other Jean stares defiantly at her sister-in-law.

Cissy's mouth doesn't gape open. Instead, her face is like a mask, the muscles pulled together, her composure flawless.

'I'm never going back,' says the other Jean. 'And I'm taking Ava with me.' She starts to wheeze, gulping like there's no air, holding back breath till the muscles strain on her neck. It's enough to make Cissy forget to lock the door.

'Water. I need water.'

Cissy gives me a long hard stare then disappears along the corridor into Mr Thomson's office. The other Jean follows. I marvel at where she came from, this woman, born with the rattle of machines in her bones, her nerves and sinew made from that same grinding steel, her brain a muscle of the mills, raw and relentless. There's a pitcher of water on the desk and a glass. Cissy fills it and hands it to her. 'It's him, isn't it?' she says.

The machine woman says nothing.

'I knew it, though I'm surprised even you have the brass neck to declare it outright.' Cissy sighs, steps closer. She smells of coffee and polish. 'I don't care what you do, Jean Owen. In fact, it's probably for the best. Tommy's better off without you. Eventually he'll realise it. But one thing is sure, you're not taking that wee lassie. Over my dead body.'

That's when it happens. A noise at the front door, not loud, and the creak of footsteps up the stairs. Cissy turns her head. Suddenly the machine woman is gone, and then there's only me, my heart thudding so hard it feels like a balloon about to burst. The room begins to swirl. I need machine woman to come back, with her strong bones and steely nerves. I don't know what to do. I can't let Cissy go up there. My glass of water flies through the air and hits the wall behind her head. Cissy lets out a yelp. Then I'm watching as this other Jean races in front, goading Cissy, blocking her path. 'You never liked me, did ye? Well, I hope ye're pleased wae yerself. You got whit ye wanted. The morra I'll be gone. And Ava too. And there's not a bloody thing you can do about it.'

'What on earth are you playing at, Jean?' Cissy puts her hands on her hips and raises her voice. 'Mr Thomson, can you come down here, please?'

There's a thud from upstairs.

Cissy's expression turns to alarm.

Another thud. Then furniture scraping and clattering across the floor, followed by a muffled shout.

'Mr Thomson?' calls Cissy. She turns to me, her lips drawn back in a hiss, 'Something's wrong. This is your doing, Jean Owen.' She pushes past me, into the corridor, then up the stairs.

'Cissy, don't go up there.'

It's too late. The front door clicks open. There's nothing I can do. In she comes with her wide hips and slow rolling gait: Una McMenemy. 'I'm here tae see Mr Thomson aboot my pension,' she calls out. 'And tae give him a piece of my mind. Forty years I've worked in this place and I'll no be leaving withoot my long service certificate –' She stops. 'Jean McParland, whit you daein here?'

Footsteps on the floor above. Billy will be down with Harry's men any second. Trust Una. It had to be Una. 'Whit's going on?' she says.

Una doesn't know it's not Jean McParland standing before her, but the machine woman. 'Get out of my way, Una.'

Just then Billy and his men come downstairs. They shove Cissy against the wall, her hands covering her ears, screaming like a pack of devils are after her.

'Hurry,' I shout.

They've got tights over their heads. American tan. But you can still see it's Billy. He's carrying a brown satchel under his arm. Una's face is red, her mouth loose and her cheeks quivering with fear. But for all she's shrinking back into the doorway, her face is defiant, angry. 'You'll no get away wae this, Jean McParland. Over my deid body.'

That's two deid bodies to climb over in one day: Una and Cissy. I see the van outside. Una hasn't moved. Her heavy bulk is barring the way, her hands gripping each side of the doorframe.

'Jean, for fuck's sake,' shouts Billy.

I'm still wearing my overalls under my white coat. Machine woman reaches into the pocket. They're still there: the scissors for splicing the thread. She grips them in her fist, like an arrow, and rams the hard point into the back of Una's left hand, piercing the soft flesh between the bones. I don't know which is the real Jean and which isn't. It's like I'm floating above, watching the concentration on machine woman's face, the twitch in her muscles as she yanks the scissors free. Una sinks to the floor, howling, holding out her wounded hand. The other Jean stands above her holding the scissors. Then everything goes quiet. Billy and his accomplices push me through the door and out towards the waiting van. My legs are running, though they're not sure which way to go. A hand shoves the small of my back, and a distant voice says, 'Fucking move, eh?' Then I'm inside the van, the doors slamming on all sides, brakes screeching as we speed past the north gatehouse and out onto the road.

Gradually the sound comes back. There's a panic inside the van, raised voices, swearing, shouts of, 'Jesus fucking Christ.' It's like my ears and throat, my whole head is burning. We turn into Thomson Street. I feel myself pushed out the van and into a waiting car. I don't see who's driving. I don't recognise anyone except Billy. He's sitting beside me in the back, the satchel on his knees, his head turning constantly over his shoulder. His jaw is grinding so hard I can hear his teeth. The car skids onto Ferguslie Walk. I pick up snatches of talk. Mr Thomson got a hold of a phone, threatened to call the police. Billy had to hit him over the head, then tied him up to stop him screaming. My face feels numb but my cheeks are wet. I didn't realise I was crying. 'Ava,' I say. 'Ava. Ava.'

We're in Argyle Street and outside my mother's close. Billy opens the car door to let me out. 'No fucking about, Jean. I mean it.'

I lurch from the car, half-running onto the street, my legs trembling beneath me. I stagger up the close like I'm drunk, banging on the door. 'Mammy. Mammy.' This time she answers quickly. 'Ava,' I say, struggling to draw breath. 'I'm here for Ava.' My mammy doesn't move. I barge past into the house. 'Ava, love. It's time to go.' There's no one there. The television in the front room is switched off. I run into the kitchen. Empty. 'Ava,' I screech. 'Ava.' Mammy stands watching me from the hall, that twist of a smile on her lips. 'Where is she?' I say. 'Where's Ava?'

She reaches inside the pocket of her apron and unfolds a piece of paper. I snatch it from her. The writing looks like shaky spider-legs. But I know it's my mother's hand. *Tommy*, it says. I look up. 'No, Mammy, she canny be. Tell me she's no wae Tommy.'

My mother nods her head. This time I feel the tears. 'Why, Mammy? I asked you tae watch her fur me. I wis counting on ye. One thing, that's all I asked.' It's the hug, that's what it is. I should never have given her that hug. Ever since the day of her stroke, she's been suspicious. Maybe both of them have known all along. Tommy's coldness, the white coat neither of us could afford.

'Jean, come on!' Billy's voice from the foot of the close. My mother stiffens. I wonder if she'll shut the door, but she doesn't. I hear him climb the stairs, two at a time. He reaches the landing. 'Jean. Now!' he says.

I rush towards him. 'Oh, Billy, she's gone. Ava's gone.' I grip the lapels of his jacket. 'She's wae Tommy,' I say. 'We have to go and get her. I canny leave withoot Ava. I can't.'

'There's nae time, wumin.'

'Billy,' I say. My voice is calmer than I feel. 'Please, I'm begging ye. It'll no take long, I promise. You said, Billy. That wis the plan, you, me and Ava.' I'm cold and shaking all over. My face is wet. There's stuff running from my nose into my mouth but I don't care.

Billy's voice is clipped, impatient. 'Ava will be awright wae Tommy. She'll be looked efter.'

My mother makes a noise, like a self-satisfied click, in the back of her throat. It's not a sentence, not even a word, but its effect is stony and coarse and I know exactly what it means. Selfish Jean. Got exactly what she deserved. I feel like I've been thrown against the rocks. There's a sound in my mouth, like a siren wailing. A force rises within me, carrying me with it like a wave. I want to smash through my mother, knock her aside. Her hair is in my hands, my words flying up in the air then drowning again. Something pulls me back, Billy's arm, wrapped around my body. 'Stop it, Jean. Stop it.' Spit flies from my mouth. 'Ava,' I say. 'I want Ava. Help me, Mammy. Help.'

This time she lifts her good arm, tries to push him back and shut the door to stop him dragging me out into the close. She's too slow. Billy shoves her hard in the chest and she staggers, falls onto her side. 'Mammy.' I can hardly see in front of me anymore. I can't turn round. It feels like my feet aren't touching the ground. We're heading down the stairs, Billy's breath in my ear, hot and struggling. There's daylight at the bottom of the close. When I see it, I cry out. I know as soon as I enter that light, it will take me away from Ava. Forever.

Annie is watching us coming down the stairs, standing back, keeping the weans safe inside. 'What's going on, Jean? Why's Billy here? Where are you going?'

I don't have time to answer. I catch her eyes as we pass. 'Ava,' I say. 'They've took Ava.'

'Tommy's got her,' Annie shouts after us. 'Your mammy asked me to take her round earlier. Jean?'

'Tell Ava –' I don't get to finish my sentence. Billy presses down my head, shoves me into the back seat. The door slams and we're off. 'Where's the wean?' says the driver. He looks familiar, one of the guys from Harry's bar next to the docks.

'Forget it,' says Billy, his chest rising and falling. He grabs my hair. 'Don't ever dae that tae me again,' he says. I feel my neck being jerked round so I'm facing towards the men in the front. 'Tried to attack her own mother,' he says.

The men glance at my tear-stained face and turn away. Billy releases his grip and I sink into the seat, wiping my cheeks with my palms, sniffing back the tears that keep on coming. Billy looks at me and laughs. 'This'll stop you greetin,' he says, and lifts the brown leather satchel onto his lap. I turn away, squeezing my eyes shut. 'Come on, hen, don't be like that.' This time his palm clamps onto the back of my head, forcing my face down. I open my eyes. The satchel is full of notes, green and blue and brown, not bundled in neat rows but crammed on top of each other, edge to edge, filling the space like leaves. 'Look at it, Jean, that's whit it's all about. The fruits of yer labour. Jist like you wanted. You and me, Jean.' His hands scoop my damp cheeks, lifting my face to his, his lips pressing hard against my mouth until I can't breathe.

2013
Pickering, Ontario

Ava is glad to be back at the old house, with its familiar weathered cracks. Removing her dark glasses, she unwraps the scarf she's been hiding behind for the past ten hours. She couldn't face talking to Wanda, so she waited until she got off the plane before calling her to say she was on her way.

It's strange seeing the place so empty. Even the Steinway has gone, the sound of its tinkling keys nothing but memories. All that remains in the front room are the two dark forbidding urns on the mantelpiece, and a dank earthy smell, like the onset of mould. At least the kitchen table and chairs are still there. Ava traces scratches on the surface of the wood. 'Scott played with his Matchbox cars on this table, do you remember?'

'Yup,' says Wanda. 'Cissy didn't let nobody get cute with her except him.'

Barney pours a Scotch and hands it to Ava. It's blended and cheap and stings the back of her throat. 'What's the occasion?'

Wanda's voice turns low and confidential. 'Sit down, honey.' Ava doesn't have the energy to argue. She takes a seat and finishes the rest of the Scotch in one gulp. The warmth soaks into her chest and up the base of her neck. 'I've been trying to call you,' says Wanda.

'I'm sorry, things have been… hectic.'

'It didn't seem right to leave a message. We thought you should see it for yourself.'

She follows Wanda's gaze to a slim brown envelope on the table. It's addressed to *Ava Newport*. The handwriting is different from the other envelopes, deliberate like a schoolchild's. A tight ball forms in Ava's stomach. Part of her wants to get back in her hired car and drive the hell away. She couldn't stand another anonymous missive from the past. Whoever this is better have something to say; she's done with games. Pouring herself another drink, she grits her teeth and gingerly removes the paper from its sheath.

November 2013

Dearest Ava,

I've never been that good with words, so I'll just try and speak plain. Jean, your mother, is still alive.

That will come as a shock, but I swear it's the truth. Now that Cissy's gone, it's up to me to put the record straight. Not that Cissy didn't have her reasons. At the time I thought it was for the best. I just wanted to brush it all under the carpet, pretend Jean never existed.

But a girl needs her mammy. As soon as you were old enough to understand, I should have let you know the truth. I was your Dad after all. I said as much to Cissy. But it was too late. I think that's why she told you I was dead, it was her way of protecting you. She wasn't daft. The longer it went on, the harder it got, and so I kept my gob shut. But there's no two ways about it. We failed you. And that's all there is to it.

I'm not asking for forgiveness. There's too much water under the bridge. The phone number at the bottom of the page is in case you want to get in touch with Jean. Though I should warn you that she's not how she used to be. The years have been kinder to me. I don't know why.

There's someone else you should meet too. In fact, if it wasn't for her, I'd never have had the guts to write this. But I suppose she'll be in touch in her own time.

In case I don't hear from you again, I want you to know that those short years when you were my wee lassie were the happiest times of my life.

Yours Tommy

A shiver runs through every vein and hair on her body. It's not what she expected, not what she expected at all. She bites her lip in a futile attempt to stop it trembling. Wanda's rosy face grows pale and she reaches across the table. 'Oh Ava, I can't imagine what you must be feeling. Your parents alive after all this time. But try to see it as a blessing. If there's anything we can do... if you need our help...'

'Cissy told me they were dead. How can that be a blessing?'

'God guides us and we have to put our trust in Him because, honey, we don't know the plan.' Ava's breath quickens. It's the *let's pretend everything is okay* voice, the kind you use on a child to stop it being afraid of the night, only it makes the darkness thicken.

Barney attempts to refill her glass, but she covers it with her hand. 'God? What's God got to do with anything?'

'Cissy was a good woman,' Wanda says, struggling to get up out of her chair. 'I don't think she meant to deceive anyone. Whatever she did, she thought it was for the best.'

If it wasn't for the fact that Wanda was here, with Cissy, while Ava was busy living her life, attending meetings, being Mrs Bruce Newport, then she wouldn't have time for this Wanda version of the world, all apple pie and rainbows. She exits the kitchen to avoid Wanda's arms – she can't breathe, can't surface. All she wants is fresh air.

In the garden below the porch, pale yellow flowers bloom in spite of the November rain. Gladioli. She remembers when Cissy planted them. Lies. All of it. It's selfish. Goddamn selfish. Who do these people think they are? They made their choices, based on their own needs, not hers, and suddenly, when death rattles the door, they want to put wrongs to right. Well, what if she doesn't want the truth? What if she was fine the way she was?

A memory of Cissy hanging a picture next to the coat stand: a watercolour of daffodils in a wooden frame. Whenever Ava came home and took off her jacket, her aunt would call, 'Mind the picture.' Stupid place to put a painting. There's nothing left for her here. This isn't her home, it never was. For all she knows, Tommy might not be her real father, and so what does that make Cissy? Nothing at all.

She goes back to the kitchen to gather her things. 'I'm tired. I need to find a hotel.'

Barney's mouth creases. 'There's more. I found these when we were clearing out the place.' He empties a Jiffy bag and they cascade onto the table: Christmas cards and birthday cards, faded pictures of butterflies and reindeer, one after another, like moving images: teddy bears – balloons – a robin. The writing inside is so like her own, but the words don't make sense, each card the same: *To my darling Ava. Love Mammy.* As though mammies were ten a penny, like they were falling from the clouds.

The firm but gentle grip of Wanda's wrist eases her into the chair, like she's a cloth doll, baggy and hollow, with no will of her own. The seat is surprisingly solid, her own voice strange in her ears. 'Where did you get these?'

'Under the creaky floorboard in the hall,' says Barney. 'It came loose when I was fixing it.'

One of the cards is ripped in two: a bicycle, with a red number thirteen. Cissy had bought her ice skates that year. She'd promised to take her to the rink downtown, Ava racing from the front door into cool April sunshine, only to look back and find Cissy shuffling frantically through the mailbox. Most of the mail she shoved back inside, except for one card. 'Is that for me?' Ava had asked, her thoughts full of secret admirers. 'It's nothing. Junk,' said Cissy, her hands swiftly ripping it in half. Later Ava had looked for the card in Cissy's bag, but it was gone.

The amount of times she stepped over that creaky floorboard in the hall, carrying Scott on her shoulder, rocking him to sleep. That's what makes her sick – other people knowing more about her life than she does.

'I wish there was something I could say,' says Wanda. 'All I know is that Cissy was my friend, and she was good and kind; she must've thought there was no other way.'

'It's not enough.'

If Scott was taken from her -- it doesn't bear thinking about because she wouldn't let it happen – but if it did, she'd go to the ends of the earth to find him, to know he was safe. It's not like she's had it easy with Scott. She had nothing. A teenage mother with a small kid. Even after she married Bruce it wasn't exactly a stroll on the beach. Watching her son lie all day in the dark, his eyes like two holes, not eating, not speaking. It was terrifying. She'd never been so powerless, so empty. But she wouldn't have left him. Not for anything.

Ava tips the cards and letter into the sink. The matches Cissy always kept in the kitchen drawer are still there. She strikes one up and holds it to Tommy's letter, the heat singeing her skin. Outside, the light fades and the sky becomes heavy with rain. In the muggy distance, a car door slams. What was it Cissy used to say when she got a bad feeling, that she'd just crossed paths with *auld Nick*? There's the sound of footsteps approaching, then a knock. 'I'll get it,' says Barney.

Ava grips the edge of the sink, her eyes on the floor. It's like her blood has stopped flowing, her legs tired of holding themselves up.

'I hope I'm not interrupting,' says a voice.

The furry ankle boots come into view first, followed by a blue suitcase. Then Susi.

The corners of Ava's mouth tighten. 'What do you want?'

One of the cards has fallen to the floor. It has a pink dress on the front, outlined with scissor-marks, the kind you cut out and hang on those old-fashioned cardboard dolls. There's a ribbon with a tiny silver key and the number eighteen: her last birthday before they moved to Pickering. Scott was born a month later. Susi picks it up and turns it in her hand, her face breaking into a smile. 'You haven't answered my question,' says Ava.

'We need to talk –' Susi's gaze shifts from Wanda to Barney.

'It's okay, they can hear anything you have to say.'

'Actually,' Wanda's cheeks flush. 'We've got to be going, haven't we Barney?'

'No, don't,' says Ava.

Wanda gives her arm a gentle squeeze. 'You know where I am if you need anything.'

Slumping into a chair, Ava pours a large measure of scotch. She waits till the front door clicks shut, then gives Susi a hard stare. Susi unzips her suitcase, takes a piece of paper from the inside pocket and pushes it across the table. It's the rubbing of her mother's inscription, the missing page from the book. Until now, no one has set eyes on it but her. She starts to smile, then her happiness turns to suspicion. 'Where did you get this?'

'I found it – the night Bruce got taken to hospital.'

Ava lifts the scotch. 'I think we better have a drink.'

★

She's on the floor in the front room, her coat covering her legs, something soft under her head. It's still dark, but the light in the window tells her dawn is not far off. Christ, how much did she have last night? She rubs her eyes and winces; they feel like two soft sponges of nerves. A recollection of sitting at the table, laughing at a word Susi used to describe Bruce; her mother had taught her it. Sounds like a slap. Twat. That was it. Bruce is a twat. For some reason, Ava found that hysterical.

The room swirls when she levers herself up. The inside of her mouth is bone dry. A suitcase is lying open on the floorboards. Susi's. There's not much inside, a few items of clothing and a toiletry bag. Ava wonders if it's a Zen thing, the sparseness of Susi's existence. Then it all comes into focus with a sharpness too real for this time in the morning: the faded greetings cards; Tommy's letter. *Your mother is still alive.*

Ava eyes the suitcase and has a feeling she's forgotten something important. A cold dread creeps under her skin. A misty image of a sweater being tucked under her head, an arm hugging her body, and a voice, like her mother's, telling her it's all going to be okay. It must have been a dream, an hallucination conjured in that fine line between alcoholic stupor and sleep. She gropes her way in the dark, past Cissy's urn, still unable to escape that feeling her aunt always gave her, that she was being watched, judged.

The hall is empty, the kitchen door shut. It reminds her of the door to her parents' bedroom in Paisley, reaching up as a small child to turn the handle, then climbing in beside two warm bodies. Both laughing because Ava had grown big enough to let herself in: *now there'll be trouble.*

The kitchen flickers with the light of a single burned-down candle, another of Cissy's emergency supplies. 'God, you startled me,' says Susi. 'What are you doing up?'

'I could ask you the same question.'

Susi's cheeks are hollow and her eyes wide. 'Couldn't sleep.'

The bottle of Scotch is empty. Ava runs the tap, cold water hissing into the sink. She catches it in her palms, its icy cleanness abrasive in her mouth. It's a moment before she takes it in: Susi hunched over the birthday card with the silver key, candlelight making it look like the dress is moving. 'It's beautiful.'

'You're still drunk,' says Ava.

'I'm sorry.'

'Look, forget it. I understand why you didn't tell me about finding the inscription, especially after everything with Bruce. Believe me, I've got other problems.'

'You accused Scott and it's all my fault.'

'What do you mean?'

'I wish he told me he was going to write to you.'

'Who?'

'Tommy.'

Ava feels her shoulders stiffen. 'What do you know about Tommy?'

'Yesterday I could see you were upset. The last thing you needed was me barging in with my size tens.' Susi gazes at the card and her face softens. 'Then I saw these. I'd no idea she'd sent you these.'

'Those cards are my personal property.'

'Not just yours.' Susi turns to face her.

'Pardon?'

'It's my life too.'

Ava rubs the bridge of her nose. 'Look, it was nice being friends, and I'm sorry if it seems unappreciative, but you've got to get on with your life.'

'It was *me*,' says Susi. 'The letters from Jean. I sent them.'

The words are like punches. Ava feels sick, can actually taste the bile rising from her stomach.

The candle sputters and the light dims. 'Jean is my mother.'

A heavy silence settles in the room. '*Your* mother – but?' Ava tries to finish the sentence. No sound comes out.

The sky outside has lightened, revealing dark hollows under Susi's eyes. 'Ava, I'm your sister.'

★

Gazing at the tables with their paper flowers and doilies, Ava wonders why she didn't choose somewhere else. Cissy used to drag her to this same café. They'd sit at the window while she examined the crockery, fussing over chipped cups or specks of dust. Ava sits in the corner, near the old Wurlitzer. Music drifts through the speakers above her head: *Only Sixteen*. At least it's not The Andrews Sisters singing about sitting under the apple tree. Cissy used to love that one. If she hummed it, you knew she was happy. The thought of it, Cissy's fake happiness, is enough to make her skin prickle.

For the past couple of days, she's been staying at a small hotel on the waterfront, not what she's used to, but it'll do. Bruce's twenty-four hour deadline has expired, and the first company-approved reports are already finding their way into the press. Most of them use the word, 'ordeal.' *Mrs Newport is very tired after her ordeal. A statement will be issued in due course.* No comments from Bruce himself. It'll take a couple of days for them to catch up with her, time enough for her to deal with this mess, with Susi. Wanda said she should give her a chance to explain. 'Try and see it as a blessing.'

The cafe starts to fill up, mostly elderly ladies on daytrips, shaking their wet coats, ordering tea and cakes, arguing about who's going to pay. From the corner of her eye she watches Susi wind her way between the chairs, waiting while this one sits down, or that one stands up. Ava doesn't acknowledge her, not until she's standing at the table. Even then she only steals discreet glances, watching Susi hang her coat on the back of the chair – trying to recognise something of her mother. All these years Ava hardly gave her mother a thought. No, that's not true. In her darkest moments, when she was pregnant and alone, or when Scott was at his worst, she'd think: if only her mother were here… *if, if…* but it hardly matters now, so much time has passed. The face in the black and white photograph means nothing to her anymore. Whatever happened to that woman, wherever she went, it's got little to do with Ava.

Susi gives a nervous cough. 'How are you?'

Ava shrugs. She can still hear it: the crack of her hand on Susi's face. She didn't have to think about it, just slapped her. Hard. No apology. Susi didn't say anything, just quietly gathered her things and left. Afterwards, Ava had sat staring into space until Wanda turned up that afternoon.

A waitress approaches and takes their orders. Despite the chink of crockery, the hum of café conversation, she can hear Susi's breath, is aware of the movement of her chest, in and out. When the waitress leaves, Ava says, 'Well, you wanted to explain. I'm waiting.'

'Where to begin…' Susi chews her lip. 'I understand how you feel. When I found out Mum had been married before, it was a shock. I had no idea I had a sister.' The words sound alien, as if Susi is talking about someone else's life, nothing to do with her. The waitress returns and clangs the tray onto the table: a cappuccino and Susi's herbal tea that smells like cut leaves. She's ordered a fairy-cake with a swirl of cream on top. As she lifts her cup, there's something defiant about her, a firmness in the line of her jaw. 'I thought me and Mum were close,' she says. 'But when I read the letters, knowing she could keep all that from me, I was angry. I wanted answers.'

Ava tightens her fist. 'You lived in my home under false pretences. You realise I could go to the police?'

Susi nods. 'None of that was meant to happen. You won't, will you? Go to the police, I mean?'

'Depends on what you have to say.' Ava stirs another sugar into her coffee and clinks the spoon loudly. There's enough sugar in it already but her hands need to be occupied. 'You said your father was from Hong Kong and has a restaurant in Chinatown. Is that true?'

'My stepfather.'

Ava doesn't blink, a hard-ball technique she learned from Bruce.

Turning her plate so that her cake rotates, Susi licks a spot of cream off her thumb, then shoves the plate aside. 'He had this saying, my stepfather, about secrets lying in shallow soil. He knew you existed, but Mum swore him not to tell.' Susi leans back in her chair. 'I know what you're thinking. But he can't be *your* father; they didn't meet until long after you'd gone to Canada.'

Ava has to hand it to her: she's quick. She takes a sip of coffee and it burns the back of her throat. 'Then who is?'

Susi smiles gently. 'I wish I could tell you.'

There's a long silence, filled by Pat Boone, *Ain't that a Shame?* It's difficult to bring up her name, to even introduce her into the conversation, though she's the reason they're both here. Ava's mind drifts back to Scott when he was little, rocking him to sleep, cooing into his ear, *'Mamma's little baby loves shortnin', shortnin'...'* She'd wonder if her own mother had kissed her toes the way she kissed Scott's, or rubbed her nose in her hair just to drink in that precious baby smell, like warm almonds.

'She talked about you, you know.' Susi's voice is quiet. 'At the time I thought it was all part of… part of her condition, the rambling, not knowing where she was… who *I* was.' Susi sighs deeply and her eyes wander over the table, over Ava's head. 'I used to put a piece of paper in her purse, with her name and number on it, whenever she went out, just in case. One day the police called; she'd been caught shoplifting, just walked out and forgot to pay. She was hysterical. Wouldn't let them touch her. It was the uniforms, they terrified her. She kept shouting, "No, no. Ava, Ava." It was the first time I heard her say your name.' Susi pauses as if to gather her thoughts. 'After that it got worse. One night I found her on the bathroom floor. The water in the bath was stone cold. She'd been there all night. I couldn't do it anymore, look after her on my own. I had to sell the flat to pay for her care. It wasn't much. Small. You could fit a hundred of them into your house in Victoria.' A half-baked smile.

'So she's –'

'In a nursing home. I was going through her paperwork when I found her letters, most of them written to you, tucked away in an old envelope in the back of a drawer – by then it was too late. I couldn't ask her about it, have any sort of conversation. The only person who I could go to, who might know something, was Tommy. It was a shot in the dark. I looked up the Voters' Roll and found his address in Paisley. I don't know who was more shocked when I turned up at his door, me or him.'

'You asked him about me?'

'It was like he'd seen a ghost.' She searches through her bag and pulls out a crumpled scrap of paper. 'At first he wouldn't speak to me, or couldn't. But I begged and begged. He told me to come back the next day, and then he gave me this.' She lays it on the table between them. 'It's Cissy's address. They used to write to each other. He knew you were married, was glad you'd made a success of your life.'

It makes Ava shiver, the thought of her aunt scratching secret words to Tommy, discussing *her* life, *her* son. Whenever she'd asked about the past, Cissy always bristled, so that not talking about it became normal. Ava put it down to grief, her aunt's belief that suffering was between a person and God. But it wasn't grief, it was guilt. Well, she's done with tiptoeing over creaky floorboards. This woman sitting in front of her knows nothing about who she is. 'You didn't need to come to Canada,' says Ava. 'You could have emailed, contacted my secretary, followed me on Twitter.' She glances down, feeling her cheeks flush. 'The way I see it is you thought you'd find your rich sister, get your feet under the table.'

'It wasn't like that.' Susi's eyes skim the vase, its single cloth carnation. 'I spent weeks drafting a letter, trying to explain who I was but it sounded so complicated, so implausible. In the end, I figured it wasn't my place. So, I sent Jean's letter to Cissy in an envelope with your name on it, and a note begging Cissy to tell you your mother was alive, that you had a sister. I hoped that would be enough; that Cissy would tell you the truth.'

'And we'd all live happily ever after?'

'Stupid, really.' Her eyes shift to the window and there's that same sad look – Jean in the photograph – then it's gone.

Ava sighs, fidgets with her napkin.

'I waited for months,' says Susi. 'When nothing happened, I decided if I could see you in person it would be easier, the right words would come.' She snorts. 'I decided to work in my stepfather's restaurant until I figured out what to do. I walked by your house sometimes. It was a whole other world – the gates and security cameras. I took one look and knew I couldn't find the guts. Just as I was about to give up, Bruce started coming into the restaurant. He joked about not being able to find a good housekeeper, actually I think he said "goddamn English-speaking housekeeper," and I offered my services.'

Ava coughs. It's like she's talking about finding a twenty-dollar bill in her pocket, not conning her way into someone's life.

'I remember when I saw you for the first time. I was in the kitchen. You had just got back from a function. Together you both looked – like something off TV, I suppose. Bruce kept calling me Susan, and complaining about how long I took to make his coffee. I was so nervous. "Don't mind him," you said. "His bark's worse than his bite.'"'

Outside, a loose gutter gushes rain onto the sidewalk. Ava flexes her fingers. 'The anonymous envelope that arrived at my home, with Jean's letter to Tommy? That was you too?'

Susi's fingertips trace invisible patterns on the table. 'The longer it went on, the harder it became. I'd no idea Cissy had left you Jean's letter in her will. I thought that if I didn't tell you, no one would. I needed a way to break the ice so it wouldn't come as such a shock. I hoped you'd confide in me, talk to me about it.'

'I never realised I was so intimidating.'

'Formidable is the word I'd use. Plus you have a mean right hook.'

Ava almost smiles, then stops herself. 'I trusted you, Susi. In all that time, you were the only friend I had.'

'I am your friend.' Her voice is loud enough for other customers to turn round. 'It was real. All of it.'

The waterfall running from the gutter has lost its confidence, become more of a dribble. 'I don't know what's real anymore.'

Susi lowers her eyes as if the answer might be under the table. *Furtive*, that's what Cissy would call her. 'Mary, Queen of Scots,' she says. 'We had that book on the shelf at home. I was never allowed to touch it. I used to read it secretly until, one day, it disappeared. That night, after Bruce's heart-attack, when I found the rubbing you made of the inscription, it changed everything: it meant you knew she'd tried to find you; that she hadn't stopped looking. When I got upstairs, the page was still in my hand; I don't know why I held onto it, maybe because it was a piece of her, how she used to be. It's what links all three of us together –' She clasps Ava's hand. 'In a few days, I'm going home, back to Paisley. Mum isn't doing so good. I want to be there, in case...'

Her muscles contract, and Ava pulls away. 'I don't see what that has to do with me.'

Across the table, Susi slides a small hardback book: a photograph album with a red fabric cover, frayed at the edges, the spine barely holding the pages together. 'Mum wanted Tommy to pass her letters on to you. But he didn't. Instead, that job has fallen to me. You'll find the rest of them inside. Along with my forwarding address.' Her smile is serious, but not unkind. 'This could be your last chance. If you change your mind, you know where to find me.'

★

The hotel room has a view of the marina. Wind lashes the sea, the little boats daring the waves to sweep and crush them beneath the current. The conversation with Susi reverberates in Ava's head as she scrolls through the business headlines. It's worse than she thought. One journalist has 'acquired' information about Scott's medical records, the usual kind of muck-raking. Bruce is getting nervous. To have one 'unstable' member of the family jump ship is unfortunate, but if he were to be followed by the boss's wife, that sort of thing suggests a loss of control. Not that Borealis couldn't weather that little storm, but it's the rocking of the boat; it makes shareholders want to offload their precious cargo. There's a voice message from Bentley, nothing overtly threatening, of course: 'Still waiting to hear from you about that matter we discussed.' Then a significant pause. 'By the way, how's Scott?'

It ignites all her worst fears. She has to know if her son is alright. Eventually he replies to her barrage of texts, his answer typically glib. *The only thing worse than being talked about is being ignored. X.* She admires him for the way he can laugh it off. Either that, or it's another manic phase. She couldn't deal with that right now. No, he's signing his texts with an X; that never used to happen. Things are good between them. If she tells him now about Bruce's threats, it'll ruin everything. *Hold tight*, she replies. *Love, Mom.*

Stretching out on the bed, she grabs Susi's album from the side-table; she needs a distraction more than anything; something to take her mind off things. The paper is old and brittle. Some photographs come loose and fall from the pages. Kodaks, square and compact. Most are black and white. A little girl with wisps of dark hair curling beneath a woollen hat. She's in a buttoned-up coat, holding onto a toy pram with a teddy bear perched inside. A woman kneels beside her. She has a scarf on her head and light hair that tumbles to her shoulders. Her face is sharper, more lined than in Ava's old photograph. She puts her hand over the woman's face so that only the eyes look out: sad, scared, the only place her smile hasn't reached.

In other photos, the little girl is a few years older, sitting on rocks at the beach, at the entrance to a castle, or at a picnic table surrounded by trees. In each of the pictures, Jean is beside her, her unsmiling expression searching the distance, as though waiting for someone or something to appear. There's a man, too, small, like Jean, with smooth dark hair and Asian features, wearing an outsized suit with huge lapels: Susi's stepfather. In the centre of the album there are no pictures, just two envelopes pressed between the pages, like the dried flowers Cissy used to keep in her gardening books. Thumbing open the first envelope, Ava gets that feeling all over again, like her blood is full of static.

April 1965

Beloved Ava,

I hoped I might have heard something by now. But Canada is that far away and I suppose it must be easy for letters to get lost in that big place. I can't believe it will be your birthday soon. Seven years old. Imagine. I wish I was there to see you open your presents. How on earth did you end up with a silly mother like me? I'm really sorry. I miss you terribly. I found this photo of me. It's outside the picture house in Paisley, taken on the day I met your father. I was much younger then, or at least it feels that way. I hope that sometimes you'll look at it and think of me. Be a good girl, love always,

Mammy.

She takes the photo of Jean from her wallet. In the background is the bottom edge of a poster: *Starring Elizabeth Taylor...* Ava switches from Jean's face to the letter, and tries to imagine her crouched over the page, but all she sees is the image of a tree, shedding its summer leaves, changing slowly year after year. Moisture fills her eyes and blurs everything into one. Then she hears a voice, her mother crouched in front of her, a loose strand of her hair brushing against Ava's cheek. There's a smell of hairspray and smoke. Always cigarette smoke. Then she's on the sofa, Jean patting the cushions for Ava to lie beside her, nestled in the warm curve of her hip. She's telling a story about how Mary, Queen of Scots was imprisoned in a big castle. Ava must have asked how big, because she says it was just as big as the mills, only instead of having concrete and chimneys all round, there was water, a big lake as far as the eye could see. In the middle of the story her mother closes the book. 'Do you know what I did today?' she says. 'I stuck my head out the window of the mill, right up on the sixth floor, and screamed, loud as, just emptied my lungs into the clouds. I don't know what came over me. Nobody noticed.' She giggles and Ava giggles back. Then her mother shifts, and Ava rolls into the warm empty cushions.

December 1968

Beloved Ava,

I know I've not written for a while. Tommy keeps sending back my letters. He wouldn't give me your address though I begged and begged. In the end I gave up. Anyway, I shouldn't blame Tommy. It was me who caused this mess. But things are going to change now. I'll find you again if it takes me months, years. I've done some terrible things, but the biggest mistake of all was losing you. My beautiful daughter.

I love you with all my heart,
  Mammy

Ava drops the letters on the bedside table. The past is like a mould that spreads and spreads, multiplying its tiny spores deep into her heart, till here she is, sitting alone in some hotel room, wondering what the hell to do with her life. She needs to put a stop to this once and for all. Fetching Tommy's letter from her bag she scans the number at the bottom of the page, then punches it into her phone and waits, staring out the window at the bobbing boats. The line clicks. A phone rings out somewhere across the grey Atlantic blur. Her heart is leaping against her ribs. Hair prickles up all over her skin. It's a recorded voice: 'Hello. You have reached Craigton Care Home. Press one...'

She hangs up. Outside, one of the little boats knocks blindly against the jetty, the ocean swell tugging at its keel, pulling at it.

PART TWO

2013
Paisley, Scotland

The cold hits me as soon as I get off the plane, like my lungs are breathing ice. I should be used to this. Winters in Montreal regularly plunge to minus ten. Cissy used to drum on about how wonderful it was to have a white Christmas every year: 'Look, Ava, look at all the snow.' But after Alex died, even she got sick of clearing the path every morning. I think she wanted me to love Canada more than any place on earth: if I was happy there, I'd have no need to think about the past, to wonder what might have been, or how the grass looked on the other side of the Atlantic.

She was right. I wish I could feel something about the town where I was born, but I don't. It's like I'm here on business, only instead of spreadsheets and projections, my briefcase contains letters, a bunch of tacky greetings cards and a dusty book about some long dead queen. Nothing to declare.

Susi has given me the address of a hotel not far from where she stays. She offered to meet me at the airport, but I didn't want her waiting for me in Arrivals, waving and pretending like we're the *Brady Bunch*.

Five o'clock. I glide down travellators, past the airport coffee bars, and hail a cab outside. Through the windscreen, everything has an oppressed look. The low clouds, the concrete, the roofs of the buildings, all huddled together in a grey haze, far removed from the brightness of Vancouver, where snowy peaks and steel towers gleam against a blue sky.

Here, night comes on fast, and eventually all I can see is my own reflection in the window of the cab. The hotel, The Rowan, is at the top of a small hill. Its namesake is in the courtyard out front, a gnarled ancient tree with branches that twist every which way, giving it the appearance of a hunched old woman carrying a sack of twigs. Compared to the straight-backed cedars and firs of British Columbia it's nothing more than a bush. Looking at it makes me smile. She's like the lone survivor of earlier days, of centuries long forgotten.

I'm checked in by a tall dishevelled man. This isn't one of those modern hotels with corridors like apartment blocks. It's an old building, Persian rugs on the floor, a wide staircase, and ghostly draughts that seem to come from nowhere.

As soon as I dump my bags I go down to the lounge. There's a roaring fire, and a red leather armchair that I sink into, then I order some tea. I've turned into one of those people who live in hotels. I used to wonder how they ended up that way. Now I know. They're nowhere people. Extras. Floating between the past and the future. People who, somewhere along the line, have been uprooted and haven't quite figured where they belong.

After half an hour staring into the flames, the thought of spending the evening alone, lying on a hotel bed, makes me claustrophobic. I finish my tea and go outside. A few stars poke through rags of grey cloud. The old tree has a copper glow, and I stroll towards it across the grass, my breath loosening clouds of steam. Removing my glove, I feel the texture of the bark, patting it in a friendly way. It's the sort of thing Ginny would do. God, I'm definitely losing it. I slip my glove back on and walk briskly down the hill.

It's cobbled and not easy to navigate in heels. At the foot, I turn onto what appears to be the main boulevard. Kids are yelling at each other across the way. I recognise the harshness of the accent, more Alex than Cissy, but they're talking too fast and I can't make out the words. Further along is a building in a simple neo-classical style, with a notice advertising library hours. Light shines from inside. I climb the steps to a glass door. Under a high ceiling, people click quietly at computers, or browse the shelves, some reading at tables or on soft chairs. There's a coffee machine, adverts for knitting groups, computer classes, mother and toddler mornings.

At the foot of a metal staircase a bucket collects drips from the ceiling. I climb up to the gallery and look down, trying to imagine Jean, with her pinned up hair, flicking through the pages of the books, reading the spines. I descend the staircase on the other side and find the biographies section.

There she is, Mary, Queen of Scots herself, sandwiched between Nelson Mandela and Marilyn Monroe. A modern, revised version, less wordy and with glossy photographs of castles and objets d'art, but it's still the same tragic tale, the spirited queen brought down by scheming men, only this time she's painted as less of a heroine, and more of a flawed human thwarted by her own perceptions.

She was forced to abandon her son when she fled. Or maybe she was just a bad mother. That's the trouble with the past, it can be manipulated so many ways, told and re-told till it's hard to know which version is true.

Craigton Care Home. The name has a glutinous sound, like it's sinking in mud. When I say it aloud, I get a horrible sticky feeling in my chest. Susi says it's best to 'take things at my own pace.' The trouble is I can't. What if I look at Jean, my mother, after all this time, and I feel nothing? Numb.

I sit on one of the soft chairs. A blonde librarian, her hair in a ponytail, gives me a concerned smile. 'Are you ok?'

'Just browsing.'

'Canadian, right? I have a cousin out there. I recognise the accent.'

'I was born in Paisley, but it's been a long time.'

'We have a heritage department if you're interested in tracing your ancestry.'

I hesitate. 'Do you keep a record of lost books?'

'Depends how far back. Why?'

'No reason.' I fasten my coat, and head outside.

The moon is slanted in the sky. Where the road bends, a large sandstone building rises out of the shadows, its gothic tower piercing the frozen clouds. I cross the street for a better look, warming my hands in my coat pockets. A man walking a small white dog nods as he passes. 'Bit cold the night, eh?'

I dig my hands in deeper. 'Sure is.'

He gives me a curious look. 'Impressive building, isn't it? Coats Baptist Church, the biggest in Europe, built by the mill owners –'

'Really?'

'Aye, so was the library and museum. Well, the owners made the profits, but the sweat of the workers built this toon. Only there's no many left that remember. They're all gone now, the mills. This used to be a thriving wee place, and look at it now.'

'My mother worked in the mills.'

'Oh aye, whit was her name?'

'Jean. Jean McParland.'

He stands still. I think he's going to speak, then I realise he's just waiting on his dog to finish peeing against a lamppost.

'Bye then,' I say.

'Aye, cheerio.'

My bones are warming up. The sky is crisp and cold and full of stars. I take a turning on the left, past a funeral parlour and another church, and find myself in a narrow street lined with Victorian sandstone apartments.

The tarmac on the road is worn, the smooth heads of the cobbles poking through. The apartments seem to enclose the narrow strip of sky and there's a dark dense feel, like walking through deep fog. I jump when a car pulls up to the pavement. A woman hurries from a doorway and cuts across me, dragging a small child. They bundle into the car, and I watch it disappear.

It gives me a strange feeling, like waking after a dream when all the images have faded. I don't know why, but I push the door of the building where the woman came out, and find myself in a dim passageway illuminated by moonlight shining through the back window. A flight of stone steps leads up to the next floor, where the window looks down onto a small square of grass and some drying poles. A low stone wall marks the boundary into the next yard. I have the silly urge to run along it, to go out onto the grass and spin round in the moonlight like nothing matters but this moment. Upstairs, a door creaks open and a voice calls, 'Is sumbody doon there?'

Part of me wants to answer, 'It's me, Ava,' but I say nothing, tiptoe quietly from the building, and out into the cold night.

★

For breakfast I have poached egg and toast that I cut into soldiers, just like when Scott was a boy. I've half a mind to switch off my phone. The news has been coming thick and fast all morning. Borealis is to be the subject of a government enquiry. I was notified by an intern; it seems I don't merit the attention of anyone above tea dispenser these days. The latest footage from Vancouver shows Sue Brash standing before the indomitable Captain Hastings, assuring the public of full transparency.

Bruce won't take this sitting on his haunches: he was so sure he had it under control, that the protests over Temple Grove would disperse with the injunction. 'We can only wonder,' says one reporter, 'how different the situation would have been for Mr Newport if his wife hadn't switched sides.' My appetite for breakfast evaporates, and I retreat to the lounge, rifling absent-mindedly through the display of tourist leaflets. Apparently, the last witch executions in Scotland were in Paisley. There's a tourist trail, culminating in a trip to the middle of a road junction where their bones are buried under a horseshoe to prevent them wreaking revenge on the town.

I imagine telling Bruce that story, though he doesn't believe in ghosts. Perhaps if I reminded him of that little boy he rescued on the seafront in Pickering, of the yachting trip they took on Lake Ontario where they called each other 'Captain,' or the sheer glee on Scott's face when he'd been allowed to take the wheel. Surely *that* means something. No matter how much time has passed, or how we might disagree, we're still a family, aren't we?

The wind shakes the sash windows and, outside, the old rowan tree surrenders a clutch of pale yellow leaves. I think of all the storms it's weathered. While I was living my life thousands of miles away, breathing in summers in Montreal and winters in Lake Ontario, that tree was still here, rooted to the exact same spot. I fling myself into the big red chair by the fire. The heat warms my skin, enfolding me like a protective body. Sleep comes swiftly.

When I wake, Susi is sitting across from me. I check my watch. An hour has passed since breakfast. 'How was the flight?' she says.

'Fine.'

She inspects me for a moment. 'It's good to see you. I wasn't sure you'd come.'

My eyes drift to the fire. 'It's not exactly the best time.'

'The enquiry?'

I nod.

There's an uneasy pause. 'I'll get us some tea,' she says.

'Old habits die hard, eh.'

She returns carrying a tray. I tip orangey liquid into my cup, add plenty of sugar and stir.

'Funny how neither of us takes milk,' she says. 'It's like those TV reunion shows where long lost sisters discover they have the same hairstyle, or drive the same car.'

'Those shows are set-ups.' I pour a drop of milk and stare as it turns the tea a weak beige. 'It's just DNA. I don't know what the fuss is about. We're like mountains that were once part of the same continent. It doesn't mean anything.'

She stares at me dumbly.

'I'm just saying, don't get too carried away.'

The skin on her neck flushes. 'You do want to see our mother, don't you? You haven't changed your mind?'

My tea tastes like it's gone off. We sit in silence for a moment.

Bright shards of light slice through the window and across the floor. Pushing away her cup, Susi coughs. 'I called the care home this morning. Mum's not too good. She needs bed rest. Best leave it a couple of days till she improves. If that's alright with you.'

I glance at my knees, wishing the whole thing was over with.

'Don't worry.' Susi stretches her fingers and beams a smile. 'It's nothing serious. We could go for a walk. Take your mind off things.'

I hesitate, then nod. There's nothing like a bit of fresh air to clear the head. It'll do me good.

In my fan-tailed coat I feel slightly overdressed. There's no sign of the sun-tanned women you see in downtown Vancouver, with their Aviator sunglasses and coiffured poodles. In Canada, these kinds of towns get turned into giant carparks. It's what Bruce would call 'under-developed.' Colourless, too, most of the buildings made out of the same drab sandstone, decaying under a flat grey sky and dirty-looking clouds. 'Mum says this used to be a great town, back in the day,' says Susi. 'There were shops, cinemas, dance halls. Now it's full of ghosts.'

The people look pasty. Uncle Alex was right about the sidewalks, hardly room to spread your arms. Cissy used to say there was no point in getting on a plane and flying halfway round the world when Canada had everything right on its doorstep: beaches, mountains, lakes, canyons, fourteen-lane highways and giant malls with escalators and automatic doors. 'Didn't you ever want to come back for a holiday?' says Susi.

'Not really. Bruce would go to London sometimes on business, but the rain depressed him. He preferred the Canary Islands, Monte Carlo.' I pause. 'He said Scotland was full of sheep and peat bogs.'

I can feel Susi's long, sympathetic stare, the kind of expression she wore when she made me those smelly teas, back in Victoria. 'You know, if you want to talk about it, I –'

'I'm fine, thanks.' I recognise for the first time that she has

Jean's round face: we both do, but Susi is darker, leaner, her jaw more set. She winds her green woollen scarf tightly round her neck and tucks her hands into her anorak. 'Show me where she worked,' I say.

'The mills? But –'

'Just take me.'

We cross a dual carriageway with a quaint little church up on the verge. I notice the witches' horseshoe in the middle of the junction, but say nothing, telling myself I don't believe in omens. Past the streetlights, the sidewalk is so narrow I could almost reach out and touch the traffic. We come to a shell of a building covered in graffiti, its front wall supported by scaffolding. A dilapidated pediment depicts a marble frieze of children and a schoolmistress gathered around a globe. 'This was the Half-Timer's school,' says Susi. 'Built in the Victorian era for the girls who worked in the thread mills. The only education they got.'

I look around, but all I see are streets and houses. 'So where are the mills?'

'Gone. Demolished.'

I feel slightly disappointed that we should have walked all this way for nothing.

'I'll show you where they used to be.'

More narrow roads. We turn down a street of identical houses with tiny square windows. At the end, a short wooden bridge leads over a stagnant river. In the reeds near the bank, a family of ducks swims through a film of green algae. On one side stands a red brick building with a clock tower, in the Victorian style. 'This was the Bridge Lane gatehouse,' says Susi. 'The big spinning mill was just behind it, on the edge of that housing estate. There were nine mills in total, storage depots, vans, even a fire station. Hard to believe it's all gone.'

Now I remember. This is where I stood when I came looking for my mother. I stop outside the arched entrance to feel the sandy brick, warm under my palm. Perhaps Jean's hand touched this stone, or that one, or that one. A gull flies overhead and lets out a screech. 'Come on,' says Susi.

The houses on the estate look bland, with identical porches and featureless strips of lawn. Somewhere, a car door shuts and an engine starts then fades into the drone of distant traffic. We follow the canal until we come to a large building made of buff sandstone, with pediments and tall sash windows. Rose bushes line the paved entrance, and there's an annexe with a roof garden and wisteria trained along the balcony. 'This used to be the Counting House,' says Susi. 'Where they kept the money, made up the wage packets.'

I picture Cissy going in and out the glass doors, her heels clicking efficiently on the stone steps, her glasses on a chain round her neck. I can almost hear the sound of her thoughts, ticking off her A to Z of tasks, immersed in the bustle of business. She would have thrived in a place like this. When I struggled with accountancy at university it was Cissy who told me which numbers went where. In the blink of an eye, she made neat little columns of income and expenditures, all standing to attention. It surprised me that she knew all that stuff. She could have run a business blindfolded, but she gave it up. For me. So she could bring up a child that wasn't hers. Now all that's left of that part of her is this one small outpost. Just a building.

We keep walking and soon the canal widens into a large pond. 'The twisting mill was right behind us,' says Susi. 'That's where Jean worked. Right up on the sixth floor.'

Reflections shimmer on the water: a row of box-shaped houses and blue sky. The mill has been erased from time; but knowing this is where it stood, the building that loomed over the first few years of my life, awakens something inside. 'I suppose you must have come here a lot.'

Susi thrusts her hands into her pockets. When she lifts her eyes they have a long saggy look that reminds me of a lost dog. 'Mum couldn't stay here, not after –' She looks at her feet.

'After what?'

'After she lost you.'

I stare into the pond. There's a bench along the bank and I sit down. Susi searches the water, then perches beside me with a loud sigh. 'Mum got a job as an orderly in the hospital at Perth, about seventy or so miles from here. My stepfather owned a restaurant and takeaway. She used to go there all the time. Mum was never keen on cooking.' Susi laughs. I notice how she relaxes. In Victoria there was always something apologetic about her. 'In a way they were a perfect match. Mum worked in the restaurant, serving customers, cashing up.'

'What happened?'

'He started going to the casinos, getting home late; she didn't like that. I used to hear them arguing. He got into debt, the business folded and – he went to Vancouver.' Her eyes cloud and she tucks her chin into her scarf. 'I'm sorry,' she says. 'It must be difficult – all this.'

Silence gathers. Clouds charcoal the horizon. On the pond, one of the ducks takes flight, clacking at a rival up in the shadows. 'She had an affair, didn't she?'

I sense the tension as Susi breathes in. 'Once, when I was ten years old, I asked Jean for a baby brother or sister. She covered her eyes and turned pale. I knew she was crying and I ran from the room. I thought I'd done something wrong. Other times I'd talk to her but it was like she wasn't there. I'd be tugging at her sleeve, then she'd notice me and smile, like she'd woken from a dream.'

'I don't get it.'

Loosening her scarf, she twists it in her fingers. 'Look, there are things that happened before I was born. Tommy can give you the answers you want. You need to hear it from him, get his side of the story.'

'It won't make a difference.' I get to my feet and walk towards the water.

'Maybe not, but at least you can decide for yourself.'

My feet are sore. I blow warm air into my hands, desperate for a hot drink. 'Come on,' I say. 'It's getting cold.'

We follow a cobbled road until we come to a terraced row of brick houses even tinier than those on the estate. Each block has a communal door and a threadbare patch of grass. The one Susi stops at has a wooden bird table out front. She presses an intercom. A curtain shifts in one of the lower windows.

An elderly man, with watery red-rimmed eyes, opens the door. He's wearing scruffy slacks and a red knitted top over a blue shirt. There's a look of pain about his stooped body, the muscles taut over his bones. 'Ach Tommy,' says Susi. 'You didn't have to come out.' A little dog yaps and runs onto the path, and I recognise the man from the Baptist church last night. He stares at me for what seems a long time. An image of arms and rolled up sleeves. Faces at the kitchen table. A man winking as he steals an extra piece of sausage from my plate.

'Ava.' His voice is papery and quiet. 'You must be Ava.' When he smiles, the teeth look too big for his mouth. 'I recognised the eyes. You have your mither's eyes.'

I bite down on my lip. My father. This small unassuming man, who chose to let me believe he was dead. I thought I'd know what to say, but I don't – I don't feel anything.

We go through a cramped passageway and into a room that smells of dog. There's a radiator on the wall, turned up full, and another heater in the middle of the room, giving off an orange glow. The air is frying. A game show plays silently on a TV in the corner. On a shelf are some china dogs and a wooden box shaped like a treasure chest. Most of the space is taken up by an armchair and a beige sofa with sagging cushions. Someone's head is visible over the backrest. 'Son,' says Tommy.

The face turns and a pair of hands circle the eyes like binoculars. I hold onto the door to keep me steady. 'Scott?'

'Hi, Mom.'

'I don't understand. What are you doing here?'

'I'm making my film.'

'Did you know about this, Susi?'

'No, I swear.'

'Aunt Susi, awesome,' says Scott.

Awesome is not the word I'd use to describe it. My thoughts are all over the place. Before I can formulate another word, Tommy wheezes and stumbles against the shelf. Susi settles him into the armchair and mutters her usual, 'I'll make some tea, shall I?'

In a shrunken voice, he whispers, 'Thanks, hen.'

The tiredness hits me all at once. Scott is staring at the ceiling, open-mouthed, as if it were St Peter's dome instead of lumpy artex and a dusty shade. 'So, Mom, how does it feel to be back in the street where you grew up?'

'Actually,' says Tommy. 'Our old house was demolished in the sixties when they got rid of all the slums, but it's still Newton Street.'

Slums. I've never heard them called that before. I imagine Bruce's face if he knew he'd married a Scottish slum girl.

'I'm fond of this place,' says Scott. 'It's got none of the gloss of Vancouver, but it's real. There's a truth about it, don't you think?' His limbs are bunched up, like he's too big for the room.

I'd wanted to keep him out of things, thought I'd be home before he noticed I was gone. 'How did you find out I was here?'

'Tommy told me. Surprise, huh?'

The air feels stuffed and awkward. I throw Tommy a look and he scratches his head. 'I'm sorry, hen. I thought you knew. It's as much a shock to me, as it is to you.'

'I doubt that.'

His eyes start to well. 'I thought I'd never hear my grandson's voice, then he phoned and said he wanted me for this film.'

'Working on a project together; it's the best idea I've had in years,' says Scott. 'We're the same, you and me, Mom, we both have parts of us missing.'

'What are you talking about? What project?'

'Ava Newport, successful businesswoman, meeting the mother she thought was long dead, discovering the past she never knew she had. *That's* my film. Pure dead brilliant, isn't it? That's what they say in Scotland.' He laughs, a vibrant, ringing sound. I remember Cissy used to say he had a *rare* laugh. 'And the best thing is, it's just making itself. It's a small production company called Carhorn, but I'm exactly what they're looking for, real stories made by real people.'

'You pitched them this idea?'

'No. *They* contacted *me*. A little thing called the internet.'

'These things don't just fall out of the sky, Scott.'

'In case you haven't noticed, we're all over the news right now. I guess that makes us kind of topical.'

'I'm only thinking of you. Do you even have a contract?'

'I'm an artist, Mom, not a businessman. When the contract's ready, I'll have a lawyer check it over. Promise.'

'I'm sorry. It's great, Scott, really great.'

There's the chink of plates and cups in the kitchen, the noise of a kettle being boiled. I lean into Scott and lower my voice, 'It still doesn't explain how you know *him*.'

'You mean Grandpa?'

Scott beams at Tommy, whose neck reddens under his collar. I think back to that day in Pickering when we found my birth certificate, how strange the word had sounded on Scott's lips: *Granddaddy*. Susi returns with a tray of cups and a plate of biscuits. Scott jumps up to catch the door, holding it open with his shoulder. 'I'll tell you later,' he says.

I dig my nails into my palms, tired of all the guesswork.

The old man takes the plate and holds it out. At the centre of each biscuit is a small red heart. 'Jammy Dodgers,' he says. 'These were your favourite.' I can't bring myself to take one. His hands are shaking and the tray makes a rattling sound. 'You'd go through these ten tae the dozen at yer Granny Senga's.'

I get a feeling of déjà vu. Then a memory of running up a flight of stairs. I'm wearing my favourite shoes: red leather with white soles. There's a blue and cream linoleum floor, and a mustard-coloured cupboard with a navy-blue biscuit tin inside. My hands are small and smooth. I have a biscuit in each one: white mallow and pink mallow with a strip of jam down the middle. There's a woman in an apron, something planet-like about her. She pats me between the shoulders. A mole on her cheek I'd try to avoid when I gave her a kiss. Then I'm in another room, sitting on the floor. In front of me, a small white dot comes to life. Pictures bloom on the screen: black and white puppets. A feeling of glee. I lick the coconut biscuits and laugh at the silly talking flowers. Behind me, someone is leaving. 'Bye,' I shout, without turning round.

Then the moment is gone, and I'm aware of Scott in the corner of the room, fiddling with a tripod. He makes a speech about seeing the camera as part of the furniture. But the possibility of this film becoming a reality, however remote, sets my teeth on edge. 'I'll no mind it,' says Tommy. 'I forget whit I said two minutes ago.' A feeble attempt at a joke. Breaking the ice only works if it's thin enough to crack. I try not to look at him, but I'm aware of his face shining on me, like a small moon. He attempts a gummy smile, and I shift my gaze to the ceiling.

It would be easier to talk to this man if we were total strangers, but we're not; I don't know what we are. For a while, no one speaks, then Susi stretches and rises from the sofa. 'It's probably best if you guys talk to each other alone. I'll make myself scarce.' She gives us all a sheepish smile and slips out the door. The dog gets up and pads around. It slumps in front of Tommy's chair and he rubs its neck.

Scott breaks the silence. 'Tommy was explaining what a double nugget is.'

'I'd get you wan fur a treat.' Tommy addresses the air between us. 'Chocolate coated wafer wae ice cream in the middle. You made a right mess –'

'She told me you were dead.' The words are out before I realise I've opened my mouth. I'm surprised at how childlike I sound, almost pleading.

There's a squeaky noise while Tommy shuffles in his chair. He's like one of the game show contestants on his TV, squirming under the lights, desperate to give the right answer. 'I suppose, by then, she thought it wis too late.' His voice is a whisper.

'Too late for what?'

He blinks, his eyes all big and doughy. Now it's his turn to sound pleading. 'Life goes by that quick. Ye try tae do things fur the best, but then it's too late and you've got tae live wae yer mistakes.'

I jab my finger into my chest. 'You let a child think her parents were dead. This child. So don't expect me to feel sorry for you, Mr McParland, because you don't deserve my pity.'

The old man's voice falters. 'I don't know where tae start.'

'The photo,' says Scott. 'The one of Grandma. Show him the photo, Mom.'

Reluctantly, I fish the faded image from my purse. Tommy gazes at it, hand shaking. 'Aye, that's her. On the day we started courting.' He pauses for breath, his voice soft and wheezy. She wanted you to have it. It wis the only thing a hers I asked Cissy tae give you.' He grips the armrests, and swallows. 'Letting you go tae Canada wis the biggest decision I ever hud tae make, and I regretted it every day. Ye're right tae be angry.'

The dog stretches languidly in front of the heater's orange glow. I look at Scott, his eyes absorbed in the camera's LCD screen. There's a determination about him, an energy I haven't seen in years. Despite everything, I'm glad he's here. 'Alright,' I say to Tommy. 'I'm listening.'

He takes a deep breath. 'Yer mither wis jist a wee thing, a right looker, mind. I thought I'd nae chance. I met her first at the dancing, stood on her toes aw night. Then I heard she'd taken up wae this Billy character. It wis a sin, a lovely lassie like her running roon wae his type, strutting aboot like he wis gallus. I suppose she thought he wis exciting, like Marlon Brando or something. Who knows whit wimin like?' He shakes his head and smiles. A pink glow rises in his cheeks. 'My pal, Archie, said it widny last. He wis right. Billy got the jail, best place fur him, and I took my chance. Right pleased wae maself I wis. Mairrit in two months. Thought I'd swept her aff her feet. Then you came along. It wis the best day a my life. My own wee lassie.' He grins, straightens the collar of his shirt.

My throat closes. It's too hot. The ceilings are low and I feel squashed, like I've been stuffed inside an old cardboard box. My palms are sweating. I stand up and try to open the window, but the catch is stuck. Tommy ambles over and undoes the latch. He smells of soap, like he's tried to scrub himself clean. Like all the years of lies could be washed off.

I sit back down.

The old man rubs his watery eyes and totters to his chair. 'After Senga had her stroke, that's when I knew. Jean told me some pack a lies aboot being at night school. The way she cuid look me in the eye wae the lies pouring out of her mouth. It wis him. He made her that way. It wis like I cuid smell him on her. She disgusted me after that. I didn't know whit tae dae. I thought it wid fizzle oot, like before.' He clenches his fist, an edge of anger in his voice. 'I should've known that bloody morning, dragging ye tae yer granny's at the crack a dawn, whit wis she thinking a? I thought maybe you wurny well and she wis keeping ye aff school, though Senga wis in no fit state tae watch a wean. I'd jist finished a shift and I wis lying in bed when Annie brought ye back roon. "Senga says ye've tae keep her here," she said. "And don't let her oot yer sight." I asked her whit wis going on, but Annie jist shrugged. "I don't know, Tommy. Best wait till Jean gets back." I cursed Jean under my breath, wondering whit in the blazes she wis playing at.' He pauses. There's something taut about his posture, hard and flinty, throwing out small invisible sparks. 'I made you egg and chips, only the egg wis burnt underneath and the chips were half-cooked. There wis a wee cake on the table that you'd left fur me that morning. I couldny look at it. A while later, the door went. Annie again, staunin there pale as snow. I knew whit she wis gauny say afore she opened her mooth. Jean and Billy. Run off thegither. Jean wis wanting tae take you with her – with *them* – but Senga pit a stop tae it. I didny say anything, jist shut the door and sat back down at the kitchen table. You dipped your breid in the yoke. "It's lovely, Daddy," you said. That broke my heart.'

The dog gets up and wags its tail, puts its paws on Tommy's knee. He rubs behind its ears. 'What's his name?' says Scott.

'Polson.'

He films Tommy petting the dog. When Tommy finally goes to sit down, he pats my shoulder, as though I need to be petted too. I keep perfectly still. Tommy shifts in his chair. 'I knew that you were better off wae Cissy, that I couldny look after ye. I didn't ask her to tell you Jean wis dead. Or me fur that matter. I didny find out till it wis too late. Cissy convinced me it wis fur the best. There wis nothing I could do after that. There wis no going back.'

'You could have told the truth.'

He doesn't answer. Instead, he stares absently at Polson. 'After a while, Jean stopped wae the letters. She knew it wis useless, that I widny pass them on. Then one day, six years later, there she wis oan the doorstep.' He takes a sharp inward breath. 'I knew it wid happen, but the sight of her wis still a shock. I'd got mairrit again, ye see. Tae a lassie she knew fae the mills. Wee Angie. God rest her. Jean jist walked right intae the hoose, like it wis her ain, and stood by the window. Angie wis out, thank Christ. I thought of how you'd stood by that same window the night yer mither ran off, waiting fur her tae come hame, and I cuid feel the anger rising in me. She looked older. No wae age, mair a sort a weariness, like the lines roon her mooth and eyes had hardened. Her hair wis tied back, and it made her face look sharp. Bit there wis a sadness tae. Fur a moment, I felt pity. Then she said, "Tommy, you know whit I want. Jist tell me where she is. I've a right. I'm her mither."

I told her she couldny jist turn up and expect everything tae be the same, that she made her bed the day she took up wae *him*. Of course, she claimed it wis nothing tae dae wae Billy. "A girl needs her mither, Tommy," she said. I grabbed her arm, pushing her down the hall. I can still hear her voice, the way it cracked when she spoke: "You're her faither. Honest you are. You're the one brought her up. She's your name. Jist like me. Your name, Tommy."

"My name? Is that aw?" I said. She didny answer. I wis having none of it. I said, "The lassie's wae Cissy and that's where she'll stay."

She wis crying and begging me fur an address, saying how sorry she wis and that Billy meant nothing. I mind how her body stiffened like a rod and her legs buckled as I forced her tae the door. "Get out and don't come back," I said. "Ye're no wanted here." I slammed it shut. She banged and banged, shouting, "Please, Tommy, she's my daughter, my own wean." Then efter a while, it wis silent again. That wis the last time I ever saw yer mither.'

Tommy's chest makes rapid jerky movements as he tries to catch his breath. He slumps back in his chair. Scott goes to fetch him a drink of water, but Tommy can barely hold the glass and Scott has to keep it in place. There's a tenderness about him that I've never seen before.

'Surely you could have stopped her?' I say.

Tommy's old face shines back at me. 'Jean wis her ain wumin.'

'I'm talking about Cissy.'

He shifts his gaze to the shelf with the china dogs. 'She had her reasons.'

Scott sits down. 'You asked me how I knew about Tommy? There was some stuff in a box in Pickering. I wanted to tell you about it, but –' He jerks his head, like he's trying to shake something out of his hair.

'Talk to me, Scott. I'm your mother.'

He stares into the worn carpet. 'You know it's not easy, being your son. Ginny said I should give you a chance. All this stuff from the past, finding out Grandpa and Grandma are still alive –' He slaps his head, making me jump. 'It's happened for a reason, Mom. It's meant to bring us together. Don't you see?'

My heart sinks. We've been here before, Scott looking for signs, like life is all a big game, a great mystery that he can solve by attaching meaning to some random set of coincidences, followed by the inevitable crash, the disappointment when he realises it's just not that easy.

Tommy pats his shoulder. 'Give her the box, son.'

Lifting the treasure chest from Tommy's shelf, Scott holds it towards me at arms' length, like he's poking it through the bars of a cage. It's heavier than it looks, with a rusted clasp and engraved seaweed, mimicking something that's been buried at the bottom of the ocean. 'Open it,' he says.

I unfasten the clasp and lift the lid. There's a musty smell, like a second-hand book store. Inside is a bundle of blue airmail envelopes wrapped in an elastic band. They're addressed to Cissy in Montreal.

'I found it in that yellow suitcase under Cissy's bed,' says Scott.

'This isn't Cissy's.' I put it on the table. 'I've never seen this before.'

'Come on, Mom, it's real. Everything you want to know is there, inside that little box.'

A feeling of panic swells inside me. The more I try to hold it back, the more it threatens to engulf me. 'If it's so important, then why didn't you tell me you'd found it?'

Scott pushes the hair from his face. 'I wanted to, but the things you said that day in the car, and then the way you accused me of sending those letters. I was angry. I decided it was up to me to choose what to do with it. It was like having something all of my own, that you couldn't control.'

'You make me sound like a monster.'

'Not all monsters turn out to be bad, Mom. Not even Cissy.'

'It's been a shock fur us aw,' says Tommy awkwardly. He reaches out to grip my hand. I don't have the strength to let go. 'I'm so sorry,' he says. 'Losing you, Ava, it wis the worst thing that ever happened tae me. But, please, don't be angry wae Cissy. Read the letters. Try to forgive her.' His red-rimmed eyes look into mine.

'Tommy,' I say. 'Are you my father?'

His face softens and melts. He glances at the black and white image of Jean on the table, and I think if he could climb into that picture to stand beside her, he would. I feel sorry for him then, can't help it. Despite everything, there is love in those eyes, after all these years. He flings me a helpless look. 'I don't know.'

Dark spots of rain splash the pavement. This is the same street I found myself in last night. I go to the door where I saw the woman and child, and push it open. I know this place well. The apartment on the lower floor used to have a pram in front of it. An older woman sat by the fire, all dressed in black with a scarf over her head. I was scared of her, the way she always dribbled.

Upstairs was my nana's house. I remember that evening when I found her lying on the floor, her mouth slack and drooling like a baby. How I'd run downstairs and gulped for air. There was a game I used to play on the back green where I'd mount the low brick wall and pretend to be a tightrope walker, arms spread and chin held high. Driven by impulse, I go down the short steps and out the back. The wall is still there, only smaller. I hitch up my skirt and stretch my arms for balance. As I hobble gingerly along the uneven surface, that old memory flashes through my mind: my mother pulling me behind her, the vapours of her cigarette floating above us like steam, her plastic coat brilliant white against a dim sky; me wishing she'd slow down, a feeling of excitement, of knowing something was different.

A window opens and a voice shouts, 'Whit you daein doon there?' Quickly, I jump off and run into the street. I don't stop till I reach the corner, gasping for breath.

The library is still open, lights blinking against the darkening sky. There's a door marked 'Heritage Centre' just inside the entrance. Its only occupants are an elderly man reading a newspaper, and a student scribbling notes beside her laptop. Taking off my coat, I sit at one of the long wooden tables and place the treasure chest in front of me. It's not a treasure chest at all but a vintage sewing box with two tiers inside. The letters are on the top and, underneath, is a skein of navy embroidery thread labelled with the same circular chain logo as on Alex's tie: *J & P Coats*. I loosen the envelopes from their elastic band. There's a card with a single lily on the front and the word 'Condolences,' signed 'from all at the Counting House.' It must have been posted to Cissy after Alex died. I realise I miss him, more than ever.

Most of the letters are in Tommy's deliberate hand, written not long after we moved to Montreal. The old Newton Street address is in the corner of each one. It would have been easy enough for Scott to trace. A simple matter of checking the voters' register. Tommy never moved from that address, as though he spent his whole life waiting to be found. The first letter mentions my nana being in hospital, how it's *touch and go*. A few months later, he says simply, *Senga died*. After that, there's nothing, not for four years, when he writes to announce he's getting married again.

Tommy said I should forgive Cissy, but this only makes it worse. I never saw my nana after we left. She took her away from me too. I'm about to give up hope of finding anything significant, when I notice a brown envelope with heavy handwriting that isn't Tommy's. It's dated January 1963:

Dear Cissy

We haven't spoken much, except maybe in the office once or twice. We all thought your Tommy was a fine fellow. I wish my man was more like him but he spends most his time seeing double. The office gave me your and Alex's address. We thought you might want to see this. I hope it reaches you ok. I put an extra penny stamp on it just in case. Una is doing alright. It's quite a bad wound on her hand and she can't move it but she says it's no worse than her shingles and at least it's not infected. She sends you her best. We'll look out for Tommy.

Maggie (from Twisting)

There was something attached to the top corner, but whatever it was is long gone, leaving only a rusty staple. I don't understand what's so important about someone's shingles, and I've a good mind to call Scott and ask him what he's playing at. But there's only one more letter in the box. It's in matching cream stationery, stamped with a fleur de lis. Inside the envelope is a newspaper clipping of a woman holding a big bunch of flowers, with others gathered on either side, dressed in their best hats and coats. She wears a determined expression, and has big beefy arms that look like they'd rather strangle the flowers than hold them:

December 1968

Dear Cissy

There was many times I thought to write but, I never did. I can't check at the office if its the right address because I'm not at the mills anymore. I was the last worker to get a long, service certificate but they made an exemption just for me probably they knew the fuss I could kick up if they didnt. Sorry I've not told you my name yet its Una McMenemy. I worked with Senga Owen and youknowwho. Poor Senga every time I think about her I feel like greetin God, rest her. I'm getting on myself now so I'll likely be joining her soon but I didnt write to tell you all about me. Theres bean a bit of trubble here not that I'm one to tattle but I saw it all with my own 2 eyes or as much as I can see at my age. All those years splicing skinny bits of threid has made my peeper's go doolally. I bet its nice in, Canada. I declare you wouldn't know the place, here. Theyve recked most of George Street and built a big block of flats on the corner at Maxwelton that are quite welltodoo. If you were in Paisley you might be in one yourself though I said to Maggie I wouldnt fancy going up and down in the lift what with my blood preshure but I'm still not bad on my pins. Anyway I'll get on with why I'm writing. I like to go and watch them put up the new houses and sometimes I bring a bit of stale breid and keep going up the canal and feed the duck's. That's what I was doing this day only when I go past the old school I hear the carryon and there is Maggie and Myra Broon and Aggie and others on the bridge. Maggie has her arms folded and she only ever does that if shes about to have a go so I look across the bridge and who do I see but youknowwho all dolled up to the elevens in one of those mini-skirt's. Not that I'm surprised the front of her. She wants to know where the wean is and starts greetin for them to tell her. Maggie says that she should leave well alone and that Tommy and the lassie are the better without her but Jean Miss Nibbs threats to go to the office and ask your address from Mr Green so Maggie says and I think shes quite right just try and come across that bridge and see what happens. She starts greetin but Maggie says they were alligator tears and thats a fact, anyway she wasnt excepting to see me standing right behind her because Maggie saw me coming the whole time but never let on. I say if she wants to go near that mill she will have to go through me. Well she didnt know what to say and this is the best bit Cissy. Bold as brass she says how are you Una. Am sure you agree its a front asking me how I am after all thats gone on. Thats when I do it. I crack her one across the cheek, its been a long time coming and I have to hold on to the wall of the bridge so I dont fall because I wouldnt give her the satisfashion. Then I tell her to go back down Maxwelton Street and keep walking and never let us see her in this Toon again. I think she might start greetin again but she doesnt which I think shows her true colours because if it was me I'd be black affronted. She runs away which is all she is good for and the last we see of her is at the corner. I don't mind telling you Cissy my hands were shaking. My scar which you probably have heard about was as red as John Knox in the poolpit. Theres not much more to tell than that. Please dont mind my writing to you only if it was me I'd want to know. And If your Tommy happens to ask you can tell him Jean Owen will be bothering him over my deid body.

Una

PC. Herewith is a photo from the mill paper of me on my retirement day just so you can put a face to the name.

I look at the woman's hard stare, and try to remember what I was doing while my mother was being slapped across the face by Una, strangler of flowers. I was at school. Even by then Scotland had become a mythical place. The Old Country. Just words.

I think of the Counting House with its big windows and double doors, of Cissy working behind a sturdy Victorian desk, surrounded by wooden cabinets and drawers, filing away folders, keeping records of wages, job descriptions, pensions, her forwarding address. I think of the birthday cards under the floorboard. Her ashes still on the mantelpiece in Pickering. Cissy, whose only dream was to travel across Canada on the Canadian Pacific line and see the great lakes, the prairies, the mountains. She never did understand how it could be snowing in one province and blazing sun in another. How taking away someone's child can have consequences.

'Hello, here again?'

I look up. It's the librarian from the other night. 'Can't keep away,' I say.

She glances at the sheets of crinkled paper strewn over the table. 'If there's anything I can help you with –'

'That's alright.' I smile.

'Have you lived in Canada long?'

'Yeah, most of my life. My mother is from Paisley, a mill worker.'

'My grandmother was a mill girl,' she says. 'Who knows, if things had been different, you could have been one yourself.' She laughs a big toothy laugh, and walks away, her ponytail swinging. Well, this was a waste of time. I'm about to tidy away the letters and shut the box, when I notice a small envelope, the size of a gift card, in the lower compartment. It's blank, weightless. There's no letter inside, just a yellowed section of newsprint. I open it and read:

Mother Sent to Prison

Jean McParland, mother of one, from Newton Street, Paisley, was sentenced at the High Court yesterday to six years in prison, on charges of aiding and abetting a robbery, with additional charges of assault and grievous bodily harm. The robbery took place in November at the premises of J&P Coats Ltd, Ferguslie. Mrs McParland admitted allowing three armed men into the premises. The men then proceeded to assault the finance manager, Mr Thomson, causing grievous bodily injury. Mrs McParland also seriously injured a mill worker who attempted to gain access to the premises during the incident. The men, accompanied by Mrs McParland, made off with three thousand pounds in cash before being apprehended by police the following week. William McBride, also of Paisley, was sentenced to ten years imprisonment for his part in the robbery. The other two men are from Glasgow and due to be sentenced next week.

I read each word again, thinking I might be mistaken. I can barely focus, there are so many questions bubbling through my brain. Part of me wants to blank out the whole thing. The corner of the paper has a small rip. Then I remember Maggie's letter. Wedged beneath the rusted staple is a very small sliver of paper. I work it loose with my nail, then try and fit it to the clipping's wrinkled edge; it's a match.

The clock ticks slowly. Nearly ten minutes pass before I can stand up. It's like I'm seeing the room through the wrong end of a telescope, the librarian's desk miles away. I inch forwards, one foot then the other. My mouth is so dry I can barely speak. 'I'm looking for – local paper – 1962.'

'Are you okay? You look a bit pale.'

'I'm fine.'

The ponytailed librarian crosses the room and disappears through a set of double doors. I sit down at the nearest desk until she returns with a hardback folio, the size of a broadsheet. She tucks a book rest under it and places it on the table. 'Can I get you anything? Water?'

'Please.' The folio weighs a ton. It contains every edition of the *Paisley Daily Gazette* for 1962. I turn the pages in thick bunches, skipping over columns of narrow print. How did people read stuff this small? Then I find it, glaring at me from the December edition: the same report. That name again. William McBride. Billy. A shiver runs through every nerve. They knew all along, Alex, Cissy. They knew and they didn't tell me. *Read the letters, try to forgive her.* But how can I? All I feel is betrayal. Anger. I'm gripping the paper so tight my knuckles go pale, the veins on my hands popping like elastic. I wish the wind could blow the words off the page, make them nothing to do with me. My mother. An armed robber. Una and her angry red scar. She did that. It doesn't make sense. The photograph with the sad eyes and soft face. The white coat, and me tagging along behind. I think of how I lashed out at Bruce when he threatened Scott, but could I actually hurt him, cause grievous bodily harm? Then I remember Susi, the clapping sound of my palm against her face, but that's different. Isn't it? I was upset, confused. Desperate.

I start to feel cold, as though the big library windows have been blasted open, letting in swirls of stinging Arctic air. My stomach aches like it's been punched from the inside. So this is why Cissy lied; better for a child to think her mother is dead than to tell everyone she's a convict? 'Did you find what you were looking for?' says the librarian.

I jump. She hands me a plastic cup of water but I can't hold it steady. There's water all over my shoes, the floor. I run from the room with my hand covering my mouth and a stomach-full of nausea, the sour taste rising in my throat.

When Scott comes down for dinner, he looks freshly showered, his hair still wet. We managed to get him a room in the hotel. The restaurant is small, only six tables. I've chosen the one nearest the window. There's a display of photographs, a local society's exhibition of nature scenes: white streams, purple hills, bronze sunsets. He squints closely at a group of funny looking birds gathered on a cliff. Then he pulls out a chair and sits down, his elbows on the table. 'Did you read the letters?'

'I –'

'Mom.'

'Yes, I read them.'

'Who'd have thought it?' he says, taking a bread roll and ripping it with his hands. 'The daughter of Bonnie and Clyde. Well, Bonnie anyway. Tommy's not exactly outlaw material.'

'Scott!'

'Come on. It's kinda cool.'

'Cissy didn't think so.'

He rubs his fingers on his napkin. 'I didn't know what to think. Part of me believed you'd known about the robbery all along; I mean you were acting kind of strange in Pickering.'

'You misjudged me.'

'I'm not the only one with poor judgement. You actually believed I was capable of a hoax – on my own mother – that hurt.'

'I'm sorry, I was wrong.'

'So, don't make a decision until you know the facts.'

'This isn't the same.'

'Why not?'

'She's a criminal, Scott.'

He studies my face. 'And what about you? This whole enquiry thing?'

'That's different.'

'Really? Illegal logging is against the law. That's what makes it illegal.' He widens his eyes. 'You know Kelly has resigned?'

'To spend more time with his family.' I pick up the menu.

Scott plucks it from my fingers. 'He's jumping ship, trying to wash his hands of the whole thing, preserve his ministerial legacy. You know it's bullshit.'

It's true, something stinks. I'm familiar with Bruce's opinions on ancestral land rights, how prime forest has got too much value 'for a bunch of alcoholics to build their wigwams on.' Kelly and his predecessors haven't enjoyed Bruce's backing for nothing. All it takes is one leak. Any evidence of malpractice and Bruce can say goodnight to his licence for Temple Grove. 'If it's to do with the latest allegations,' I say, 'I handed over those contractors on a plate. If Bentley can't make that story stick –'

'Then it'll be you who takes the heat.'

'Better me than –'

'Than who?'

I shrug and fold my arms. 'When you take on something like this, there are consequences.'

'So act if it bothers you that much.'

'What can I do?'

'Speak at the enquiry.'

I lean back and cross my arms. 'Absolutely not.'

'That's not the mom I know. I thought you had more guts.'

I snort. 'How can I appear as a witness when my own mother is a convict?'

'Once this film comes out, you'll be like...' He points at me across the table. 'Who's that dude in the Bible who turned right-eous on the road to Damascus?'

'Paul?'

'Yeah, him. People will see you for who you really are.'

'Great. The daughter of an armed robber.'

Scott laughs and steals the roll off my plate. 'What's wrong with that?'

'Seriously, Scott. I don't want you getting involved. Bruce has influence. He can make things difficult.'

But Scott's not listening. He beckons the elderly waitress, who's been waiting patiently on our order. 'What's your impression of my mom?' he says.

Her cheeks pinken. 'Oh, well, I –'

'You don't think she's a serial killer, do you?'

'Oh no, of course not.'

'Did you know she's here to meet her long lost mother? Hasn't seen her since she was four years old.'

'My goodness, that's a long time.'

'She was an armed robber, you know.'

'Scott!' I apologise, making excuses that the air's got to my son's head. We order traditional steak and kidney pie and the waitress disappears to the kitchen.

'See,' says Scott.

'See what?'

'Here you are, about to meet your dead mother for the first time in over fifty years. That's what my film is about. Besides, what better way to gain back public sympathy? Play Bruce at his own game. It'll be the making of us.'

After dinner, I flick through the papers in the lounge, glancing up now and then to watch Scott taking shots of the ceiling, tables, vases of flowers.

My mind drifts back fifty years, to that big liner with its red and black funnels, sailing across the Atlantic, crowds of people waving from the docks, and how, while I was asleep in the bunk, my mother was in a cell somewhere. A draughty cell, like in the old movies, with a barred window that lets in the wind and cold, her only furniture a narrow bed pushed against a bare stone wall. All that's missing is Jean herself; she's the only thing I can't picture.

When the waitress walks past, Scott gets her to say her name into the camera. She blushes. I never knew he could be so charming, and I think of what he goes through to reach that point, the mania, the self-doubt, the depression. He's not like me, not really. Despite my hippy artist phase, I've always had a sensible side, a practicality that kicked in when it was needed. Maybe Scott is more like her, like Jean: impulsive, restless.

The window reflects his image so that he seems to be walking towards me on both sides. Manoeuvring the camera, he says, 'How do you feel about your mother, now that you know what she did?'

I stare into the lens, see my upside-down reflection, and imagine the topsy-turvy world being captured within. For a split second, I'm a child again, in Newton Street, my mother showing me how to dance, twisting on the balls of her feet so that her hips shake; she looks like she's from another world. When she throws her head back and sings, it's the best feeling ever. I want to press my face into her swinging hips and never let go.

That's all it is, a collection of images. The truth is that the entire course of my life is the result of somebody else's mistake. The newspaper clipping flashes into my head. *Mother Sent to Prison.* It gives me a strange shiver to know the word refers to me, even obliquely. That somehow I'm part of this crime, this robbery. If it wasn't for me, she'd simply be *Woman Sent to Prison.* But she's not my mother. Mothers organise birthday parties, help with homework, explain to their daughters the awkward ritual of menstruation, warn them about boys, listen to their daily tribulations. My mother is nothing more than ink on a page. These letters, these articles belong to her life, not mine. They're from another time and place. I've got my own problems. 'Disappointed,' I say. 'I feel disappointed.'

'A few weeks ago you were in a prison cell, just like her.'

'It's not the same thing.'

'Why not?'

My cheeks grow warm. 'That was an accident, I wasn't irresponsible.'

'Wow,' says Scott, and laughs.

'What?'

'You sound exactly like Cissy.'

★

I'm walking through the corridors of the hotel. It's windy and I need to fight the draughts. I'm searching for something I've lost, but each time I open a door, a gust from inside sucks it shut. Hundreds of sheets of paper are blowing past my ears, sticking to my arms and legs. Pages and pages. I try to catch them, but they slip through my hands. It's late. I have to get to work. But I can't find the right door. At the end of the corridor, I make out someone playing a piano. Cissy. She turns towards me, her mouth opening and closing, but I can't hear a word.

Gradually I'm aware of light entering the room. My eyes open and I sit up in bed and check my phone. Ten o'clock. A vacuum cleaner whines along the corridor, there's the sound of footsteps and the tinkle of distant crockery. A hotel has rituals, routines. Life goes on. Inescapable, exhausting. I curl into the foetal position and imagine my mother waking up on that fateful day, how she felt knowing she was about to take part in a robbery; whether any part of her told her it was wrong; and how she silenced that ghost of a voice.

Eventually I roll over and get out of bed. I get dressed and go to find Scott, but his door is locked. 'Scott, it's Mom.' No answer. Downstairs in the dining room the waitress is arranging fresh cups and napkins on the tables. 'Excuse me,' I say. 'Has my son been down today?'

'Yes, he left a message at the office. It's through the lounge and on the right.'

The tall, dishevelled man who checked me in is sitting at an equally untidy desk. I knock on the half-opened door. He begins rifling through a drawer. 'This is for you, I believe.' It's a piece of hotel stationery on which Scott has scribbled a hastily drawn map with a set of footprints leading to an address, and the words: *Susi's house.*

'Up the cobbled path and around to the left.'

'Thanks,' I say.

'An unfortunate business that.'

'Excuse me?'

'I saw your photo on the news. We quite often get celebrities staying here. I have to say, you look much better in the flesh, which isn't true of all of them, you know.'

I almost thank him for the compliment, then remember my status as Bruce's conspicuously absent wife. The corners of my mouth twitch.

He gives a discreet smile. 'We had Lance Armstrong once,'

he says, as if to assure me that all kinds of the fallen are welcome.

The path is enclosed by high walls that amplify the sound of my heels. I follow Scott's map, passing an observatory of all things – a Victorian structure with a bronze dome – and, next to it, a small building with 'Philosophical Society' etched in gold on a pane above the door. Susi's apartment is two blocks down. I buzz the intercom and enter a tiled hallway that smells of dust and dried grass. Susi opens the door of the apartment to my left, and a strange chanting sound drifts from inside. 'It's Mongolian throat singing,' she says.

'Whatever floats your boat.' I'm not in the mood for small talk.

Going inside is like walking into some weird cult. I haven't burned incense in years, and the spicy taste hits the back of my throat. 'Scott says you went to the library yesterday?' She stares at me expectantly. 'I gave him a massage to calm his nerves. I could do one for you as well if you like.'

I cough. 'No thanks.'

The door opens on one of the rooms, and a barefooted Scott emerges, wearing a Paisley scarf and some kind of wooden beads. 'You're such a prude. Did you know Aunt Susi is a qualified aromatherapist? That Mongolian chanting is *soo* dope.'

'It's about finding your own frequency,' she says. 'Once we release that blocked energy, things just click into place.'

'Well,' I say. 'Things sure have clicked into place.'

There's a high-noon moment, each of us looking at the other, and I wonder how it came to this, all of us standing in an apartment in Paisley, brought together by an event that happened years ago, that few people probably remember.

'If you don't mind, I think I was on the verge of enlightenment,' says Scott, and retreats again, shutting the door.

Susi shows me into a room with laminate flooring and a corniced ceiling. A tiled fireplace has been painted white and filled with fat candles. There's a Buddha on top of the mantelpiece, framed calligraphy prints, and incense sticks in elephant-shaped holders. I sit down on the sofa. After a minute she returns with two cups of spicy-smelling tea. The steam clouds my face. Folding her hands in her lap, she says, 'I wasn't trying to be flippant – about Scott I mean. I know his condition is serious, that it takes more than meditation and chanting –'

'It's okay. It's been a stressful couple of weeks.'

'I take it you know about the robbery.'

I don't reply.

'She made a lot of mistakes, our mother.'

My throat sticks. I'm not even sure if I still want to meet this woman, *our* mother. I look at Susi. 'How long have you known?'

She shrugs. 'A while. Mum has a way of surprising people.'

'Yeah, well, you're doing not bad yourself in that area.'

She returns my smile. 'You know, the first time I went to Tommy's he nearly shut the door in my face. He had no idea I even existed. It was only after I showed him Mum's letters that he let me in –' Susi pauses and looks into her cup. 'For months I cut myself up about how she could be this whole other person and not tell me. I suppose she thought I'd reject her. It took me a while to realise – she was just scared.'

'Of what?'

'Losing a child all over again. You have to understand, the years after she got sent to prison were hard. Not knowing where you were.'

'She committed a robbery. Surely she must have known the risk she was taking.'

'It wasn't just that.' Susi pauses.

'What then? Billy?'

Her eyes gather moisture. There's a fragmented air about her, like she's been patched together. I wonder what age she is, maybe late forties, early fifties. Her skin is pale, too pale; it darkens the shadows round her eyes. I notice there are no photographs in the house, none of Jean, no children, no partner. She has the self-containment of a person used to her own company, and I get the impression that all this stuff about the past means more to her than it does to me, that she needs it. She tosses her head slightly as if shaking off a sudden memory. 'All these years, Mum had one true friend. Her only friend. When she got out of prison, it was her who helped trace you to Montreal. She's old now, but still sharp as a tack. Scott said he'd like to meet her, that it would be good for his film. And I know she'd love to see you again.'

The film. I heave a deep sigh. All Scott's hopes are pinned on this film. For a moment, I consider telling Susi everything, about Bruce's threats, and how I was up all night researching the production company, trying to find out who's pulling the strings. But there's no point going over it all again; I've made my decision. 'What about *your* family?' I say.

'There's no one else.'

'Didn't you ever get married?'

Susi shakes her head. 'Men aren't my cup of tea, if you get what I mean.'

I take a sip of my drink. 'Ah, you prefer the more intelligent sex.'

She smiles.

'There must have been someone special?'

'No.'

'So you've never been with –'

'Never. Not even a woman.'

I can't imagine what that would be like, not to have experienced that kind of intimacy with another person. I remember when all the girls in class had been kissed, except me, and I used to pray to God not to let me die without ever knowing what it was like to feel that lingering taste of someone else's lips on mine. 'It's never too late,' I say.

One of the incense sticks has burned down. She takes another from a packet on the mantelpiece and lights it with a match. There's a smell of sulphur and wood, then the cloying vapours of incense. 'Mum was always strict when it came to boys,' she says. 'I wasn't allowed make-up, had to be in by nine. Not that I ever went out. I studied nursing in Edinburgh. At the weekend I'd come home. Mum would get a box of assorted biscuits and we'd watch *Dallas*, *Dynasty*, all those ridiculous soaps. I told her I was waiting for the right person. "You can't wait forever, Susi," she'd say. But I couldn't bring myself to come out with it. Back then, things were different. People got shocked. Anyway, I'd always been shy. When it comes to love, I suppose I just missed the boat.'

'Some people might say you're lucky.' A nerve twitches in my cheek. Jealousy, I can't help it. It's like looking into a parallel universe, how things could have been if it had been me growing up with my mother, if I was the one who'd sat beside her watching trash TV. *No point crying over spilt milk*: one of Cissy's phrases.

'I think Mum was disappointed, not having grandchildren. She never said anything, but I could see her looking at other grandmothers in the street. In a way, Mum and me, we couldn't be more different. I always thought that you'd have had more in common – that you'd have been the one she was close to –'

'Well, I wasn't around.' I didn't mean it to sound so bitter.

Susi's mouth tightens in a sort of helpless smile. 'When she became ill I learned aromatherapy because I thought it might help her, but she didn't believe in that sort of thing. It's a different generation.'

The door opens. Scott crosses the room and sits down in the middle of the floor. When he opens his mouth, a low rumbling noise comes out. It seems to grow from his belly, the sound vibrating through every cell of my body, wrapping itself around my skin. He stops and leans forward, then gives his hair a shake. His eyes are bright and shining. 'Whoa. I feel better now. Nothing like a bit of Mongolian chanting to get you motivated.'

It's cold but there's hardly any wind and the river looks grey and solid. Scott leans over the fence and films a swan as it swims round an overturned shopping cart and disappears under the bridge. We're on the opposite side of town from Newton Street and the mills where Jean worked. There's another bridge that looks over a wide but shallow waterfall. Susi says it's called the Hamills. Hunkered on the bank is a large six-storey brick building with rows and rows of windows. These were once the Anchor

Mills, she says, owned by the Clark family, but eventually they all became part of Coats. The building has been converted into flats, all that's left of Paisley's thread industry. We take a path around the side, and Scott walks backwards, filming us coming towards him.

There's a pungent smell that Susi says is the tannery. The Thread Museum is in another old building at the opposite end of the mill complex. I realise how big the place is; even Bruce would be impressed. We're going there to meet this woman, Jean's one true friend, apparently. I can't think who it might be or what will come of it. Susi keeps asking me if I'm alright, as though I might break down at any minute. But even if I did, what good would it do? What's the point in getting worked up? She was a shit mother. She left me. End of.

We go through a set of gates and towards a red brick building with a tall chimney, and in through a set of doors that leads down to a basement. At the back of the room are textile machines, and display cabinets showing samples of cotton at various stages of production. On the walls, faces wrapped in shawls gaze out from centuries past into an unfathomable future. Scott is already working his way round the room, filming the different coloured threads, bobbins, boxes and photographs. 'Hello,' calls Susi. 'We're here.'

A glass door opens and out comes a short, stout woman. She must be in her eighties. She's dressed in trousers and a long coat, wisps of silver hair poking out beneath a scarf. 'It's bloody freezing in here,' she says. 'Come intae the office and get warm.' We follow her to a small room with a table and chairs, surrounded by filing cabinets and a photocopier. A convector heater blows warm breath. With a wave of her hand, she invites us to sit down. I notice liver spots on her skin. 'If you're filming fur profits we'll have to ask you fur a donation,' she says, eyeing Scott with his tripod. 'We run this place oorselves, ye see. No government funding.'

'Annie is curator of the museum,' says Susi.

'Don't worry,' I say. 'I'll make a donation.'

The old woman humphs, but seems pacified. Susi takes her arm and nudges her towards me. 'This is Jean's daughter. Remember I was telling you about her?'

'I know who she is,' says Annie. 'She has her mither's eyes.' Annie gives me a long look. The skin on her face is crinkled, but there's something about the mouth and nose; a memory returns of a set of full rosy lips leaning over me, her hair pinned back from her face, a baby perched on her hips. 'The last time I saw you…' Her eyes are shiny and moist. 'I'll away and get us some tea.'

She returns with a tray of cups and saucers and a plate of biscuits. I add sugar to my cup and stir. I haven't had breakfast and I unwrap a chocolate biscuit, devouring half of it at once. Annie laughs. 'Some things don't change. You always could snaffle a biscuit.'

I feel myself blush, then it all comes flooding back: the building where my nana lived, the pram outside the door on the bottom floor, the woman in black who ate ice cream by the fire. I realise what I remember about Annie is her calmness. She was always surrounded by people who needed looking after, but no matter how many demands they made, Annie would be at the centre, unruffled, her voice smooth and steady, as though in time everything would sort itself out. 'I remember you,' I say.

'I should think so,' says Annie. 'You were never away fae my bloody door.' A warmth rises inside me. Annie's gaze lingers on my face, measuring me with her eye. There's a kindness in those eyes, years of life. Grabbing my hand, she smiles. 'Ava.' My body relaxes. I expect her to let go, but she doesn't. Instead, she squeezes. That one simple gesture is all it takes: I start to whimper like a little girl. 'There, there,' says Annie, and passes me a tissue.

'Sorry,' I say. 'I don't know what's come over me.'

'Susi tells me you've done quite well for yerself.'

I mumble that it's not so bad out there. If she knows about Bruce, the corruption allegations, she doesn't say anything.

'Go and get me that book, love,' she says to Susi. 'The one on the long table.'

Susi returns with a thick black album that Annie opens in front of us. It's full of photographs, most of them black and white:

women in plain wrap-around overalls standing by machines, or sitting at tables, surrounded by teacups and cakes. My eyes linger on the faces, the exchanges of smiles and glances, signs of real friendship, the kind that, despite all the functions and corporate dinners, I've never had. Looking at the pictures gives me a feeling of longing, like I want to crawl amongst the nylon-wrapped legs, the green overalls, and hide.

Annie's eyes grow clouded as she points out a photo of four women seated round a table in a canteen. 'That's her.' Sliding the album towards me, she taps a face near the back. The figure is half-hidden, as if the others have sat down without noticing her, like she doesn't quite belong. Her hair is piled up in a beehive, elbow resting on the table, a lit cigarette in her hand. Only one leg is visible, the crossed leg, wearing a dark calf-length boot. I think of the photo I found in Cissy's house of me sitting at the piano and, at the edge of the picture, the anonymous leg. The same boots.

Soon she's reminiscing about the other women in the picture: Angie, the small one with freckled skin opposite my mother, 'Her and Tommy wur mairrit thirty-eight years afore she died,' and Maggie, plump cheeked and with laughing eyes, seated at the front, next to the indomitable Una with thick arms folded across her body and a business-like demeanour that eclipses everyone in the picture. I look again at Jean's pale face. She doesn't seem any match for this woman whose hands are like spades.

'How long did you know her?' My lips can't form the word.

'Your mammy?' Annie shifts in her seat. 'Too long.'

'And Una?'

'She was a friend of your Granny Senga's.'

My fingers tremble when I take out Una's letter and put it on the table. Annie fetches a pair of glasses from a drawer. Puffs of air and grunts of affirmation escape from her lips while she reads. When she's finished, she turns the letter face down without a word, and leaves the room. A siren wails in the distance and I resist the temptation to say anything about robberies or mills.

Annie returns with a large ring-bound folder under her arm.

'They called it the mill's darkest day,' she says, laying it on the table. It contains copies of *The Yarn*, the mill newspaper. There are articles relating to the robbery: a picture of Una, her hand bandaged and in a sling, her mouth grimly down-turned. The article reads: *Mill Worker Injured in Attack*, and describes Mrs McMenemy's brave attempt to stop the robbery by blocking the thieves' exit, only to be viciously attacked by former mill worker, Jean McParland, who stabbed her in the hand with a pair of thread scissors. The finance manager, Mr Thomson, received a severe blow to the head and is currently in hospital. Police are doing all they can to find the suspects. 'Mr Thomson's a good man and he didn't deserve that,' says a quote from Mrs McMenemy. 'They'll get what's coming. Let them try and keep me away from that witness stand.'

'It was the talk of the toon for months,' says Annie. 'No one could believe it had happened. Mr Thomson wis clubbed ower the heid wae a typewriter. They say he wis never the same efter that. He didny work again, died a few years later.'

I don't know what to say. Pushing the folder away, I look into Annie's soft eyes. 'I'm glad we got this chance. Meeting you again has been lovely, but all this reminiscing, it can't change anything. What's done is done.' I lean back and press my fingers to my temples.

A crease forms in Annie's brow, but it's Susi who speaks. 'I know how you feel. When I think about what she did, it doesn't seem real. But she's still my mother.'

Annie squeezes her hand. Without knowing why, I'm envious of the gesture, the closeness between them. 'So why did she do it?' I say.

'Why do people do anything?' Scott steps out from behind his tripod. 'I don't think she meant to hurt anyone. If an animal feels threatened, it bites.'

'She's not an animal, Scott.'

'No, he's right,' says Annie. 'I saw her that day. There wis a van out front, the engine running. I saw it through the curtains. I didn't know whit wis going on, of course. There wis a cairry-oan and, when I opened the door, Billy wis shoving Jean doon the stairs. That morning wis the last time she ever saw you. Her eyes were wild, panicked like an animal's. She wis screaming your name, clawing, begging him. Then he shoved her intae the van and they were gone.'

I look into Annie's face, the way her eyes crease gently at the corners. Then I think of Jean's letters, the desperation, the pleading. 'It's not like she didn't have a choice,' I say. 'No, as far as I'm concerned, she got what she deserved.'

Annie crosses her arms. 'When I found out aboot the robbery, I wanted nothing tae dae wae Jean. She'd gone too far. Billy wis behind it, of course. We all warned her, bit she widny listen. Efter the van drove off, I rushed upstairs and found Senga. She cuid hairdly breathe. She'd hud anither stroke. Never left the hospital after that. Aye, Billy McBride or no, yer mither had a lot tae answer fur.'

Susi gets up from the table. 'I need some air.' Her expression looks tight and drawn. Annie stares after her, through the door and out into the carpark. I think of Susi's apartment, the smell of incense, the music.

'You're not much alike,' says Annie.

'What?'

'You and Susi. You were the spit a yer mither, liked pretty dresses and playing at being a princess. She wis a quiet wee lassie, introverted ye know, kept herself tae herself. I mind when Archie used to send her oot fur his fish supper. Every Friday night it wis the same. He liked a pickled egg bit she'd eat it oan the way hame and no say a word. Ach, we didny mind taking care of her. It wis like having you all over again.'

I pause. 'You took care of her? But I thought Susi grew up in Perth.'

'That wis later.' Annie turns to Scott. 'Now, you're more like Jean than the ither two put thegither,' she says. 'No in looks, mind, bit – ach, I canny explain it. Spirit, I suppose.' Annie shuts the photo album and stands up.

'Annie. Wait. What was he like, this Billy?'

There's a pause as she lays the album on the table and sits back down. 'Jack-the-lad, you know. Gift a the gab. Hair like Frankie Avalon. Always up tae nae good.'

'They must have been in love, to want to take such a risk, to run off and be together.'

Annie snorts. 'Jean wis a romantic, and he knew it. Played oan it. He wis good-looking, if you like that sort. Jean wis never happy wae Tommy, no really. She thought marriage wis supposed tae be aw fairytales and tiaras. But Billy wis nae Prince Charming. Nothing bit a small-time crook who got in ower his heid. Thought if he robbed the mill he cuid impress the big boys. Aw he needed wis someone oan the inside. Someone like Jean.' She offers us a shortbread finger. Nibbling the top off her own biscuit, she wipes the crumbs from her chin. 'Filled her heid full a big dreams aboot America. She wis that daft she thought he'd be the new Frank Sinatra and her the next Marilyn Monroe.'

'How did they get caught?' Scott snaps his stick of shortbread.

'After the robbery, every police unit in Scotland wis oan the lookout fur them. They'd planned tae lie low at some friend a Billy's, Harry something or ither. He wis in oan it, bit when it aw went wrang he didny want tae know. Billy said they should go right tae Edinburgh and catch a boat fae Leith. Oh, I canny mind the details. It aw came oot at the trial. Jean kept begging Billy tae go back fur you, bit he said it wis too much of a risk. They got to some hotel. There wis an argument and, when she woke up in the morning, he wis gone. The money tae. Jean didny know whit tae dae. She handed herself intae the police, thinking at least that way she might get tae see her daughter again. That evening they caught Billy trying tae board a ship to the States.'

'But you stayed in touch all these years,' I say. 'You must have seen some good in her.'

Annie stares out the window into the clouds. 'She sent me letters, begging me tae visit her in prison. I wouldn't go. Every time I thought about her, all I could see wis Senga lying in her hallway, gasping fur breath.' Looking down, she shakes her head. 'But I had to make a decision. In the end, I'd nae choice.'

'Why?'

The door opens and Susi stands in the entrance, her face wet with tears. 'Because Jean was pregnant.'

There's a canteen in the foyer of the mill selling pre-wrapped sandwiches and shrivelled-looking food in metal trays. Susi sits down at one of the flimsy aluminium tables. In the harsh fluorescent light, the grey roots of her hair show through. We're alone; she didn't want this part to be filmed.

I order fries but Susi isn't hungry. All the same I put some from my roll into hers, and push it across the table. 'Cissy used to make chip butties every Saturday night,' I say. 'Uncle Alex called it traditional Scottish food. I made it for Bruce once and he thought I'd gone mad. I've never had a butty since.' I bite into the warm stodge and lick the butter from my fingers.

'Mum used to make butties too. I got sick of them.' She pushes it back.

'It was you, wasn't it?' I say. 'You were the baby.'

She smiles weakly. 'Do you know what people tell children whose parents are in prison? They tell them they're at work. I used to look up at that big dark building, its rows of tiny windows, and think my mammy must be really important to work in such a place, to be in charge of so many people.'

'They have to tell them something I suppose.'

Susi gives me a stony look.

I cough. 'So what happened after you were born? Who looked after you?'

'Annie.' Susi sighs and stretches her feet under the table. 'If it wasn't for her I'd have been taken into care. She brought me up like I was one of her own. It was Annie who was there when I took my first steps, said my first word.'

My butty stares up at me from the plate. 'It seems we both had guardian angels.' I'm surprised at my own words; I've never thought of Cissy as an angel before.

Susi's face relaxes briefly, then her muscles tighten. 'We'd visit

Mum in prison. I didn't like it. I was scared of the noise, the men in uniform, the clanking doors. Scared of *her*. I always had this feeling that I'd done something wrong. She'd tell me not to worry, that we'd soon be together in a nice house with a garden, and we'd make up names for a puppy or a kitten. She'd tell me she loved me and teach me to blow kisses through the glass.' Her eyes dart round the room as if the tea ladies might suddenly transform into prison officers. 'My earliest memory is of that place. I needed the toilet and the guard wouldn't let us go, so I wet myself. Mum was crying, the man shouting at her to shut up. After that I didn't want to go back, but I had to. "Smile," Annie would say. "Look, it's Mammy."'

I lick the grease off my fingers, wipe my hands with the napkin and take a deep breath. 'She might have been in prison, but at least she was there,' I say. 'At least you had her.'

Susi exhales slowly. 'When she got out, I was nearly six. I didn't want to live with her, not at first. We went to stay in Perth.'

'It must have been difficult,' I say. 'For both of you.'

'When I got older, we used to have these arguments. I'd do anything not to be like her. I dressed differently, cut my hair short.' She stretches and I see something of Scott in her lean frame, that looseness of limbs. I think of all those times Scott pushed me to the edge, the accusations, the doubts, the screaming. There were times I wanted to do it, just one hard slap. Then the hours I spent afterwards, hating myself.

Susi fishes beneath the neck of her sweater and removes a chain with a tarnished silver locket in the shape of a heart. 'Open it.'

Inside is the picture of a young man with a set jaw and a grin that challenges you to talk back. The picture is faded so the eyes aren't quite in focus, yet there's an energy behind it that crackles with life. Next to it are the words, *Forever Yours*. 'That's him,' she says. 'My father. Billy McBride.'

I close the locket in my fist, then open it again, watching his face blink out at me from its tiny window. The man who changed everything, whose actions altered the course of my life. Forever. The man who might be my father.

'It's the only thing he ever gave me.' Taking a tissue from her pocket, she blows her nose. 'Mum never talked about my real father. We used to have arguments. She said he was a waste of space, a mistake. I didn't even know his name. Then one day, when I was about fifteen, I overheard her and Annie talking in the kitchen. Mum was upset. "I should have told her about Billy from the beginning," she said. "She must hate me, Annie."

Annie said that he'd have been no father to me. "If you'd ended up with Billy McBride," she said. "You'd be stuck in that old flat in Bank Street living a dog's life. Turned out just like his old man."

The next day, I skipped school. I caught the coach from Perth to Glasgow, then a bus to Paisley. I went down Bank Street, checking the names on all the doors. I remember going up a flight of dark stairs. There was an awful smell, like urine. I saw the name McBride scratched in pen on one of the walls, and knocked. A voice inside rasped, "What do you want?"

"Are you Billy McBride?" I asked.

"Aye, what of it?"

I dug my nails into my palms and blurted out the words, "I'm your daughter."

A man opened the door. His vest was stained down the front, his hair receding and his face unshaven. I remember thinking he didn't look like anyone's dad, but that didn't stop me feeling scared. He scanned me up and down, then grunted and showed me in.

The place was a mess, nothing in the room but an armchair surrounded by empty beer cans and bottles, and a TV with a broken aerial and fuzzy picture. I sat on a cushion on the floor, next to some old newspapers and dirty plates. He slumped into the chair, clicked open a can, and studied me with one droopy eye. "So you're the lassie they were telling me aboot," he said. I nodded. He said he was sorry the place was such a mess, I'd caught him at a bad time, between jobs and so on. The conversation didn't last long, if you could call it a conversation. I asked him about Mum. He said they'd met "up the dancing," and that she was "a nice bit of stuff." But when I asked what had happened, where he'd been, he just said, "here and there" or "this and that, you know the way people lose touch."

I remember there were lots of silences, then he'd say, "How's yer mither" or "Are you working?" When he'd finished the can, he went out the room and returned with the locket. "I gave this tae yer mither once, but I suppose she didny like it after all because she sent me it back when I wis in the jail.'"

Susi pauses. Her lips are dry and her skin almost transparent. 'I remember feeling afraid because he'd been in jail. Ironic isn't it? Mum used to call it "being away." Even when I was sixteen, she still insisted the place Annie had taken me to was a hospital and she'd stayed there so she didn't have to travel to work. We both knew the truth, but it was just easier to pretend. She never talked about the past. "If you're happy," she said, "that's all that matters." But she wasn't happy.'

Susi takes a long slow breath. 'And I didn't want to pretend anymore. So I asked him right out, I asked Billy McBride why my mother had been in prison. He laughed like I'd made a joke, then he realised I didn't know. "Ask yer ma," he said.

"I'm asking you."

He sucked at his can till there was nothing left, then crunched it in his fist. "Alright. But don't blame me if ye don't like whit ye hear. She tried tae rob the mill. We both did." The way he said it was matter of fact, like it was normal. I just sat there. "If she hudny grassed me in, yer old da cuid have left you some money. I cuid have been somebody instead of stuck in this auld flat." He glanced at the yellowed walls. I could see his hands starting to shake. "You better go," he said. At the door, he emptied the locket into my palm, asked if I was good to lend him a fiver, then I never saw him again. About a year later he died of liver disease. Drank himself to death. A pauper's burial.' She blinks.

For some reason, I'd expected her to describe a large man, tattoos on his arm, the kind of criminal you get in movies, tough and witty. Not this pathetic figure, a greyed-out shadow, a bum. I pass her back the locket. 'Did Jean ever find out?'

Susi nods. 'I told her like it was some kind of victory. She went spare. Grilled me over every word he said. But she let me keep the locket. After that, it didn't matter anyway. That was all I ever knew of him.'

'I'm sorry,' I say. 'Maybe we're two of a kind after all.'

She leans across the table and gives me a long steely look. 'At least Tommy wanted you, at least he wished things were different.'

'Come on, Susi, let's not fight about this.'

'Why not? You think you've had it tough? What about me? I saw the way you lived, the house, the cars. You think you're better than us, don't think I haven't noticed. What was it you said? We're like continents that drifted apart, and it doesn't really mean anything?'

'I'm sorry, that was a stupid thing to say.'

'You can always go back to Canada, you still have money. What do I have?'

'You have your aromatherapy, your mother.'

'Great.' She laughs. 'You've no idea what it's like looking after a sick old woman, washing her after she's wet herself, feeding her when she won't eat. It's been years of hell. At the nursing home it's no better. Half the time, she doesn't know who I am. Do you want to know why I didn't tell you who I was straight away, why I lived with you all those months in Canada? Because it was an escape. Away from Mum, from the constant worrying, feeling like I wasn't good enough, like I'd missed out on life. For a while, I could be someone else. A new person. Ava Newport's housekeeper. I liked it, got off on it even. I wanted to see what kind of person you were.'

A shiver runs down my spine. 'You wanted to get back at me?'

She shakes her head. 'Maybe. I don't know. I was confused. Finally, I saw things the way Mum did. Every time she looked at me, she had to face the consequences of her actions. She wasn't a bad mother. She tucked me in at night, held my hand, but never too tightly, and never too long. Because, all my life, I reminded her of one thing: that she didn't have you. That was my greatest crime: I wasn't you.'

I can't hold it back any longer. 'Susi, please. None of this is my fault. Whatever happened with Jean, I'm sorry. But at least you knew her. You know who your father was. What about me? If you know anything about who my father really is, if Jean ever mentioned it, you have to tell me.'

'I'm sorry.' She stands up. The metal chair leg clangs against the table as she gathers her things and rushes outside. I stare after her, the gap into the carpark opening then closing again, narrowing each time until the doors finally swing shut. On the table is Susi's half-finished tea. I pick a greasy fry from the plate and bite into it. Cold.

I go back to the Thread Museum alone. I hear Scott's laughter as I go down the stairs. He's huddled next to Annie at one of the tables, two large photo albums open in front of them. I notice a small bottle of whisky next to their mugs of tea. Annie turns to face me. 'You forgot your phone. At least I think that's whit it is. I'm nae good wae these things.'

'We'll get you one, Annie, won't we?' says Scott.

'Would you like a wee dram?' Her eyes twinkle. 'I pit a drop in yer tea earlier. Tae melt the ice. Crafty old bugger aren't I?'

She pats the chair beside her. I sit down, my eyes drawn towards the photographs. I recognise the Counting House, two rows of office workers standing in front of it with serious expressions. The one in the middle is older, with glasses and a thin moustache. Annie taps his forehead. 'That's Mr Thomson.'

My eyes wander over Mr Thomson's skull, and imagine the bone cracking under the typewriter's impact, the soft grey matter underneath. I push the album away and stand up. 'How did she do it?' I say. 'How did she live with herself knowing she'd caused so much damage?'

Annie hands me a cup of warm whisky-laced tea. 'I'm an auld wumin noo. Things happen and you pit up wae it, you live wae it because it becomes normal. The strangest things in the world can seem normal after a while. I'll never forget Jean's face that day I went to the jail, after she told me she wis pregnant. She looked so frightened. I never understood whit she did, bit I pitied her. I had to help her. I even wrote her letters oot fur her –'

'That was *your* handwriting?' I picture the tightly-jammed script, the one part of my mother I thought I was beginning to know, yet even that isn't real. But somehow it fits, the measured strokes of the pen, Annie's reliability, her kind heart.

'Aye, Jean didny want you getting thon prison-stamped paper, see. Archie said I wis soft, but I talked him round.'

'Compassion,' says Scott. 'It's what makes us human.'

I take a sip of sugary liquid, taste the hint of spirit. Annie glances over her shoulder towards the door. Her eyes, filled with concern, search across the carpark. 'Where did Susi go?'

I flop into the chair with a groan. 'I might have upset her.'

Annie shakes her head. 'It's not your fault.'

I stare into my lap and feel the weight of her eyes on my face. 'It must have been hard,' I say. 'Letting her go after you brought her up all those years.'

She humphs under her breath. 'At least I knew where she wis. We never lost touch, no like –' She looks at me apologetically and purses her lips. 'Susi's always been a bit, you know, up and doon. It wis hard for her, wae Jean the way she wis. When she told me she wis looking fur ye, well, I didny think anything wid come o it. Too much time had passed.'

'And now?'

She shrugs. 'I can't tell you whit to do, hen. Jean made her mistakes and she suffered fur them, bit she's yer mither, and ye're stuck wae her, like it or not.'

'Just like I'm stuck with you,' says Scott.

I ignore the comment, not sure if he's only half-joking. Annie gives a hearty chuckle. 'I mind I used to call you Ava Maria, like in the song. You were a nice wee lassie, never any trouble. A wee angel.'

'Jean wanted to name you Scarlett,' says Scott. 'After Vivien Leigh in *Gone with the Wind,* but Tommy wouldn't have it so she called you Ava instead.' He tips more whisky into his cup and with a mischievous smile says, 'Ava Gardner was in her second favourite film: *Killers.*'

It's strange, having my son tell me things about my own past, the kind of things that should get passed from parent to child, not the other way around. I recall what the doctors said about the importance of stability and routine, and I hope all this isn't having a negative effect.

'He's been bending my ear,' says Annie. 'Wanting to know aboot you and Jean.'

'Your favourite shoes were red with white buckles,' he says. 'And when she went to night classes you'd visit Annie and she'd give you a penny for an ounce of rhubarb and custard candy.'

In the well of my mind, I see the white paper bag, the last few sweeties stuck to the inside. 'You'd tell me to suck them slowly and not crunch or I'd break my teeth.'

'Aye,' says Annie. 'And you always forgot.'

Scott's laugh brightens the room.

'He's been pointing that thingmy at me,' Annie goes on, nodding at the camera. 'If I'd known I wis gauny be a film star I'd have pit my teeth in.'

'By the time I've finished you'll look twenty years younger,' says Scott.

She pats her scarf. 'Cheeky bugger.'

When she looks at me there's recognition in her old face, like she still knows the essence of me, despite the distance. Suddenly I want to tell her everything, about Bruce, the enquiry, Melanie; I want to ask her why people do these things, act in a way that makes it impossible to be with them. But I don't. Instead, I go into my bag and lift out the birthday card. The little silver key spins and catches the light. 'This was sent to Montreal,' I say. 'Cissy kept it all these years.'

Annie takes it in her gnarled hand. 'We were in that shop ages afore Jean settled on this one. She minded Cissy taught piano, so we went tae the big library in Glesga that had aw the Canada phonebooks, and went through every piano teacher in Montreal until we found you. It took us hours.' She heaves a deep sigh. 'We wur back and forth tae the phone box a dozen times afore Cissy finally answered. As soon as Jean heard her voice she hung up. "It's her, it's her," she said, her whole body shaking. I had to hold her up so she cuid walk.'

Annie rests her hand on my arm. 'Every year she sent ye a birthday card. She put by every spare penny she hud fur gaun tae Canada wae. And when a letter finally arrived fae Cissy, she cuid hardly sit still she wis that excited. This wis it, she thought, aw the letters and cards had paid aff. Cissy wis going tae let her see you again. Bit it wisny an invitation. She said you were moving house. Didny say where, only that Jean wis tae stay away. *As far as Ava is concerned, you're dead*, said Cissy. *It's better that way.* Fur Jean, it wis like losing you all over again. It finished her, that did.'

The photo album is next to my elbow. Cissy's face stares up at me from the Counting House. She was always so certain about everything, so unimpeachable. Now it's like a layer has been rubbed away, and there's something doubtful in her eyes, the self-consciousness of a person aware of being watched. I think back to that day in our kitchen in Montreal when I told her I was pregnant. She'd been about to say something and I'd interrupted her. There was a pale haunted look in her face. I was so sure she'd found out. But what if I was wrong, what if she'd been about to tell me I had a mother who was alive and on her way to Canada?

I imagine Cissy's hands, so neatly restrained in the photograph, opening the Queen of Scots book, tearing out the inscription and crumpling it into a tight ball. Then I look at Scott sitting beside me and it all makes sense. Cissy needed me. Without any children of her own, she'd have had nothing. She saw Jean's desperation, and knew what it was like to lose the child you loved. That's why she couldn't throw away those cards. It was too cruel, even for Cissy.

I turn to Annie's honest round face. 'Why are things so complicated?'

The warmth of her hand closing over my fist is reassuring, strong. 'One thing is simple: Jean loved you. Bit she wis so full of whit might be, or whit could've been, that she missed whit wis standing there in front of her.' Annie winks. 'You're still my little

Ava Maria. Don't you make the same mistake.'

The sky is darkening by the time we reach the river. Scott walks along silently, his head bowed. It's the first time we've been alone all day. I'm sweating despite the cool air. I joke that it's his turn to buy dinner. 'What do you fancy?' I say. 'What about haggis? Or a fish supper?'

I say it in my best Scottish accent, *fish suppur*, and wait for him to laugh. But his muscles tense, his shoulders hunched. 'So, when are you leaving?'

'What?'

'God, do we have to go through this, pretending that you don't know what I'm talking about? I saw your phone. You've been checking flights to Vancouver.'

Cold air fills my lungs. 'You went through my phone?'

'It was on the table.'

The abbey, with its gothic arches and jutting facades, towers over us. It looks silver in the twilight, like something out of a fantasy tale. Gargoyles peer down with bulging eyes and gaping mouths. 'Bruce wants a public statement.'

'And you're going to give it to him?'

'What choice do I have?'

Scott leans over the railings beside the river, lights shimmering like scales on its surface. 'How can I make a film about you when you're not here?'

'It's – complicated.' I take a deep breath. 'I made some enquiries about that production company of yours. The CEO of Carhorn was at King's College with Sue Brash. They graduated together.'

'So?'

'It's a connection to Bruce. This could affect your entire project.'

He walks towards me and drapes his arm round my shoulder. 'Bruce is desperate. Any minute now he'll be playing the super-hero card, all that stuff about how he saved me when I was a kid. There's no way he's going to ruin his family image. It's the best publicity he's got.' His mouth widens into a grin. 'Trust me. I know how to get them.'

'What are you talking about?'

'Promise you won't tell anyone.'

The moon peeps over the floodlit tower of the abbey. I nod.

'There was a report.'

'Report?' The word sticks in my mouth, like one of those giant pieces of candy, *gobstoppers*, Alex used to call them.

'An environmental impact assessment. It shows how increases in the selective cut zone will damage the Grove. They *know*, Mom. They've known all along. He's got a PR woman, Melanie something or other, denying its existence.'

'Melanie?' A flush of heat in my chest.

'If you turn up with a copy of that report, people will listen –'

I hold it in my mind: this moment, my son standing beside me, the way I always wanted it to be. I was there that day, I remember the look of panic on Dave Winterbourne's face when Bruce ordered the report be buried. If Scott finds out, he'll never forgive me. Scrolling to the business section of the *Vancouver Sun*, I pass him my phone. There's an article questioning my 'erratic' behaviour and fitness to take the stand. 'I'm not going to testify, Scott.'

'Why?'

I stop walking. 'It doesn't matter.'

He scrutinises my face. 'You knew, didn't you?'

I bite my lip.

He's walking away from me. Panic surges through my body. I go after him but I can't keep up. 'Stop, Scott. Please. I was trying to protect you. Jean, the enquiry. It's all one big mess going around in my head. I'm sorry, you shouldn't have to deal with any of it.'

He freezes. 'So you've seen the report?'

'It's on the internal system, password protected, but I don't have access; I'm locked out.'

As if on impulse, he comes back and squeezes me tight. 'It's okay. *I'm* okay, you don't have to protect me.' I touch the softness of his hair, feel the warmth of his cheek. 'Promise me you'll stay,' he says, 'that we'll see Jean together.'

'I promise.'

'I forget you're getting old.'

'Shut up.' I give the back of his head a playful scuff, the blood heavy in my veins, each cell weighted down with guilt.

The moon scuds the rooftops, big and golden, but with a shorn edge. We bypass the hill leading to the hotel, and walk along the main street. The route seems familiar now, like an old map uncovered of dust. At the Baptist church we turn off, walking silently along my nana's old cobbled road, then down past the horseshoe and towards the park, its trees silvery and bare against the starry sky. I know these trees. I've played between their trunks, tossed their leaves in the air. They were part of me once. Strange how something as solid as a tree can become so fragile, so easily removed; how the very roots of you can be whisked away, like they'd never existed.

I press firmly on the intercom. 'It's Ava.'

I go through and find Tommy in the hallway. He ushers us to the front room, his eyes bright, the little dog wagging at his heels. A clock on the mantelpiece ticks loudly. Tommy returns to his chair and I sit on the sofa, Scott playing with Polson on the floor, tickling his tummy, the dog letting out joyous yaps. 'I'm glad you came back,' says Tommy, quietly. 'After the last time I thought –' He gives a helpless shrug.

'Don't you get sick of the view?' I say.

'I suppose it's become a habit.' He laughs, and scratches behind his ear.

I sigh, dimly aware of Scott shifting onto his knees, positioning the camera. I turn to Tommy. 'I had a chat with Susi earlier. About her father.'

He drums his fingers and lifts his head, as if watching for something behind the clouds. 'Billy McBride,' he says. 'That man took everything that wis precious tae me and threw it away. I'd lie awake at night hating every part of him, his voice, that cocky smile he hud, thinking he wis aw the useless evil bastards under the sun. Even when I got mairrit tae Angie it didny stop. If anything, on the day of the wedding, I thought aboot it more. I knew Angie wisny like Jean, bit ye canny help wondering: whit if it turns oot the same? It didny, bit I couldny bring maself tae want anymair weans. I jist wanted it tae be me and her. She didny mind, she wis a good wumin.'

Lifting a picture from the corner table, Tommy hands it to me. A wedding photograph. Angie is small and pink-faced, in a white dress with button-up sleeves. Tommy's in a suit, his cheek pressed next to hers. 'I mind one day, I went fur a pint efter work, like I always did on a Friday. They'd knocked doon the Lighthouse so we went tae the Bull Inn. Me and Archie and a few ither lads. I wis fur gaun up the road, when a voice behind me said, "I hear ye've a new wife, McParland." I turned roon. He wis leaning against the bar. He hud they sideburns that wur the rage at the time. Never did like them, made a man look untidy. "Works at the mill, doesn't she?" he said. The whole place had gone quiet. It had been ten years, but folk still remembered it, hauf the toon worked in the place and ye don't forget a thing like that.' Pinpoints of sweat break out above Tommy's lip. His hand forms a fist. 'I asked, what did it huv tae dae wae him? Well, he finished his pint in wan go, took a step forrit and started oan aboot how Angie didny huv Jean's looks bit you can't have everything. "Jean always did like a real man," he said. "Bit, if ye're lucky, this one might be jist as handy wae a pair a scissors." That wis it. I caught him wan oan the jaw. He went tummlin backwards. People wur shouting, drinks flying. He hit his heid against something, I don't know whit, only I saw blood oan the side of his face. Not wan person helped that man up. They got on wae their business, and let him lie there, groaning. The barman jist gave me a nod and said, "See you later then, Tommy." "Aye," I said. "Later."'

Folding his hands into his lap, Tommy sighs. 'That wis the last time Billy McBride ever bothered me. Efter that, he'd walk past me and no look up, no even say a word. Course, the drink had him by then. Anyway, my point is, ye canny carry bitterness and hatred aroon forever, sooner or later it'll eat ye up.'

All the time I'm listening to Tommy, his words cast long shadows over my heart. The emotions I've been trying so hard to keep down swirl upwards like black choking dust. My eyes sting. It's like the ground under me is shaking, slipping away piece by piece. 'How long did you suspect – that I might not be your daughter?'

He heaves a leaden sigh. 'We wur mairrit quick, yer mither and me. I suppose that's why Senga always liked me – fur doing right by her. No many men wid take oan anither man's wean. The truth is we used it against her though. And Jean knew it.' He sighs. 'There wis part of me that always expected her tae be grateful. Bit that disny mean I wis right. You cuid still have been mine. And I let that chance go – naebody else. Me.'

I picture us, me, Tommy and Jean, bobbing on the surface of the Atlantic in our fragile little boats, drifting away from each other, blown by the currents. I want to crawl inside myself. I'm sick of being Ava Newport. Sick of her decisions, her responsibilities, her big sorry mess. I make an excuse and go outside. The cold air catches in my throat and quickens my breath. I head towards the trees, the shelter of their branches. Leaning my head against a trunk I bury my nose in its earthy scent.

Behind me there's a scurrying noise. Polson scrabbles past me on the path, Tommy at his back. He's wearing a light-coloured jacket and moving slowly, a slight limp making him dip and rise. The lamplight casts a fragile glow onto his grey head. When he reaches me he's almost out of breath. 'I always liked it here. The trees,' he says.

I sniff. The moonlight illuminates his face, making his eyes shine, and I remember those same eyes looking down on me, leaning closer to kiss my cheek before he left for work. Tommy. The man in the moon. The night man. Eternal. Mysterious. Father. All at once my lips tremble. I look into his face and feel my own begin to crumble, like I'm dissolving into little bits. Tommy catches me in his arms. 'Ach, hen, whit's wrong?'

The cold air flows into my lungs until my whole body heaves with heavy choking sobs. 'My marriage is over, and if I don't do what Bruce wants it could ruin Scott's future.'

Tommy pats my shoulder. 'Ach, hen, it'll be alright.'

I give a violent shrug. 'Don't, Tommy. Too much time has passed. It'll take more than a few lame platitudes.'

'Nah, that's no whit I mean.'

'I'm so confused, Tommy. I came here for answers, but every day I end up with more questions. I don't know who I am anymore.'

Gently, he turns me to face him. 'When Cissy told me aboot you, whit ye'd achieved, I wis that proud. There's a grit aboot ye, Ava. Ye get it from Jean. It's whit she gave you. Believe me, it'll take mair than this man and his threats tae bring ma lassie doon.'

No one knows patience more than Tommy. The cracks and lines on his old face are full of pain. Yet there's a composure about him, an ability to bide his time. 'I want you tae know that I'm here fur you, as long as I've got breath. I'll even do wan a they DNA whatsits,' he says. 'I promise ye lass, we'll get tae the truth.' Polson is sniffing between the trees. Tommy whistles and the dog scampers over. From somewhere, an ice cream van plays its hurdy-gurdy melody. He hands me a handkerchief.

'Thanks.'

'Fancy a double nugget?'

I wipe the strands of hair from my cheeks. A smile forces itself across my face. I want to stretch this a while longer, the stars flickering brightly from those same places where they've always shone, above these trees and across the same wide ocean. 'Can I stay here tonight?'

A ruddy glow brightens his cheeks, 'Course you can, hen. Anything.'

In the distance, the ice cream van picks up its tune. Tomorrow the sun will rise, and I'll be Ava Newport once again. But just for tonight, I can be that little girl: I'm Ava McParland. And I'm having a double nugget.

★

The morning is bright and cool and I shiver slightly as Tommy opens the back door and Polson comes skidding towards me, his tail wagging. I rub the dog's ears. 'He's taken wae ye,' says Tommy. Outside, garden birds flutter at a feeder hanging on a small tree. 'I like to watch them while I'm having my breakfast,' he says. 'Course, they'll be different than the ones you get in Canada.'

I tell him I've never noticed. Tommy whistles while he fills the kettle and feeds Polson. The dog licks greedily at his bowl. 'Where's Scott?' I say.

'He left early this morning. I offered him breakfast bit he wis in a hurry. Apparently Jean's recovered enough wae the antibiotics to get out of bed.' Tommy turns to me and smiles. 'I'm a wee bit nervous, you know.'

'Why?'

'You sitting here in the kitchen, jist like when you were a wee lassie.' He puts a few slices of bread under a grill. 'Efter I wis oan the night shift, I'd sometimes make you breakfast. Dae ye mind?'

I nod. 'Egg with toast soldiers.'

'And you'd always ask fur mair sugar in yer tea.'

'Only you never put enough butter on the toast.'

'"Mammy butters it right tae the corners," you'd say.' He sighs. 'Ye're a bit big fur sodgers noo.' The smell of toast fills the room, and the only sound is his knife scraping across the bread. The minutes pass slowly, then he says, 'So ye're going tae see her the day?' His back is towards me. I can't see his expression, but I feel the weight of memory bearing down upon him.

'Looks like it,' I say. 'If Scott says it's been arranged.'

I picture the woman in the photo. She was so young, not much older than me when I had him. It's the reason I came here, but I don't know what to think, how to feel. I chew the side of my nail.

Tommy puts a mug of hot dark coffee in front of me. The bitter smell wakens my senses. The coffee is followed by a plate of toast, then jam and sugar. His movements are slow. It seems to take forever. I get up to help but he shoos me back to my seat. There's silence while we stir sugar into mugs, then he says, 'It's no her fault.'

'What do you mean?'

'She was young, foolish.' He shakes his head. 'I should've known she wisny happy, bit back then you jist got oan wae it. People didny get divorced, they gritted their teeth and made the best a whit they had. Bit no Jean. *That's* whit folk resented, not the robbery. They couldny stand the fact that she tried to get out. Bit in the end it wisny Jean who paid the price. It wis you.' He wraps his hand around my wrist, his old eyes gazing into mine. 'Whit we did, me and Cissy, it wis worse than any robbery. We committed the greater crime.'

Inside me, it's like a fist has slowly started to open. The confusion, that feeling of betrayal, of thinking you know somebody, know yourself, eventually it loses its grip. 'Do you want to come with me?' I say.

He stares at his mug of coffee, as though the answer might reveal itself in the rising steam. 'We had our time,' he says. 'It wis over long ago. This is aboot you. She wis your mither, whatever she did. And she loved you. Don't forget that.' He passes me a slice of toast, buttered all the way to the corners, just how I used to like it. 'Thanks,' he says. 'For listening tae an auld fool like me.' His lips form a slanted smile. 'I'd like it if you stayed in touch.'

I bite off a corner of bread. Smiling, I pat his hand.

After a quick change of clothes at the hotel I head over to Susi's. In her small kitchen, she fills the kettle, a classical station playing from a digital radio on top of the fridge. Her face is bright and her cheeks ruddy. 'Lovely morning, isn't it?'

I shrug.

'Are you okay? You look a bit flustered.'

'I lost my room key and had to get another from the office.'

'Never mind, you're here now.'

It's like a different person from the one who left the café yesterday with her shoulders sloped, as though the life had been emptied out of her. I wonder what's changed. 'Am I still public enemy number one?'

She plucks teabags from a tin and turns the music down. 'I'm sorry. All that stuff I said yesterday, I didn't mean it.'

'That's not the impression I got.'

'Scott helped me realise a few things.' She pours water into two mugs and leans against the worktop. 'What happened in the past, none of it is your fault. I'm Billy's daughter whether I like it or not. With you it's different. You have another chance; you can have that happy ending. I suppose I was jealous.'

'Scott said that?'

'Not in so many words.'

'Did I hear my name being mentioned?' Breezing into the kitchen he steals a mug from Susi's hand. She giggles and fills another. I'm glad they get on. When all this is over he's going to need someone and it might as well be her. 'Well, ladies, I hope you're ready for your close-ups,' he says. 'Today is all about details: eyes, mouths, hands. I want to give this moment the depth it deserves.'

'By filming my hands?' I say.

'Body language, Mom, remember?' I laugh and shake my head. Tommy is right. Whatever happened in the past, it wasn't for lack of love. You do what you think is right at the time. I can understand that. I only hope Scott does. His ringtone goes off, one of those screeching guitar bands. 'I gotta take this.' I watch him disappear into the hall.

Susi studies my face. 'You look nervous.'

'Wouldn't you be?'

'Try not to worry. Some days are better than others. Mum can sit for hours and not say a thing. Then a wee glimmer comes into her eye and she'll ask me what's on at La Scala, like it was yesterday.'

I listen to the cadence of Scott's voice, mostly grunts and murmurs; whoever is on the other end has a lot to say. Susi hesitates. 'It's not just Jean, is it? There's something else bothering you, I can tell –'

'I don't want to talk about it. Let's get through today first.' I smooth my hair and take a sip of tea. Susi turns up the radio. It's a cello concerto, something Baroque, perhaps Bach or Vivaldi. I'm rubbish when it comes to composers. I close my eyes and the long melancholy notes make me think of brightly coloured fishes darting through plumes of coral. My muscles relax. I lean against the wall and, for a second, it's easy to believe what Tommy said about things working out. Then the strings stop dead, as if all the fishes have been yanked out of the ocean in a great net. Scott is standing in the middle of the room, a disgusted look on his face.

'What's wrong?'

He drums his temples.

'Peanut, you're scaring me.' Blood drains from my limbs and I sit down. It's one of those folding tables and the half-moon section knocks against my thigh, but before I can swing my legs under, Scott's phone lands in my lap.

'Play it.'

'Play what?'

The gush of the tap makes me flinch. Susi pours the remainder of her tea down the sink. The phone is showing a video from CBC news. 'Ginny called me as soon as she heard. At least there's one person I can trust.'

My finger hovers over the screen. This is the lull that comes before the hurricane. I press play. There's a dramatic fanfare before the newsreader, a woman with an expression of condescending contentment, twirls her pen in her hand and announces the words I've been dreading, 'A surprise twist in the Borealis enquiry.' The announcement wasn't supposed to go public for another twenty-four hours. I made up my mind this morning and called Sue Brash from the hotel. 'You can have your statement,' I said. 'But leave Scott out of it, and don't pretend you don't know what I'm talking about.' I should have known not to trust Bruce. At the very least I thought I had a day's grace with my son before the shit hit the fan. The newsreader delivers her oracle with a faint smile:

Mrs Newport, who is recuperating from exhaustion at an undisclosed location, has confirmed that her purpose at the riots was to open a dialogue with the protestors, and that her arrest was a mistake on the part of the police, and one for which they have apologised. Mrs Newport fully supports Borealis's strategy on Temple Grove, and states that Borealis will continue to comply with government regulations and to work closely with all agencies to ensure a sound environmental policy for the future.

Scott's stare freezes my blood. 'You said you were on *our* side. I believed you.'

I hear myself telling him, 'It's for the best,' but instead of noble sacrifice, I feel emptiness, the inward shrinking of a coward. 'I did it for you,' I say.

'Liar!' he screeches. 'Don't put this onto me.'

'Try and understand, Scott.'

His hands tremble as he shields his eyes. 'You've ruined everything, Mom.'

My stomach churns, and the buttered toast Tommy gave me for breakfast rises to my throat. 'You don't get it, I had to make that statement.'

'You're right.' He strikes his forehead. 'I don't get it.'

I reach to calm him, but he jerks away like he's been winded. 'It wasn't supposed to happen like this. I thought I had it under control,' I say.

'Yeah, your precious bonus, I forgot.'

'Bruce threatened you. He engineered the offer from Carhorn. Don't you see, if I didn't sign up to his demands there wasn't going to be any film.'

A laugh escapes his throat.

'Bruce has what he wants now. You can still make your film.'

The laughing stops. 'You've just publicly supported Borealis. If I do this film now, it'll be like a publicity ad. This meant everything to me, Mom. Finally, I'd stopped being that failure, just another thirty-plus dude on meds. But you know what I think? It suits you to have a lost cause for a son; then you can make speeches about me at fancy functions, and talk about *your* sacrifices and *your* corporate donations. God –' He squeezes his fists. 'I actually believed I was getting to know the real you, the mom I had before money became so fucking important.' The laughing starts again and he backs out of the kitchen. We follow him into the front room where he grabs his camera. 'Why am I even doing this? It's a fucking waste of time. I'm deleting everything. Delete. Delete. Delete.'

'No.' In one swift move, Susi wrestles the camera from his hand. 'I can't let you do that. It isn't just your story in there, it's mine. All of us together, everything that matters, our history, is captured in those files. Don't throw it away, Scott. Whatever your mum did, I'm sure she had her reasons. Right, Ava?'

A drop of water splashes on the floor. Then another. The sight of Scott, his lashes wet with tears, rips me in two. If his work is destroyed, he'll never recover. 'Listen to Susi,' I say. 'This is *our* film. You can't give up now.' She has her arm around Scott, nodding encouragement. He's tense as a wire, but he's not pushing her away. Just then my phone vibrates. 'It's Bruce.'

'Answer it,' says Scott.

I take the call. 'What do you want, Bruce?'

'Ava, darling, I knew you'd come through.'

'I didn't *come through*; you threatened my son.'

'Hell, I don't like playing hardball. We're a team, always have been.'

'Get to the point, Bruce.'

'It was nothing… that thing with Melanie… it's over.'

'I don't care about your sordid little affairs.'

'If that's how you want it.' I hear him swallow. 'I need your help, for old time's sake. It's this damned report. Winterbourne is the leak, I'm sure of it. Goddamn hippy. I should have known he was an asshole when he turned up in that Chevrolet Volt. If he'd taken the cash and sold the report to every rag in the country I'd have had more respect, but he's too spineless to take the heat. Still, you know what these hackers are like, think they're goddamned superheroes. If you or anyone else has a version of that bullcrap, you've got to tell me.'

'And what if I don't?'

'Kelly will milk me like a fat cow. They'll crucify me, Ava. I could go to jail. Not just me – everyone who saw that report. My – our – whole future hangs in the balance.' He sighs. 'Try and think, Ava. Who has access to your devices? Your files? What about that whippet of a girl, you know, the one with the hair? She's no good for him, by the way. No one who doesn't sniff coke could be that skinny. All I need are your drives. Let's put this thing to bed and get on with our lives.'

I feel like I'm sinking, like all the air is being compressed out of me. 'Why should I? You promised me one day's grace.'

'Shit, you know the markets. Shares are up one percent since your statement.'

One percent. The price of my son's love. I wipe my eyes and imagine Bruce drifting away from me, downriver, becoming nothing but a speck. 'I don't have your report. It's been wiped.'

'Listen, I'll come to Scotland. Pick you both up. We'll go to Europe, the Sistine Chapel, the Black Forest. Spend more time as a family, all three of us.'

'You threatened my son, Bruce.'

'I'll explain, tell Scott it was all my fault. Hell, I don't like doing any of that stuff, Ava. But it's not just me. I have responsibilities. Shareholders, directors. It was out of my hands. You understand?'

I catch snippets of words, jagged and cold-edged. Bruce is mad now. I hold the phone from my ear, his voice receding into the distance. 'Thirty years of marriage has got to count for something, Ava. All I want is a piss-assed report. Be reasonable –' My thumb hovers above the screen.

'Tell him to go to hell, Mom.'

'Goodbye, Bruce.' I cut the call.

Scott is breathing fast. I feel guilty for putting him through all this. I should have warned him, told him what was going on. Instead I treated him like a child. 'I'm sorry,' I say. 'I thought if I signed the statement, it would be over.'

'With people like Bruce, it's never over. Power is nothing if it's not absolute.'

When I look at my son, it's like I'm seeing him for the first time. There's a fierce intelligence behind his eyes. Self-assured, strong. 'I have to tell you something.' He takes a plastic card from his pocket and waves it in front of me. It's my room key.

'I was looking for that.'

'I took it out your bag at Tommy's. Sorry, but we needed a way. Winterbourne signposted us, but he didn't give us the file – said it would compromise his integrity.'

'His career, more like,' says Susi.

'Ginny knows some activists who specialise in, um, data retrieval. This morning, we went to the hotel and accessed your laptop.'

'Who's *we*?'

Susi dangles a pen drive between her thumb and forefinger. 'We transferred the data from the internal system.'

The grin on Scott's face is wide, mischievous. 'Now you can testify at the enquiry. This is all the proof we need.'

'Do you mean to say you followed me to Scotland to get those files?'

'No. That was an optional extra. I came to make the film.' He tilts his head in that cute way that used to get him out of trouble when he was a kid. 'You're not angry, are you?'

I take the pen drive and close it in my palm, marvelling at how a weightless piece of plastic can change everything. 'Yeah, I'm angry. It's morally reprehensible.' A pulse runs through my body, like a surge of electricity. 'It's also genius.'

'So, what are you going to do?'

'Time for me to stop running,' I say. 'We need to end this on our terms. Let the world see Borealis for what they are.'

Susi glances from me to Scott. 'Let's do it.'

A mix of sleet and rain spatters the cab. It drives us through a run-down part of town, houses with the windows boarded up. A woman pushing a pram hurries past some boys on the sidewalk. Their dull eyes follow her along the street. I try to imagine how my life might have turned out if Jean hadn't left Tommy. Maybe she and I are more alike than I thought. We both bit off more than we could chew. It's not easy, that moment when you realise you're not what you thought you were and there's no going back.

The cab pulls into a driveway with lawns on either side. The sight of a fox and cub makes me start, then I realise it's only a statue. There are fake sparrows on the roof of the birdhouse too. This is what's in store. A world of make-believe. The flowerbeds are shrivelled, the last of the year's roses hanging their heads. I think of Tommy this morning, putting out birdseed. *She's your mother, she loved you.* It seems like an age away.

We get out of the cab. Above the entrance there's a sign that says, Craigton Care Home, with a rising sun behind it. Or maybe it's a setting sun. Susi smiles nervously and punches a number into the intercom. The door opens.

A cloying antiseptic smell, mingled with a faint aroma of warm food. The odour clogs my nostrils, the soft carpet yielding under my feet. We go up in the elevator, through another set of locked doors, and down a cushioned hallway. Frank Sinatra, *New York*, blares out from tinny speakers. A few elderly people are sitting on chairs. One woman hugs a pillow, singing to herself, another stares ahead, completely still, except for her hands which rip apart a tissue, small paper fragments floating onto the floor. Susi knocks on an office door and a nurse in a blue tunic comes out. 'I have visitors today,' smiles Susi. 'This is Ava, my sister from Canada.'

The nurse widens her eyes. 'You'll be looking forward to seeing your mother.'

She waits, as if expecting an explanation. *Yeah, I'm the one who thought she was dead.* I nod. 'It's – been a long time.'

The nurse retreats back to her cubbyhole, and we follow Susi down another bright corridor. It's like a parallel universe. A television blares loudly from a beige lounge where two or three residents sit slumped and snoozing in chairs. I try to imagine my mother sitting in one of these chairs, Susi treading these soft floors, while all the time I was in Vancouver, oblivious. At the end of the hall we stop outside a closed room. 'Are you ready?' says Susi.

My mouth feels dry. I glance along the hall where a vase of dried flowers, dark reds and browns, is framed by a large window. Before today, Jean was where she'd always been, far away. Now all that separates us is a sliver of wood a few inches thick. I turn to face the door. It feels impossible that she should be behind it. I picture her in her white PVC coat and brown boots, walking with quick hurried steps, dragging me down the street, away from all that I knew.

I'm not ready. How could anyone be ready? Yet I've come this far, crossed a lifetime, just for this moment. Susi gives my hand a brief squeeze. I nod and breathe in.

The door opens silently into a darkened room. 'Ach, Mum,' says Susi, mumbling something about it being too early to shut the curtains. I make out a bed and, opposite, the dim bulk of a wardrobe and a chest of drawers. Facing the window is a high-backed chair. It looks empty, but, as Susi draws back the drapes and light slowly diffuses the gloom, I notice an arm, pale and thin, perched on the rest. Scott moves soundlessly, filming the framed picture of a sunlit Scottish glen, the veneer dressing table and its single photograph of Susi as a child, sitting next to Jean under a row of tinsel.

He films over my shoulder as I move towards the chair. I don't think I've ever felt so small. Every muscle in my body is taut. I daren't blink. All I can focus on is that corner where Susi is crouched down, talking softly, saying things I can't hear.

When I reach the foot of the bed, I stop. The chair is a dull burgundy colour with a high back that engulfs the tiny body within. There's a footrest and two little feet burrowed inside pink fluffy slippers. The legs are thin and bony, bare knees sticking out like twigs above a pair of thin nylon socks. The dark skirt and pale blue cardigan hang down like scarecrow's clothes, yet there's something about that colour of blue. It pulls me towards her face. How small it is, how birdlike, her white hair short and wiry and flecked with grey. It's her, it's really her. The eyes shine through. They reflect the sea-blue of her cardigan and are the only part of her that moves, following the drift of clouds across the sky, as though it was new, something she'd never seen before. In the glow of daylight her skin looks silvery, translucent even.

Susi smiles. 'I've brought a visitor.'

The face turns slightly. Her eyes lift towards mine, and the breath catches in my throat. I try to swallow but can't. 'Are you here to give me my bath?' she says.

At the sound of her voice, shrill like a child's, my throat contracts. I open my mouth but nothing comes out.

'Mum,' says Susi, smiling down at her. 'She's here. It's your daughter, Ava.'

We all watch her face, scanning for a reaction, a flicker of recognition. A bird swoops onto the windowsill outside, her eyes dart towards it and seem to widen in delight. I notice she's wearing red lipstick that gives her a kind of clownish effect. I glance at Scott's face, his muscles screwed tight in concentration. I'm glad he's here, like a thread connecting me to the real world, stopping me from tumbling headlong into a dark tunnel.

Jean's lips close together. She lets out a puff of air, like a baby trying to make a sound, her mouth slowly tightening, puckering until finally a whistle escapes. It's followed by another, half air and half noise. Then two more, arriving in stops and starts. At first I think she's trying to communicate with the bird. Then Scott whispers, 'It's a tune.' The rhythm is difficult to make out until he starts to snap his fingers and hum along: '*So plea-ea-ea-ease... Love me do.*'

A smile splits Jean's face. Her teeth can't be real, I think, they're too perfect, too white. She starts to sing, her voice croaky and broken, like a smoker's cough, but there's something else, a spark at the corner of her eye that comes alive when she looks at Scott, the two of them singing in unison, '*Love love me do.*'

Then she stops and the room falls silent again, Jean turning back to the window like nothing happened. I look at my watch. I don't know how much time has passed but it feels like ages. 'Do you want to say something?' says Susi, motioning me to come closer.

'Yeah, Mom, say something.'

I glance behind me out the window, then at the small woman ensconced in the chair, her birdlike bones, the empty blue eyes. I shake my head. 'I can't.'

Holding Jean's hand, Susi says, 'Here, take it.'

I let the tips of her fingers rest in my palm. The skin feels papery and cold; a strange sensation crawls up my arm. This isn't my mother, the woman I remember, who used to sit at the kitchen table in Newton Street. We're strangers. I don't belong here. The past is buried too deep, a shipwreck on the ocean floor. I let go, and her hand drops limply into her lap.

Susi squeezes my shoulder. 'Are you okay?'

I shake my head. 'This was a bad idea. She doesn't even know me.'

'Wait.' Scott hunches down beside Jean's chair and leans towards her. It's odd seeing them like that, so close together. He shows her the digital screen, playing back what he's just filmed. 'See, that's you, Grandma.' She turns to him and smiles emptily. He rewinds the footage. 'And this is Tommy. Remember Tommy?'

The vacant smile fades. A tiny-sized Tommy walks across the screen, Polson at his heels. She screws up her small blue eyes. A bubble of saliva forms at the corner of her mouth. 'And look, there's Ava,' says Scott. I'm standing at the door to Tommy's house, waving into the camera. Only now it's like we're waving at Jean. He pauses the image. Jean reaches out a bent finger and touches it, then looks questioningly at Susi, who puts her hand on my arm. 'It's Ava, Mum. She's really here.'

'A bit older than I used to be,' I say, stupidly.

I unzip my bag and take out the book. It feels strangely solid in my hands. 'Remember this?' I hold it in front of Jean. 'You gave it to me for my eighteenth birthday.'

Her eyes flicker over the burgundy cover. I read the title aloud, '*The Life and Times of Mary, Queen of Scots.*' She's watching my face. Even as I place the book on her lap and crouch down to read the inscription, she doesn't take her eyes off me. Slowly, her mouth breaks into a smile. She points at the dressing table. 'What is it, Mum?' says Susi.

'She wants something,' says Scott.

Susi goes over to the table. 'There's nothing here. Just your hairbrush and jewellery box.' She turns towards me. 'I don't know why she needs jewellery. It's not like she goes anywhere.'

'Just bring it,' says Scott.

The box is chipped and fading. I recognise the cat on the lid, the cracked tabby fur slowly vanishing into yellowed vinyl. When Jean opens the clasp, up pops a tiny plastic ballerina, arms in a pirouette, showing off her dress, a piece of tattered netting. My legs wobble. I'm a child again, sneaking into my mammy's bedroom, holding my breath while I wind up the box and watch the little ballerina rotate round and round to the music of tinkling bells. I try the mechanism at the back, but it doesn't turn. The years have made her still.

There's a clatter as Jean empties out the contents, necklaces and earrings spilling across the pages of the book. Most are made of plastic, not worth anything. Among the jewellery is some make-up. She searches until she finds a lipstick and holds it between her yellowed nails for me to take. 'Scarlett,' she says, in a soft voice. 'Scarlett.'

'Mum!' says Susi. 'I'm so sorry, Ava, I don't know what's got into her.'

I freeze. 'My birth certificate. Scarlett is my middle name.' I reach out to take the lipstick, painting my mouth with the colour. Jean smiles and claps her hands then makes a circle with her fist and, holding it to her lips, sputters a broken fanfare through an invisible trumpet. Susi says I don't have to amuse her, that it's okay. 'No,' I say. 'I understand this. I know what she's doing. The memory comes back, of making-up my face when I was a little girl. The dress and pretend crown, my mother holding up the silken cloak while I parade around the room. Now, the same tiny woman grins at me from her high-backed chair, her hand making the royal wave. I wave back, my fingers stroking invisible air. My mammy. Grief and joy. Like water rushing into an empty space. It swells over me and I can't stop crying. I didn't expect this – this loss of control. Until now, I never realised how much of me was closed off, neglected: whole chapters locked inside a tiny box. Now she's here, in front of me. Breathing. Alive. And I'm a child again, my throat choking back big baby sobs.

I want it to stop. She's not allowed to do this to me. I won't let her. Sunlight filters over the roofs and through the window, catching the top of Jean's head in a golden glow. I'd forgotten how much I wanted to be like her. I squeeze her hand. The skin is sallow, worn. I let go and rush towards the door. It sticks. I rattle the handle, not knowing whether to push or pull. Damn thing. 'Will somebody let me out of here?'

'Mom!' calls Scott.

'What?'

I turn round. His eyes are on Jean. She's sitting with the box on her lap, the tiny ballerina spinning slowly to a tinsely refrain from *Swan Lake*, the notes like little stars falling through the sky. In her hand is the cardboard base, its lining threadbare and rose-coloured.

'Look,' says Scott. 'She's taken it apart.'

I walk over slowly. Hidden under the base is a clutch of banknotes, faded pink. He unfolds the bundle. 'Look how big they are, like newspaper pages.' He counts three hundred pounds. 'It must have been jamming the mechanism,' he says, and laughs.

'Where did this money come from, Mum?' says Susi.

The music has slowed. Jean doesn't seem to notice any of us. She turns the key at the back of the box and watches the ballerina rotate, her vacant smile broadening, like the tinkling music has lulled her into a dream.

Susi sighs. 'She probably doesn't remember.'

'Wait.' Gently, Scott leans over her and reaches into the box. 'There's something else.' He scoops out an envelope and holds it up. A single word is scrawled on the front: *Ava*.

A lump rises in my throat. 'What does it say?'

'You read it.'

I rip it open and unfold the paper. I notice my mother's hand-writing is almost exactly like my own. The letter is dated is 1981, four years after Scott was born. I swallow, then start to read:

Dear Ava

I wish you could meet your sister. Her name is Susi and she reminds me so much of you. You have the same shape of face, the same smile. She's at college now. I have to pinch myself every time I think about it, that a daughter of mine could be at college. You've both grown up so fast. I dread to think of the day she'll leave home. I don't know what I'll do without her.

It was a shock to see you, after all these years. All grown up and a woman, with a bump the size of a football! Cissy didn't mention that in her letter. I had it all planned out. Annie told me ages ago that Alex died, so I called up the mill in Canada pretending to be Cissy, asking them to confirm they had my new address for sending on his pension. I'm not as daft as I look. You don't spend six years in the jail and learn nothing.

I'd never been on a plane before. I felt ever so important, drinking a gin and tonic way up in the sky. I spent one night in Toronto then got the train straight to Pickering. It's a nice place, Pickering. There's so much forest, so much space, and that lovely big bay. Much nicer than Paisley. A taxi took me to the corner of your street. My heart was clanging inside my chest, I can tell you! I kept on whispering to myself, 'She's your wean, Jean, you've a right.' I took deep breaths, working up the courage to knock on that door and say, 'Here I am, your mammy, back from the dead.'

Then, before I could get near, it opened and out you came. It was like looking at myself all those years ago, carrying you inside of me. How scared I was. I knew then that I couldn't do it. Who knows what might have happened? You could have fainted, anything. Cissy was right. I was being selfish. I would only upset things. All those years of wishing and waiting, it was just a dream. You've your own life, your own responsibilities. Whatever I think of Cissy, whatever she did to me, she loves you, wants to protect you, I can see that now.

When I got back home I tried to carry on as normal. Tried to forget. But all I could think about was my grandchild, what they looked like, if it was a boy or a girl. Not knowing was like losing you all over again. I borrowed money. I know it was wrong but what else could I do? My husband started gambling to pay it off. I suppose it's my fault, and it's put a strain on us, but it was worth it, all of it, just to see you one last time.

It was all so accidental, the way it happened. I was on the beach, wondering what to do, when I happened to look up and there you were, walking along the promenade. He was beside you, so beautiful with his curly hair and innocent blue eyes. He looked straight at me. I waved and, I don't know why, but he ran towards me. Just once, I wanted to hold him, to know what it felt like. I scooped him up in my arms. I'll never forget the smell of the sun in his hair. You started calling his name, "Scott," and I ran towards you, Scott's wee hand in mine, thinking God had given me a second chance, that I'd been forgiven. Then this man, smart-looking as the devil, accused me of trying to steal him, said if I didn't let go he'd tell the polis. I knew then, it was too late. He grabbed the wean and took him to you, but not before I'd pressed a shiny coin into Scott's hand, 'Remember your Nana,' I said. I watched you sail off in that big yacht. The way you look after him, protect him, you're a good mother, Ava. A better mother than I ever was.

There's some money I managed to hide from Billy, and the polis. I used to fancy that one day I'd give it to you, but I realise now that was stupid. That money can only ever bring bad luck. I only keep it to remind me of what I lost. This letter is my way of saying goodbye, I suppose. I'm not going to send it. I'll keep it locked away, next to the money, in a place where it can't do any harm.

When I think of you both out there in Canada, I feel happy. More peaceful than I ever have since... then. I want to tell you that I'm sorry for what I did. But you're stronger than me, smarter. Never forget how special you are, and that I love you always,

Your doting mother, Jean.

She's staring out the window again. Blue eyes, blue cardigan. 'Mum,' I say. She doesn't answer. For all I know, she didn't hear a single word. She's watching the pigeons land on the rooftops. Occasionally, her eyes lift when there's a squabble, or when the gulls swoop down from above. 'Mammy, you wrote this letter. Do you remember? Anything at all?'

I shake my head and turn to Scott. He focuses the camera on Jean, then on my hand as it grips the letter, but behind the lens I see his eyes are red, his cheeks smudged with tears. His hands start to shake.

Susi gets up. 'Here, let me take that. Sit with your grandma.' She takes the camera from him, and he sits opposite me at the other side of Jean's chair. 'I've never forgotten that day.' His gaze wanders up to the ceiling. 'Kids remember that kind of stuff, don't they? Getting lost, that fear of being truly alone. But there was something about her, how her eyes twinkled, her funny accent; it's always stuck in my mind. When she picked me up I felt safe, until Bruce arrived. Then she was gone.' He rubs his forehead.

My heart beats faster as the lost pieces click into place. 'I wiped your hands, told you not to talk to strangers. "Nana," you said. "Nana-nana." I thought it was just baby-talk.' I sit down on the edge of the bed. 'I can't believe it. All that time she knew about us, where we lived. She knew.'

The banknotes are still on the floor. No one touches them. 'I had no idea she went to Canada,' says Susi. 'I must have been studying in Edinburgh at the time. She acted like nothing was wrong. How could she keep all that in? It must have been awful.'

My mouth trembles when I see Susi reach across and caress her mother's fragile knuckles. That picture in my mind again, of the kitchen in Newton Street, Jean sitting at the table, smoking, the tea in front of her growing cold. That feeling I had of being half-afraid, yet of wanting to go to her, to fall asleep in her lap, bury my head in her smoky scent and never let go.

I decide to do what I never could before. I crouch beside her and rest my head on her knees, feeling her thin bones under me, the soft touch of her hand on my head, brushing my hair in long smooth strokes. 'Poor lassie,' she says. 'My wee lassie.'

I look up. She's sitting perfectly still. Then she turns, dips her head towards me, and the golden light from the window melts away, leaving her eyes, forehead, in blueish shadow. 'Hello, hen.' She smiles. 'Is it time for my bath?'

★

Below the bridge, a family of ducks shelters in the reeds, sharing each other's warmth. Their ancestors may have lived here generations back, when Jean worked in the mills, or maybe some of them are like people, and fly to distant places, never to return. The river mirrors the clouds that hang above the roofs of the housing estate. In my mind I can see it, wavering on the surface: the reflection of the old spinning mill, rising like a ghost behind the manicured lawns and neatly parked cars. I can hear my mother's footsteps on her way to work, passing between the gatehouses and depots, the smoking chimneys and rattling machines.

Susi made us breakfast this morning: tattie scones, fried eggs and mushrooms. 'You can take the girl out of Paisley,' she said, 'but you can't take Paisley –'

'Out of the girl,' we chimed.

Our flight leaves tonight. I needed to have one last look at the town where I was born, that made me who I am. Flakes of snow fall from the sagging clouds and dissolve, and one of the ducks lifts its head and quacks then snuggles back under its feathers. I offered to take everyone for dinner later, no expense spared, but Tommy says he doesn't care for fancy restaurants. He's taking us to a place he used to go with Jean when they were 'courting,' an Italian fish restaurant in the centre of town. I open my mouth and tilt my head skywards, letting droplets of sleet melt on my tongue. I think of Jean at the window of Craigton Care Home, mesmerised by the white drifts, smiling softly to herself, her mind as blank as the snow. It's a blessing in disguise, how her gradual disintegration has allowed her to forget, relieved her of the burden of years, the pain of regret she carried for so long. Yet I can't help hoping that, deep down, she'll know that she got what she'd been waiting for, a sense of something being complete, even if it's only for a passing moment.

Leaving the bridge, I go back through the streets and head towards the main road. I brace myself against the wind, hurrying past the gothic spire of the Coats Baptist Church, and on until I reach the library. The air is warm and alive with the hum of soft voices. I login at one of the computers, my breath quickening as I take Susi's pen drive from the pocket of my bag and insert it into the USB slot. Then I upload Dave Winterbourne's environmental report into an email, and copy in every major newspaper editor in Canada. 'Mary, Queen of Scots,' I whisper, and click *Send*. An act of rebellion worthy of Jean herself.

I wander over to the biography section, imagining how the library would have looked fifty years ago when she first cast her eyes on the leafy gold lettering of the book she loved so much: the story of a life lived long ago, but that somehow touched her own.

'Hi again,' says a voice at my shoulder. It's the librarian with the blonde ponytail. 'Tracing family, wasn't it? A mother who worked in the mills?'

'That's right.'

'Did you find anything interesting?'

'Yes. I believe this belongs here.'

I remove *The Life and Times of Mary, Queen of Scots* from my bag and hand it over. She examines the half-torn library ticket inside. 'Yes, this is one of ours. Looks like it's been gone a long time.'

'I like to think it's come back home.'

'A bit like yourself?'

'Yes,' I say. 'I suppose you're right.'

I turn to leave, but a pang of guilt makes me reach into my bag and take out the page with the inscription. 'This belongs with it too,' I say. 'I wanted to keep it, but I suppose I shouldn't.'

The librarian reads my mother's words and smiles. 'So you're Ava?'

I nod. 'For my sins.'

'Well,' she says, handing me back the page. 'I won't tell anyone if you don't.'

EPILOGUE

June 2014
Canada

Four days ago, I boarded *The Canadian* in Toronto. It was Cissy's dream to travel in this train. She'd cut pictures from magazines of it carrying its passengers through the western prairies, river plains and great lakes, the narrow valleys and majestic forests, and on towards the towering peaks of the Rockies. Occasionally, I reach out and touch the bag on the seat beside me, with its dark blue urn inside. It's comforting to know we're together again, one last time: Cissy, Alex and I.

Scott says I look happier these days that the single life agrees with me. I have a new apartment in West Point Grey, with a balcony where I sit sketching the view over the water. I even got a red tint put through my hair. Last week we launched his company, Polson Productions, in the Vancouver Lookout. His documentary about me was broadcast on one of the mainstream channels. These days, I'm regarded as a whistle-blower and campaigner for Green Alliance, an occasional talking-head on environmental issues. I'm lobbying for a complete ban on selective cutting. The Borealis enquiry resulted in the usual corporate slap on the wrist and a two hundred page waste of paper recommending 'a review of internal systems.' But it was enough to make shareholders run with their tails tucked under them, and for Kelly to fast-track a Chinese takeover bid; Bruce is on borrowed time and he knows it.

The train enters a tunnel, and that image flashes through my mind again, the one I've seen a thousand times, of Jean in her shiny white coat, and me tagging after her in my red and white shoes. Then it's replaced by a vision of her in that soft blue cardigan, sitting still and peaceful in her chair by the window, exactly the way she looked when I laid eyes on her for the last time. Such a short span, a life. It's been ten days since I got the call from Susi. I knew before I picked up the phone. Died peacefully in her sleep. According to staff, the night before she passed, Jean said, 'Tell Cissy it was nice of her to come.' Maybe when our time arrives it's the dead who surround us, whom we feel closest to. The funeral was small, just Susi, Annie and a few of Jean's carers. And Tommy. Till death do us part. That's what he promised her. I don't think anyone could have meant it more. I picture his old watery eyes watching her coffin being lowered from the catafalque, how he'd go home afterwards to sit by the fire, Polson, his faithful companion, at his side.

The train bursts into daylight again, and I feel my blood vessels heating up, expanding. The railway hugs the mountainside. The people who built it are long gone, but the steel tracks remain, glittering into the distance, winding between glaciers and tree covered slopes. Susi says it would be good for Tommy to come out here, get away for a bit. I floated it to him over the phone. 'Ach, I don't know,' he said. 'I've only ever been as far as Troon.' I think of him watching the milestones of my life: Scott's arrival, my graduation, marriage. From a distance, he shared every success and disappointment. In his eyes, I was always his little girl. 'It'll be good for you,' I said. 'You know Scott would love to see his granddad.' There was a silence, then Tommy mumbled something about knowing what to call him properly once the 'science people' had sorted it once and for all.

Mount Robson rises in the distance, its summit wrapped in cloud. I glance at the urn and think of the two women who shaped my destiny. Both of them gone. 'Here goes, Cissy,' I say. I fish the letter from my bag. It has a double helix and the heading, 'DNA Test Report.' I wanted a hard copy, something I could touch. I read the words and let out one long breath. Last time I spoke to Tommy I said: 'You're my father. And you always will be.' To see it there in black and white, 99.998% probability, gives me a certainty I've never had before.

The train hurtles between mountains and mist, through deep valleys and snow-frosted pines. Eventually it pulls in at a small station, signposted with a wooden board that swings in the wind, like in the days of the old timber towns: Valemount, the Valley in the Mountains. We're at the junction of four ranges: the Rockies, Monashee, Cariboo and Selkirk. I remember how Cissy would say the *Selkirk Grace*, and how I'd press my lips together, trying to mimic the strange words. *Sae let the Lord be thankit.*

I put the urn in my rucksack and leave the station, filling my lungs full of clean air. I'm travelling light, just a set of warm clothes and anorak, and a crampon to help me up the steep paths. I follow the straggle of other hikers through the village main street with its low buildings and flat roofs. Eventually I come to the Alpine Lodge where I'll spend the night. Tomorrow I'll lay Cissy to rest, where the sun sets over forested valleys. This place has a permanence about it, something solid, lasting.

A family at the Lodge give me a lift, their trunk piled high with tents and rucksacks. They have two kids: blonde-headed sisters who handclap rhymes in the back seat: *A sailor went to sea, sea, sea, to see what he could see, see, see.* They persuade me to join in. 'It's alright,' I say when their mother scolds them to stop pestering. 'I have a sister of my own.'

After Jean died, I invited Susi to come and live in Vancouver. She turned me down. 'I've been in other people's shadows too long,' she said. 'I need to work things out on my own.' She's running an aromatherapy business from her spare room, and goes to community centres treating pensioners and young mothers. I came across a CD of Mongolian chanting in a store in Chinatown and posted it to her for good luck. I imagine us as little girls singing rhymes: *Miss Mary Mack, all dressed in black, with rows of silver buttons, all down her back.*

The car nears the entrance to Mount Robson Provincial Park

with its giant white caribou on a plinth. The family drops me off, I cross a wooden bridge over the Robson River and take the trail through a sun-dappled forest of hemlock and red cedar. The air is cool and wet. I walk for an hour before the path opens onto a shimmering lake. A narrow suspension bridge spans the teal waters, and I make my way to the steep track on the other side. After a while, my legs start to ache. Sun shines on the back of my neck as I scrabble between patches of rock. Through a gap in the trees, a spectacular waterfall cascades into a pool, then tumbles downwards into the valley below.

I find a broad ledge amongst the trees and stop. 'Well, Cissy,' I say. 'It's as good a place as any.' Taking off my rucksack, I stop to catch my breath. Below my feet, spruces and cedars descend the steep slopes, their crowns visible through the mist and spray. I think of all the people who brought me to this moment. Cissy and Jean. Alex and Tommy. Senga and Una. I think of Paisley and the mills, their tall brick chimneys tumbling to the ground in clouds of stone and ash.

I remove the urn, and pause a moment before tipping its contents into the cool valley. Dust spirals downwards, coating the leaves in an ivory glow. 'So long,' I say. I remember the old Steinway and that tune Cissy used to play, her back rigid and straight, her voice breaking slightly on the high notes, those elongated vowels cracking beneath the surface: '*There was a mill girl, a Paisley mill girl, who travelled far away…*'

THE END

Acknowledgements

I'd like to thank:

G2 Writers for encouraging me in the original idea for the novel, as well as Paisley Writers' Group, and Read Raw Ltd. for constructive feedback and support.

Everyone who took time to read the unfinished manuscript: my Mum, Angela, and sister, Shirley, Rachel McJury, Stephen McBride, Fiona Lindsay, Sheila McLachlan, Donal McLaughlin and Brian Whittingham.

Evelyn Hood for her book, *Mill Memories*, The Thread Mill Museum, and Sheila Millar and Stewart Millar for invaluable assistance with the research.

Rebecca Johnstone, Andrew Forteath, and especially Fiona Lindsay for making the process of publication so enjoyable.

Dave Manderson for helping me to believe in myself as a writer.

The Paisley mill lassies.

About the author

Tracy Patrick was born in Paisley in 1972. Her father worked in Coats's, printing labels, before joining Paton's. Her grandfather was a weaver in Stoddard's carpet factory, and her grandmother worked in Chrysler. Tracy joined Paisley Writers' Group in 2000, and has continued writing ever since. *Blushing is for Sinners* is her first published novel and she is author of *Wild Eye Fire Eye*, a Celtic-themed poetry collection.